"Ms. Shinn knows full well the power of appealing characterization and uses it most skillfully to reflect her ingeniously piquant imagination."
—*Romantic Times*

PRAISE FOR SHARON SHINN AND THE SAMARIA TRILOGY . . .

Archangel

"Taut, inventive, often mesmerizing, with a splendid pair of predestined lovers."
—*Kirkus Reviews*

"Displaying sure command of characterization and vividly imagined settings, Shinn absorbs us in the story . . . an interesting SF-fantasy blend that should please fans of both genres."
—*Booklist*

"Excellent world-building, charming characterizations. A garden of earthly delights."
—*Locus*

Jovah's Angel

"Shinn displays a real flair for [music and romance], giving music a compelling power and complexity, while the developing attraction between Archangel Alleluia and a gifted but eccentric mortal should charm the most dedicated anti-sentimentalist and curmudgeon . . . [A] book of true grace, wit, and insight into humanity, past and future."
—*Locus*

"Some may raise eyebrows at Sharon Shinn's less-than-saintly angels, but they make for far more interesting characters than the winged paragons of legend. Many will no doubt find her end results quite heavenly."
—*Starlog*

"Romantic . . . delightful. I'm eagerly awaiting her next novel."
—*The Magazine of Fantasy and Science Fiction*

The Alleluia Files

"A warm and triumphant close to Shinn's Samaria trilogy."
—*Publishers Weekly*

"A tale that makes for exciting, suspenseful, romantic, frightening and even amusing reading."
—*St. Louis Post-Dispatch*

continued . . .

ALSO BY SHARON SHINN . . .

Wrapt in Crystal

"Taut, realistic police work, an involving love story, and a fetching backdrop . . . well up to Shinn's previous high standards."
—*Kirkus Reviews*

"Shinn deftly combines mystery, high-tech SF, and romance with a layering of fantasy in a fresh and innovative tale full of surprising turns of plot." —*Library Journal*

"Offers a convincing view of human impulses toward both worldly and unworldly passions with a touch of the otherwordly to bring it into the realm of science fiction." —*Locus*

"It doesn't get much better than *Wrapt in Crystal*—interesting characters, an intriguing mystery, a believable love story and a satisfying ending." —*Starlog*

The Shape-Changer's Wife
SELECTED BY *LOCUS* AS THE BEST FIRST FANTASY NOVEL OF 1995

"Ms. Shinn takes a traditional romance and wraps it in a fantasy . . . rousing." —*The Magazine of Fantasy and Science Fiction*

"The spellbinding Ms. Shinn writes with elegant imagination and a steely grace, bringing a remarkable freshness that will command a wide audience." —*Romantic Times*

Heart of Gold

"Will appeal to readers who enjoy unconventional romances and strong women protagonists." —*Science Fiction Weekly*

Summers at
Castle Auburn

SHARON SHINN

ACE BOOKS, NEW YORK

This is a work of fiction. Names, characters, places, and incidents either are the product of the author's imagination or are used fictitiously, and any resemblance to actual persons, living or dead, business establishments, events, or locales is entirely coincidental.

SUMMERS AT CASTLE AUBURN

An Ace Book / published by arrangement with
the author

PRINTING HISTORY
Ace edition / April 2001

All rights reserved.
Copyright © 2001 by Sharon Shinn
Cover design by Jean Pierre Targete
Book design by Tiffany Kukec

This book, or parts thereof, may not be reproduced
in any form without permission.
For information address: The Berkley Publishing Group,
a division of Penguin Putnam Inc.,
375 Hudson Street, New York, New York 10014.

The Penguin Putnam Inc. World Wide Web site address is
http://www.penguinputnam.com

Check out the ACE Science Fiction & Fantasy newsletter
and much more on the Internet at Club PPI!

ISBN: 0-441-00803-8

ACE®
Ace Books are published by The Berkley Publishing Group,
a division of Penguin Putnam Inc., 375 Hudson Street,
New York, New York 10014.
ACE and the "A" design are trademarks
belonging to Penguin Putnam Inc.

Printed in the United States of America

10 9 8 7 6 5 4 3 2 1

*To Theresa, Donna, and Andrea, who have all known Bryans,
And to Robin, who knows even more than Corie.*

CONTENTS

Summers at Castle Auburn

PART ONE

Excursions

1

The summer I was fourteen, my uncle Jaxon took me with him on an expedition to hunt for aliora. I had only seen the fey, delicate creatures in captivity, and then only when I was visiting Castle Auburn. I was as excited about the trip to the Faelyn River as I had been about anything in my life.

I had been surly at first when Greta insisted that I could not go alone with my uncle such a far distance from the castle. "People will say things," she pronounced in her hateful voice. "A young girl and an older man gone off together for three nights or more. It will cause talk."

"He's my uncle," I pointed out, but Greta was not appeased. She did not like me, and I assumed her ambition was more to thwart my glorious adventure than to protect my reputation.

However, when I learned who my traveling companions were to be, I stopped complaining and began dreaming. Bryan of Auburn was everything a young prince should be: handsome, fiery, reckless, and barely sixteen. Not destined to take the crown for another four years, he still had the charisma, panache, and arrogance of royalty, and not a girl within a hundred miles of the castle did not love him with all her heart. I did, even though I knew he was not for me: He was betrothed to my sister, Elisandra, whom he would wed the year he turned twenty.

But I would be with him for three whole days, and say clever things, and laugh fetchingly. I expected this trip to be the grandest memory of my life.

The others who were assigned to us I accepted with passable grace, though only one had come my way often. Kent Ouvrelet was Bryan's cousin, a thin, serious young man whom I had known since I first began visiting the castle eight years ago. Damien, a peasant's son, was Bryan's food taster, and never more than three feet from the prince. However, I could hardly say I knew him since he almost never spoke. The last member of our party was a young guardsman, tall, sandy-haired, lanky, and freckle-faced. He was new to the castle since my last summer there, and I did not even know his name until we set out.

Which was the hour before dawn, a time both dark and wet. We all met at the stables behind the castle, myself, at least, skidding on the slick cobblestones that spread a hard carpet around the entire grand citadel. I had tied my heavy black hair back in a thick braid and dressed in boy's clothes (a more flattering look for my slim figure than some of my court gowns, and I hoped Bryan noticed).

Jaxon laughed when he saw me. "Don't you look like the gate-keeper's urchin!" he exclaimed, not letting this prevent him from giving me his customary bone-cracking hug. "What was Greta about to let you out in public dressed like this?"

"She wasn't awake when I left my room," I said breathlessly.

"Well, your sister's maid, then. I can't imagine that she— Come to think of it," he added, breaking off to look about him in an ostentatious way, "where is that girl? Didn't Greta tell me she would be coming with us to chaperone you?"

I gave him one long, guilty look as I tried to think of a response. There was no good answer: He laughed again, more heartily this time.

"She's still sleeping, I'll wager," he said shrewdly. "Thinking that our little caravan's not leaving till noon or some such hour."

"Nine," I said.

"Well, that gives us plenty of time to travel beyond reach. Bryan! Kent!" he shouted out the stable doors, as if expecting his voice to carry to the turrets and corridors of the castle. "Where are those boys? I should have hauled them out of bed myself."

Five minutes later, as Jaxon and a sleepy groom double-checked the saddle packs on the horses, we heard footsteps running over the wet stone. Bryan was in the lead, tossing back his dark red hair and calling to someone over his shoulder.

"Told you I could outrace you, even in my boots," he crowed and burst into the stables. It was as if dawn had come early and forcefully, an explosion of light. I caught my breath and fell back against the wooden walls. Three whole days!

Kent entered at a more leisurely pace, apparently having given up the challenge some distance back. "You win," he said in an even, indifferent voice, as he pushed his straight dark hair from his eyes. "I think poor Damien fell down somewhere back there."

Bryan shook his head. "I'll never make a man out of him."

"He doesn't have to be a man, he just has to be a stomach," Jaxon said, and then roared with laughter at his own joke. Bryan snorted, amused at this picture. Kent just looked around.

"Are we ready? Where's Roderick?"

"Who's Roderick?" I asked.

"Guardsman. Just up from Veledore," Kent answered. He nodded over at Bryan. "My father won't let the young prince off the property without some protection, so Roderick's our sword."

On the words, Bryan whipped out his own weapon, a wicked silver blade with a gorgeous filigree grip. "I'm sword enough for my own protection!" he cried, thrusting toward Kent and slashing his blade three times through the air. "If we're set upon by rogues or outlaws—"

"Which I doubt, since there are no trade routes cutting up toward the Faelyn River," Jaxon said dryly.

"*I* could defend myself," Bryan continued, a little more loudly. "I could defend all of us."

"Well, and don't forget I've some skill with a sword myself," Jaxon said, still in that same cool voice, "not to mention young Kent here, who's even better than you are."

"Who's—he is *not*!" Bryan exclaimed. He fell into a fighting stance just two yards before Kent. "On your guard, then, man! Let me prove once and for all—"

"Lord, Bryan, just put away your sword and shut up," Kent said impatiently. I almost jumped a foot in the air. I had never heard anyone talk to Bryan that way—so dismissively, so cavalierly. Usually everyone hung on his words as though diamonds would spill from his mouth. At least, that's how the girls in the castle listened to him.

Bryan didn't like the tone, either. He paused in his crouching dance forward and brought his sword up to his nose, bisecting his face. "Are you telling me you refuse my challenge?" he asked in an ominous voice. "Are you telling me you refuse to test my mettle against yours?"

"I'm telling you we should get on the road before the sun comes up and stop wasting time fooling around here," Kent said. "You're a great swordsman. Everyone knows it. If we're attacked on the road, I'll personally let you defend me."

"If we're attacked on the road—" Bryan began, but before he could finish, the last two members of our party hurried through the stable door. Poor Damien looked wet and bedraggled, as though he had fallen more than once. He held his head down and said nothing as he sidled in. Roderick glanced around once, quickly, as if to assess the situation in every detail.

"Sorry I'm late," the guardsman said briefly. "The captain had some last-minute advice for me."

"Well, are we all ready, then?" Jaxon demanded, touching each of us with his gaze. "All right! Mount up! Let's get out before the sun actually rises."

Everyone moved with alacrity except Bryan, who somewhat sullenly sheathed his sword and glowered at Kent. Who completely ignored him. Managing to pass by the prince on my way to my own horse, I whispered, "*I* think you're the best swordsman in the eight provinces." That made him laugh, and he looked quite sunny as we finally headed out through the stable doors.

The guardsmen at the gate saluted us, fists to forehead, and all the men except Bryan saluted back. I, too, raised a hand in the official gesture, wondering if the guards thought I was a boy as well. Probably not. Everybody knew everybody else's business at the castle, and the servants knew more than anybody. We had talked of this expedition for weeks, and even the lowliest scrub maid had heard that I would be on it. Before Greta was even out of her bed, someone would bring her the news that I had left the castle in the company of five men and no female companion. I hoped it ruined her day.

We had not gone half a mile before I brought my horse alongside Jaxon's so I could talk to him as we rode. Despite the fact that I adored Bryan with all my heart, my uncle Jaxon was the most important man in my life. And I rarely saw him, for the summers that I spent at the castle were his busy time; he was seldom there. A landowner, a trader, a hunter—and, Greta would say, a reprobate—he was a man who never stayed still for long.

"Thank you so much for inviting me on this trip, Uncle Jaxon," I said prettily, though I had thanked him a hundred times already. "I'm sure it will be the most exciting journey of my life."

He looked down at me with a wide grin showing through the thick bush of his beard. He was a big man, burly even in satin court clothes; when dressed for hunting, as he was now, he seemed massive and untamed and dangerous. His black hair, now beginning to gray, was tousled and nearly shoulder length; his eyes were a bright black, and wild as a wild boar's.

"Do you think so?" he said, and laughed again. "I doubt we'll so much as spot an aliora through the branches, let alone come close enough to catch one. But the ride should be pleasant and the weather's fine, and it won't hurt young Bryan to explore to the limits of his property. So, I don't mind the wasted trip."

"Why won't we see any aliora?" I wanted to know. "Why won't we catch them?"

"Because it takes stealth or guile, and a party of six doesn't possess either one," he said comfortably. "That's all well enough, though. I don't have time to be riding out to Faelyn Market with a few aliora in tow. Not this month. I'll go back later in the summer and see what I can catch."

He was the richest hunter in the eight provinces. He could live off his wealth acquired from this one harvest alone, but I had heard him say more than once that it was the thrill of the hunt, not the gold on the market block, that drove him again and again to Faelyn River.

"How many aliora have you caught? You alone?" I asked him.

"Exactly thirty. I've been doing this damn close to twenty years now, but I remember when a good year was catching three aliora all told, and a bad year was the third year in a row when I caught none. They're as smart as you or I, Corie, maybe smarter. That's what makes them so valuable."

I glowed a little to hear him call me by my common name. At the castle, it was a rare pleasure for me to be so addressed. Greta always called me the more formal Coriel, and everyone else followed her lead. Except my sister, Elisandra. Like Jaxon, she had asked me early on how I wished to be addressed, and ever afterward, she had called me nothing else. It infuriated her mother, of course, but then, everything about me did. My existence troubled Greta. No help for that.

"Their intelligence and their rarity and their beauty," I cited, for he had taught me that eight summers ago. He laughed again.

"And their gentleness and their teachability," he added. "Yes, all these things have made the aliora greatly sought after—and me a wealthy man."

"Greta is afraid you will die and leave all your money to me," I said. Just recently I had overheard this conversation and had been impatient to have a chance to repeat it to my uncle. "She says the money and property should go to Elisandra instead."

He looked at me with those bright trickster's eyes. "Oh? And what do you think?" he asked.

I smothered my giggles. "I think my grandmother would turn into smoke from astonishment if I inherited a penny of your money,"

I said. "She has the lowest opinion of you—and everybody in your family."

Another sideways look. I couldn't tell what he was thinking. "I would like to see your grandmother turn to smoke, I must admit," he said. "Though, if I were already dead, it's unlikely I'd have the chance. But hold a moment! She's an old lady, ninety if she's a day. I—"

"Sixty-five," I said.

"I am a young man of fifty and will surely outlive her. So I will have to give you all my money while I'm still alive."

I wrinkled my nose. "We don't have much use for money in the village," I said. "My grandmother usually barters her services when she needs anything in the shops."

"Ah, but who's to say you'll always live in the village?" Jaxon asked. "Perhaps you'll marry a fine young man and move off to his estate. Perhaps you'll stay at the castle, wed to one of your sister's friends. Then you'd need plenty of gold."

I opened my eyes very wide. "Once grandmother dies, I'll be needed in the village," I said. "There's not another wise woman for thirty miles. It's hard on her even when I'm gone for the summers."

"Time to train a new apprentice, then," Jaxon said.

"*I'm* her apprentice," I replied.

He laughed softly at a new thought. "No wonder she dislikes me so much, then! She's afraid I'm taking you away. Well, but I'm not the only man who might do that. She has not realized just how pretty you are."

I smiled at the compliment, and the talk turned to other things, but later I thought his words over and realized he was right. Eight summers ago, Jaxon Halsing had showed up at my grandmother's cottage and changed my life completely. He was my father's brother, he said, and my father was dead. He had come to honor a promise he had made at my father's deathbed, that I would be found and brought to my father's household, introduced to my scattered relatives and given some semblance of the birthright I was due.

"She's a bastard," my grandmother had said flatly. "And the child of a bastard at that. I don't see her taking her place in some lord's fancy household."

"I promised my brother," Jaxon had replied calmly. "She is his blood, after all. She deserves to be treated as such."

My grandmother watched him with her narrowed witch eyes, familiar with all evil, all strong desires. "My daughter came upon him in the village tavern, fed him a potion, and seduced him against his will," she said. "He was not the first man she tricked this way. She cared nothing for him, nothing for her daughter. I have not seen her myself for five years. I do not think your brother deserves the scorn he will get for siring such a child."

"My brother is dead," Jaxon said lightly enough, but he had loved his brother; that I learned later. "No scorn can be felt by him."

"But to his legitimate daughter? Born to his lady wife?" my grandmother shot back at him. "What of their mortification and pain?"

"His lady wife would improve upon the application of a little mortification," Jaxon said imperturbably. "And Elisandra—" He paused, and seemed to think it over. "I think she would like to have a sister."

Even I had not believed that, credulous six-year-old that I was. But he had been right about that; Jaxon was right about many things. Following that first visit to the castle, where the royal family and their retainers lived, I had returned every summer. I could not exactly say I had been welcomed into this most sophisticated of societies, but everyone except Greta was at least civil to me. I looked forward to the visits, for I was infatuated with Bryan and I worshipped my sister and my days there were filled with pageantry and color. But I never forgot where I belonged. I never forgot that I was a bastard's bastard, a wise woman's apprentice, nobody special. Exciting though my days at the castle were, I knew that my own story would be a placid one.

WE RODE FOR three hours through the gentle green countryside that was so lush and so fertile that it made Auburn the richest of the eight provinces. Close to the castle were a number of small towns designed to cater to the gentry traveling toward the court, but farther out most of the land was privately owned. Acres and acres of abundant farmland would surround some majestic stone mansion, barely visible from the road. Such sights always amazed me. Cotteswold, where I lived most of the year, had few such noble estates. It was a poor country of hardworking farmers who would stare, as I did, at such wealth belonging to a few men.

Eventually we left the main road that would have taken us to Faelyn Market if we followed it the next hundred miles straight north. Instead, we turned in a northwesterly direction along a badly kept track, and headed toward the forested lands on the borders of Auburn, Faelyn, and Tregonia.

Bryan was the one who demanded a halt, which I knew Damien and I both appreciated. I was determined not to be the one to slow the party down, so I had not volunteered the information that I was thirsty and in need of some private moments behind a bush. But I was not in as sad a case as Damien, who was unused to traveling. Bryan himself rarely ventured beyond the castle for an overnight expedition; when he did, he traveled in luxury, and Damien rode along in the coach. The rest of us were more used to the saddle.

"We'll have a few bites to eat, then, while we're stopped," Jaxon said, and passed around hard rolls fresh from the kitchens. Damien took a small bite from Bryan's bread at least ten minutes before Bryan would touch it; since he did not clutch his belly and fall to the ground, Bryan ate the rest of it.

Jaxon watched this with interest. "At the formal meals—yes, I understand that any number of people could pour poison into your food," he said to the prince. "But here? We're in the middle of the wilderness! No one around for miles!"

"Cooks in the kitchen have been traitors before this," Bryan said darkly. "And everyone in the castle knew we planned to set out today. Anyone could have snuck into the bakery to fold poison into my bread."

Kent had flung his long thin body to the ground, and now he lounged on the fading summer grasses. "And you yourself have carried the food around in your saddlebag all day," he observed to Jaxon. "Plenty of opportunity there to do away with your future king."

Bryan scowled at his cousin. "I didn't mean to say *Jaxon*—"

"Oh, why not? I'm as likely as the next man to murder you," Jaxon said cheerfully. "I just didn't realize you suspected."

Bryan's frown grew blacker. "It's not *funny*," he insisted. "Do you know how many kings and princes have been done away with by treachery? My own father had a taster every day of his life—"

"And died when an edgy stallion threw him, so where's the moral there?" Jaxon asked. "He'd have done better to worry less about spies in the kitchen and more about how to hold on to his horse."

Bryan was furious now. "He— My father was a *wonderful* rider!" he exclaimed. "My father could outrace you any day of the week! He could ride any horse in the stable! Yes, and the wild stallions they brought in from Tregonia, my father could tame those in a day—"

Kent came to his feet, giving my uncle a level look. "Jaxon was only teasing you," Kent said, putting an arm briefly around his cousin's shoulders. Bryan shook him off. "Everyone knows what a gifted rider your father was. Also a great hunter. And a swordsman. The horse was lunatic. Everyone said so."

"Yes, and the head groom shot it that very afternoon," Bryan said. "It deserved to die."

I hadn't known this story. I felt sorry for the horse, but sorrier for Bryan, who still looked both angry and forlorn. I stepped closer to him, trying to think of some way to soothe him. "Are you much like your father, Bryan?" I asked. "You ride and hunt so well yourself. Do you resemble him? What was he like?"

He turned to me eagerly, pushing back that deep red hair. "Yes, everyone says so, I look exactly as he did when he was my age. My fencing instructor also taught my father, and he says I hold my sword just the way my father did. He says I make the same mistakes, too—but they are not many!"

Again, I caught that exchange of glances between Kent and my uncle, which annoyed me to no end. Did they have no conception of how hard it must be to be the young prince, trying to live up to the shadow of a dashing king, and watched on all sides for any sign of weakness or inability? I thought he should be encouraged, not baited. So as we mounted our horses again, I rode alongside Bryan for the next few hours, asking him questions and listening with unfeigned pleasure to his answers. I told myself that Elisandra would not mind; she had heard all his stories before, and she would want him to be happy on this ride. I knew that I had achieved the pinnacle of happiness myself.

We took a longer break at noontime, though this rest passed without incident. By this time, we were within sight of the forest, the great dark cluster of woods that spread from the river in every direction.

"Slower going once we're in the forest," Jaxon observed, bringing us all to a halt. "We'll ride as far as we can, though we might get knocked about by a few low branches. Eventually we'll have to walk."

"How far in the forest before we reach the river?" Kent wanted to know.

"The rest of the day, I imagine, and we might not reach it by nightfall," Jaxon said. "Best not to, in any case. You don't want to be camping by the Faelyn River more than one night. Not in these woods."

"Why not?" Bryan demanded.

Jaxon gave him a sidelong look. "Aliora," he said. "They'd steal you as soon as we would steal them."

Bryan sat up straighter on his horse, laying his hand upon his sword hilt. "I'm not afraid of a few scrawny aliora," he said. "If one came to me in the middle of the night—"

"She wouldn't try to win you away with brute force," Jaxon said mildly. "She'd whisper in your ear—crazy things, lovely things— she'd paint you a picture of Alora so beautiful you would weep to be taken there. How many times have I woken in the middle of the night to see my hunting companions leaping to their feet, their faces covered with tears, and watched them go running across the Faelyn River no matter how I called to stop them? Charm and seduction are the weapons the aliora use on men. Your sword doesn't stand a chance against them."

We were all mesmerized by now. "Have you ever had an aliora whisper in your ear, Uncle Jaxon?" I asked.

He laughed. "Often and often. But I know how to protect myself. And as for letting one of them touch me—ah, that's the fatal mistake to avoid, boys!—it's never happened. None of them has ever laid a hand upon my head."

Bryan's eyes were huge. "What happens if they touch you?"

Jaxon turned slowly to look at him. "You don't know? You came hunting aliora, and you don't know the dangers? If an aliora touches you with the least little tip of her finger, you will be enchanted. You will rise to her call, you will answer to the sound of her voice, you will follow her across the river though you drown, though you never return to your family and your loved ones. If she lays her hand across your cheek . . ." He put his palm upon my face and, against my will, I leaned toward him, hypnotized. "If she feels the bone of your face with the flat of her hand, you will be dazzled—you will think of nothing else but her. She will put a fever in your blood that nothing can cure. You will splash across the river to Alora and never be heard from again."

There was a profound silence when he finished speaking. I felt half-bewitched myself, and it was only Jaxon who had touched me. Kent was the first one to shake off the mood.

"But we have aliora all over the castle, and we touch them all the time," he said practically. "There's no magic in their hands."

Jaxon pulled away from me and turned to look at Kent. "Their magic is inhibited once the golden cuffs are placed around their wrists," he said. "They can't abide the touch of any metal, but gold most especially. That is why I warned all of you to wear gold talismans—to protect yourself against the touch of the aliora. Did you do as I told you? Will you be safe?"

Damien and I instantly felt around our necks to pull out necklets and medallions of the finest gold. Kent extended his right hand, where he wore a fat signet ring bearing the Ouvrelet family's crest. Bryan wore a haughty look and displayed no such amulet.

"I'm not afraid of the aliora," he said proudly. "I wore nothing."

Jaxon quickly smothered an expression of irritation. "I brought a couple of extra wristbands, you can wear one of them."

"No," Bryan said, shaking his head, "I need no protection against the lures of the aliora. I am the prince. I am not afraid."

"Well, and you'll have very little to be afraid of, out here on the edge of the forest," Jaxon agreed. "Though at times the aliora do venture out this far, but rarely at this time of year—"

Bryan's face darkened. "What do you mean? If you think—"

"I think I'm head of this expedition, and responsible to your uncle for your well-being, and that if you don't wear a gold talisman into the forest, and keep it on, you're not riding in any party of mine."

Bryan balled a hand into a fist. "And I say we ride on! You cannot tell me what to do! I am the prince, and I—"

Jaxon turned his back on him to address Kent. "Your cousin is very wearying," he said. "Everybody mount up! We're heading back to the castle."

Dead silence greeted this pronouncement, broken only by the jingle of Jaxon swinging back into his saddle. On horseback, he looked down at us. "Well? Mount up. Time to head home."

I found my voice first. "Uncle *Jaxon*!" I cried. "No! You promised. You said you would take me to the river to see the aliora—"

He kept one hand on his reins and spread the other in a gesture of futility. "And I'd like to, but not unless the prince is safeguarded. You and I will return some day, Corie. Just the two of us. Things will go more smoothly then."

I turned to Bryan beseechingly, but Kent had moved faster. "Put on the damn bracelet and try not to ruin everything," he said in a rough voice, punching Bryan on the shoulder. "Jaxon's right, and you know it. My father would hang all five of us if something happened to you in the forest. If you won't do it for yourself, do it for Corie. There's some honor in being gracious for a lady."

Bryan turned a smoldering look on his cousin, but Kent ignored him. "Give me the wristband," Kent demanded of Jaxon, and Jaxon handed it over. It was a thick cuff, hinged at the middle and closed with a key, looking like nothing so much as a shackle. This was not an ornamental piece of jewelry; this was a fetter that would be clamped to the wrist of any aliora we happened to catch in the wild. "Hold out your hand," Kent said.

"I'm not wearing that," Bryan said through clenched teeth.

"Then we go home," Jaxon said.

"Put it on," Kent said, grabbing for Bryan's arm.

Bryan slapped him away and danced backward. "I'm not wearing that—that slave's chain," he said more loudly. "I will wear gold, since Jaxon insists, but I will not dress like a prisoner."

On the instant, I had stripped my own necklace from around my throat. It was a flat, heavy piece, a gift from Elisandra, and I rarely went without it. "Oh, Bryan, please, would you wear my necklet? I'll wear the wristband—I don't mind."

Kent turned on me impatiently. "You shouldn't have to—"

But Bryan interrupted. "I will be glad to," he said in a stiff voice, and made me a small, formal bow. "I will accept the loan of the lady's favor. I would not want to deprive her of the pleasures of our sojourn into the forest."

I was instantly suffused with relief and exultation. Bryan to wear my necklace! And to return it, alive with the scent of his body! I had never been so happy to lend an object in my life. He even allowed me to fasten the chain about his neck, stooping a little so that I could close the clasp under the fall of his red hair. When he straightened, he bowed a second time, a little more fluidly.

"My thanks, kind lady," he said, and gave me the smallest smile.

I turned back to Kent, who fastened the band around my arm. The gold felt sleek and rich against my skin, though the hinge scraped unpleasantly against my wristbone. I twisted it to a more comfortable position and gave Kent a blinding smile. He shook his head and grinned slightly in response.

Jaxon swung back to the ground, a most sardonic expression on his face. "Well, that's all nicely settled, then," he said. "Can we continue on with our journey?"

And then a most unexpected voice spoke up, slightly apologetic but more than a little ironic. "Sorry, noble sirs and lady," Roderick said, "but I didn't come equipped with gold. It hasn't come my way that often," he added, and I could have sworn I saw a hint of laughter in his hazel eyes.

I turned on him, reproof on my face and tears starting to overrun my eyes. "Oh, Roderick!" I cried, using his name for the first time. "How could you not tell us till now?"

He shrugged. "The king will not care so much if I'm snatched by the aliora," he said. "I don't mind risking the ride into the forest unprotected."

But Jaxon was rooting through his saddlebags again. "Nonsense, I came prepared to reap a bountiful harvest," he said, and pulled out a second shackle. He held it out to Roderick with a huge grin on his face. "Now you too can be a slave in the service of Coriel," he said. "I trust it doesn't offend your sensibilities."

Roderick was grinning back as he snapped the fetter in a most businesslike way about his wrist. "I have none to offend, sir," he said. "Thank you kindly."

Jaxon swept the whole group with one comprehensive look. "Any more surprises?" he demanded. We all shook our heads. "All right, then! Into the forest!"

The track into the woods was much narrower than the road we had followed so far, though wide enough for two to ride abreast. Bryan, of course, waited for no one; he was the brave young prince, he wanted to show us all the way. Jaxon grinned and guided his horse in next. I found Kent beside me as I first rode into the green shadows of the wood.

"So how are you enjoying yourself so far?" he asked, ducking a little to avoid a low-hanging branch.

"Oh, it's wonderful! Better than I had even hoped! Three days with—" I stopped abruptly and shot him a sideways look.

"Three days without hearing the dulcet tones of Lady Greta," he completed suavely. "Yes, I can see where that would improve your life somewhat."

"I don't blame her for not liking me," I said fairly. "But to tell you the truth, I don't think she likes anyone except Elisandra."

"That's because producing Elisandra was the most significant thing she'd done in her entire life," Kent said with an edge of cynicism. "A Halsing daughter! She'd fulfilled her destiny."

This made no sense to me. "Why would she be so interested in bearing a Halsing daughter?"

"Because men of the royal family traditionally marry women of the Halsing line. It has happened for generations. And with Jaxon himself so adamant against marrying, it fell to Greta and your father to perform that particular duty." He looked at me again, a sleepy smile in his gray eyes. "And then, who could believe the luck? Your father produced *two* daughters."

I could not restrain my laughter. Jaxon glanced back at me but did not pause to ask what the joke was. "Oh, yes, the royal court was glad to learn the news about *me*," I exclaimed. "I'm exactly the sort of bride they were looking for."

"Don't tell me it wouldn't be a dream come true," Kent said, still smiling. "All the girls are mad for Bryan."

"Bryan is betrothed," I said a little breathlessly. "It does not matter who else adores him."

"Bryan has always been a little willful," Kent said dryly. "It is hard to gauge how heavily his betrothal weighs on him."

I frowned. "What? What do you mean?" But quickly thinking it over, I understood, and frowned more severely. "Don't say such things! You are unkind to Bryan—you and Jaxon both. You tease him when you know it will only stir up his temper."

"It is true he has a temper, but neither of us deliberately tries to rouse it," Kent said a little more sharply than I expected. "He is to be the king, after all. He should learn to guard his emotions a little more closely."

"Like you, I suppose," I said in a huff. "*You're* never edgy or out of sorts."

He grinned lazily. "I am, all of the time. There is much about the way the world is ordered that does not please me at all. But I think it foolish to vent my displeasure on every poor soul who happens to cross my path."

"Bryan does not vent—"

He flung up a hand for peace. "And Bryan is still young. I am three years older than he, and I have learned some calm in those years. Perhaps by the time he weds your sister and takes his crown, he will be ready to be a good king—still quick in temper, but quick in thought, too, and moved to easy generosity. He has a great deal of energy, which a king needs. What he lacks is the means to control it. But that may come with time."

I gave him another sideways look, this one more considering. He was, after all, so close to the throne himself. "Do you wish you had been named king instead?" I asked him outright. Greta says I am rude; Grandmother says I have no guile. I suppose they mean the same thing. "Your father is regent for Bryan—do you wish he was regent for you?"

He looked straight ahead at the path before him. "You realize that if something were to happen to Bryan before he bore an heir, I *would* be king—my father abdicated all hope of the throne when he agreed to be regent. So do I wish I was to be king? That is not the question I ask myself. I ask myself, Would I be a good king? Would *I* be quick-witted and generous of spirit and full of that boundless energy? Or would I be clumsy and stupid and dulled by my own prejudices? I try to be a good *man*, since I am alive at all, and hope that that teaches me what I would need to know if I was ever faced with a higher challenge. Some days I am more successful at it than others."

I did no such thing as sit there with my mouth open, though I may as well have, since I felt as if my mind was gaping. It had simply never occurred to me to wonder what kind of person I was, what kind of person I wanted to be. I had not envisioned this as something I had any control over, just as I could not alter the round shape of my face or the dense black curl of my hair. If I wanted to be angelic and sweet-tempered, could I achieve that? I thought my grandmother would laugh if I mentioned such a notion to her.

Now Kent was watching me. "I didn't mean to silence you completely," he said. "Or are you trying to keep from saying I have made no headway at all?"

I shook my head to clear away the cobwebs and grinned up at him. "I was wondering if I could turn myself into someone Greta would like," I said with a laugh. "Who could I model myself after?"

"Lady Greta herself," he suggested. "She seems tolerably well pleased with her own personality."

"No, if I wanted to be like anyone, it would be Elisandra," I said.

But now Kent, unexpectedly, had turned sober. "I would not take Elisandra for my model if I were you," he said.

I was completely taken aback. "What? Why not?" He only shook his head in answer. I exclaimed, "I thought you admired her!"

"More than anyone I know, perhaps. But that does not mean I think you should try to be her."

"Why not?" I said again, and this time he replied, giving me a small, crooked smile that did not make him seem happy in the least.

"Perhaps it is because I like you the way you are."

That did not seem like the truthful answer, but before I could press him again, Bryan called out a warning of bad trail ahead. Jaxon immediately swung off his horse and pushed ahead of Bryan to examine the track before us.

"I think we'll be on foot before long," Kent said. "Just as well. The way seems to be getting narrower all the time."

And, indeed, ten minutes later when we resumed our journey, we were all dismounted and Jaxon was in the lead. The way was rough with exposed roots and the occasional bramble, not to mention unexpected patches of mud, but I did not really mind. I had spent plenty of time on trails like this, hunting herbs with my grandmother. However, I made sure I did not fall too many paces behind Kent, and glanced behind me now and then to see if Damien and Roderick were still nearby. Damien had his eyes trained on the ground and looked comprehensively miserable. Roderick—who caught my glance every time I looked his way—grinned and nodded encouragement. Despite the fact that he had scarcely spoken this whole day, I found myself liking him just for the cheerfulness of his face.

We continued in this way for more than an hour before Jaxon

called another halt to rest. This time, there was even less conversation than before, except when Roderick asked Jaxon how much longer we would continue.

"Another two hours, I would think," my uncle replied. "We should stop before nightfall and take a little time to make camp. No use exhausting ourselves before we've reached our destination."

"I know you brought provisions," the guardsman said, "but the woods are full of game. Would you like fresh meat?"

Jaxon eyed him speculatively. "We're making a considerable noise with our passage," he said. "I doubt there's any game for three miles all around us."

"Well, if I see something, then," Roderick said, and let it go.

Soon enough, we were back on our feet and back on the trail. I was tired enough by this time that I would not have minded dropping to the mud, curling up in a small ball, and sleeping right there in the middle of the trail. But Jaxon forged on ahead, and we all followed. I watched my feet and tried not to think about feather beds.

I glanced back less often during this stretch of the journey, but when I did, Roderick was missing. I halted my horse and waited for Damien to catch up.

"Where is he? Did he fall? Should we go back?"

Damien shook his head as if he were almost too exhausted to speak. "Hunting," he said breathlessly. "Said he'd catch up."

"What if we lose him?"

Damien shrugged. "He seems," he said in a thin voice, "able to care for himself."

I hesitated, still troubled, and wondered whether I ought to call out for Jaxon. But Damien nudged me forward. "They're gaining ground," he said, and I wearily set myself in motion again. Roderick would be fine, I knew it; just looking at him you could see his easy competence. It was just that I would not want to be alone in these woods myself. I did not want to abandon anyone else to such a wretched fate.

Roderick still had not caught up with us by the time Jaxon

mercifully called a halt. It was some hours before nightfall, but he had come across a shallow clearing not far from the trail, wide enough for us to build a fire and pitch three tents.

"Time to make camp," he said. "Where's Roderick?"

"Hunting, Damien says," I replied.

That caught Bryan's attention. "Hunting! *I* could have caught us some game if we needed more provisions."

"I think he was just bored," Kent said gently. "He's a country man. Used to rougher land than this."

"Well, he's supposed to be guarding me. How can he guard me if he's off somewhere looking for game?"

I couldn't help myself, I smiled at my prince. "But Bryan, he knows your sword is as good as his," I said earnestly, and I meant it. "He knew he didn't have to be worried for you."

"Well," Bryan said, mollified a little, "he probably won't catch anything this afternoon. Not with all the noise we've made."

"Doesn't matter," Jaxon said practically. "We'll need a fire anyway. Who wants to gather firewood and who wants to pitch tents? And who wants to dig a pit for garbage?"

It was clear by the expression on Bryan's face that he didn't think the prince should have to do any of these tasks, but since it was clear from Jaxon's voice that everyone would have to do something, he made his choice. "I'll build the fire," he said.

Jaxon pointed. "There. We'll put the tents around it. Corie, let me set up my tent first, and then I'll help you with yours."

"I can settle myself, thank you," I said, and proceeded to unstrap my bags from my horse's back. Jaxon could set up Bryan's tent if he was so eager to be helpful.

In fact, I was the only one of the group to have a tent to myself, since naturally none of the men could sleep beside me and the maid was back at the castle. Bryan had not been happy to learn that he would have to share his quarters with someone else, though he had agreed to allow his cousin to join him. The other three would crowd into a third tent, unless Jaxon slept under the stars, which he expressed an interest in doing. I didn't mind sleeping in the open myself, unless it rained. In my experience, a tent did very little to keep away insects or shield you from the cold, so you might as well settle on the hard ground and stare up at the fizzing night sky. But a tent had been provided for me and a tent I would use, and in fifteen minutes I had it snugly pegged in place.

Just as I had turned to offer assistance to the others, Roderick materialized from the trail behind us. He had three game birds slung across his saddle, tied together at the feet, and a pair of rabbits over his shoulder.

"Had a little luck," he said, when Jaxon admired his kills. "Should feed us all."

Bryan looked miffed, but Damien and Kent crowded around Roderick to help him dress the game. That left me to set up a spit across the fire and see what else Jaxon had brought in the way of food. Despite the frequent breaks for refreshment along the way, I was suddenly starving, and the smell of the roasting meat made me nervous with hunger.

Although it seemed like hours later, it was really not too long after the fire started that we were ready to sit down to our meal. We all ate like barbarians, devouring bread, meat, and dried fruit without saying a word. Only Bryan ate with caution, ten minutes behind the rest of us, after Damien had tasted his food. Even I thought this was a little too cautious, since only the five of us could have had a chance to poison the food before he ate it, but perhaps we were among the people he suspected of having designs on his life.

Well, he had already as good as accused Jaxon of considering such treachery. Kent had admitted to me that he would inherit the throne if something happened to the prince. And who knew anything of the young guardsman, so fresh from Veledore? Perhaps he was right to risk nothing, even at a campfire in the middle of the woods.

Jaxon was the first to finish, emitting a loud belch and leaning back against his saddlebag in loose satisfaction. "Ah, that was a good meal," he sighed. "Hunger is the spiciest seasoning."

Kent raised his canteen in my direction, since we had nothing so fancy as wineglasses at our disposal. "A splendid job done by the chef," he said, although all I had done was turn the meat on the spit.

I gestured at Roderick. "And the hunter." Roderick grinned, shrugged, and said nothing.

Jaxon reached behind him and pulled up an oddly shaped fruit or tuber, something that glowed deep red in the tricky light of the fire. "Found this earlier as we were riding along," he said. "Any of you know it?"

Kent took it from his hand, examined it, and passed it along. "No," Kent said. "Is it edible?"

Bryan gave it a cursory look and handed it to Damien, who almost immediately laid it in Roderick's palm. The guardsman looked at it curiously, turning it over and hefting it to gauge its weight.

"Nothing I've seen," Roderick said, and gave it to me.

"It's edible," Jaxon said, answering Kent, "but worth your life to eat it if you aren't careful."

I smothered a yelp and dropped the smooth, waxy globe on the ground before me. Jaxon laughed.

"This dayig fruit's the sweetest you ever tasted—like honey and strawberry and melon all packed in one," he said. "You could gorge yourself on it and not care if you ate another thing in your life. Only grows a few places in the eight provinces, this being one of them. But nobody farms it and nobody harvests it, because you can't sell it. Everyone's too afraid to eat it."

"Why is that?" Kent asked.

Jaxon held out his hand, and I laid the dayig in it. He'd pulled out a pocketknife, and now he slit the fruit in two. "See that?" he asked, holding up one of the halves. The inside was feathered with oblong white seeds too numerous to count. "Poison, every single one of them. Eat just one of these seeds, and you'll die in ten minutes. Fifteen at the most." He shook his head. "Pity, for the fruit is the most wonderful thing I've ever tasted."

Kent took the dayig from him and studied its interior structure, holding it closer to the fire to get a better look. "If it's so dangerous to eat," he asked, "how is it you know how it tastes?"

Jaxon's laugh boomed out. "Because I ate it several times before I knew what the risks were, and obviously the meal had been prepared by a careful hand. But let me ask a question of all of you. Say you wanted to try a dish of dayig fruit—but you knew the seeds were poison. What would you do? How would you avoid the chance of death?"

"I would have my taster eat several bites first," Bryan said instantly. "Only if he survived would I try the food."

Jaxon nodded. "Fair enough. What about the taster—eh, Damien? Suppose you weren't eating on Bryan's behalf. What would induce you to take a bite?"

Damien looked pale and defiant by firelight. "Nothing," he said. "I would not take the chance."

"Even for the most delicious forkful of your life?"

Damien shook his head vigorously. "Not even then."

Jaxon looked at me. "Corie? I know you've got courage."

I took the dayig back from him and tilted it this way and that. Under my grandmother's tutelage, I had learned the names and properties of a good number of poisons, and this was not one I was familiar with. I half-suspected he was tale-telling, just to watch our reactions, but I intended to show some caution nonetheless. "I'd want to know if any antidotes existed before I risked the poison," I said. "If I had the remedy at hand, I'd probably sample a portion."

"There's a good answer," Jaxon approved. "Kent? What about you?"

Kent laughed. "I'd eat it," he said, "if I prepared the recipe with my own hands. I would trust myself to remove every last seed."

Jaxon liked that answer best of all, though Bryan snorted. "Cook for *myself*," the prince said. "I never expect to see that day come."

"Well, then, resign yourself to the services of a taster the rest of your life," Jaxon said pleasantly. "But I do think every person's answer illustrates something about the individual."

"*You* haven't answered," Kent pointed out, but I spoke up before my uncle could.

"Neither has Roderick," I said.

Roderick looked over at me in surprise, though a smile quickly gathered up the corners of his mouth. "I can't imagine anyone going to the trouble of preparing a fancy dish to kill me off," he drawled.

"I'm more likely to die with a sword in my belly or a knife in my back."

Jaxon roared with laughter and the rest of us smiled. I urged, "But if you *were* offered such a concoction—"

He merely shook his head. "It will never happen. I don't fret over things like that."

"So how about you, Jaxon?" Kent asked again. "What would you do presented with the dilemma of the sweet and bitter fruit?"

Jaxon took the dayig half from me and balanced it in his hands. "Why, what I've done before," he said, and crammed the entire portion in his mouth. The rest of us gasped with horror as he chewed noisily and swallowed. I half expected him to fall dead at our feet within the minute, but the instant his mouth was clear, he began laughing again.

"I've never seen such faces," he said. "If I only had a mirror so you could stare at yourselves."

"Uncle *Jaxon*!" I burst out. "The seeds—the poison—you'll die—!"

"It was a lie, meant to test us," Bryan said loudly. "Your uncle Jaxon makes a game of all of us."

"Not so. The poison's very real, as you'll find out soon enough if you try it," Jaxon said. "It's just that I've a hardy dislike of being at somebody else's mercy. So over the years I've fed myself the fruit a little at a time, seed by seed by seed, till I grew immune to its toxin. Now I can eat a whole one and its hundreds of seeds and suffer no ill effect. But more than one"—and his grin gleamed through his beard—"and I am sick for days. I have learned to be content with that little taste, though that I am determined not to give up."

"Nothing could taste that wonderful," Damien said with conviction.

"Oh, but it could," Jaxon said, and caught up the other half from where it lay on the ground. With his pocketknife, he scraped all the seeds out, then cut a sliver of the ruby fruit and offered it to Damien.

The taster shivered and leaned backward. "No. Thank you. No."

Jaxon offered the slice to Bryan. "A taste? It's safe, I assure you."

Bryan came fluidly to his feet. "I think this game has gone on long enough," he said. "I'm for bed." And he stalked the few yards over to his tent.

Jaxon watched him go, then shrugged. "Anyone else?" he asked.

"I'll try a piece," Kent said, holding out his hand. When he put the dayig in his mouth and chewed, an indescribable expression crossed his face. "Ah," he said finally. "I understand why you would risk so much."

"Let me try some," I demanded, and Jaxon peeled off a piece for me. I ate it, and everything Jaxon had said was true. Honey and wine and late summer flowers and the special cake that your grandmother bakes to celebrate your birthday—these things and more were rolled into the taste of this one small piece of fruit.

"Let's pick some more," I said, when my mouth was free for more mundane things, like speech.

"We'll look for it tomorrow," Jaxon promised. "But be very careful when you bite—"

"I'll have another taste right now," Kent said.

"Give Roderick a piece," I suggested.

Again, the smiling look of surprise on the guardsman's face. "You don't have much left," he said. "I wouldn't want to deprive you."

I leaned across the fire to lay the slice in his hand. "I'm a country girl myself," I said with a smile. "I know what it's like to have a rare treat. Eat it."

He thanked me and ate, then his eyes widened with astonishment. Wiping his mouth he said cheerfully, "I know what *I'll* be hunting for tomorrow," and we all laughed.

There was a sliver left, and it was in my hand. Once again, I turned to Bryan's taster. "Damien?" I asked. "The last piece?"

But he shook his head and, like Bryan, climbed hastily to his feet. "Not tonight," he said. "I'm tired. I think I'll go to sleep." And he headed to the other tent set aside for the men.

So we cut the remaining slice into four tiny pieces and each took our final share. But even the wonderment of the dayig fruit couldn't keep me awake much longer, for I yawned through my final swallow.

"Bedtime for me, too," I observed, rising. Then I laughed. "Snug and comfortable in my own roomy tent. The rest of you will be a little crowded."

Jaxon shook his head. "I'll be sleeping by the fire," he said. "I prefer it."

Roderick nodded. "Me, too."

Kent glanced at the two of them. "Then so will I," he said. "Bryan will prefer the solitude anyway."

Jaxon hauled his sleeping blankets out of his saddlebag. "Whoever wakes in the night, throw another branch on the fire," he said.

The others also began unrolling their blankets and looking for flat places to spread them. I stooped over to kiss my uncle on the cheek.

"Goodnight, Uncle Jaxon," I said. "Goodnight Kent—Roderick. I hope you all sleep well."

Five minutes later I was curled in my own blankets, not entirely comfortable on the cold ground. I wondered if the others would stay awake a few hours, talking idly around the glowing fire. I wondered if they would send me back to my tent if I ventured out to join them, laying my blankets alongside Jaxon's for additional warmth. I wondered if we would really find more dayig in the morning, and if there would be enough to have a whole one for myself. I fell asleep.

2

In the morning, some of the glamour of the adventure had worn off. Nothing like insufficient sleep on a damp and rocky bed to dim your excitement on a journey. We all thrashed about for privacy in the woods and wished we had more water for washing. The men had kept the fire burning all night, so we were able to have a hot meal for breakfast, but only Jaxon was made truly cheerful by this fact. I was irritable, Kent was taciturn, Damien was withdrawn, and Bryan was downright sullen. It was hard to tell if Roderick had any sort of mood upon him; he did not seem like the type to inflict his humors on his companions.

We were all just as happy to leave the camp behind when Jaxon gave the signal to march out. Once again we went on foot down the pathway, in single file even when the trail was wide enough to accommodate two. No one particularly felt like talking. Once again, Roderick disappeared for brief periods of time, departing and returning with so little fuss that I was never sure when he was with us and when he was not. The great trees dripped incessantly upon us—drops of water from ancient dews, bits of bark and dead leaves, curious insects, feathers, seeds. The sky, barely visible through the thick mat of branches overhead, looked faraway and mournful. In the distance, birds called and unidentifiable animals chittered and growled. My feet stuck in the mud with each new footfall and had to be pulled out with a conscious effort. I considered flinging myself like a rolled saddle blanket over my horse's back, head flopping down on one side and legs down the other, and cursing away the rest of the journey.

We traveled awhile, stopped briefly, traveled on. I lost track of time and distance, so I had no idea how long we had been on foot before I caught the faint, distant rumble of rushing water somewhere before us. I glanced around to see who else had noticed. Roderick, directly behind me, smiled when I caught his gaze.

"Rapids, do you think?" I asked.

"Sounds too loud for rapids," he said, and I realized that he had not only caught the noise long before I had, but assessed it automatically. "Falls, probably. Didn't know there were any on this stretch of the river."

"Do we cross the river?" I asked.

Roderick shook his head. "Not this party," he said. "Maybe if your uncle was by himself."

"And, anyway, it's dangerous to cross this river," I said a little breathlessly. "Aliora on the other side."

"Aliora on this side, too, if the stories are right," Roderick said, looking a little amused. "Though I doubt we'll see them. We're safe enough."

"*Safe!*" I exclaimed. "*We* have come hunting *them*. It's they who ought to worry about being safe."

He looked at me a moment as if he had some contradictory thought in his head, but he made no answer. Just then, Bryan brought his horse to a stop. As he was following directly behind Jaxon, he brought the whole line to a halt.

"What's that? That rumbling noise?" Bryan demanded.

Jaxon looked back over his shoulder. "The Faelyn River," he said. "You'll see it in a few moments. Come on."

We all picked up the pace then, for ahead of us we could see a dazzling white expanse of blankness that must mean a break in the interminable wall of trees. The river ahead, yes, but at the moment we were even more interested in seeing sunlight.

In another ten minutes we were free of the woods, which splintered into smaller stands of trees as the land sloped down toward the water. The banks were both mossy and muddy, so we skidded a bit, but we didn't mind that. All of our attention was on the river.

It wasn't particularly wide, as rivers go—I had seen broader, more impressive waterways in Cotteswold. The things that held our attention were the current, racing along so quickly that it foamed joyously past every rock and submerged log, and the color, a brilliant blue that at first we mistook for a reflection of the sky. But the sky overhead was a milky white, strung with filmy clouds and leached of color. The river was a jewel of its own making.

Kent took a deep breath. "I've never seen—down by the castle, it doesn't look like this."

"No, and nowhere else that you come across it," Jaxon agreed. "But these are enchanted waters, running across magical ground. Taste it here and it'll taste strange to you. You won't be able to say why—but you'll never forget its flavor."

Roderick was glancing up and down the small stretch that we could see before the river curved out of sight and back into the forest. "Where are the falls?" he asked.

Jaxon gestured upstream. "Quarter of a mile that way. Sort of a rough hike, though the sight is magnificent. Think it's loud now! You can't talk over the sound of rushing water."

Bryan, too, was looking around. "So, where are the aliora?" he wanted to know.

Jaxon laughed and pointed across the river. The woods grew instantly thick on the other bank, crowding down toward the water and stretching away limitlessly into darkness. "Somewhere over there," he said. "How far from the river is a matter of some speculation, for no hunter has gone that far—and come back."

There was a short silence. "No hunter has found the aliora settlements and come *back*," Kent repeated. "What makes you think they went looking?"

"Well, we all went looking, one time or another," Jaxon said. "I've tried more than once to find the fabled home of the aliora. Never came across it, though I went fifty miles into the forest once.

Who knows how I missed it? Perhaps it was just a mile to the east
of me, or ten miles to the west. Perhaps I strolled right through it,
but the aliora had taken on fabulous disguises and looked to me
like nothing so much as a stand of trees and a fall of ivy. Perhaps
Alora is a hundred miles beyond where I made my final camp. All
I know is that I could not find the place the aliora call home."

"So? Then none of the other hunters found it, either," Kent said.

Jaxon tilted his head to one side, as if he was unconvinced. "Did
they not? Cortay was a hunter every bit as good as me, not a man
likely to get lost in the woods. He set out to find the aliora one
summer, and never came back. Same with Fergus and Elliot and five
others I could name you. Brave, smart, strong, ruthless men, all of
them. Went looking for the aliora and never came back."

As always, when Jaxon spoke in that slow, lyrical storyteller's
voice, I felt my heartbeat race and my throat close with tension.
"What happened to them, Uncle Jaxon?" I whispered.

He shrugged. "Who knows? Twisted an ankle and fell to the
forest floor, unable to walk for help, and died there. Got eaten by
wolves or lynxes. Fell sick of a fever. Tumbled into the river and
drowned. There are many ways a solitary man can perish in the
forest."

"But?" Kent said.

Jaxon shrugged again. "But I think some of them found Alora
and were prevailed upon to stay. Perhaps they were thrown into
chains and bound into slavery. Perhaps they succumbed to the glamour of that place, the bewitchment of those aliora voices, and they
threw down their weapons and petitioned for admittance. I only
know that, once lost, these men have never been recovered—and
Fergus, at least, has been missing for fifteen years. A long time to
be gone for a man who meant to come back."

I put my hand on my uncle's arm. It was the hand with the
golden fetter. "Perhaps he was not careful," I said in a small voice.
"Perhaps he did not wear his gold charm when he went hunting.
But you'll be safe—you'll be careful, won't you, Uncle Jaxon? You'll
wear a gold band always, you'll not stir a step without gold around

your wrist? You won't let the aliora mesmerize you and carry you away?"

He laughed down at me, covering my hand with his big warm one, and the brief spell of the story was broken. "I'm safe," he promised me, but I noticed he did not answer the question. All of us had been forced to wear gold into the woods, but not once had Jaxon showed us a talisman of his own. Did he fear that wearing the gold would prevent him from getting close enough to an aliora to catch one? Or was he, like Bryan, so sure of his prowess that he scorned to stoop to the measures that would keep him protected? I vowed right then to stick closely beside him while we were in the woods, to guard him with my own body, my own gold, whatever weapons I had.

Jaxon patted my hand once again, then turned toward his horse. "Let's make camp here. Strip down the horses, have something to eat, clean ourselves up in the river."

Kent glanced from Jaxon to the water and back to Jaxon. "But— the river," he said cautiously. "If it's enchanted, as you say, are we safe to step into it?"

Jaxon nodded. "Oh yes. Swim in it, drink from it, it's just water. Sweeter and purer than any water you'll ever taste again, but there's no harm in it. I've drunk from it many times."

We all hesitated a few moments, covering our uncertainty by unloading the horses and setting up a rough camp. But, now that we were free of the dismal overhang of the trees, we began to grow hot in the summer sun, and the turquoise water looked unbeliev- ably enticing.

"Oh, fine, I don't care if I *am* bewitched," I said finally, and began stripping off the outer layer of my clothes. I hadn't exactly packed for swimming, but I was wearing a dark shirt under my man's jacket, and it hung to my knees. *Modesty enough with my uncle as chaperone, don't you think, Greta? Yes, I think so, too!*

I was the first one in the water, Kent and Roderick right behind me. The river was not as cold as I'd feared, so it must have lain quiet in the sun a mile or so before it raced down the falls, but it was frothy as a cauldron bubbling over the fire. It boiled past me with a delicious tickling effect, and I squealed with chill, sensation, and delight.

"Careful! Don't go too far in!" Kent shouted, splashing over beside me and spraying water everywhere. He had stripped to his breeches, and as he strove with the river, his pale chest seemed more well-muscled than I had expected. "It's probably deep farther in."

"I can swim!" I called back.

"Not in this current!" he replied.

So I was careful to go no farther than my feet could find a purchase on the sharp rocks of the riverbed. Roderick had instantly dived for a handful of those same rocks, and now he came up, his sandy hair sleeked back from his face. The sudden severity of the hairstyle threw his broad cheekbones and strong chin into relief; he looked like nothing so much as a model for good, sturdy, yeoman strength. I watched him as he began skipping rocks into the lively water. The current swallowed his first two stones on his first two throws, so he adjusted his stance and sent the next one skipping downstream, along the face of the moving river. This time the rock leapt back into the air, two times, three, four. He had got the trick of it already.

Jaxon and Bryan joined us in the water, both of them splashing around mightily. Damien hung back on the shore, watching somewhat plaintively but afraid to jump in. Myself, I was delighted with a chance to get clean, and I ducked under the water again and again so that my thick hair would let go of its day's store of dirt and twigs. Every time I surfaced, I found Kent nearby.

"I'm not going to drown!" I informed him over the steady roar of water. "You don't have to be ready to snatch me to safety!"

"You look so small—like the current could sweep you away!" he called back. "I'll just stand right here."

We played in the water till we all started shivering, then climbed back out to warm ourselves in the sun. By this time we were all starving, so luncheon was the next item on the agenda. It was only then it occurred to us that there wasn't much else to do but wait.

Bryan was the one who brought that up first. "So, now what do we do?" he wanted to know. "How do we find the aliora?"

Jaxon lay back on his blanket with a sigh of pure contentment. Roderick had found three dayig during his foraging that morning, and those of us who weren't afraid to try them had split two for lunch. "We wait for them to find us," Jaxon said. "We stay here very quietly, and watch for them to come to the river. Usually one will come alone, first, to make sure all is safe. Then they'll come in twos and threes, and splash in the water just as we did. Eventually, they'll come over to this side of the river, searching for food or fruit or—who knows—maybe even for dayig. I've never asked. I've just taken them unawares."

Even I could see that a raucous party of six, which had just cavorted loudly in the river, had little chance of catching aliora unaware. Even if none of us moved a muscle from now until the next century, we were a hard group to overlook by anyone with reasonable caution. I smothered a sigh, for I had always known we were unlikely to actually capture an aliora, but I had hoped. Bryan, on the other hand, seemed to realize for the first time that this trip might all be in vain.

"They'll never be fools enough to cross the river while we're all camping here!" he exclaimed. "If there were any aliora for miles around, we've scared them off by our shouting! I thought we would press on across the river—I thought we would track them down in their own territory."

"Well, we won't," Jaxon said sleepily. He shut his eyes. "It's possible that none will be brave enough to cross the river while we're camped here—but you may yet see an aliora in the wild, drifting through the forest across the river, or even coming down to the water to take a drink. That's a sight that most men cannot boast of. That's a thing to make the whole trip worthwhile."

Bryan was on his knees, furiously repacking his saddlebags. "Well, it's not enough for me," he said hotly. "I came to hunt aliora, and I'm going to *hunt* them, not lie here tamely waiting for them to fall over my sleeping body. I'm going to cross the river now, that's what I'm going to do, and I—"

Jaxon opened his eyes and gave Bryan a single level look. "No, you're not," he said.

"Well, I will," Bryan said, but his hands stilled in their packing. "I never saw anyone like you. A hunter, you call yourself. You're a lazy coward who doesn't even bother to set a trap. If you catch any game, it's through sheer luck—or because your prey is stupid enough to walk over and beg you to take it captive."

Jaxon continued regarding Bryan with steady eyes. "If you cross the river," he said, as if Bryan had not spoken, "I will leave you there, do you understand? You will never find your way back to the riverbank, let alone to the track that brought us through the forest. You will be lost on the enchanted side of the river, and you will either be taken captive by aliora or you will starve or you will break your neck on a fall over some hidden root. If you cross the river, I will say goodbye to you forever."

Bryan stiffened. His face took on that rigid, bony look it acquired when he was trying to be regal in the face of great fear. "My uncle—" he said.

"I don't much care what your uncle says, at this point," Jaxon said softly. "If he wanted a nephew who would live to be king, he should have raised one with better sense. I've told you the dangers. You're a young man with some rough intelligence. Make your own choice. I'm taking a nap." And he closed his eyes again and, to all appearances, fell instantly asleep.

The rest of us all stared at Jaxon's still form because we couldn't bear to look at Bryan. The prince sat absolutely motionless, ready to explode or ready to weep, we did not know. No one liked to be talked to in such a tone of voice—in effect, dared to be stupid enough to die—and Bryan was not used to such treatment from anybody. I did not for a moment believe that Jaxon would allow Bryan to die witlessly in the enchanted forest, but he had certainly made it sound as if he would. Bryan was hotheaded and brave, but he was not a fool. He did not want to be lost here on this silly, romantic pleasure jaunt. He sat still as a forest tree, and said nothing.

It was Roderick who broke the tableau, shouting, "Pheasant!" and streaking off through the forest. Kent followed him instantly, and I went crashing after them though I had no idea what any of us hoped to gain. Certainly not a meal for dinnertime, since we made so much noise that not even the most oblivious bird would loll around for us. But Roderick surprised me. I had not realized he had a small crossbow with him, which he had snatched up upon his cry; and in two swift shots he had brought down two good-sized birds.

"Well, now I am impressed," Kent said, fetching the downed birds and inspecting the shots. The arrows had gone cleanly through, and there had been no wasted ammunition. "I don't suppose you could teach me to shoot like that?"

"Maybe," Roderick said, with that habitual slight smile. "Depends on your eye. Depends on your aim."

Kent gave the slightest laugh, seeming to measure Roderick for a long minute. "Probably not as good as yours," he said slowly, "but I'll wager I could improve, at least."

"Wager what?" the guardsman asked.

"What would you learn in return?"

"My letters."

Kent's eyebrows went up, either surprised that Roderick could not read or write—or surprised he wanted to. "Done," he said. "As soon as we return to the castle."

We loitered in the woods a while longer, loathe to rejoin the others at the campfire. Roderick found two more dayig and let another half dozen pheasant fly by unmolested. I showed them some of the herbs I knew, reciting their formal names and their healing properties.

Roderick squatted by a scrubby tiselbane bush, all hunched and scraggly in the insufficient sun of the forest floor. "For headaches and other pains, you say?" he repeated. "But it's a spice, too, isn't it? For chicken stews and such."

I shrugged. "That I don't know. I don't cook much."

He looked up at me from his crouch on the ground. "Don't cook?" he asked. "All girls can cook."

I was tempted to reply "All men know their letters," but that seemed too cruel. Besides, unlike Kent, I knew it wasn't true. "Elisandra can't cook," I said. "Greta can't cook. None of the fine ladies of the court can cook. What you mean is, all village girls can cook."

He rose to his feet, brushing his hands together to loosen the tiselbane's distinctive smell. "Maybe that's what I meant," he said cautiously.

"Corie's not a village girl," Kent said, with more heat than I expected. "She's a nobleman's daughter."

Roderick spread his hands. "I apologize."

I gave Kent a stern look; he had no reason to jump to my defense. "I don't have any interest in learning to cook," I said. "I want to be a healer."

Now Kent moved his frowning gaze from Roderick's face to mine. "You could have a higher goal than that," he said.

"It's my goal," I said. "I'll make it as high as I like."

After that, we continued through the forest for a while in silence. Eventually, by common consent, we turned back toward our camp-site. Jaxon appeared to be sleeping still, and Damien lay on the ground a few yards from him, eyes also closed. Bryan was standing waist-deep in the river, a fishing line in his hands and his eyes steady on the racing water. Three gleaming silver trout lay on the riverbed nearby.

"Oh, Bryan, how clever of you! You've been fishing!" I cried, running down to the river to exclaim over his haul. At first he seemed annoyed that I had interrupted his concentration, but at my words, his face relaxed into a smile.

"I thought to add something to our dinner table," he said.

"Oh, yes! And Roderick's shot some pheasant and we've found more dayig—it will be the most wonderful meal! I'm so impressed! I shall never starve if you're with me in the forest."

These words pleased him as well, though he cautioned me, in a friendly voice, to be quiet or risk scaring the fish away. So I knelt on the muddy riverbank for the next hour, as motionless as I could become, and watched him pull in two more trout. I regretted now that I could *not* fry up the meal. I would have liked to impress him as much as he had impressed me, but it was a little late to be gaining accomplishments that I had for so long resisted.

Soon enough it was dinnertime, and a fine meal it was. Bryan ate more than his share of the trout, which no one minded since they were, after all, his trout—and I noticed that for once he did not require Damien to taste them before he ate. I supposed he realized that, with his hands alone touching them, he was completely safe.

After dinner, as night drew on, we settled around the fire and began to tell stories. Well, Jaxon told stories as only he could, in that lilting, seductive voice that made far-off cities and exotic princesses seem so real and so magnificent that you ached to see them for yourself. Kent then told a few stories of his own, tales which he claimed he had read in the history books about past kings of Auburn. Roderick surprised me then by raising his quiet voice to repeat old bits of folklore about brave woodsmen and ensorceled maidens and strange dark villains who lurked in mysterious towers. My grandmother had told me similar stories when I was a child, and I had loved them then. Now, lying under the indolent stars and listening to the murmuring race of the river, I loved them even more.

By this time, the fire had died down and everyone was trying to smother yawns. Jaxon looked at us all and laughed.

"I think it's bedtime for this group of adventurers," he said. "But one word of caution! Make sure all of you wear your gold bands as you seek your beds, for aliora love to creep up upon sleeping men and steal them away in the night."

"We're safe," Kent said, extending his hand to display his ring. Roderick lazily flexed his hand to show off the band on his wrist, and I held mine up to the firelight. Damien tugged on his gold chain to prove its existence. After a moment, Bryan did the same.

"Good!" Jaxon said. "Now, who's sleeping where? I'm at the fire again tonight. It's such a fine night."

Kent shrugged as if to dislodge a clammy palm along his back. "I woke up to find a spider in my hair," he said. "I think I'll try the tent tonight."

"I'll bunk with Damien," Roderick said. "Perhaps the two of us together will be able to fight off any aliora who come sneaking up on us in the night."

I caught Damien's look of relief, as I had earlier caught his look of fear when Jaxon mentioned that particular danger. So Roderick was a kind man, in an offhand, undramatic way. That impressed me even more than his skill with a crossbow.

We all said our goodnights and settled upon our chosen beds, but I, at least, had no intention of closing my eyes. I waited till I thought the others would be sleeping, then crept from my tent, my blankets over my arms.

Jaxon's whisper caused me to leap nearly a foot in the air. "And where exactly do you think you're stealing off to in the middle of the night?" he inquired. "Crossing the river, like the young prince threatened to do? I'll have you know I won't go after you, either."

I stifled a giggle and spread my blankets on the ground across the fire from where he lay. "Well, the regent would scarcely notice that I was missing, so you'd have no worries there. And Greta would be delighted," I whispered back. "But no, I didn't think I'd go so far. I just wanted to sleep under the stars this one night."

I heard his blankets rustle as he turned his big body. "I'm glad of the company. I haven't had much of a chance to talk to you these two days. Are you enjoying the trip?"

"Oh, so much! I can't imagine anything more fun!"

He chuckled softly in the dark. "It's not such a terrible thing to be the only girl among so many men, now is it?" he observed. "Keep you on the trail much longer with this lot, and you'd be choosing among your suitors."

"I hardly think so," I said primly, though my voice trembled with laughter. Jaxon knew as well as I did that there was no suitable match for me in the young men of this group. Bryan and Kent were leagues above my social station; because of my noble blood, bastard though I was, Roderick was below it. And Damien could hardly have been to any woman's taste, though I tried not to despise him for his wretchedness. I had long ago resigned myself to an unmarried life. I truly fit nowhere, and I was not about to try to force myself somewhere I did not belong.

Jaxon chose to misinterpret my reply as disinterest in my choices.

"Well, you're young yet. You'll meet many attractive men. One day one of them will appeal to your wayward fancy."

"It's not the appealing that's the problem," I said drowsily.

I heard him chuckle. "Then there's really no problem." If he added another syllable, I did not hear him, for I was fast asleep.

I could not have said later what woke me up, for stray sounds were swallowed by the roar of the river, and the dying fire did not give off enough light to flicker across my eyelids. But one minute I was sleeping, the next I was awake, rigid and breathless on my hard bed and convinced I should not open my eyes.

I was lying on my side, one ear against the ground, so with my other ear I strained to hear any signal of danger or alarm. No night birds called, no hungry wolves sent out warning ululations; there was only the river, rumbling, murmuring, chuckling past.

Was that the faintest sound of voices overlaying the low monotonous chatter of the water—?

With infinite caution, I opened one eye—and then stared in absolute stupefaction, though I was clever enough not to move a muscle. Across the fire from me, a shadowy shape in the near-complete darkness, Jaxon sat crosslegged on his blankets. Before him appeared the most beautiful creature I had ever seen.

She had skin so pale that it glowed milky white against the darkness, illuminating the features of her face and the long, impossibly black fall of her hair. She was dressed in some sort of iridescent clothing that wrapped her in a net of silver glitter, and she looked in every way to be a thinner, sleeker, more elegant version of a human woman. When she gestured, the grace and fluidity of her long, frail arm was birdlike; when she smiled, her face seemed overlaid with tragic poetry. She moved once, turning to look at the river, and I saw that her feet did not touch the ground. She had no wings to keep her aloft, but she was so delicate that the air itself supported her; it was so enamored of her that it held her close and would not let her fall.

When I had finished staring at her, I remembered that I had senses other than my eyes, and once again I strained to hear sounds over the rush of the river. This time, but faintly, I could catch the soft interplay of voices.

"A more than ordinarily risky venture, Jaxon Halsing," the beautiful creature said, and her voice was as primitive and full of echoes as the voice of the river itself. "Or did you wish us to steal the young prince? Did you bring him to my riverbank just to tempt me?"

"If I thought such a bait would make you careless, I would have brought him years ago," Jaxon said. "Go ahead—try to take him. It will give me just the edge I need."

She laughed, and I heard the sound above all others in the night. I wanted to hear it again, I wanted it to be the last sound I heard in my final living moments. "Oh, no, I have not yet grown so tired of my life that I wish to turn it over to your safekeeping, Jaxon Halsing," she said. "The prince stays with you."

"Some other member of my party, then," he suggested. "The prince's cousin. He's a fine young man, intelligent and good-hearted. Try for him. Not an ill prize if you should win him. Or Roderick, the tall one with the good aim. You might take him back to your encampment and make a fine slave out of him."

"Unlike you humans, we do not take slaves," she said in her musical voice. "Those who live with us do so by choice, and are glad to be among us. They are treated as equals, valued as friends, and loved because we love all our people."

"No way to prove that," Jaxon retorted, "since not one of them has returned to sing of your glorious treatment."

"Unlike the aliora who have escaped from your confinement," she said swiftly, "who tell tales of wretched captivity."

I thought I saw Jaxon's teeth gleam in a smile. "There is little wretchedness in the prince's castle," he remarked. "Even the aliora sold at the Faelyn Market go to homes of refinement and wealth. No one would mistreat an aliora. They cost too much on the open market."

"And no aliora would enslave a human—or any creature," she responded, and again her face seemed to me more tragic than beautiful. "How could you be so cruel to a nation who has done no harm to you?"

"Ah, yes, you with your soft words and sad entreaties can almost make me forget," he said. "But I know the hunters who have disappeared into your woods. I know the children who have been lost wandering the edge of the forest in Tregonia. I know the tales that go back long before men like me began setting their traps for creatures like you. You began to steal us before we began to steal you. And we have lost many more loved ones than you have."

"You have lost them because they chose to come to a world far more gracious and wondrous than yours," she replied. "In Alora, the streets run with magic—you inhale rainbows when you breathe. The air is scented with cinnamon and decorated with song. No man lives in want, no child goes unloved, and the contentment of your heart makes every day a joy. This is true for the aliora, and it is true of the humans who have chosen to live among us. Come to Alora. See for yourself."

Jaxon laughed shortly. "Yes, and be taken prisoner myself! Never to return to tell my family and my friends about my wonderful new life."

"Come with me," she repeated, extending one spider-thin hand. Moonlight glowed along its long, white length, glinted at the fingertips. "I promise you that you will be allowed to return if you so desire."

"And to how many men have you made that promise?" Jaxon scoffed, but there was something odd about him now. He seemed to be leaning toward her as if a terrific force inclined him in her direction, mightily though he resisted; his arms and his back seemed knotted with tension.

"To all I have invited with me to Alora."

"And how many of them have returned to the haunts of man?"

"Not one," she said, "but not one of them wished to."

Now Jaxon rolled to his knees, as if impelled by that great external coercion; still he seemed to struggle silently against some impossible desire. "And you think I would not want to?" he said, what I could hear of his voice sounding scraped and raw. "You think I would cross the boundaries of Alora with you and choose to stay forever?"

She still had her arm extended toward him. Now she came a

pace nearer and turned her hand palm-up in invitation. "Ah, Jaxon, you wish to come with me," she whispered, but even so I heard the whisper. "You have long wished to see my home, to live with me among the beautiful people. You would not be lonely another minute, my friend—you who are so lonely now that you stay awake night after night for the companionship of a campfire. I know your heart, you see. It is bitter and empty and full of regret. Come to Alora, and all that will be washed away."

"I cannot come," he said, his voice very low.

"You want to come," she replied.

"No."

"You do. You wore no gold into the forest, Jaxon. Why was that?"

"So you would be unwary enough to approach me. One step nearer and I will snatch you up and bind you in chains."

She floated closer by an inch, maybe two. It was then I realized that the aliora's pose was as tense and painful as my uncle's, that she yearned toward him with an equal longing. Her pale fingers trembled in their own ghostly light, and her face seemed shut tight against both dread and desire. "Is this close enough, Jaxon?" she asked. "Can you touch me now?"

"I warned you," he said.

"Closer still?" she murmured. "Would you like me to lay my hand across your cheek? Would that convince you to follow me across the river?"

"If you touch me, you are lost," he said.

"If I touch you, and you with no gold upon you, you are mine," she retorted. "Is that what you want? Do you want me to touch you?"

He made no answer. The night was unbearable with stress; I could not move nor breathe. Both of them seemed to tremble with an uncontrollable emotion that kept them weighted in place even as it propelled them forward. Then suddenly there was motion too swift for me to follow. It seemed as if Jaxon leapt for her and she shot away, for there was a whirl of gowns and blankets and suddenly she was twenty feet from him. Jaxon was on his feet, breathing hard and staring harder, his hands clenched at his sides and his face a study of anguish.

She was laughing. "Not this time, Jaxon," she called to him, her voice carrying over the distance and over the sound of water. "Not for you—not for me."

"I'll return," he said. "Often and often."

"I will await you," she said, and disappeared.

Yes, she did, she disappeared, because I did not take my eyes off of her. One moment she was there, white and glowing against the streaky blackness of the night, and the next moment she was gone, not even a sparkle left behind. My tiny gasp was covered by the gurgle of the river, and by Jaxon's sudden stomping around the campsite. He stalked some distance away as if to release some frightening energy, and he rubbed his hands up and down his arms as if he had suddenly grown cold. I could not tell if he was disappointed at missing the chance to capture the aliora, angry that he had come so close to surrendering to her—or if some other emotion, mysterious to me, kicked him down to the river and back. He did not look any happier or any calmer as he came close enough to the fire for me to see his face, and I was wise enough not to let him know that I was awake.

What could you say to a man, after all, after witnessing such an encounter as that?

He had brought some logs back with him and built up the fire, so I was careful to lie as motionless as possible. He sat there for some time staring into the flames, then he dropped to the ground again and rolled himself in his blankets. Though I lay open-eyed for another thirty minutes or so, he did not make another sound, and eventually I fell asleep.

IN THE MORNING, Jaxon made no mention of his adventure from the night before. Roderick was the first one to rise, but just by emerging from his tent he startled Jaxon and me awake. The guardsman crept to the fire with a few branches in his arms, and then moved less quietly once he saw our open eyes.

"How'd you sleep?" he asked, squatting on the ground and feeding fuel to the coals.

"As well as a man can on a hard ground," Jaxon said cheerfully enough. "You, Corie?"

"Oh—I don't think I stirred all night," I said a little hastily. "Just fell right asleep and stayed there."

Roderick slanted me a sideways look. "So much for admiring the beauty of the stars," he commented.

I was tempted to reply that the beauties of the night were very impressive indeed, but I didn't want to rouse Jaxon's suspicion. "Maybe next time," I said vaguely.

A few promising young flames were licking at the wood, and now Roderick added a good-sized log. "No aliora dropped by unexpectedly, I take it?" was his next question.

Jaxon glanced around. "Well, not that I know of," he drawled, "but who knows that they didn't go raiding the tents? I guess we should wake the others just to make sure they're safe."

"Let them sleep," Roderick suggested. "If they're not safe now, they're beyond our help."

Jaxon laughed and agreed. The two men set out to make a breakfast meal while I headed down to the river to freshen up. While I splashed vigorously in the water—*much* cooler at this time of day and not nearly as much fun—I pondered over the strange events of the night before. Clearly Jaxon did not want any of us to know about his odd conversation with our midnight visitor. Clearly Jaxon and the aliora had met often before, had sparred and whispered to each other across many campfires over many years. Clearly each wanted desperately to get power over the other.

Was it possible he had brought us all to this campsite at this river solely and specifically for a chance to meet up with this aliora again?

I scrambled up the bank to find all five men heading down. "Watch the fire," Kent told me as he passed me, "and keep your eyes turned away from the river. All of us need to strip down and clean up."

Soon enough, we were all washed and reassembled, eating the porridge that Jaxon had concocted. No one was too talkative and it was clear to us that the adventure was on the downward slope of excitement. Now we faced the long trip back without the illustrious goal before us. It was hard to be entirely lighthearted.

"Might be one more night on the road," Jaxon observed. "Depending on the time we make today."

Bryan rose to his feet. He had not so far said a word. "Then let's strike the tents and be on our way."

INDEED, THE TREK out of the forest seemed five times longer than the journey in, and no one made much effort to alleviate the others' boredom. As before, Roderick amused himself, drifting off to hunt or merely enjoy the scenery while the rest of us trudged down the endless green miles of forest.

Once we broke clear of the woods, we had a collective improvement of mood. Kent fell back to discuss something with Roderick, while Damien actually ranged ahead of the group. I, by some great and never to be sufficiently appreciated stroke of fortune, found myself riding beside the red-haired prince.

"The fish you caught yesterday were the best part of the dinner," I said, partly to open the conversation on a note of praise and partly because it was true. "How did you know to bring fishing line with you? I would never have thought of that."

He glanced down at me with the slightest frown. "We were going to a river, after all," he pointed out.

I smiled—my best oh-I'm-just-a-silly-girl smile, in which I very rarely indulge. "Well, maybe I'll think of it next time. But you caught so many! What bait did you use?"

He laughed shortly, suddenly and deeply pleased with himself. "A few slices of that dayig fruit," he said. "Everyone else seemed to find it so delicious, I thought the fish might."

I laughed with him. "Well, the fish was wonderful—the dayig was wonderful—the whole trip was grand. But maybe you missed all the formal dinners and meetings with ambassadors."

"There will be plenty of that waiting for me when I get back," he said. "Dirkson of Tregonia will be there with his daughter,

Megan, and I'll be expected to squire her around for the next week or so. She's a tiresome girl, always trying to get me to flirt with her. I swear, her only notion of a conversation consists of me telling her how beautiful she is and her replying, 'Why, thank you, Bryan!' "

Coming from Bryan, this was actually exquisite humor, but I was shocked nonetheless. "Flirt with her!" I exclaimed. "But you're betrothed to Elisandra!"

He flicked me a smiling glance, and I saw a touch of that arrogance that had been missing since the night before. "She doesn't want me to *marry* her, she wants me to pretend to be in love with her," he said. "You are not at court often enough. You do not know how these games are played. A little dalliance in the garden—a few whispered words in the hallway—everybody does it, and it means nothing."

Unexpectedly, he held out one imperious hand. I laid mine against his palm, wondering, and he squeezed my fingers lightly.

"I'll show you how it's done," he said. "I come across you in the breakfast room, perhaps, and you've just finished your tea. 'My, Lady Coriel, don't you look fresh this morning?' I say. 'The color of your gown so exactly matches your eyes—I feel like I could drown in them, they are so blue and so deep.' And then you say—"

"My eyes aren't blue," I interrupted. "Brown eyes. See?"

"Well, brown eyes aren't poetic," he dismissed them. "And then you say, 'Oh, Prince Bryan, I was just about to go to the stables for my morning ride. But I'm so afraid to ride out by myself, for the countryside is so vast and I'm so silly that I get lost even at home—' "

"You can't get lost within twenty miles of the castle," I said practically. "You can see it from every road—"

He ignored my interjection. "And I say, 'Why, of course, Lady Coriel, I would be happy to ride with a woman so beautiful as you.' And then you take my arm as we stroll down to the stables, and you pretend to be afraid of your horse so that I have to personally hand you up into the saddle, and then you extend your hand to me to thank me. And I kiss it on the knuckles," he said, suddenly and unexpectedly raising my hand to his mouth.

I actually gasped aloud; this was the last thing I had expected, and it was over before I had truly grasped the fact that *Prince Bryan of Auburn was kissing my hand*. I willed the heat of his mouth to sink through my flesh and imprint upon my bones so that for the rest of my life I would carry the outline of that salute within the cells of my body—but he had dropped my hand, laughing carelessly and urging his horse forward, and my hand had already forgotten the precise texture of his lips against my skin. Numb, I kicked my horse forward to catch up with him again.

"So that's what I've got to look forward to when I get back to the castle," he said, relapsing into a glum mood. "It wouldn't bother me if we were to spend another night on the road."

I could come up with no answer. He had kissed my hand. The forces of gravity came unraveled; there was no cohesion at the core of the world, no order in the universe. Clouds and trees and birds and suns spun around of their own volition, freed from their laws and routines. Bryan had kissed my hand. I could not be rational; and so nothing in the world would make sense again.

WE PUSHED ON as late as we dared, but were forced to camp eventually because Jaxon didn't like this particular party to travel by night. We had been quiet as we traveled, and we were nearly silent now. I went to bed inside my tent and dreamed the night away.

In the morning, a few hours of steady riding brought us in sight of the castle. A commotion at the stable yards and Bryan and Damien were gone before the rest of us were dismounted. Roderick, Jaxon, and Kent lingered to discuss the horses with the grooms, and I was left somewhat forlornly alone to gather up my belongings and trudge back to the castle. Greta was no doubt waiting to give me a terrific scolding, and Elisandra was no doubt busy with some of those visiting dignitaries. The Grand Adventure was over.

3

Late in the day, refreshed by a nap and still unable to locate my sister, I headed for the upper level of the castle, where the aliora lived. I had discovered this place on my very first visit to the castle, when I felt small, lost, and unwelcome—by everyone except Elisandra, of course. You could encounter aliora throughout the castle, gliding soundlessly down the marble passageways intent on some errand or another, but I only knew a few of them to talk to. In particular, I was fond of Cressida, who belonged to Greta and tended to my sister and—when I was at the castle—me. Aliora were not human, of course, so it was hard to tell, but she seemed matronly and middle-aged, more substantial than the willow-thin young aliora who moved with such grace it was like watching a sunbeam walk. Cressida was kind. She had comforted me more than once when she found me crying, taking me into her long arms and holding me until I was calm.

That was the thing about aliora, I learned later—that was the reason they were so sought-after, so richly prized. It was not just their beauty and what I had described to Jaxon as teachability—it was that sweetness, that gentleness, that great tangible aura of kindness that they could wrap around a weeping human child, a fuming princess, an angry lord. They brought civility to humans. They could make us happy.

So that day long ago I had gone to seek out Cressida, and toiled up miles of narrow stone stairs to find the aliora quarters at the very top of the castle. One wide doorway, guarded only by a curtain, admitted anyone to their chambers. Outside the door on a long golden chain hung a single golden key. It was a key that would turn the lock on every single shackle that the captured aliora wore around their wrists. But they could not abide the touch of gold; they could not lift the key from the wall and free themselves from their fetters. The key hung there as a reminder of the castle's wealth—and the castle's power.

Through the door was one great room, loosely divided into smaller rooms by hanging blankets and groupings of furniture. That first day, I had stepped into the big chamber and stared all around me, but I did not focus on the arrangement of bed and dresser and wall. What I noticed was the glow, milky and iridescent, that coruscated through the room and laid a faint patina over the air itself. You did not see it on the individual aliora as they slipped through the castle—but here in this room, all gathered together, they glimmered with magic.

Cressida had welcomed me that day, had let me play with strange colored-glass beads while I lounged on her bed and listened to the soft chirruping speech of the other aliora. She introduced me to her fellow prisoners, giving me both their true names and the names by which they were called by humans. I tried, but I never caught the exact syllables of her true name. The others' I did not even attempt. After that, I frequently went back to the aliora quarters whenever I was lonely or miserable, and I never failed to leave that place feeling happy and refreshed.

Today I burst through the doorway with my usual abandon. "Cressida!" I called. "Cressida! Oh—hello, Andrew. Bryan's back, he's probably going to be looking for you soon."

Andrew, like Cressida, had been in captivity ten years or more; his dark hair looked to be thinning somewhat, and his pale skin to be growing muddy and clotted. A sign of age, I thought. I had never come up with a polite way to ask any of them how old they were.

"I have seen him," Andrew said softly. All the aliora spoke softly, with these delicious, whispery voices that made you feel as if you had been dipped in champagne. "I am to attend him more fully later."

He was seated on a dilapidated sofa, his legs folded crosslegged before him, seeming to be merely a collection of angular arms and knees and elbows. Not for the first time, I wondered how furniture in Alora was built, and if it accommodated the aliora any better than these castoffs did.

I climbed up next to him on the sofa and leaned against his chest; his arm came around my shoulder. I took a deep sigh and released it on a sound of pure contentment. Troubles fall away when you're in the arms of an aliora. No worries nag at you; even your physical aches lessen. The excitement of the journey had worn me down, but now I felt relaxed and at ease again.

"He wasn't always in a cheerful mood on our hunting trip," I volunteered. "You might find him a little difficult."

I heard the smile in Andrew's voice; he lifted a hand to pat my head. "Bryan is always difficult," he said. "But he rarely takes out his ill humors on me. He allows me to charm him."

I felt Andrew's copper shackle bump against my skull, though he held his hand carefully to avoid hurting me. The aliora were so sensitive to gold that they would perish if they wore for long the gold shackles with which the hunters trapped them. Once the aliora were sold, their fetters were exchanged for baser metals—which still inhibited their movements, but pained them less.

"I charmed him, too, once or twice," I said, smiling happily at the memory. "Jaxon and Kent *would* tease him, but I was nice to him, and I could usually cheer him up."

"You could cheer anybody up," Andrew said. "It always cheers me to see you."

"And he kissed my hand," I said blissfully. It was no secret among the aliora that I was desperately in love with the prince. "It was such a wonderful journey!"

Andrew laughed softly. "And did you and the great hunter Jaxon catch any unlucky aliora on your trip?"

"No. But we—" I sat up. "But, Andrew, we saw—"

Before I could complete my sentence, Cressida swept into the room. This had happened more than once, but it astonished me every time I saw it. One pace outside the room, she looked ordinary, frail, a little weary—one step inside and she seemed to expand, grow taller, gain a certain brilliance, just from the pooled magic in the room. It didn't happen just with Cressida. Every aliora was transformed upon entering the communal chamber.

"Corie! You're back!" Cressida exclaimed, coming over to kiss me on the cheek. My sense of well-being increased a hundredfold. She pulled up a small stool and sat before us, taking my hand in hers. "How was your trip?"

"Bryan kissed her hand," Andrew informed her.

Cressida looked amused. "Ah, then it was most successful," she said. "How is it you have not died of the ecstasy?"

"Perhaps she believes that if she lives, she will experience the ecstasy again," he suggested.

I shook my head. "Oh, no. I know whose hand Bryan should be kissing, and it is not mine. But it was wonderful all the same."

"And the purpose of your journey? The hunt? How did that go?" she asked me.

"They captured none of our people," Andrew said before I could answer. Cressida's hand, which had been tight on mine, relaxed a little. I frowned slightly, for it had not previously occurred to me—

I shook my head. I was too content and happy right now to worry over odd little moral dilemmas. Like what my friends the aliora thought about my hunting trip to trap more aliora.

"No, we did not capture any aliora—but Andrew, Cressida, the strangest thing happened," I said, my words tripping over each other in my haste to get this mystery answered. "The night we camped by the Faelyn River, Jaxon and I slept by the campfire, under the stars. And in the middle of the night, I woke up to find him speaking to the most beautiful aliora woman, and she invited him to come back to Alora with him, and he wanted to, I know it. Then suddenly he tried to grab her, and she sort of flew away. Then she laughed, and she was gone. And the next morning, he didn't say a word about it to anyone. He pretended like we had not encountered any aliora at all."

Andrew's hand had come back up to stroke my hair. Cressida's fingers had once again tightened and loosened on my own. The two aliora exchanged one long, meaningful glance before answering.

"So. She is still hovering on the banks of the Faelyn River, waiting for her loved ones to come back," Cressida said very quietly. "That is a dangerous place for her to wait, with Jaxon Halsing prowling the forest."

"That is why she waits on the riverbank," Andrew said, in a voice even lower than hers. "Because Jaxon Halsing hunts there."

They made no sense. I drew my hand away. For the first time while sitting in that room, I felt a faint sense of unease and premonition. "What are you saying? What do you mean? Do you know who that woman is?" I demanded.

I was looking at Cressida, but she was looking at Andrew. Finally he answered. "She is the queen of the aliora, as you understand the word 'queen,'" he said at last. "She has led our people for longer than you have been alive. Everything that is good about us is magnified in her—her beauty, her gentleness, her intelligence—"

"Her strength," Cressida interjected.

Andrew nodded. "Her strength. It has been her goal since she attained rulership to see a halt put to the depredations of the humans upon the aliora. She has done what she can to close Alora, to keep our people from wandering outside its protected borders. But the young ones are foolish still, wandering where they will and getting caught in the nets of hunters such as your uncle."

"And she wants them back," Cressida said.

Andrew said, "So she drifts closer and closer to the human settlements, studying their buildings, studying their ways. And the closer she comes and the longer she stays, the more danger she puts herself in. And if the queen of Alora is captured by Auburn hunters, I do not know how long Alora itself can survive."

"But they are slaves, these captured aliora," I pointed out, my voice sounding harsh and stupid against the melody of theirs. "And they wear metal shackles that can only be undone by a golden key. Even if she could find them all, she could not free them. She only puts herself at risk."

"She is strong," Cressida murmured again. "If there is a way, she will find it."

"If Jaxon Halsing is in her way, she will find nothing but bondage and misery," Andrew said darkly. Again I felt that curious, unwelcome sense of disturbance and unease. I gave Andrew a troubled look.

"What you said before—about Jaxon—why does she look for him?" I asked diffidently. "Why does she seek him out?"

"Because, like any foolish girl, she is drawn to the thing she should most fear," said Cressida in the hardest voice I had yet heard her use. "Because she knows danger when she sees it, but thinks it looks like euphoria instead."

"I don't understand," I whispered.

She bent a stern look on me. "Don't you? You of all people should."

My face must have shown my fright and anxiety, because suddenly her features smoothed out and Andrew gathered me into a close embrace. "Ah, child, words I should not say, words you should not hear," she said gently. She patted my hand and then let me go so I could curl up more tightly against Andrew's side. I felt safe again, comforted; worry slipped from my mind like sand through a sieve.

"But what is her name?" I asked. "The aliora queen?"

Cressida spread her hands as if considering. "In a tongue you can pronounce? The closest word would be Rowena, I suppose."

"And will she be safe, do you think?" I asked, for though I had gone hunting aliora just a few days ago, this one somehow seemed precious enough to deserve her liberty.

Cressida looked as if she might give an equivocal answer, but Andrew smoothed my hair with his long, thin fingers. "She will be quite safe," he said soothingly. "Do not worry. All will be well."

*   *   *

THREE STEPS FROM my own chamber door, I was unlucky enough to run into Greta. When she saw me, she actually stamped her tiny foot and pointed a finger in my face.

"You!" she exclaimed, and wrath drew her patrician features into the most dreadful scowl. Her face was as pretty and delicate as Elisandra's, but she was fair where her daughter was dark, and so small that, if she would ever be silent for even the shortest period of time, you could overlook her completely. But she was never silent. "How dare you disobey my *explicit* orders and leave this castle without a chaperone? Do you know what kind of censure you have laid yourself open to? Do you know what damage you have done to your reputation—which is fragile enough, being who you are, but for you to shred it like that for no good reason—"

It was hard for me to even pretend to look contrite, though I tried. "I thought we were to meet at the stables. When I arrived there, she was nowhere in sight, and we needed to leave immediately—"

She shook her finger at me even more angrily, though she had to glare up at me, which ruined the effect somewhat. "Don't lie to me, you idiot girl! I know full well that you left her behind on purpose—to make a mockery of me and a hoyden of yourself! But it's not me you're hurting. Oh no, it's yourself. What respectable young man will take you if you persist in such antics? What hope do I ever have of finding you a husband?"

I stood stock-still. Why had this topic come up so repeatedly in the past few days? "I have no thought of marriage," I said stiffly. "And even if I did, I would not look to *you* to find me a husband."

"Then the more fool you," she said tartly. "Why else do you suppose your stubborn uncle drags you to court year after year except to introduce you to the eligible men of the eight provinces? He does not want to see his own flesh and blood—bastard though she be!—thrown away on some half-wit yokel from down in the southern swamps. The Halsings are too proud for that. He wants you wed, and wed well, and I have promised him I will do what I can. But if you continue to thwart me as you have—"

"And why would *you* care if I marry a lord or a stablekeeper?" I demanded, losing my own temper. "You can scarcely stand the sight of me!"

"I know my obligations," she said stiffly. "I know what is right."

"Well, you have no obligations to me," I declared. "I would not marry a husband of your choosing if there were no other men—"

"Be quiet!" she exclaimed, furious again. "You will *listen* for once, and you will do what I say! You have come to court to meet your future husband, but it will not be this week. I am too angry with you. You will not join us for the grand dinner honoring Lord Dirkson of Tregonia. In fact, you will not be permitted at any of the festivities for the rest of your stay here until you can prove to me that you can behave like a lady. *And*," she added, as she saw me draw breath to say that I did not give a damn about the court festivities, "if your behavior continues unchecked, you will not be permitted to ride, you will not be permitted to leave the castle grounds, you will not be allowed to wander even about the castle unescorted. Do I make myself plain? Guard your actions, or they will be guarded for you."

I could have killed her, right there in the hallway, pummeled her tense little body into bits of bone and taffeta. But very clearly she meant every word; and she had the power to enforce her threats. I could feel my very blood grow brittle as I replied in a shaking voice, "Yes, Greta, I understand you very well." It took all the willpower at my command to keep from adding all the epithets I knew, especially since she watched me a long moment to see if she could goad me into some further indiscretion. But I held my tongue and stared balefully at her, and finally she turned to leave.

"You will come to my chambers in the morning," she said over her shoulder, "and we will plan your lessons for the day. There are parts of your education that have been too long neglected."

With that parting sally, she moved quickly down the hall, smoothing the front of her dress as if by that action she could smooth down her own ruffled emotions. I stared after her with bitter resentment, then stormed into my room where I stomped around until I wore myself out.

It was not until early evening that I finally saw Elisandra. I had flung myself on my bed and was reading a badly written romance when she knocked on the door and called my name.

"Come in! Come in!" I cried, sitting up and nearly bouncing on the bed. "I have been looking for you all—oh, but you can't stay, can you? You're all dressed up for dinner."

Crossing the room to my side, Elisandra pirouetted once, slowly and gracefully as she did all things, to allow me to see the full glory of her gown. It was a glittering silver net laid over a dove-gray silk, and at every diamond-shaped intersection of heavy thread there was sewn a pearl. Her black hair was braided back from her face and pinned in place with silver and diamond combs; great icy scallops of the same gem hung around her throat and wrists.

"How do you like me?" she asked, dropping to a chair beside my bed. "Will Megan of Tregonia be jealous and impressed? Will Lord Dirkson call me the Treasure of Auburn, as he has before?"

"Will Prince Bryan fall to your feet and declare you the most beautiful woman in the eight provinces?" I asked.

"That, too," she said serenely, and folded her hands carefully in her lap.

I studied her for a moment, for my sister was a woman it was impossible to look away from. She was beautiful, of course, with the night-dark hair and eyes that characterized everyone in the Halsing line; she had her mother's fine features and regal bearing, and an innate elegance that I had simply never seen falter. But there was something else about Elisandra that was even more striking, and that was her air of absolute, unbreakable calm. Even when she spoke and gestured in the course of an ordinary conversation, a great stillness lay behind the animation of her features and the glances of her eyes. Even when she danced, she seemed to move as a figure in a frieze would, stately and frozen in place from panel to panel. There was no exuberance in her, no matter how she laughed or smiled. There was a great watchfulness that hung about her like a curtain of light or shadow, and filtered out any thoughts, any expressions, that she wanted no other to see.

I wanted nothing so much as to be like her, and I had no hope of it. My one consolation was that she loved me and never failed to show it. She was courteous to everyone, and she never spoke in anger; but to me she showed a deep affection that left me glowing and grateful by turns. She had no cause to love a bastard half sister foisted upon her by a determined and wayward uncle, but she did— and that was the real reason I was eager, every year, to return to Castle Auburn.

"How long will this horrid Megan be here?" I asked presently.

Elisandra looked mildly amused. "What makes you think she's horrid?"

"Bryan says she flirts with him."

She nodded. "All the girls flirt with him."

"Well, I thought she sounded worse than most."

"You just say that because she's here."

"So is she horrid?" I asked.

"Not particularly. A little insipid. Her father is very powerful and thinks that makes up for his own deficiencies in intellect, as well as his daughter's." She shrugged lightly. "Who knows? Perhaps he is right. So did you enjoy your trip?"

"Oh, it was the most wonderful time ever!" I exclaimed. "We rode and rode, and then we were in the forest and we had to walk, and we camped by the Faelyn River and ate dayig—"

"Dayig?"

I nodded enthusiastically. "Yes, it's a poison fruit, and Jaxon—"

"Poison!"

"Well, only the seeds are poison. Jaxon taught us how to eat it, but only Kent and Roderick and I would try it."

"Who's Roderick?"

"A new guardsman from Veledore. He came along to protect us, although Bryan said he didn't need any protection. And I never saw him use a sword," I added, "but he was very clever with a crossbow. I liked him. He smiled a lot."

"I'll have to watch for him, then, although guardsmen don't often come my way. Did you find any aliora?"

I hesitated, but in actual fact, we had not found any—though one had come across us. "No," I said. "But I don't think Jaxon expected us to. I think you have to be much quieter than we were."

She smiled faintly. "Just as well, maybe. I don't think I would enjoy being along on a trip where wild things were trapped for the purpose of being sold into bondage."

Just this thought had begun to nag at me that afternoon. Still, it was new enough that I felt free to argue. "But I love having the aliora at the castle!" I exclaimed. "Cressida braids my hair for me when no one else will take the time, and she sat up with me for three straight nights last summer when I was sick—"

Elisandra nodded. "Yes, impossible to imagine life without them. I just sometimes—" She paused, shrugged, and then smiled the thought away. "So what else happened on this wonderful trip? Did you argue with Kent? Flirt with Bryan?"

I had planned to keep this great betrayal a secret, but the words built up like a storm force inside my chest, and then burst out in one swift, guilty rush. "Oh—Elisandra—I *did*!" I admitted. "Flirt with Bryan, I mean. We were riding back, and he was telling me about Megan of Tregonia, and how the lords and ladies talk to each other and he—he kissed my hand! I'm so sorry, I'm so sorry, but I didn't know he was going to do it and it made me so happy, but I know it was wrong—"

Elisandra was laughing. She reached out and took both my offending hands in hers. "Oh, silly Corie, Bryan kisses lots of girls on the hand. On the mouth, too, when there aren't four or five other people watching nearby. Bryan's a terrible flirt. He can't help it. All the girls are crazy for the handsome young prince."

"So you don't mind?" I asked anxiously. "Because I try not to adore him, you know—and of all the girls in the castle, I'm glad that it's *you* who gets to marry him, because you're so beautiful and so kind that you deserve him more than anybody else does—but I can't help it. My heart just hurts sometimes when I look at him. I do try to get over him every winter when I go back home. Maybe this year I'll be able to manage it."

She was laughing still, but now she looked a little sad, though

I couldn't tell what in my tumbling speech would have sparked that emotion. "It is not for my own sake that I wish you wouldn't love Bryan," she said softly, refolding her hands in her lap. "I hate to see you hurt or heartbroken. Bryan knows very well what his life holds. Nothing in your adoration will change that."

"I know—I know," I said unhappily. "Even if he was not betrothed to you, Bryan would not love me. I'm not the kind of girl that princes marry."

Now she looked even sadder, though she smiled and leaned over to kiss my cheek. "But you're one hundred times more lovable than Megan of Tregonia," she whispered. I laughed. She straightened in her chair and glanced at my bedside clock. "Almost time for me to go," she said. "I wish you were to be dining with us. But my mother tells me—"

"I am not to have any fun for weeks," I said glumly. "And if I don't behave—"

"I know. She told me. I know you don't like her, Corie, but in a way she's right. While you're here, you do owe it to yourself to behave a little bit more like a lady."

"So she can find me a husband?" I demanded. "Who ever thought that's why Jaxon brought me here?"

"Everyone, silly," she said, smiling again.

"Well, I'm not going to be forced into some stupid marriage with some stupid boy from some northern province that I've never even been to," I said sullenly. "I don't even want to marry! I want to live at my grandmother's cottage and become a wise woman to be useful and good. I don't need to marry to do that."

"No one wants to marry you off to someone you don't care for," she said. "And anyway, all that is years away."

"And who would marry me, that's what I want to know," I said next, regaining my spunk. "No lord's son is going to marry some witch woman's daughter born out of wedlock—"

"You're a Halsing," she said with gentle pride. "It's the second most famous name in Auburn. And your uncle is one of the richest men in the eight provinces—and he's shown that he has your welfare at heart. You are much more marketable than you realize, my dear."

"When you put it like that," I said deliberately, "I'd rather marry a stablehand."

She laughed and rose to her feet. "Many days, so would I," she said. "But some of us don't get the choice."

"Don't go yet," I begged. "I haven't seen you for days."

"I must. I'm late already. But tomorrow—"

"Tomorrow morning your mother says I must come learn lessons in her chamber."

"Tomorrow afternoon, then. We'll go riding. I can teach you just as much as my mother can about how to be a lady."

She kissed me again and was gone in a swirl of silver skirts. I stretched out on the bed again and thought over everything we'd said. So they really planned to marry me off to some minor lordling who wished to curry favor with my uncle. Elisandra, who had been promised to Bryan on the day of the prince's birth, knew better than anyone what it meant to be bartered away for lands and bloodlines. But Elisandra, at least, was slated to marry the most eligible and desirable man in the entire kingdom; no reason there for any complaining.

I rolled onto my stomach and rested my fist upon my chin. But perhaps the boy they found for me would be handsome and dashing, too. Not as spectacular as Bryan, of course, but broad-shouldered and fierce-eyed, brilliant in battle and tempestuous in love. They might find me a lord's son who matched that description. I might even develop a fondness for him, though no one would replace Bryan in my heart.

And if I was not fond of him, no one could make me marry him, and that I resolved at that very minute. I might be half Halsing, but I was half woodwitch, too, and the women of my mother's family had always proved a little hard to coerce. No one would make me do anything I did not want to do. Comforted by that thought, I turned on my side and resumed my reading.

THE NEXT FEW days were trying in the extreme. In the mornings, I sat with Greta in her chamber, allowing her to drill me in manners, deportment, and speech (she didn't like my southern accent and had said so more than once in the past). Elisandra escaped her own duties only once to go riding with me; and Kent, who could sometimes be counted on to play a game of cards with me, was nowhere to be found. Off squiring Megan around, I supposed. I despised the young lady even more.

I did come across Roderick one day, finishing up sword practice in the yard with the rest of the young guardsmen. I was not enough of a judge to determine whether he did well or poorly, but he was still standing at the end of the final bout, while some of the men were not. I had joined about a dozen other spectators sitting or leaning on the broad wood fence that circled the weapons yard. Most of the others were kitchen maids, who were making eyes at the young men, or old soldiers, who had come to watch with a critical eye. There were no others of noble blood, or even half noble blood, anywhere in the vicinity.

I was surprised when Roderick came over afterward to greet me, pulling off his helmet to reveal his matted sandy hair. I had not thought he would notice me among the others, dressed in my plain daytime gown.

"Well, you've learned the trick of hunting aliora," he remarked, leaning his elbow on the top railing of the fence. I had perched precariously on top, and was swinging my legs rhythmically despite the very real possibility of overbalancing and falling off. "Are you next going to take up swordplay?"

I wrinkled my nose. "Ugh," I said. "So I can learn to kill people? I don't think so."

He gave me that lazy smile, and his whole freckled face looked amused. "Well, you wouldn't have to kill them all. Just disable them. Discourage them a little."

"Are you any good?" I asked directly. "I can't tell."

He shrugged. "I'm improving," he said in a laconic voice. Which told me nothing, since Roderick did not seem the type to boast of his prowess. I would have to ask Kent. "Yesterday I got a cut in the shoulder because I was careless." He flexed his arm experimentally and frowned briefly in pain. "Hurts more than I thought it would."

Now I was interested, in a professional way. "Have you bound it? Put salve on it?" I asked.

He shook his head. "It didn't bleed so much as all that. It'll heal in a day or so."

Most of the onlookers had dispersed by now, and the guardsmen still in the yard were talking amongst themselves. No one appeared to be paying us any attention at all. "Let me see it," I said.

Again that smile crossed his face, but without any protestations of modesty, he unlaced his leather vest and unbuttoned the cotton shirt beneath. The wound on his shoulder had started to bleed again with the afternoon's activity, and it did not look to me quite as minor as he had made it out to be. Nothing that would kill him— unless it got infected—but it was a cut that would cause him great discomfort.

"I have something I can give you for that," I said, swinging my legs to the outer edge of the fence and hopping to the ground. "Come up to my room and I'll give you a salve."

He did not move. "Come up to your room?" he repeated. "I don't think so."

I stopped with one foot already on the path back to the castle. Of course, stupid girl. Even Kent, who was close friends with my sister, rarely came to the suite of rooms reserved for Greta, Elisandra, and their attendants. Bachelor men and their valets resided in rooms on the other side of the castle, while the royal apartments were in the central portion. And guardsmen of Roderick's status were almost never in any of these wings; they lived in barracks situated nearer to the stables than the ballrooms.

"Lady Greta is right," I said with a smile, pivoting back to him. "I'll never understand the etiquette of the royal household."

Roderick was relacing his vest. "I'll be fine as I am."

"No, I'll get you something. Meet me in the stables in twenty minutes."

He still seemed reluctant, and his next words explained why.

"Are you really sure you can concoct some ointment to soothe this? You're a very nice girl, I'm sure, but—"

I laughed out loud. "My grandmother is a wise woman, and I'm her apprentice," I said. "Didn't anybody tell you that? I know a lot about herbs and medicines—and other potions, too, when it comes to that."

"What other potions?" he asked immediately.

I smiled, already sorry I'd mentioned it. "Nothing you need right now. But a healing salve—that I've got up in my room. I know you don't think I can help you, but I can."

He shrugged. "I'll be in the stables. Twenty minutes."

I scurried up to my room, careful once I was near my quarters because I didn't want to encounter Greta, and ran back down to the stables as quickly as I could. Roderick was waiting for me and, to my surprise, Kent was with him.

"You didn't believe me!" I exclaimed to Roderick. "You had to go off and find Kent to ask him if I could be trusted!"

"No, I was just coming in from my afternoon ride," Kent said. "I wanted to know why he was loitering here, looking so worried."

Roderick was grinning. "I said, 'Yon Halsing wench, eh, is she be studying the blacker arts?' " He croaked this out in a perfect north-county accent. We all dissolved into laughter. " 'Be she about to poison me, eh lad, were I to give over me blood into her hands?' "

"I could, too," I informed him. "A few dayig seeds ground up into powder—"

"If you had any," Kent said.

"I kept them all. Any good witch would."

"Well, and we've only your uncle's word that they're poison," Roderick said with a shrug. "I'm not so all convinced that he wasn't making a game of us."

"And are you the one who's going to test his story?" I demanded. "Not today, anyway. Now, unbutton your shirt again."

While Roderick was so engaged, I glanced over at Kent. "I really won't kill him," I said somewhat tartly. "You don't have to stand guard."

The young lord looked sheepish. "No, I thought perhaps—I myself stand in need of a little doctoring. I thought you might be willing to give me some ointment as well."

I opened my eyes wide. "You? You got hurt? Doing what?"

"Much the same thing Roderick was doing," he admitted.

Roderick was now stripped to the waist. His long, lean torso sported a few old scars, trophies of similar encounters in the past, and he smelled faintly of leather and sweat. I was suddenly aware of him as a seminude man standing not two feet away from me, but he seemed completely unself-conscious. I opened the satchel I had carried down with me and busied myself poking among the bottles and vials.

"You were practicing swordplay?" I said, my voice a little gruff.

"With Roderick here, no less," Kent said. "I thought my lofty status would protect me from actual blows, but I miscalculated the brutality of the career swordsman."

"You told me not to spare you," Roderick said. "Had I known you wanted to be treated as a baby after all—"

"Spell 'Auburn'!" Kent challenged him, cuffing Roderick on his uninjured arm. "Spell out Corie's name!"

As Roderick recited the correct letters, I suddenly remembered their bargain on our trip. Roderick would teach Kent the crossbow, and the lord would teach the guardsman how to read. Apparently they had decided to expand into swordfighting as well. I was glad, somehow, to learn that they were adhering to their promises.

By this time, I had composed myself and pulled out a vial of antiseptic and a medium-size jar of dark red salve. "This will not feel entirely pleasant," I said to Roderick, wetting a clean cloth with the antiseptic. As I touched the medicated cloth to his shoulder, I saw all the muscles of his chest tighten in response, holding their coiled protest while the cleanser worked away at the skin. The sticky smell of sweat was even stronger.

"It was poison, after all," he said somewhat faintly. "But I had hoped it would not be quite so painful."

I wiped the rag once more across the cut, then laid it aside. "But the salve will feel very good," I promised. "It even has a nice smell."

With a businesslike air, I dipped my finger in the cream and smeared it carefully across the wound. His flesh felt slightly hot to my touch—perhaps the beginnings of infection in the cut.

"You'll need to apply this twice a day for three or four days," I said. "I've brought you a spare jar."

Roderick flexed his arm muscles and looked surprised. "It does feel better," he said. "How can it work so fast?"

"Something in there that numbs the skin," I said. "It doesn't mean you're healed yet. It's just that you don't feel it."

I turned to Kent, who had rolled up the sleeve of his left arm. His gash was even nastier, perhaps a day old, and rimmed with a crusty red inflammation. "Well, that must hurt," I observed.

"Enough that I was considering going to Giselda in the morning," he confessed. Giselda was the motherly old woman who resided in the castle and called herself an apothecary. She had trained in healing in Faelyn Market, but I had spent more than one morning with her, going through her medicines, and I knew that she was a witch woman at heart. There was almost nothing on her shelves that my grandmother did not have at home.

"Well, she would probably do what I'll do, but since I'm here, let me get you started healing," I said, treating him just as I had Roderick. First I cleaned the wound—which he took much less stoically than the guardsman, yelping and jerking away from me so that I had to grab his arm to keep him still. Then I smeared it with salve and bid him to let it go to work.

"How exactly did this happen?" I wanted to know. "Fencing?"

"It's not fencing when you're using a broadsword," Kent said. "But I didn't move quickly enough."

"I was thinking today. Might be time to go back to practice swords," Roderick said.

"It is not!" Kent said indignantly. "I haven't fought with a wooden sword since I was—well, since before I was Corie's age."

This was all very interesting. I said to Kent, "I thought you were such a brilliant swordsman. Jaxon said so."

"He did? I doubt it," Kent said dryly.

"He did. Right here in these stables. He said you were better than Bryan."

"Oh. Well. I suppose I am."

"You're not bad," Roderick interposed. "A good man to have in a fight. It's just I've carried a sword almost since I could walk. Trained for it since childhood. I'm bound to be better than a man who's only played at it."

"I've done more than *play*—" Kent began.

"And you've other skills," Roderick said swiftly, smiling a little. "It takes all manner of men to run the kingdom."

Kent looked a little ruffled at that patronizing comment, and I had to hide my smile. "You can roll your sleeve down now," I told him in as serious a voice as I could muster. "I'll get you an extra jar of salve, too. You'll need it more than Roderick."

Wiping the exasperation from his face, Kent adjusted his sleeve then rotated his wrist back and forth. "It does feel better!" he exclaimed. "Who made this? Your grandmother?"

"*I* made it," I said. "Hasn't anybody been paying attention? I live with a wise woman. I'm her apprentice. I'll be a wise woman myself in another ten years."

"She says she knows other magics," Roderick said. "Potions, she said, but she wouldn't say what."

"Potions, is it?" Kent said. Suddenly, who knew how it happened, I was no longer the professional healer with a calm demeanor, but the silly young girl being teased by the neighbor boys. "Can she give a man something to make him sleep?"

"Make him strong?"

"Make him fall in love?"

"All those things," I said curtly, repacking my satchel and hating both of them. "I can cure his headache and help him remember his dreams. I know how to make the babies come—and I know how to keep the babies from coming, too."

I stopped abruptly, because all at once talk of babies and falling in love seemed dreadfully embarrassing as I stood unchaperoned in a stable talking to two attractive men. Certainly this would not be on Greta's short list of acceptable behavior. Kent looked embarrassed, too, but Roderick was laughing

"Well, I'll know who to go to about those pesky babies," he

said. "What other helpful medicines do you have in that little bag?"

"Things you'd best not be asking about," I said darkly, and baldly turned the subject. "You should both make whatever effort you can to keep your wounds rested in the next few days."

"That I will," Roderick said, grinning. "I'll just tell Kritlin, 'No sword practice for me, old man, I've a little gash on my shoulder.' He'll pat my head and set me on the sidelines for sure."

Kent grimaced. "Not much chance here, either. There's the ball tonight, and my father expects me to do my part dancing." He looked over at me with a smile. "You're only fourteen this year, aren't you, Corie? Still too young for the balls, I expect. Elisandra didn't start going until she was fifteen."

Too young for the ball and too much a hoyden for the dinners, I thought but did not say. "Well, do what you can, both of you, to avoid more injury," I said. "I'll check on you two later." And before there could be any more talk of balls, behavior, or babies, I slipped out of the stables and headed back up to my room.

THAT EVENING, I crept down to the ballroom to watch the festivities. There was a long, narrow balcony overhanging one wall of the dance floor. This balcony was only accessible from the servants' corridors, as the railings were frequently hung with flags, banners, or great ropes of flowers. Elisandra had shown it to me on my very first visit to the castle, when I was six and she was nine and we were both too young to be invited to events. We had stretched out on the floor and peered through the railings for hours, watching the dip and sway of the dancers, the glances between lovers, the indecorous embraces, and the haughty refusals. Although Bryan knew about the balcony, he had never joined us there, but from time to time Kent had sat on the floor and watched with us. In fact, more than once, he and Elisandra had practiced their own dance steps in time to the waltzes played below.

Tonight I sat cross-legged on the floor and watched closely to see who partnered with Bryan. Naturally he was committed to Megan of

Tregonia for the first dance, and I studied her with a critical eye. Elisandra had called her insipid, and certainly, against Bryan's dramatic coloring, she looked pale and nondescript. She was fashionably thin, but to my mind her bare arms looked sticklike, not dainty, and her small face seemed gaunt and woebegone. Even her hair, a struggling brown, looked sick and undernourished.

Still, Bryan smiled at her and bowed most elaborately when the dance ended, and I had every reason to hate her.

I minded less when he danced with Elisandra, dressed tonight in a forest green that made her dark hair preen with luster. They seemed to have less to say to each other than Bryan and Megan, though they were obviously better suited to each other in their style of dancing. They never held each other too close, never missed each others' cues; they could have been two statues dancing, viewed now from one angle, now from another, caught for an eternity with all the sculptor's skill.

After that, all the silly girls of the castle and the surrounding countryside did their best to draw Bryan's attention by placing themselves in strategic spots on the edge of the dance floor, or letting loose their most winsome laughs just as the music ended. I swear I saw blond Lady Doreen bump Marian Grey aside with her hip, to make the younger woman look awkward and ungainly the minute Bryan turned his eyes their way. In any event, Doreen was the one with whom he chose to dance. But I had watched these events in the past; before the night was over, Bryan would have danced with every woman who had a pedigree. His uncle the regent demanded that measure of courtesy from him, and Bryan always observed it. Once I was old enough, he would even dance with me.

When I lost track of Bryan in the throngs, I looked for Elisandra and Kent. I saw them dance together twice, easily, comfortably, laughing at each other's observations. No one ever seemed to amuse Elisandra quite as much as Kent could—and once in a while, when she was with him, she actually relaxed her usual watchful guard. They had known each other since she was born; neither had ever lived anyplace else. I wondered what it would be like to know someone else so long, so well.

Elisandra was dancing with Dirkson of Tregonia and I had lost track of both Kent and Bryan when I heard a noise at the servant's door behind me. I spun around on my knees in time to see Kent come through the door with a questioning look on his face. This cleared up the instant he saw me.

"You *are* here. I thought I saw your little face peering through the rails," he said. "Are you having fun?"

"Counting the girls Bryan dances with," I said. "He seems to be enjoying himself."

"He does like entertaining," Kent agreed.

"And you? Are you enjoying yourself?" I asked.

He shrugged, and leaned his shoulders against the wall. He was not so tall as Roderick, but in his black formal clothes he looked almost the same height, heavier in the shoulders and more serious in expression. His dark hair had been styled tonight in some approximation of fashion, and all in all he looked rather imposing.

"I know what the purpose is, and I know how to play my part. There are things I prefer doing, but it is not hard, after all, to dance and smile and say polite things."

"Sometimes it is," I said, reflecting on my sessions with Greta.

He smiled, and the seriousness vanished from his face. "For you, it seems to be," he said. "But Greta may civilize you yet."

"Turn me into Megan of Tregonia," I scoffed. "I don't think so."

"No, I doubt you'll ever be entirely tame," he said. "I wait for the day you turn the entire castle upside down through some passionate and ill-advised action. Elisandra says it will never happen, but I'm certain that it will."

I could not imagine how such a conversation might ever have transpired; it made me feel peculiar to think of it. "How is your arm?" I asked, to change the subject. "Is it bothering you?"

He shook it twice. "A little. That was the excuse I gave my father, anyway, when I pleaded for a break from the dancing. He can't decide whether to be pleased or angry that I'm studying the sword on my own, so he can't tell how annoyed to be that I've hurt myself. But he permitted me to take a rest. So I came to look for you."

"I'm glad you're teaching Roderick to write," I said. "I would guess he's a quick learner. He's country-smart. I see it all the time in the village. Boys who don't have a chance to get real tutoring but who manage to learn things all the same. Girls, too."

Kent nodded. "He learns fast. Kritlin thinks highly of him, I know. I think with a little education Roderick could rise quickly through the guards' ranks and be captain someday."

Kritlin had been captain of the guard ever since I could remember. Kent's father trusted him absolutely and even invited him to the dinner table from time to time, when more exalted guests were not at hand. To rise to such a position would be an honor indeed for a young man from Veledore.

Before I had thought of a reply, the orchestra segued into a lively waltz. "Oh, I love this song!" I exclaimed.

"So do I," Kent said, holding out his hand. "Dance with me."

I had done it often when I was first learning my steps: Kent would partner first my sister, then me, and I too had always been at ease with him. But we were alone on the high balcony, no Elisandra nearby to critique my performance, and I was suddenly shy.

"You should rest your arm while you have the chance," I said in a reproving voice. "I'm not one of the court ladies you have to impress."

"You're one of the court ladies I wish to dance with," he said, still extending his hand. "Come! Show me you haven't forgotten your steps."

I shook my head. "You'll be missed at the ball," I said.

He dropped his hand and swept his dark coat back from his hips as though about to sit on the floor. "Very well, then—"

"Don't!" I said sharply, and he froze in mid-bend. "The floor's dirty," I explained to his look of surprise. "Look—I've got smudges all over my gown."

Slowly he straightened, watching me all the while. "I won't stay if you don't want me to," he said.

"I didn't say that," I said, enunciating clearly. "I said the floor is dirty and you'll be missed at the ball. Did I say I wanted you to go?"

He smiled. "Then dance with me," he repeated.

Silly to be embarrassed about dancing with a man I had danced with a hundred times in my life. I jumped to my feet and held out my arms. "Oh, very *well*, then!" I exclaimed. "I'll dance!"

He twirled me into his arms, and we romped up and down the narrow confines of the balcony with great energy. I was laughing so hard that all my embarrassment melted away, and once or twice I thought I might skid across the floor, tilt over the railing and go wheeling down onto the heads of the dancers below. We made it through the piece without serious mishap, however, and when the music ended, Kent bowed over my hand with a flourish.

"Thank you for the dance, kind lady," he said.

I curtsied, having practiced this art for three days running. "You're most welcome, gentle sir."

He kissed my hand with great flair, bowing again as he did so. I giggled and pulled my fingers free.

"I guess Bryan's not the only one who flirts with the court ladies," I said.

"Ah, but I only flirt with some," he said solemnly.

I waved my hands to encourage him toward the door. "Well, time to go back to those others, then," I said. "Your father will really begin wondering where you are."

He turned toward the door, but lingered on the threshold, seeming to want to say more. "You should not let just anyone kiss your hand, you know," he said, the mock seriousness still in his voice. "Greta will tell you that. And definitely no kissing anywhere off the dance floor—in the gardens, for instance, or in empty hallways when no one else is near."

"I believe she's covered that in one of her lectures," I said demurely.

"Only old friends. Trusted old friends. Not already engaged to be married to one's sister or one's acquaintances."

"I'll remember that," I said. "Now go."

Still reluctant, he bowed again and left. I turned immediately back to the railing and leaned over it, looking for my sister, looking for the prince.

It was silly and pleasant and even a little breathtaking to dance with Kent, of course; and I had been surprised and a little electrified when he kissed my fingers—but it was nothing like being kissed by Bryan. In your life there will only be a few circumstances that overset you completely, and for me that had been one of them, and no other similar experience, however exhilarating, could ever successfully compare.

THE FOLLOWING DAYS were better because Dirkson and his tiresome daughter were gone, which meant my sister had more time for me. Two mornings, she joined me in her mother's parlor, and her soft instructions were easier to obey than her mother's curt ones. One afternoon, she and Kent and I played in the gardens that edged the northern wing of the castle. We took turns hiding behind the rich summer greenery of the shrubs and seeking each other out. More than once, gardeners and parties of court ladies were startled by our shrieking laughter and sudden eruptions into their midst. We nearly knocked down an old man I'd never seen before when we had a three-way race from the rosebeds to the lilac bushes. Kent won, and all three of us collapsed in a heap on the rich grass under a spreading oak.

Elisandra laid a hand to her chest and looked dramatic. "I shall grow faint," she said. "My heart is pounding."

Kent stretched out full-length on the grass, though Elisandra and I sat more modestly, our skirts spread around our ankles. He gazed at her critically, throwing an arm up to shield his eyes from the sun. Even the race had not disturbed her dark hair, pulled back in its usual coiled braid, or ruffled the habitual serenity of her face. "Your color's healthy, though," he observed. "I don't think you'll die. Anyway, it's good for you."

"Good for me to go yodeling through the gardens like the hoyden my sister is?" she asked. "I'm not so sure."

"It's good to hear you laugh," he amended. "You don't much, these days."

She plucked a long blade of grass and split it slowly down the middle with one perfect nail. "There's not much to laugh about," she said.

"I know," he said.

I was mystified. "There's plenty to be happy about!" I exclaimed. "That horrid Megan is gone, and Greta says I can join the dinners again. And tomorrow we're to go riding—"

Elisandra looked over at me with a sad smile. "But the summer is almost over and in a few short weeks you will be leaving again," she said. "*That* I'm not so happy about."

"But I'll write," I said. "I always do."

She reached out a hand to brush the softest of caresses on my cheek. "It's not the same," she said. "I miss you so much when you go."

"You could come visit me," I said. "The cottage is small, but you could stay in my room. I'd sleep on the floor. My grandmother could teach you herbs, and then you could help Giselda when there's fever in the castle—"

She smiled again, this time with a little more sparkle. "Actually, I think it would be fun," she said. "I could tie my hair back in a scarf and wear a patched cotton skirt, and walk into the village on market day."

"Well, it's a lot of work, because Grandmother makes you memorize the names of all the plants, where you can find them, how to prepare them, what to put them in if you want to cover the taste, and what you should never mix them with. There's so much to know, and sometimes she's not very patient. But it's more fun than learning about the heraldry of the eight provinces," I added darkly.

"Maybe *I'll* come," Kent said. "You'll have to leave a map."

We sat there awhile longer, talking idly, till the golden quality of the air told us that the summer afternoon was reaching its final somnolent hour. When we finally returned to the castle, we found we didn't have much time to clean up and change before dinner. Cressida rushed through Elisandra's toilette so she could help me finish mine. I was wearing a new royal blue dress that Greta had promised me if I was good. It made my dark eyes seem huge and my dark hair rich.

"Aren't you pretty," the aliora said, patting a curl behind my ear. "Let me see you smile. Yes, you'll be as lovely as your sister when you're a year or two older."

I shook my head vigorously. "No one is as beautiful as Elisandra."

Cressida smiled at me in the mirror. "Her sister is."

Greta, Elisandra, and I hurried down to the dining hall, arriving just as the royal family did. Bryan looked quite regal, his red hair clean and combed back, his formal black silk jacket giving him a dignified maturity. He nodded toward me and Elisandra and held out his arm to escort Greta into the room. Kent extended his hand to Elisandra, and the regent offered his arm to me.

"Good evening, Coriel," the regent said in his watchful, speculative way, as if he noted every single reaction you might have to his words or his tone. He was shorter than his son, gray-haired, intense; his temper was legendary, though I had never seen him in an actual rage. He was said to be a fierce and canny negotiator, passionately devoted to the affairs of the realm, and impossible to deceive. He always made me incredibly nervous.

"Good evening, Lord Matthew," I said, giving him a little curtsey, and laid my fingers very lightly on his sleeve.

"I am glad you will be joining us tonight," he added. "We have missed you at our tables."

Not likely. "Do you entertain guests tonight?" I asked, just to have something to say.

"No, tonight it is just us. A pleasant and relaxed family meal."

Of course, it was anything but, which I knew before he deposited me at my chair. The dining hall seated three dozen people in its smallest configuration; it could be rearranged to comfortably hold six times that number. Tonight, there were just the thirty or so ranking nobles who lived at the castle either year-round or for part of the season. A small table set on a low dais held Bryan, Kent, the regent, Greta, and Elisandra; Damien sat at a small table directly behind Bryan. Jaxon, when he was present, also sat on the dais, as did any guests of honor. All of them were arrayed on the same side of the table, facing the other tables of the dining hall, which were set up in perpendicular lines to the head table. In effect, merely by turning our heads, all of us could watch our prince and his attendants eat, while they had no other view but of us.

I sat with the lesser nobles, Marian Grey and her cousin Angela, as well as both sets of their parents. Nearby were landholders from the various provinces who had some claim to royal favor. I did not know the visitors to speak to, but I liked Marian and Angela, so I was reasonably content.

The meal was delicious. I had, in two short weeks, almost forgotten the sumptuousness of even a simple "family meal" at Castle Auburn. At every plate were glasses for water and for wine, bowls for soup, plates for salad; plates for the main courses, plates for side dishes, and plates for desserts. Servants and aliora passed constantly among the diners, ladling out fresh portions, refilling glasses, taking whispered requests back to the kitchens. I ate until my stomach hurt, and then I started on dessert.

Angela, a lively young woman about Elisandra's age, leaned across the table once a servant had filled my water glass for the third time. Her curly brown hair formed a pretty frame around her heart-shaped face, and her bright blue eyes gave everything she said an exclamatory air.

"Did you know," Angela said in a low voice, "that Bryan won't drink the water anymore?"

Marian and I leaned toward her across the table to hear her better, even though no one else appeared to be listening.

"Won't drink the water?" Marian repeated in her mousy voice. She was paler and smaller than her cousin, not as outgoing but somewhat more restful. "Why not? It's the best water in the eight provinces."

This was true—Castle Auburn was famous for its well, which had been drilled three hundred feet through soil and bedrock to tap into a cold, pure, underground stream. Every day, servants rolled three huge casks down to the well to fill them with water; and every day these casks were brought back to the kitchen for cooking and serving with the evening meal. The well water was so much a part of the Castle Auburn heritage, in fact, that every toast and every bargain was traditionally made twice, "in water and in wine."

Angela spoke in a still lower voice. "He says the well can't be protected sufficiently. That it could be poisoned."

"Poisoned!" Marian breathed.

"He says he saw somebody throw something down the well the other day. He says he won't trust it ever again."

"But if Damien tastes it first—" I said.

Angela nodded. "That's what Lord Matthew said. But Bryan just shook his head. He says he'll never drink the water again."

All three of us looked doubtfully at our own water glasses, filled with seemingly fresh and innocent liquid. "But I love the water at Castle Auburn," Marian said at last.

It was a dilemma, for all of us adored Bryan and wanted to believe any action or decree of his was both sensible and incontrovertible. But to give up the water . . . "Well, nobody's trying to poison *me*," I decided, and took a long swallow.

Marian's expression cleared. "Or me," she said, following suit. Angela drained her glass, and then we three sat and watched each other expectantly. When none of us fell over gasping and choking, we all started giggling, which had much the same effect anyway. Marian's mother gave us a reproving look, so we sobered up, but wine could not have made us sillier. I was enjoying my first meal back in company far more than I had expected, and I was actually sorry when the evening finally came to an end.

4

Two days later there was a different kind of excitement at the castle. Angela and Marian returned from a morning ride reporting that they had seen a crazed wolf along the trail, foam feathering its mouth and wildness in its dark eyes. Wolves were rare this close to the civilized environs of the castle, though not unheard of. A sick one was rarer still, and more to be feared. The regent sent out a party of hunters, but though they found the animal's tracks, they could not locate him.

"That means you girls will have to stay on the grounds until the animal's been killed," Greta told us firmly. Elisandra nodded, but I protested vehemently.

"Stay on the grounds! But there's nothing to do here!"

"There's plenty to do! You can practice your dance steps, rehearse your heraldry, help Cressida with the fine mending—because, I declare, I can't imagine that you have a single undergarment that isn't in complete tatters—"

"I meant, nothing *fun* to do," I said impatiently. "And we've been cooped up for weeks!"

"Days, maybe," Elisandra murmured, for I had exaggerated; but the last two days had been wet and dreary, and we had been kept mostly indoors.

I flounced to one of the lace-edged chairs liberally scattered throughout Greta's quarters. "I'm not afraid of any stupid old wolf."

Elisandra appealed to her mother. "Maybe if we could get Kent to ride with us—"

"He and his father and Bryan are spending the day with the steward, going over tithing levels. He won't be free the rest of the week."

I bounced in the chair. "But someone? If we got someone? One of the guards, maybe?"

Greta cast me a glance of infinite weariness. She wanted nothing so much as to get me out of her way for an hour; I knew she would eventually agree if I could come up with a reasonable offer.

"They all have their duties to attend to, I'm sure."

"But if I asked Kritlin? If one of them agreed?"

She threw her hands up, at her limit. "Very well! Then go! But *only* if you have an escort, and do not go far."

"I'll be back in just a few moments," I said to Elisandra, and ran out of the room.

That was how we managed, late that afternoon, to go riding on a southern route away from the castle, my sister, Roderick, and me. The day was unbelievably fine, for the last two days of rain had left the air fresh and cool, and the breezes playful. I was so eager to get away from the castle that I set my own horse at a good gallop at the outset of the ride, forcing Elisandra and the guard to keep my pace or risk losing me to the rabid wolf. There was no time or breath left for conversation until we had ridden several miles from the castle and I was finally beginning to feel freed from confinement.

"Isn't this a glorious day!" I shouted, pulling up my horse and tossing both hands in the air. Elisandra and Roderick came up on either side of me, Elisandra looking a little windblown, though still serene. Roderick wore his usual half-smiling expression.

"It'll be even more glorious once you fall from the saddle and break your silly neck," he said agreeably. "It's the perfect day for leading a lame horse back to the castle with an injured girl on its back."

"You don't have to protect me from falls," I reminded him. "Just from wolves."

"Yes, and I'll enjoy explaining the difference to the regent when I haul your broken body back to court."

Unexpectedly, Elisandra laughed out loud. "I see you have learned already how to speak to my sister," she said. "Most people never get the trick of it."

He turned to her with his easy grin. "Well, I listened to her uncle Jaxon talk to her for four days, and I copied his speeches."

Elisandra regarded Roderick with fresh interest. "Ah! You're the guard who rode to Faelyn River on the hunt for aliora. Corie came back with stories of your kindness and prowess."

"No, I didn't," I interjected. "At least, maybe I *did*, but I take them back now if you're not going to be kind."

"I'll be kind," he said mildly. "Until you fall off your horse. Then I'll not be so happy."

"Come, now," Elisandra said, urging her own horse forward next to mine. "Ride like a lady. I know you can."

We rode at a much more sedate pace for another hour, we women in the lead. Roderick followed a few yards behind us. Elisandra and I talked idly, gossiping about court nobles, wondering when Jaxon would return, counting the few days I had left before I would return to my grandmother's. I missed my grandmother and my life in the village; but the thought of leaving Elisandra, as always, tore my heart.

"Maybe you could come back for a winter visit this year," she said. "Then the time won't seem so long."

"Maybe," I said hopelessly. I remembered the long wrangling Jaxon and my grandmother had engaged in when they first struck this bargain, and I didn't see any alterations being successful now. "Or maybe you'll come visit me, like you said."

She laughed softly, and I knew that was just as unlikely. But we both pretended. "I've got the map," she said, for I had produced one for her and one for Kent after our last conversation on this topic. "It's very detailed. Maybe one clear, frosty day, I'll get on my horse and follow the road, all the way from Castle Auburn to Southey Village in Cotteswold."

"Well, dress warmly," I said. "It will take you three days."

We both laughed, and our talk turned to other things. She was to have her portrait painted by a renowned artist who would be at the castle for weeks, rendering the faces of all the nobility. "And I asked Lord Matthew," she said, "and he said I could ask the man to paint me a quick miniature of you. So think of what dress you'd like to wear, because he'll be here in three days."

I was a little skeptical. "Will I have to sit still? Without moving or talking?"

She smiled. "I suppose so."

"For how long?"

"I don't know. An hour or two."

"It's hard to imagine," I said.

Her laugh pealed out. "That's why I want the portrait! To prove that you can be quiet!" She sobered quickly and turned to coaxing. "But you will, won't you? For me?"

"Of course I will," I said. "Well, I'll *try.*"

I wanted to ask if I could have a miniature of her in return, but I knew there was some cost involved in hiring a painter, and I had no money. Anyway, such luxuries were only for the wealthy and the royal. I would trust my memory to keep a picture of Elisandra in my heart.

We had ridden for an hour and turned back toward the castle, and still come across no sign of a menacing beast. "I think Angela was imagining monsters," I remarked. "We haven't seen anything."

"Well, she only saw one, and it was on the north side of the castle," Elisandra said. "And it may have gone back toward the woods."

"I don't think we'll need an escort if we ride tomorrow."

"I think we will," she said, gently certain. "Until they kill the wolf—or find it dead."

I glanced back at Roderick who, all this time, had followed us silently, far enough back that he couldn't hear a word of our conversation. He caught my look and smiled, but came no closer. "We won't need *this* escort, though," I said loudly over my shoulder. "We'll want someone who's more fun."

"Fine by me," he called back. "Let somebody else watch over you."

I snorted and kicked my horse forward, just to prove that I wasn't tired at the end of the long ride. I heard Elisandra call my name in a gently reproving voice, but I urged my mount faster, wanting one last gallop before the outing ended. We were on level ground and there was no reason to expect trouble, but my poor horse caught its foot in a gopher hole and pitched forward. I went careening over its head in a whirl of skirts and elbows.

Pain was the next thing I was aware of, pain and distant voices. My head, my leg, my back, my left ribs, all on fire and slivered with protest. Someone was straightening my arms, slowly, carefully; I felt fingers prod through the delicate layer of skin to the hard core of bone.

"Arm's not broken, either. If she hasn't snapped her neck, she should be all right—and there, I just saw her eyes flutter."

That was Roderick's voice, followed instantly by Elisandra's. "Corie? Can you hear me? Corie? Are you all right?"

She sounded so worried. I had never heard Elisandra sound that way. It took immense effort, but I opened my eyes and found her face hanging right above mine. "I think so," I whispered. "What did I do?"

Incredible relief swept over her face. She swooped in to kiss me gently on the cheek. "You fell off your horse, foolish girl," she said in a teasing voice; but even through my pain I could hear the falseness of the gaiety. She was still supremely terrified, but determined not to show it. "And after you promised Roderick you would not."

"I don't think you're too badly hurt." Roderick spoke again. "Concussion, maybe. Can you sit up? Or is there something really wrong with you?"

I cast him a smoldering glance and pushed myself to a sitting position, though I had to lean heavily on Elisandra's arm once I was upright. My head pounded and my vision swam; I thought I might throw up. "It wasn't my fault," I said distinctly. "My horse tripped or something."

"And your next question should be, 'And is the horse all right?' " Roderick prompted. "For you don't want it to have broken its leg, all through your careless treatment."

"I *wasn't* careless—" I began, but Elisandra interrupted, saying my name in a soft voice. "Oh, very well," I mumbled. "I shouldn't have tried to gallop off the main road. Is the horse all right?"

"Yes, indeed, a little skittish but uninjured," Roderick said. "But I don't think you'll be riding him back."

"That's stupid," I said crossly. "How else will I get back to the castle?"

I saw him glance consideringly at the sky. "Well, it looks to be a dry evening. I think if you spend the night here, lying nice and quiet on a couple of saddle blankets, you'll be fine by morning. I'll come back with a spare horse tomorrow and take you home."

I sat up straighter, though it made my head throb. "You will not leave me here all night! Out in the open! And hurt!"

He looked innocent. "But I thought you liked to sleep out under the stars. Why, when we went hunting with your uncle—"

I ignored him. "And with wolves around! Rabid wolves! You wouldn't dare leave me out here—"

"We didn't see any rabid wolves," he said dismissively. "I don't think you need to worry."

I was outraged. "Elisandra! Tell him! You're not going to leave me—"

But she had dissolved into laughter, her hand pressed against her mouth and her eyes filling with tears. I decided, later, that some of the hilarity sprang from reaction, a release from the fear of finding me dead, but for a moment I was even more furious. "And it's not funny!" I added.

She hugged me again, still shaking. "No, no, dearest, we wouldn't think of leaving you behind. I imagine Roderick will carry you back—and I'll lead your horse."

"I wouldn't let him carry me any—"

Abruptly Roderick came to his feet. "Excellent idea, Lady Elisandra," he said. "That's exactly what we'll do. I'll round up the horses, and you see if you can get your sister on her feet."

Ten minutes later, a much more slow-moving caravan continued on its way back to the castle. Despite his light words earlier, Roderick did not seem in the least disposed to leave me behind. He had Elisandra hold his horse's head while he lifted me into the saddle and quickly climbed up behind me. I swayed against him, not meaning to, and I heard the frown in his voice.

"I don't think this will do," he said. Holding me hard against him, he swung me across his lap. He cradled me against his chest with one arm and gathered up his reins with his free hand. When I gazed up at him, he was smiling down at me.

"Better?" he asked.

"Yes, please," I whispered.

"Can you handle her horse?" he asked Elisandra.

"Easily. Let's be on our way."

Roderick kept the pace to a walk, I think because I cried out in pain when he attempted a faster speed. "Is she all right?" I heard Elisandra ask more than once, as if she could not help herself. Each time he answered her gently, "I think so. She's strong. She'll be fine."

For the remainder of the ride, I caught patches and pieces of their conversation, which they seemed to indulge in for no other reason than to distract Elisandra from her fear. She asked him questions about his family and their farm, about his brothers, about his time in the royal guard.

"And did you want to join the guard, or is that where younger brothers are sent when there are too many in the family?" she asked.

It was so easy to detect Roderick's expressions by the melody of his voice. Now he was smiling. "A little of both. My father's holding is large enough to support all of us, but I was restless and wanted to make my fortune elsewhere. I trained with the city guard from the time I was twelve, and it was my captain there who recommended I come to Auburn. My mother did not want me to go so far away, but my father was proud. He packed my bags himself."

"And how often do you see them, now that you're here?"

"I've only been here a few months. At the solstice holidays, I'll be going back for a few days."

"Don't you miss them? Don't you wonder if you can spend your whole life apart from them?"

"Well, not yet," he said. "But it's still fresh and new. I've known many a wild young man who came home a sober older man and said, 'No more of this roving for me.' It could happen to me, I suppose. Right now, my eyes are still big from looking at the world."

"They say many people don't learn until too late what's precious to them," Elisandra said. "And too late they learn they've traded away something that they want more than life itself."

"I guess I haven't learned yet what would matter so much to me," he said thoughtfully. "Have you? What's the most precious thing in the world to you?"

Her voice was so low I almost couldn't catch it. "My sister," she said. "The very thing you're holding in your arms."

I SPENT THE next week recuperating in my rooms, which I thought was excessive. You would have thought I had nearly fallen through a chasm into the void of the netherworld instead of stupidly tumbling off a horse. Even Greta, who could not truly have cared if I lived or died, insisted I stay in my bed and be constantly attended.

Although I was still embarrassed by the incident, and there were days I thought my head would never stop aching, I have to admit I enjoyed all the attention that followed. My routine for that week was simple and self-indulgent. I lay in my bed till Cressida came in carrying a tray of food that might be expected to tempt an invalid: soft-boiled eggs and cream pastries and peeled fruit. Laying the tray aside, she would take my chin in her hand and study the contours of my face, asking how I had slept and how my head felt. Her quiet concern made me feel marvelous no matter how badly the night had gone. I always gave her my first smile of the day.

Once I had eaten, the aliora would assist me into the bath and wash my hair so I would not slide my concussed head under the water and drown. She had such gentle, miraculous hands that this shampooing was an ecstasy in itself, as her fingers massaged the planes of my skull and made even my brain feel relaxed. But I was troubled, now and then, by the metallic clink and clamor of the copper chains around her wrists. She did her best to keep the shackles from swinging against my bruised head, but I could not help wondering how they interfered in the daily pleasures and duties of her life. I did not ask her.

After I was thoroughly clean, she would help me out of the old ceramic tub, towel me off and assist me into whatever flowing invalid-appropriate clothes she had chosen for me out of my closet.

Generally she would stay with me for the next few hours, reading to me or telling me stories (which I preferred). All of her fables started with the same phrase, "One spring night when the full moon was luminous," and involved tales of bravery, treachery, magic, and true love. I had heard a dozen or so in the past, when I was a child and sick in the night, but I had never before heard so many told, one right after the other. I loved them all.

During this period of time, Giselda came by almost every day to feed me potions and check for swelling. She was a large, comfortable woman with wispy gray hair and a distracted manner, but she knew her herbal lore. The first day she gave me ground tiselbane mixed into a sweet syrup, for there was no other way to swallow the bitter herbs. They helped my aching head but made me so sleepy I could not keep my eyes open. The next day she brought me kinder medicines, sarafis and wotyn.

I had been familiar with the others, but sarafis was new to me. It was made of crushed red petals and smelled faintly of cinnamon.

"What is this?" I asked, sniffing the dried leaves. "I don't know that my grandmother has ever used this."

"Sarafis," she said, preening a little. "I buy it every year at Faelyn Market, for it can only be found far north, up around the border mountains. It's very dear, but it works such miracles that I don't like to be without it."

"My grandmother uses halen root for pain most of the time," I said.

Giselda nodded. "It's expensive to buy this far north, and it makes me a little nervous. You can only use the tiniest amount or you risk killing your patient. I'd like to have some, though."

"I have a little with me," I said. "If you'd like it."

Giselda could not keep the surprise from her face. Like everyone, she knew my history, but she could not entirely credit that a girl so young could know anything useful about plants—or be trusted with medicines so dangerous. "You have halen root? Well, well. I don't recommend that you use it for this type of injury, however— it's more common in the birthing bed or when a man is in so much pain he needs calming."

I knew all this. Halen was a sedative as well as a painkiller, though if you took too much of it, it would poison your body; you would vomit, lose feeling in your extremities, have trouble breathing, and die fairly quickly. I did not bother to repeat the symptoms to Giselda, however; I merely nodded gravely.

"I agree, and I am very interested in trying your sarafis," I said.

"Though, if you have halen root to spare," she said.

"I do. In my satchel there, over by the closet." She dosed my pain, I gave her the drug, and we both felt better for it.

Once I had slept off the morning medicines, Cressida would feed me lunch. Then she would support my frail body down the hall to Elisandra's sun-filled sitting room. There I would be installed on a divan where I would read (rarely), sew (badly), or hold court (which I loved). Sometimes Elisandra sat with me, often Angela and Marian came in to giggle and gossip, and Kent tried to stop by every day at least for a few minutes.

Of course, all the pain and all the mortification were worth it the day that Bryan dropped in to check on my progress.

Angela and Marian were with me that afternoon. They had just told me about the hunt being organized to catch the rabid wolf, still unfortunately at large. Elisandra sat nearby, writing a letter, and only occasionally joined our conversation.

"Lord Matthew wanted to just send a few of the guards out, but Bryan thought this would be more exciting—a challenge for all the noblemen at the castle. The prize is a gold ring that bears the royal Ouvrelet crest," Angela said.

"That seems like a large prize for so small a hunt," Elisandra commented from the corner.

"I think it's a ring he doesn't like much," Angela said.

Elisandra smiled. "Ah, well, then an excellent trophy."

"So how many have decided to join the hunt?" I asked.

"Fifteen, last I heard," Angela said.

Marian exclaimed, "Fifteen! I don't know much about hunting, but wouldn't that many men make so much noise they'd scare away any wild creatures?"

"Men *and* women," Angela corrected. "Lady Doreen and her cousin have decided to join the lists."

"Yes, fifteen riders would make an incredible amount of noise," Elisandra said absently. She was rereading her letter and was paying little attention to our conversation.

"Plus guards," Angela added. "So maybe twenty."

Marian sighed. "I wish I could go," she said.

"Which guards?" I wanted to know.

Angela gave me a blank look. "I don't know. Just some guards."

"Is Kent going?" Elisandra asked.

"I think so," Angela responded.

"And the regent?" I asked.

Angela wrinkled her nose. "He seemed to think there were plenty of others involved already."

Marian sighed again, more theatrically. "I'm sure Bryan is the one who will bring the wild beast down," she declared. "With one stroke of his sword."

"Actually, it's more likely to be one shot from my bow," said a voice from the door. If you were attuned to it, you could hear the silent shrieks from Marian, Angela, and me. Bryan! Here! We all straightened in our chairs and then froze, unable to speak or move.

Elisandra came to her feet to greet him. "Why, Bryan, I thought you would be busy with the Mellidon envoy today."

He took her hand and bowed over it. The three of us had to

shut our mouths tight to choke down little moans of envy. He was grinning wickedly; I'm sure he knew exactly the effect he had on us and was playing the gallant on purpose. He was not normally so formal with Elisandra.

"I have just spent hours with him, and must soon hurry off to some dull meeting Uncle Matthew has planned for me, but I wanted to see how Corie was doing. I meant to come by a day or two ago, but—"

Elisandra led him over to my divan, where I tried my best to look pale and interesting. Taking my hand, he bowed over it as well, and may I say that I felt more devastated then than I had after the fall four days earlier.

"How are you feeling, Corie?" he asked with a charming smile. I felt my whole face dissolve into blushing giggles.

"Fine. I mean, much better. I mean, my head hardly hurts at all anymore."

"I wanted to have that horse shot the minute I heard about the accident," he said in a regal voice. "But I—"

"Oh, no!" I exclaimed. "It was all my fault! Don't hurt the horse!"

He nodded. "Well, I do not tolerate animals that abuse humans, and so I made it very clear. But both your sister and that guardsman seemed quite certain that the beast caught its foot in a snake hole or something, and that it was an accident not a malicious event. So I had mercy and did not have it destroyed."

"Oh, yes, thank you, truly it was not the horse's fault," I said, tripping over the words now, because it had not occurred to me before that retribution could befall anyone but me. But I thought Bryan's gesture very grand—that he would sacrifice a horse because it had dared to harm me! The thought made my pulse skitter.

"And how is your head? Better?" he asked.

"Very much. Sometimes it hurts." Right now it was throbbing. "But every day I am much improved."

"Where did you hit it? Are you bruised?"

I put a hand to the back of my head, a little to the left, where I had landed with such jarring force. "Here," I said. "It's still a little tender."

And leaning forward, he touched my hair right where I had just laid my hand. Such was the glamour that attended him that I expected the ache to instantly melt away, healed by his royal caress. But in fact I felt a sudden leap in my heart that made the pain briefly more intense.

"Poor Corie," he said in a sympathetic voice. Shifting his hand, he patted me on the top of the head. "Heal quickly. We want you back among us as soon as possible."

And turning on his heel, he nodded casually to the other women in the room, and walked out.

Needless to say, there was stunned silence for about ten seconds, and then Marian and Angela and I all began squealing at once. "Did you *see* that?" "He *touched* you!" "Corie, he came by to ask after you! He was worried about you! *Bryan!*" Elisandra, who had gone back to her writing, glanced over at us once or twice with great amusement, but did not comment. To her, I knew, tokens of Bryan's affection were commonplace and received much more coolly. But I was overwhelmed with the immensity of the favor. I fell back against the cushions of the divan.

"I am immortal, and no grief can ever scar me again," I declaimed. "For Prince Bryan of Auburn touched my head."

THAT INCIDENT WAS the most momentous, but I enjoyed Kent's visits as well. He came more often, stayed longer, and did not think he conferred much honor on me by his presence.

His first visit, however, was not entirely pleasant. It was on the very first evening after my fall, my head hurt abominably, and no one had had time for me all afternoon so I was lonely and sullen. When Kent strode into the room, he looked grave and a little angry.

"I see it is true, what your sister said, that you did your best to kill yourself yesterday," was his opening remark. "I know you're careless, but I thought even you would pay more attention off the road and an hour from home."

Everyone else had been so sympathetic that his censure caught me unprepared, and my eyes filled with tears. "Well, I didn't *mean* to fall off my horse and cause everybody so much trouble," I pro-tested. "I suppose you've never in your life come unseated——"

"I have—we all have—but neither did I foolishly invite trouble by going too fast on unsuitable terrain."

It was true, and I didn't have the strength to defend myself anyway, so I just turned my head aside and did not reply. I felt two more tears gather and fall. Suddenly Kent was kneeling at the side of the divan and patting my shoulder.

"Oh, Corie, I'm sorry. That was cruel. It's just that Elisandra was so upset when she told me how you were hurt—she loves you so much and she was so worried——"

The remorseful words made the tears come faster. My head was pounding and my left shoulder, which had also taken some of the brunt of the fall, was cramping with its own unfriendly ache. "I didn't mean to do it," I whispered. "I'll be more careful in the future——"

To my surprise, he took me in a quick and comforting hug, being very careful not to disarrange me. "Of course you will. I'm sorry. Stop crying now, please? I really am sorry."

So I tried to stop and he pulled out a handkerchief—which I think I was meant to use to dry my eyes, but I used it to blow my nose. He was not interested in having it returned to him after that. Still, he pulled up a stool and sat by me for the rest of the hour. I was quite cheered up by the time he left—and even more cheered up the next afternoon when he brought me a vase full of flowers.

"To apologize," he said. "And to brighten your room. Where do you want me to set them?"

"Right there on that little table, where I can see them. Thank you so much! That was so thoughtful!"

I was feeling better, and he was still feeling guilty, so he stayed two whole hours and played board games with me. I was never much of an opponent at contests like these, but he was both patient and generous, and did not defeat me too dreadfully. I was laughing when he left. It was quite the most pleasant time I spent during my recuperation—until Bryan came to see me, of course.

I did not get another extended visit with Kent until the day after the hunt, about which I had heard very few details. The hunting party was out quite late, returning just in time for the evening meal and a small musicale to be held that evening. None of my regular visitors came by to give me any news, and when I demanded information of Cressida, she had very little to tell.

"Yes, the animal was killed. That's all I know," she said that night as she helped me from my clothes and into my nightdress. I was feeling pretty healthy this day, so her unhurried ministrations were making me feel a little impatient. "I don't know who brought it down. You can find all that out tomorrow."

And, indeed, Angela and Marian arrived the next afternoon with tales they had gleaned at supper, though they did not include the name of the victorious hunter. "No, it was not Bryan who shot the wolf," Marian said. "None of the nobles, in fact."

"I heard it was one of the guards," Angela said.

"But *that*'s not what everyone is talking about," Marian said excitedly. "Lady Doreen was riding sidesaddle, with her skirts arranged just so all around her, until they rode off the road through a little grove—"

"And her skirt got caught on a branch and the whole thing was pulled right up to her head—petticoats and all! Everyone could see her drawers—"

"And she couldn't free herself from the branch, and the horse went skittish and started turning in circles, and the skirts got more and more tangled up—"

"And she was shrieking—"

"And everyone was laughing too hard to help her—"

"Till Kent came riding up from the rear of the party and cut her loose," Angela finished. "Too bad, because if anyone deserves to be humiliated before Bryan and the whole court it is Lady Doreen."

"Did you *see* him talking to her last night?" Marian demanded of her cousin.

"*Talking* to her," Angela returned. "*Staring* at her is more like it. Well, Corie, the dress she wore—bright red and cut so low that if I ever wore it in public, my mother would disown me."

The gossip continued for another half hour or so. It wasn't until they left and Kent dropped by that I learned what I really wanted to know.

"Roderick killed that wolf, didn't he?" I asked almost as soon as Kent had stepped into the room.

He had brought me a treat from the kitchen, a chocolate confection from the night before. "One shot. He and Kritlin and I had fallen back to keep clear of the noise of the crowd. We knew we were close, though, because we'd seen his tracks, and they were pretty fresh. Still, I wouldn't have known which way to turn, but Roderick's got a natural instinct for hunting. Took us over a couple of hills and across a little creek. We waited for five minutes, and there it was. Looking pretty ragged, too, wild-eyed and crazy. Roderick just took aim and brought it down. No fuss, no horns, no dogs. Nobody hurt. Kritlin was impressed, I could tell. So was I."

"I knew it was him," I said in satisfaction.

Kent gave me a long unreadable look. "He asked after you. Said Elisandra had sent word to the stables a few days ago that you were recovering, but he hadn't heard anything since. He seemed a little worried."

This pleased me no end. "I'm fine. Did you tell him I was fine?"

"I told him."

"Did he say anything else? Send me a message?"

"Guardsmen don't usually send messages to noblewomen via the prince's cousin," Kent said dryly.

"I'm not a noblewoman," was all I could think to say.

Kent rose to his feet, though when he had entered I had for some reason thought he planned to stay awhile. "He seems to think you are," he said. "And you could be if you acted like one."

Back to criticizing my behavior. Just as well if he left, then. "Well, thank you for the dessert," I said.

He nodded. "You're welcome. I'll come by tomorrow and see how you are."

But he didn't need to. The next day I decided of my own accord that I was well enough to bathe, dress, and walk around on my own. I rejoined the ranks of the whole and healthy as they sashayed through Castle Auburn.

5

I was not much of a celebrity once I emerged from the sickroom. Bryan never thought to ask after my well-being again, and Kent was busy with the delegation from Mellidon. Even Marian and Angela were consumed with other matters. Their families were planning an extended visit to Faelyn Market, and they were obsessed with discussing which clothes they should bring and what prominent families they might meet on their sojourn.

Still, it was a relief to be back among the ordinary again, eating the communal dinners, drinking the famous waters, attending whatever event was scheduled for the evening. There were no more grand balls this late in the summer season, but there were musical evenings and card parties and informal dances. The next two weeks flew by.

I spent part of two days posing for the illustrious painter who had arrived at court while I was still in bed. He was young and very dramatic looking, with long sweeping blond hair and an accent that I could not identify. He was constantly directing me to alter my pose—"You! Lift that head!" or "You! Girl! Turn your eyes this way!"—and I tried not to let his peremptory tone annoy me. It was just as well that I was still feeling a little lethargic or I would never have been able to sit quietly for the hours that he required. Yet the finished portrait was good. Elisandra loved it, and even Kent agreed that the man had quite caught my look. He did not say it as if it was a compliment, however, so I was not sure how to take the remark.

I also went looking for Roderick as soon as I had a free hour, though at first I could not find him in any of the places that were public enough for a half-noblewoman to seek out a guardsman. But after three days of loitering near the weapons yard, I finally caught him practicing his maneuvers with a few other young men. I sat on the fence and watched. I still did not know enough about weaponry to judge his skills, but I decided to be impressed anyway.

I was sure he saw me right away—Roderick was the sort who would notice any spectators, whether he liked them or not—but he took his time about coming over to me once his bouts were ended. First he discussed some fine point of attack with his erstwhile opponent, then he inspected some imagined nick in his blade, then he conferred with the weapons master about some private matter. Finally he shrugged, picked up his discarded gloves, and sauntered to my side.

"They've let you out of your room, I see," he said in his unhurried way.

I noticed that he had not asked me how I was feeling, so I didn't bother to assure him that I was fine. "Yes, finally. I got tired of all the fussing."

"I'm not sure I'd ever get tired of fussing," he said mildly. "I've never had a surfeit so far."

"I just wanted to tell you . . ." I said. "I just wanted to thank you—for bringing me home safely."

He shrugged. "Anyone could have scooped you off the ground and hauled you back," he said, most unromantically. "Your sister could have done it if you two had been out alone."

I took a breath and held on to my temper. "But the fact remains that it was you, and I wanted to let you know I appreciated it. However ungracious you were," I could not stop from adding, "when you threatened to leave me behind."

Now his grin lit his face with a sunny halo. "That was ill-done of me," he admitted. "But I was frightened and worried, so I talked cruel to cover it up."

"You were not the least bit worried. You were angry."

"That, too."

"So I'll be more careful in the future." There seemed to be nothing more to say on this topic, so I changed the subject. "And I understand you're the one who brought down the wolf! Congratulations. Did you win the prize? A gold ring, I think it was?"

He nodded and reached inside his shirt. On a plain silver chain the decorated gold band looked glorious and out of place. I was not surprised he did not wear it on his hand; it would have gone oddly with his rough cotton clothes and battle gear. "It's pretty, isn't it?" he said, allowing himself to sound pleased. "Lord Matthew himself brought it to me, Kent at his heels. *That* made me proud, the recognition of a job well done. Some places the promised rewards don't always materialize."

I admired it a moment, then glanced back at his face with a smile on my own. "Now you can hunt aliora and be safe," I said.

He tucked the ring back inside his shirt. "I might be safe, but I don't think that's a prey I'll be hunting," he said.

"Why?" I asked.

He looked at me consideringly. I could not tell if he thought I should already know the answer or if he thought I was too witless to understand it. "I'd trap a falcon to train for the hunt. I'd catch a wild horse and break it to ride. Might even try to raise wolf cubs—some men have done it, kept them as pets, though they're wilder than any dog. But I wouldn't hunt a creature that looks and moves and talks like a man just to sell him to slavery. I'd rather kill him outright."

My breath had caught somewhere in my chest, and I couldn't breathe past the constriction. "But aliora are—they're not humans, everybody says so—and anyway, they steal *us*. Human children, I mean—"

He shrugged. "No one I know was ever taken by an aliora."

"But then—but you—if the stories aren't true . . ."

"Didn't say that, either. Just said I couldn't prove them."

"But you went with us. On the hunt," I said stupidly.

He smiled. "There was no way that group was going to bring

back trophies," he said. "Anyway, I was ordered along to protect the prince. I wasn't asked to bring in specimens. And I wouldn't have."

I just stared up at him, unable to come up with any more words. I had never before heard anyone compare aliora to men and women. It had not occurred to me that anyone rated them at such a high level. I had realized—vaguely, uncomfortably—that the aliora themselves were anxious to see no more of their kin captured. But that was fellow feeling; that made sense. Everyone in the royal household took the aliora slaves for granted, a right—even a necessity. It had not occurred to me to question the arrangement.

I was silent so long that Roderick's smile faded and returned. "New thoughts come hard to a noblewoman, I see," he commented in a soft voice.

"Half-noble," I corrected absently.

"Then perhaps they come twice as fast."

"But do you think—" I began, but he flung up a hand.

"That is the end of the subject," he said. "I was due back at the guardhouse five minutes ago. I'm glad to see you on your feet and looking a little less like death. Take care of yourself over the winter."

He smiled again, touched his fist to his forehead, and strode away.

A WEEK LATER Jaxon was back and summer was over and it was time for me to leave.

Upon his arrival, Jaxon had been gratifyingly alarmed to learn of my fall, and wanted to see with his own eyes that I was properly healed. So he stood over me and pushed back the heavy dark hair along my scalp and peered down at the bruises.

"Well, you look fine enough now," was his gruff assessment, though I'm sure he could tell nothing at all. "How are you feeling? Ever get dizzy? Ever wake up with headaches in the night?"

"No, I'm fine—no symptoms—no pain."

"I planned to have you ride back beside me, but maybe I'd better borrow a carriage and a driver—"

"No, truly, I've been riding three times since then, and I managed to do very well, thank you."

"Well, we'll take it by easy stages, at any rate," he said, still frowning. "But I've got to be back at Halsing Manor in two weeks' time, which doesn't give me much leeway for dallying on the road."

"I won't be any trouble."

I was sad to be leaving Castle Auburn, though, and the melancholy sometimes did spark a return of my headache. In her quiet way, Elisandra seemed equally heartsick. Her smiles were fewer and her eyes, when they rested on me, seemed to absorb my smallest gesture for future safekeeping. She said very little, but brought me presents almost every day of my final week in the castle—little baubles, jeweled hairpins, books, scarves. On the evening before the morning I was to leave, she offered me a small box tied with a gold bow.

"I brought you a present," she announced as she came into my room.

"Another one! You're spoiling me."

"I want to spoil you. Here. Open it now."

So we sat side by side on my bed, and I unwrapped the little box. Inside lay a ceramic pendant no bigger than my two thumbs laid side by side, and on the pendant was painted Elisandra's picture.

My mouth formed a silent "O" and I lifted the cameo out by a length of green ribbon. "El-i-*san*-dra," I managed. "This is so beautiful—"

"Lord Matthew said there wasn't time for one more portrait, but Camilio agreed to stay late one day and do this in one sitting. I told him how important it was for me to be able to give it to you. He wouldn't even take any money for it."

I instantly forgave the theatrical Camilio for all his arrogance. "I *love* it! And I can keep it? And I can wear it on this little ribbon?"

She laughed. "Perhaps not around Lord Matthew. When you're back at your grandmother's."

I sighed. "Which will be in a few days. We leave in the morning."

"I know. I'll miss you."

I gestured in the general direction of her room, where the hand-drawn map lay in her drawer. "Come visit."

Her face still held its characteristic stillness, but I thought I saw a wistful longing cross her features. "Maybe this year," she said in a low voice. "I would like to try."

She stayed late, and we sat up talking while I finished my packing. But eventually we were both too sleepy to stay up any longer, and we parted. In the morning, there was a frenzy of final orders, Jaxon striding through the hallways, the servants running in all directions, Greta arguing with someone about a matter I never did sort out. Kent dropped by to watch the commotion and managed to give me a hug before Jaxon swept me out of the room.

Elisandra stood on the side of the room, watching all the chaos, her hand against the wall, saying nothing. Just as Jaxon was insisting we leave *now*, damn it, I rushed back to give her one final fierce embrace. Then we were out the door, down the hallway, mounted on the horses, and headed past the great fountain toward the massive gate. Two guards from Jaxon's household rode with us, one of them leading a packhorse with all my possessions on it. A few people waved goodbye as we rode past, but there were not many in the courtyard to see us off. Soon enough, we were outside the castle gate and turning in the direction of home.

IN HER WAY, my grandmother was pleased to see me. It was not in her to be effusive. In fact, though Jaxon and I rode up to the cottage with something of a clatter, Jaxon shouting out directions to his guards and me laughing from excitement, she did not come running through the front door to greet us. I dismounted, threw my reins to Jaxon and ran inside. I found her in the kitchen stirring herbs into a cauldron, her eyes fixed on the recipe in some worn old hand-stitched book.

"Grandmother!" I exclaimed, throwing my arms around her. She nodded absently, her gaze still fixed on her page, and put her free arm around my shoulder.

"Yes, good. I see you're back, Corie," she said. "Are you hungry? I won't be finished here for a while, but there's plenty of food in the pantry."

Much different from Elisandra's happy hugs when I arrived at Castle Auburn every summer.

"In a little while. Grandmother, we just got here. Come out and say hello to Uncle Jaxon."

She grimaced. She didn't care for Jaxon any more than Greta cared for me. "Corie, I can't stir a step from this spot until the whole mixture is dissolved. If he wants to talk to me, have him come right in."

I sighed and disentangled myself. "I'll go fetch him."

I went back outside to find Jaxon and his men had already unloaded most of my possessions. Jaxon hoisted a stuffed bag to his shoulder and asked, "Is it safe to go inside?"

I shrugged and nodded. "She's too busy to come out and greet you."

"She always is."

Soon enough, my belongings were all stowed inside and Jaxon's men were again in the saddle, awaiting the order to ride out. Jaxon himself took a few minutes to say goodbye, promise to write, and make plans to come fetch me next summer.

"You be good now" were his parting words. Then he kissed me on the cheek, swung back into the saddle, and waved goodbye. I watched them ride down the dirt road, which was quickly swallowed up by scraggly forest, and waved halfheartedly for as long as I thought there was a chance Jaxon might look back. Then I sighed again, silently this time, and headed back inside the cottage.

"Do you need me?" I called to my grandmother as I stepped through the door. "If not, I'll unpack."

"I'm fine," she replied. "Get settled."

So I dragged the final few bundles to my room, looking around me as I moved through the cottage. As always upon my return, it seemed smaller than I remembered, its compact stone walls grayer and more dense. I noticed details as if for the first time—the way bundles of herbs hung, hundreds in a row, from the parallel beams of the ceiling; the varieties of plants clustered at all four windows of the parlor, all in bloom, all heavy with their own medicinal secrets. My eyes went to the comfortable but worn furniture, a helter-skelter arrangement of stools and sofas and rocking chairs and armoires—and bookshelves lining every wall, spilling over with books, books piled up before them, books open on every surface in the room. I had thought for years that every single one was a spellbook, filled with herb lore and potions, but once I was old enough to read, I found that many of them were novels and romances. My grandmother was not what you would call sentimental, but she loved a good story.

My own chamber was much neater than the central room, and it looked as though my grandmother had not even stepped inside it the whole three months that I was gone. It was filled with sturdy furniture and bright colors: a narrow bed covered with a scarlet comforter, a rocking chair, an overstuffed armchair, a cedar chest, a mirror, a handwoven rug of many colors, and a bookshelf of my own. Like my grandmother, I enjoyed a good story; unlike her, I was often too lazy to read.

I opened the closet and began organizing clothes into piles—dirty, dirty, very dirty, clean enough to hang up and wear again. I could see it would take me three days to get my wardrobe back in order, but I had enough clean clothes to last those three days, so I abandoned the task. I wandered back to the kitchen to assist my grandmother.

"So what are you making?" I asked. I snagged an apple from an open basket and perched on a stool close to the stove.

"Experimental. It's supposed to guard against warts. Angus wants it for his son, who spends all day in the marsh gathering thatching reeds. I read the recipe in an old book, but I've never heard of anyone using it successfully. But I added a few ingredients of my own."

"I brought you a present from the apothecary at Castle Auburn," I said, suddenly remembering.

"Oh, you did? What might that be?"

"Sarafis," I said. "She said it's very rare."

My grandmother actually looked up from her stirring when I pronounced the word. "Sarafis," she repeated. "I haven't had any of that for years. Twenty years, maybe."

"So it's good?"

"Wonderful. Heals without headaches, as my aunt used to say. Nothing like it. That was generous of her."

"Well, I gave her some halen root."

She nodded. "A good trade."

"And I brought you something else," I said. "I wonder if you've heard of it, because I never did."

"What's that?"

"Dayig seeds."

This time she was not awestruck enough to lift her gaze from the book before her. She gave a small snort. "Don't know what I'd use them for. Poison the rats, maybe, though they haven't been bad this year."

"So they *are* poison?" I asked, because I had never been sure. "Will they kill a man?"

"They will—if he eats a hundred of them every day for a month," she said. "Trace poison. The seeds can make you sick, but you'd have to be pretty stupid to die from them."

"Huh," I said, and didn't explain why I was asking. "The fruit's good, though."

She nodded absently. "That it is. Where did you come across it?"

"Out with Jaxon. Hunting."

She snorted again, more loudly. "Just the sort of man who'd go picking questionable fruit from the trees and feeding it to his friends."

I held my peace. Nothing would improve her opinion of Jaxon or any member of his family. We sat in silence for a while, if you discounted the munching sounds I made as I consumed the apple, and then suddenly she gave a small exclamation of annoyance.

"I forgot the elderberry! But it still has to settle twenty minutes or so—perhaps it's not too late—"

I hopped up from my seat. I knew right where it was. "I'll get it."

"Oh, good. Two bottles. And hurry. Thank goodness you're back."

And that's how I knew she was pleased to see me return.

*   *   *

THE NEXT DAY I was less certain. I emerged from my room later than usual to the sound of light, feminine conversation. When I made it to the kitchen, still rubbing my eyes, I found my grandmother talking to a fair-haired girl about my age. She looked vaguely familiar, so I assumed she was from one of the village families, and she looked fairly intent, so I figured she had come for advice or healing.

Imagine my surprise when my sleepy brain took in the gist of my grandmother's words, which were nothing less than a lesson in potion-making, which I had learned last spring.

"Now, if it's a cough only, you add a few leaves of sifronel, but if it's a cough and a fever, omit the sifronel. Substitute with butter hazel or lemon aliote."

"Good morning," I said stupidly to the two of them.

My grandmother barely glanced my way, but the blond girl gave me a shy smile. "You must be Corie," she said. "I'm Milette."

"Hello," I said, then waited for an explanation that did not come. My grandmother glanced over again.

"Hurry up," she said with her usual impatience. "The day's half over and you haven't even dressed. Time for lessons."

Unsure of how to reply to that, I nodded and went to clean up. Twenty minutes later I was back in the kitchen, helping myself to toast and fruit. Milette was now learning the proper way to grind the sifronel, which pestle to use and how fine to make the powder. She watched my grandmother closely, absorbed but not nervous; she must have come here often, because it takes a while to become at ease around my grandmother.

"Well, I'm ready," I said loudly, setting aside my plate. "What do we learn next?"

Milette and I took our lessons together for the rest of the day. When she finally left, my grandmother accompanied her out the door, calling to me to feed the hens and rabbits. The coop and pens were some distance from the house, past the extensive garden filled with mysterious flowers and even more mysterious herbs. I took my time about feeding the animals, dribbling corn, grain, and lettuce into their cages and watching them gobble up their meals. Then I freshened their water, petted my favorites, and walked slowly back to the cottage.

Grandmother was setting a stew over the fire, and the smells of dill and onion were comforting and strong. I sat on my customary stool and watched her for some time without speaking.

She was the one who finally offered an explanation for which I was too stubborn to ask. "Rosa's girl. You know, the candlemaker. Fifth child and no more hands needed in that house. Rosa asked if I'd take her on as an apprentice."

"And you have," I said in a neutral tone.

Grandmother shrugged. "We'll see. So far she learns pretty quickly, but I haven't given her any hard lessons. But I like her. She's a good girl, not too talky, not too stupid."

"But I thought I was your apprentice," I said.

Again that dismissive snort. "You're my apprentice when you're here, which is only three quarters of the year. And will you be here when you turn twenty or twenty-one? I don't think so. I'm the only wise woman for thirty miles. I need to train someone I can trust to be here when I'm gone."

"I'll be here!" I protested, a little heat streaking through my voice. "Why wouldn't I be?"

She cast me one quick, derisive look. "No one who's been offered a castle will choose a cottage," she said.

"But I haven't been offered a castle!"

She twisted one hand in an indeterminate gesture that meant *Not yet, maybe.* "I know what your uncle Jaxon is grooming you for, and it's not life dispensing herbs to childless village women," she said. "You have the right to make your own choice, of course, but it's not hard to see what your future holds. When you live among grand people, your ambitions change. Nothing strange about that."

How many people had made much this same prediction for me during the past summer? Yet this time it filled me with an unreasoning panic. "I don't want grand houses! I don't want to marry some nobleman that Jaxon and Greta pick out for me! I want to live with you and become wise woman to the village and never marry—or, perhaps, marry for love, some country boy with no manners but a good heart—"

She laughed at that. "And there aren't as many of those around as you would like to think, either," she said. "I'd be happy if that was the life you picked, but I'm not depending on it. So I invited Milette in, and she'll stay. You'll both just have to get used to it."

"But, Grandmother—" I said.

She pointed to the pantry behind me. "I need salt. And see if you can find any dried marjoram. This smells too bland for me."

And that was the last discussion we had on the topic. For the rest of the fall, and the entire winter, Milette was at the house as soon as I woke, and there till lessons ended at dusk. Sometimes she stayed the night, sleeping silently on the worn red couch in the parlor, never stirring, never crying out. Once I got up in the middle of the night, thirsty and looking for water, and I stood over her a long time, watching her untroubled sleep. She was everything I had always thought I was—a cheerful, intelligent, hardworking girl who knew her place in the world and had a certain ambition for her life—and she inhabited a role everyone seemed determined to push me out of. I could not hate her but I was able to resist liking her, and she was wary of me as well. Thus an unspoken but fierce competition existed between us, and we each engaged to learn every new lesson before the other. It made us better students, which pleased my grandmother no end, but it did not make life any less complicated.

When summer came around the following year and I prepared to return to Castle Auburn, I realized that I would lose ground to Milette every day of the next three months. And the thought was bitter, though it did not prevent me from making my annual sojourn. When I returned to my grandmother's that fall, I studied extra hard to make up missed time and I eventually caught up with my rival.

But the next summer I fell even further behind, and even further the following year. I was a good witch, but Milette was better, and that did not make it any easier to leave for Castle Auburn that summer.

PART TWO

Disillusionments

6

The summer I was seventeen, everything went wrong.

Elisandra was not at the castle during the first week of my visit. Her mother had carried her off to Tregonia to visit insipid Lady Megan and her vacuous family. I didn't learn this news until I arrived, late and exhausted, to find only the servants awaiting Jaxon and me in the great hallway. I, of course, rushed immediately up to Greta's suite to discover all those rooms empty and no fire in my own bedroom. The footman who had carried my luggage up two stairwells and down two long hallways hustled off to find a chambermaid who could build a fire and bring me fresh water.

Jaxon had carried one of my bags himself and glanced around my cold room while we waited.

"Not very welcoming," he observed. "I thought I told Greta when I'd arrive, but maybe she mislaid the note."

"But I wrote Elisandra. I know she wouldn't have forgotten," I said, sniffling a little, though I was trying not to cry. "That horrible woman has taken her away on purpose."

Jaxon shrugged. "Maybe. Who knows. I'll talk to her when I get back."

"When you get *back*!"

"I'm off for Faelyn Market in the morning."

"But Uncle Jaxon! I've scarcely seen you! When will you be back?"

He hugged me somewhat absentmindedly. "A month, maybe. I've got a hunting trip planned as well."

I pulled away and stared at him openmouthed. It was typical of him to be gone from the castle during much of my sojourn, but usually he stayed long enough to see me settled in. "Uncle *Jaxon*—" I said again.

"I know," he said sympathetically. "Not the best plans all in all. I'll make it up to you later on."

When he left, I cried myself to sleep, even though by now I was much too old for such foolishness. All I could think was how much better off I would be, still in the village contesting with Milette for my grandmother's affections. If no one wanted me here, why had I made such an effort to arrive?

But things were a little better in the morning. The first thing I saw when I opened my eyes was Cressida's slim shape, moving silently between my luggage and my closet, putting away my clothes.

I sat up in bed, calling out her name. She came over to sit beside me. "Good morning, Corie," she said in that sweet, soft voice that lapped over me like warm summer rain. "Look at you! You've gotten all grown-up over the winter."

I laughed and straightened where I sat, the better to show off my newly developed bustline. "And I've grown another inch taller, but I hope it's the very last time," I said. "I'm getting too tall."

"No such thing as too tall," she said. She had automatically reached for a brush and now she began uncoiling the tangles of my hair. "It's good for a woman to be able to look into a man's eyes. Then she's not afraid to tell him what she thinks."

I laughed again. "Not usually a problem I have, anyway."

She smiled. "No . . . So what else happened while you were gone? What about that Milette girl? Is she still there?"

Just her voice, just her presence, just the comforting stroke of her hands through my hair made me happier than I had been since I left my grandmother's cottage. I told her all about Milette, some of the potions I had learned, and the names of the village boys who had flirted with me during the autumn, winter, and spring.

"And here? How is everybody?" I demanded. "Elisandra?"

"Lovely as always. She was very unhappy that she would be gone when you arrived, but she should be here in a day or two. She has a new maid, the quietest little thing, but so devoted to her. It seems to have made her days easier."

"And Kent? Marian? Angela? How are they?

"Kent looks more like his father every day—getting heavier in the bones, more like a man. Marian and Angela are silly as ever, but growing up just like you."

"And Bryan?"

She was silent a moment, or so it seemed, then she laid the brush aside. "Bryan is as he always is, but more so," was the unhelpful response. "Hard to believe he will be king next year. Time for you to take a bath. I'll get a dress ready for you."

Forty-five minutes later I was clean, hungry, and in the small breakfast room where food was laid out for those who did not eat in their rooms. I was late, so I expected it to be empty, but Kent and his father strode in shortly after I had started eating.

Lord Matthew did no more than nod at me before filling his plate at the sideboard, but Kent came over to give me a hug.

"Stand up," he commanded, pulling me from my chair. "Look at you! Turn around. Amazing. You look more like your sister every year."

No compliment could have pleased me more. I gave him a quick curtsey and inspected him in turn. His dark hair looked newly cut, for the planes of his face seemed sharper, more severe than I remembered, and his gray eyes more direct. While I had grown taller, he seemed to have grown broader, though he was still trim and lean. Cressida was right; the thin, serious youth had become a thoughtful, sober man. "You look older," I said.

He smiled at that. "You had all winter to think about it, and you couldn't come up with a nicer thing to say?"

"Older, wiser, more authoritative, and better looking," I amended. "Do you like that better?"

"Much. Are you still eating? I'll sit with you."

The regent did glance over at that. "I'll need you in a few minutes, Kent."

Kent nodded. "I'll be right there."

Lord Matthew looked as if he might say something else, didn't, and set down his plate. He had eaten everything he wanted in three brief minutes. Without another word, he left the room.

"Is something wrong?" I asked.

"Something's always wrong, when you're trying to run a kingdom," Kent said lightly.

"Like what?"

He looked at me consideringly, as if he wasn't sure I was truly interested. "Eight provinces ruled by strong-willed viceroys who have always respected my father. One year from the time a twenty-year-old hothead ascends to the throne. Some of the viceroys don't want to be led by the new king, and they haven't been too subtle about the ways they've said so. Which has not made Bryan any less volatile. My father is doing what he can to soothe the waters. It's been an interesting year."

Much as I had always mooned over Bryan, I could see Kent's point: The handsome redheaded prince was much more likely to appeal to an impressionable young lady than a seasoned and wary landowner. "Which viceroys don't like him?" I asked.

Kent smiled. "Most of them, but Dirkson of Tregonia has been the most vocal. One of the reasons your sister is there now, trying to win some support from the Tregonian court. I don't think it will work, though. Dirkson has said flat out that he won't swear alliance with Auburn unless a different man is on the throne—or a different woman."

I was confused. "Different woman?"

"His daughter. Then he'd back Bryan. He'd have to."

"But—wait. He wants *Megan* to marry Bryan? But—but Elisandra and Bryan have been betrothed for nineteen years."

Kent nodded. "Ah, but he wouldn't leave her completely out of the matrimonial arena," he said, and his voice was very dry. "His son, Borgan, is a personable young man of about twenty-five who would very much like a close alliance with the house of Ouvrelet. And Halsing is close enough for him."

My head was spinning. None of this maneuvering had ever been suggested to me before; I had thought an engagement, once announced, was a settled thing forever. "But the kings have always taken their brides from the house of Halsing," I said. "You told me that."

"Which is why Dirkson considers the match good enough. Greta does not, of course, because nothing will do for her but royalty, but she agreed to go to Tregonia and play the game. Who knows? Dirkson's a widower himself, and Greta is reasonably attractive. That might satisfy him."

I put a hand to my temple. "You're making my head hurt," I complained.

He smiled again, a bit more bitterly. "Well, you did ask."

I had one more question. "What does Bryan think of all this? After all, he has always assumed Elisandra would be his bride."

"Bryan," Kent said, and fell silent as he seemed to think it over. Before he could answer—if he had even planned to—Bryan himself entered the room.

"Kent, did you oh! Corie! I didn't know you were arriving so soon!" he exclaimed. He descended upon me like red desire, sweeping me from my chair and pulling me into an enthusiastic hug. Still holding my hands, he pulled back to survey me with a frankly assessing expression.

"Well! Don't you look inviting," he said gaily. "Our little Corie has grown up to be quite a woman."

I felt myself blushing and ducking my head; I was not used to such attention from the prince. He was as beautiful as ever, that I could tell from my quick glance at his face, and his smile was melting my bones in a most peculiar way.

"I'll have to spend some time with you, getting to know you again," he said. "I look forward to that."

Leaning over, he kissed me quickly and lightly on the mouth. At my expression of stupefaction, he laughed out loud.

"Still the unspoiled country girl, I see," he said, dropping my hands. "That's what I've always liked about you. Kent, your father sent me to fetch you. He wants us both in his parlor."

"Tell him I'll be there in a minute," Kent said coolly. "I had something else to tell Corie."

Bryan nodded at both of us. "Later, then," he said, and left the room.

I turned to look at Kent. I had not said a word since Bryan marched into the room. Kent's expression was both cautious and rueful; he watched me as if unsure of my emotions.

"Bryan," he said, as if we had not been interrupted, "has discovered how very much he likes women who are attracted to the man who will be king. I don't know that, at the moment, he is too interested in marrying anybody, even someone as gracious and gentle as your sister. Perhaps especially someone as gracious and gentle as your sister."

"But he—yes, but Bryan was always something of a flirt—" I said weakly.

A shadow crossed Kent's face, as if he was disappointed at my inability to discern some very basic truth. He rose to his feet. "And perhaps it is nothing more than that," he said. "It is hard to know you are the most powerful man in the kingdom and not be interested in using your power."

"And what does *that* mean?" I said irritably, but Kent was already at the door.

"My father needs me. It's good to see you again, Corie," he said, then he too left the room.

I finished my breakfast in silence and solitude. I did not care much for my first morning back at the castle.

THERE WERE TO be more disappointments. I made my way to Angela's room, to find her being fitted for a new dress. Marian sat in the corner reading a novel, but she leapt up at my entrance. After we had all exclaimed over each other, how different we looked—how lovely, your hair looks so good that way—Angela shooed the fitter out of the room and we sat together and talked. Angela always had the best gossip, and so I hoped she would enlighten me on some of Kent's dour suggestions.

"It is so good to see you both!" I said, aiming at my goal through a circuitous route. "I could not believe it when I arrived last night and found Elisandra gone. And to Tregonia, of all places! Why there? With that vapid Lady Megan?"

Angela leaned forward to whisper, even though there were only the three of us in the room. "Lord Matthew hopes that if Elisandra's gone for a while, Bryan will miss her. He thinks the prince does not appreciate his intended bride."

I made my face look incredulous. "Does not appreciate her! Why, what do you mean?"

Angela glanced around the room yet one more time, her blue eyes very wide. "Lately, Bryan has said he does not care to marry next year, as has always been intended. He told his uncle that he will be a good and faithful husband—but not yet. The regent is absolutely furious, so he sent Elisandra away."

"But Bryan has not seemed to regret it," Marian murmured.

Angela giggled. "I can't say I'm sorry," she said. "I love to dance with Bryan five times in one night! Or walk with him through the gardens! Did you ever see a more beautiful man? And the things he says! I know he doesn't mean them, but I like to hear them. And I know he says them to other girls. I don't think the prince is ready to marry, either. And I say—let him wait. Let him see who else might take his fancy."

I had always liked Angela, but at the moment I wanted to strike her dead. I spent so much energy holding on to my black fury that Marian had time to detail her encounters, too, with the prince. I remembered that kiss in the breakfast room. All of us had always adored Bryan, but none of us had ever expected him to notice us. Now that he had, it was so much stranger than any of us had expected.

We talked awhile longer before I could escape, heading outside again where it seemed I might have enough room for my thoughts to circle around my dizzy head. There was no solving this puzzle, I knew; but a little exercise might at least calm my mind.

I strode through the gardens at a pretty good pace, disturbing a few sets of lovers and a handful of birds. My way took me without conscious volition to the back of the castle, to the guardhouses and the weapons yard, where there was even now a practice session under way.

I climbed to my usual perch and watched the combatants. None of them looked familiar. Eventually, after I had spent about an hour wishing I, too, could knock a few heads around and perhaps dissipate some of my vexation, I had a chance to speak to a pair of the younger guards who stood by me as they pulled off their vests and helmets.

"Do either of you know a guardsman named Roderick?" I asked with a pretty smile.

The shorter of the two, a fresh-faced young boy who could hardly have been sixteen years old, smiled back. "Everyone knows Roderick, but he's not a guardsman anymore," he said.

Had he left the castle and the service of the prince? My heart squeezed down. This was not news Elisandra would think to pass on in a letter. "Not a guardsman anymore? What do you mean?"

"He's a half-sergeant. Been since I came up from Mellidon," said the other man, who was taller, heavier, and a bit more surly than his friend.

Ah, a promotion. My heart billowed up again. "So that's why he's not practicing in the yard with the rest of you?"

"Not practicing because he's not here," said the second man. "Gone to Tregonia with the Halsing ladies."

My bad mood flared suddenly higher; everyone had been spirited away from me, it seemed. "Well. Tregonia. That's nice," I said shortly. "I don't suppose anyone knows when they'll be back?"

"No one's told us," said the short one cheerfully. "Did you want to be getting a message to Roderick?"

Goodness, no. What would I possibly say in a message? I slipped to my feet and brushed out my skirt. "Oh, no. I'll run into him later. Thank you so much for your help." And on those silly words, I turned and practically ran back toward the castle.

Where I suddenly did not want to be in the slightest.

*   *   *

IT WAS TWO more days before Elisandra returned. I spent those two days in the laziest fashion imaginable. I slept past noon, read novels in Elisandra's drawing room, and didn't speak to any other residents until the communal dinners. At these events, at least, everything seemed unchanged: Bryan, Damien, Matthew, and Kent sat at the head table with several high-ranking guests; I found my seat with Marian and Angela; and everyone gossiped. I tried, during these first two evenings without Greta's supervision, to drink the wine that the servants passed down the tables, but I still had not acquired a taste for it. The well water was as delicious as it always was, and I contented myself with that. I noticed that Bryan still would not touch the water, though Damien drank it when he was not tasting whatever fresh bottle of wine the prince had called for.

I was beginning to think Bryan was a little more erratic than I had ever noticed before.

After the meals, where I ate as much of the rich food as I possibly could to make up for Grandmother's much simpler table fare, I returned to my room to nap for a few hours. And, both those two nights and for most of the nights of that summer, I woke as the clocks were striking two.

Grandmother had been teaching Milette and me some of the darker magics during the last winter, potions that could only be mixed at midnight and plants that could only be cut when the moon had slivered away. So we had formed the habit of rising late, going to bed early, then rising again in the dark of night to practice our newest skills. It seemed I could not immediately retrain my body to adhere to a more ordinary schedule.

But I found I somewhat enjoyed wandering at night through the dark but far from quiet castle.

The corridors themselves were never entirely silent, even at this late hour. That first night, I crept stealthily down the halls where the permanent residents lived, and then past the rooms where the guests were quartered. Invariably, behind one or two doors, I heard the low murmur of conversation, the spike of laughter, or the run of tears. Sometimes a light spilled out at the threshold, even when there was no noise inside the room; there, I guessed, someone was reading late, or writing a despondent letter, or frightening away ghosts or memories with the aid of candlelight.

I climbed the levels of stairways to the servants' quarters, where all was deathly still; these hard-worked souls wasted none of the night in talk and superstition, but slept away every available minute. Another flight, to the highest story of the castle, to the curtained doorway through which the aliora could be found. There was no door to block my way, but I did not walk in. I stood outside listening to the strange whistling and hissing that marked the sound of aliora dreaming. Their voices sounded thin, hopeless, unraveled, and I imagined them pitched in a key and on a frequency that would carry their words to their loved ones in Alora. The longer I stood there, listening to that strange, woeful noise, the sadder I grew. I fixed my eye on the gold key hanging outside the door, and I thought about Jaxon even now hunting down by Faelyn River, and I felt colder than I had since the winter solstice.

This was too much to take for long. I hurried back down all the flights of stairs, through the grand entrance hall, and out into the warm summer night. There were guards at the main door, who were astonished to see what passed for a noblewoman roaming around at night, but they did not challenge me; they gave me a respectful salute, fist touched briefly to the forehead, and watched me go. My shoes made an odd, clacking sound on the cobblestones of the courtyard, no matter how quietly I placed my feet. It was like being followed by the audible manifestation of my own shadow. I resolved to wear my slippers if I ever went out wandering at night again.

I came to rest beside the great fountain, still spuming with water long after everyone was sleeping. I jumped to the ledge and caught my balance with my arms outstretched, then walked the unsteady circle all around its perimeter. I had done this as a child, but I had thought it too unseemly a prank to try once I turned fifteen. I was surprised at how happy it made me to walk around the entire fountain once again, feel the feather edge of spray against my face and hold my equilibrium on the slanted slope of the stone. Laughing silently, I completed the circle and hopped down.

It was a few quick steps to the front of the courtyard and the great gates that guarded the entrance to the castle. Here, there were four men on guard, all talking in low voices until they caught my clattering approach. Then they all came to attention, placing their hands on their weapons and assessing what kind of threat I might offer. I liked that; it made me feel like I could sleep more soundly at night, knowing that guards were on watch from danger without or within.

But two of them, at least, recognized me as soon as I recognized them: the young men I had spoken to briefly in the weapons yard that afternoon. I hesitated just a moment before addressing them.

"A long day for you two," I observed. "Will they let you sleep late in the morning, or is it up at dawn and back to practice?"

The short one grinned. He had curly brown hair and an open smile; he could not have been here long. "Sleep in," he said. "Cloate says it's the best part of drawing night duty. He's a lazy bones, anyway, hates to get up when the sun rises."

I glanced at his surly friend. "And this would be Cloate?"

The short boy nodded. "He's Cloate, I'm Shorro, that's Clem and Estis." Clem and Estis were a pair of evenly matched young men who looked large enough and menacing enough to give me pause; but they both nodded and smiled in a friendly way. Clearly they wondered what I was doing out at night, but Shorro obviously had already pegged me for an eccentric, so he didn't mind extending our acquaintance.

He said now, "I know who you are. The Halsing half-sister what only comes here in the summer."

I nodded. "That's right. Coriel Halsing."

Clem and Estis faded back against their side of the gate and resumed their own quiet conversation, but Cloate decided to set his observations alongside Shorro's.

"They say you're a witch," Cloate said.

I nodded again. "Studying to be one. Why? Do you need a potion?"

Even in the moonlight, Cloate looked embarrassed. "No."

"Yes," Shorro said instantly.

I could not help but be amused. I divided a look between them. "Now, who needs that potion? And what kind would it be?"

"He needs it," Shorro said. "Love spell."

"Do not," Cloate muttered. "Not interested in her, anyway."

"I can make a tonic," I said in the most encouraging of voices. "It doesn't always work, though."

They were both immediately interested, but Cloate was too proud to ask questions. "Why is that?" Shorro wanted to know.

I made a shape in the air with my hands, as if holding a large cup of water. "There are a couple different love potions," I said. "I only know one. It's good, but it only works to—how can I explain this—to open the eyes of the other person to your good qualities and charms. It can make her aware of you, but it won't make her love you. You have to do that on your own. There are potions that can create false desire, but I don't know them." I added primly, "I wouldn't practice them if I did know them. That's not the kind of herbalism I do."

Shorro nodded sagely, as if any good citizen should know those distinctions and abide by them, but Cloate for the first time looked hopeful. "That'd be good enough for me," he said. "A potion that made her—what you said. Notice me."

"Do you have access to her?" I asked.

"Have what?"

"Does she live here at the castle?" I said patiently. "I can make a preserved potion that will last till you return home again, or I can make a fresh one if you plan to use it immediately."

"Oh, she's here," Shorro said for him.

"And would you have a chance to present her with the mixture?" I asked. "Most often, it is something you would slip into her water or her wine."

Cloate looked thoughtful. Shorro said, "No, but Meekie would do it. If I asked her."

I glanced at the short boy again, laughter spilling out of me.

"Meekie? And I take it *you* don't need a potion to draw her attention?"

He grinned so widely that no other reply was needed. Cloate snorted and said, "No spells for *him*."

"Well, I can make the potion, if you want it," I said briskly. "Do you?"

Cloate hesitated, his eyes trained on the ground for a long time. When he finally looked at me again, he seemed to be struggling with his desires as well as an innate sense of justice. It made me like him a great deal. "And it won't cloud her mind? It won't make her do nothing she would be sorry or ashamed to do?"

"No," I said. "It will just open her eyes to possibilities. It won't change her nature or make her act against her best interests. It's a benign potion. In fact, if it will make you feel better, I'll mix a double batch and I'll drink half of it right in front of you."

His face cleared miraculously. "You would? That would be—but I don't want you to think I don't trust you—"

"Nonsense," I said. "You have no reason to trust me. You don't know me. I'd be happy to drink half my own vial."

"Then—yes, I'd be pleased to hire your services, Lady Coriel," he said formally—if incorrectly, for no one called me "lady." "What is the price for your work?"

I was tempted to offer the service for free, but I knew better; the village folk were too proud to accept charity magic, and insisted on paying us even when they were too poor to feed themselves. And this was a working man who was taking the prince's wage, so I certainly did not want to insult him.

"Two silver pieces," I said, for it seemed substantial enough to make the scrum seem valuable, but not so expensive he would be forced to sit out the next round of gambling with his fellows. He nodded, looking a bit relieved. He seemed to think herbal remedies came at a higher price.

"And I can bring it by tomorrow night," I said. "If you will be on duty then?"

"Tomorrow and every night till the summer ends," Shorro said.

"Good. Then that's what I'll do."

"I appreciate it."

The long walk, the conversation, and the transaction had finally made me sleepy. I gave them a drowsy smile and prepared to head back to my bed. "Tomorrow night, then." They gave me that fisted salute, and I left them.

My next day was exactly the same, down to the route I took through the castle and grounds. This time, however, I carried a small glass vial in my pocket and a basket of other treats over my arm. Cloate accepted the potion with far more reverence than he showed for the two silver coins he dropped in my palm, though I was unexpectedly thrilled to receive the money. It was the first time I had been paid for witchwork; I was surprised to discover how much I liked the sensation. I was sure Milette had done nothing to earn even so small a store as this.

"Remember—it must be poured into something she drinks, and she must drink all of it," I cautioned. "Can your Meekie ensure this?"

Shorro nodded. "She says she can."

"Good," I said. I had set my basket down when I arrived. Now I opened it and laid out its contents: a stoppered pitcher and five metal cups. "Is anybody thirsty?"

Even Clem and Estis looked interested at this. "We're not allowed wine while we're on watch," Shorro said regretfully. "Any liquor."

I uncapped the pitcher. "It's not wine," I said. "It's water flavored with dried raspberries. I mixed it up before I came out here. Are you allowed that?"

"Oh, yes, lady, we're allowed that," Shorro said enthusiastically.

So I poured measures out for all of us, then took the vial back from Cloate's hands. "Half for me," I said, and tipped some of the contents into my own cup. Smiling, I handed the other portions around and raised my own cup in a toast. We all drank quickly.

"*What* did you call this?" Shorro demanded. "Tastes wonderful!"

"Water flavored with dried raspberries. Something my grandmother taught me."

"And there's nothing in it? No magic?"

"Nothing at all," I replied with a smile. I handed the vial back to Cloate. "That's for you."

He was watching me as if to make sure I didn't turn into a dragon or a wraith before his eyes. Fleetingly I wondered if he would really have the nerve to slip the dose to the young woman with whom he was smitten. But I had provided the product I had been paid to deliver; the rest was out of my hands.

"What does it taste like?" he asked.

I shook my head. "Nothing. Water. She won't detect it."

He nodded. "Well, then," he said, and added nothing more.

"Anything else?" I asked the group at large. No one had any more questions or requests. "I'll be going, then. But I'll come back every once in a while to check on your progress. I'd like to see how this romance turns out."

As I headed back up to the castle entrance, this time forgoing the pleasure of balancing on the edge of the fountain, I did take a moment to wonder what effect the potion might have on me. It was supposed to make you sensitive to unvoiced love, allow you to pick up on a yearning you might otherwise have overlooked. It was crafted to open your eyes. My eyes would be open, but I had started to think I had already noticed things I should have seen a long time ago; so I wasn't sure witchcraft would offer any more revelations.

AT THE END of the week, Elisandra returned. I was in the north garden when the cavalcade pulled up, but I ran toward the courtyard at the sound of the new arrivals. I was in time to see Kent help Elisandra from her coach. She seemed to lean against him a moment for support even once her feet were on the ground. Even from a distance, I thought she looked weary beyond telling, and I did not rush forward to greet her since I was sure she would have many matters to settle before she had time for me.

Instead, I hung back as the cortege entered the castle, and I slowly climbed the stairs to my own room, figuring I would wait there till she sent for me. But I was not even in our own hallway when I encountered Kent coming from the direction of Greta's suite.

"There you are!" he exclaimed. "Elisandra keeps asking for you."

"She *does*? I thought she might want to rest—"

He shook his head impatiently and grabbed my wrist. "And no one knew where you were, and I had to admit I'd scarcely laid eyes on you the past two days—where have you been hiding yourself, by the way? I haven't seen you take a morning ride since you've gotten here. I loitered at the stables a good hour this morning, thinking you might show up."

I'd been sleeping, but I hardly wanted to admit that. "I've been keeping busy. I thought you were, too."

"Busier than I like," he said, towing me down the hallway and turning the handle on Elisandra's door. "But I still have time for you."

We entered into a scene of confusion. Greta was scolding some young girl, who defended herself in the soft accents of a west country native. This was the new maid, I supposed, and I was pleased to see that she did not seem cowed by Greta's bad-tempered demands. There were boxes everywhere, and two servants were just now lowering a large leather-bound trunk to the floor in one corner of the room. Fresh-cut flowers stood in vases all over the room, filling the air with the sweet scent of summer. Someone (Cressida, most likely) had known Elisandra was returning today.

Although she had been directing the men with the trunk, Elisandra caught sight of me and hurried over. "Corie! I'm so sorry I was gone when you arrived!" she cried, folding me into a tight embrace. I had the oddest sensation, that she clung to me a moment to catch her own balance—that she, always the most serene and levelheaded of women, had briefly needed my strength to assist her through a moment of despair. Then she lifted her head and smiled down at me. It was the same Elisandra as ever, calm, tranquil, no secrets to be read in the dark eyes.

"Look at you," she said, as everyone seemed destined to say on this particular visit. "You've grown up so much! You look like such a lady."

Greta broke off recriminations long enough to say, in our general direction, "But will she act any more like a lady?" Then she instantly returned to her tongue-lashing.

Elisandra ignored this interjection. "You seem taller. Are you taller? And—more filled out . . ."

I was blushing furiously. Kent was grinning. "Yes, several of the young men of the castle have already noticed her charms," he said. "I think she'll be quite the belle at the dinner next month."

A shadow crossed Elisandra's face, so faint that I almost thought I could have imagined it. "Oh, is that to come up so soon?" she said. "The dinner with all the viceroys attending?"

"Just a few weeks away," he said cheerfully. "Of course, you'll be popular, too. You always are."

She ignored this observation as well. Still looking down at me, she said, "I brought you a present from Tregonia. If, as seems impossible, we ever get everything unpacked, I'll give it to you. How was your winter? I can't believe how much you've grown."

"The winter was hard, but spring's been good. I hate Milette," I said. For, of course, she knew everything about my rival.

Elisandra laughed. "You'll have to feed her frog eyes and owl gizzards and whatever evil potions you can concoct to get rid of her."

"I can't," I said gloomily. "I don't know any of the darker magics."

Greta swirled up to us at that point, a tiny blond cloud of impatience. "This silly girl says you left behind that lovely shawl Borgan gave you," Greta said fretfully. "I know that can't be true. I want you to wear it to dinner tonight, so Bryan and his uncle can see how admired you are by other men—"

Elisandra faced her mother with her characteristically unruffled look. "It's true. I left the shawl behind."

"You *what*?" I had never actually heard Greta shriek before, though I would have guessed it to be within her repertoire. "You did not! You wicked girl! What will Dirkson think, what will his son say—"

"You did not hear the words that accompanied the gift of the shawl," Elisandra said, completely calm. "To keep it would have compromised me. So I did not keep it."

"Compromised you! In what way would it—I'll have you know, the regent will not be pleased to hear this—"

So smoothly that I almost did not notice his movement, Kent laid his arm around Greta's shoulders and turned her from Elisandra's side. "Tell me the problem and I'll inform my father exactly what happened. I'll use great tact and guile, so he will have no reason to be angry at you or Elisandra," he said. His arm still around her shoulder, he urged the protesting Greta toward the door. I caught the echo of her complaints and his soothing responses as they headed down the hallway.

I looked at Elisandra with my brows arching high over my eyes. "And just what did Borgan of Tregonia say to you when he gave you his lovely gift?" I asked.

She hesitated a moment, as if she would tell me, and then she shook her head as if shaking away a small, unimportant problem. "Oh—nothing, nothing, I just did not want to keep the gift, that's all," she said. "Corie, have you met my new maid, Daria? She's from Chillain. I just love her accent."

Daria came forward, deferential but not shy, and gave me a little curtsey. "You're Corie, then," she said, and it *was* a lovely accent. West country, just as I had suspected. "Your sister talks about you, oh, so often."

I smiled at her. She had the fair skin and blond hair common to Chillain, and her small bones did not hide her innate strength. Cressida had called her quiet, but she looked like a fighter to me. "You're new since the summer," I said. "How do you like Castle Auburn?"

"So exciting!" she said. "All the lords and ladies with their grand ways and their pretty speeches. And the aliora! I never saw one before in my life. I was afraid at first, but that Cressida—she made me feel warm as my mother's daughter, first time she talked to me."

"That's what the aliora do," Kent said, reentering the room. "Make you feel loved." I saw his gaze lock with Elisandra's before he had even shut the door behind him, and a flare of understanding seemed to briefly brighten the air between them. "*She's* all settled," he added lightly. "Any other tasks I can perform for you?"

Elisandra smiled tightly. "No, just sit and talk to me while Daria and I unpack."

"Are you sure you want us?" Kent said. "I can go away while you get settled. And I'll drag Corie out, too, if you need to be alone."

"No, stay, both of you. Tell me what's been happening. I've missed you both so much."

Kent draped his long body in one of her delicate chairs, and I seated myself cross-legged on the fluffy bedspread. "Well, the big summer ball is next month, as I've already reminded you," he said. "We've received acceptances from all eight provinces—except for Chillain."

Elisandra stood over the open trunk, pulling out wispy silken underthings and folding them into careful shapes. "Chillain," she repeated in a neutral voice. "That's surprising."

"That's what my father said. He still thinks Loman might send Goff as an envoy, instead of coming himself. Which is insult enough."

"Does Bryan know?"

"Oh, yes. He laughed. He said, 'Well, Loman's got no beautiful daughters anyway, so why would I want him to come?'"

I was surprised at this cavalier attitude, but Elisandra seemed unmoved. "That must have pleased your father greatly."

"As you say," Kent replied dryly. "But everyone else will be here. I imagine we'll have no end of intrigue."

"What about your father? Is he still feeling unwell?"

"No, the fever passed a day or two after you left. He was weak for another day, and then back to his usual strength. You know my father."

"And Tiatza?" she asked. "How is she?"

I frowned at this, for that sounded like a lowborn name. Certainly it did not belong to any court lady I knew.

"Next month, perhaps, so Giselda thinks," Kent replied somewhat mysteriously. I had the feeling they were deliberately talking in ambiguous phrases to prevent me and Daria from understanding them.

"That's early, isn't it?"

"Giselda is expecting trouble."

"I'm sorry to hear it," Elisandra said. She handed a stack of folded undergarments to Daria, who carried them to the armoire and began to store them away. "Does your father know?"

"Oh, yes. This pleases him even more than the other."

"And Bryan?"

Kent spread his hands. "He should know. He does not act as if he cares."

"I imagine he does not."

Kent was watching her. Though he sprawled in the chair, appearing completely relaxed, I had the impression that he was tense, uncertain, worried about something he was reluctant to voice. I thought, for truly the first time in my life, *Why, he loves her.* He could not have made it more plain if he had stood up, crossed the room, and put the shelter of his arms around her.

"And you?" he asked softly. "Do you care?"

She came to sit beside me on the bed. Though we sat there without touching, for a moment I felt as if she wanted to lean against me, laying her head upon my shoulder. That clearly did her need for comfort come through.

"It might be easier if I did," she said quietly. "Now, isn't that strange? You'd think just the reverse would be true."

I reached over to take Elisandra's face between my two hands and turned her toward me. "If you have private things to discuss with Kent, Daria and I will leave the room," I said. "If not, let me stay awhile so you can tell me about your trip to Tregonia. But I think you should take a dinner tray in your room tonight. You look exhausted and sad. And we should not be keeping you if you need a little time alone."

For an instant, she was so startled that her habitual mask of serenity dissolved in a look of amazement. She was not used to hearing her younger sister speak with such forthright authority. Then she laughed and put her arms around me again. Once more, I had the sense that she was drawing strength from me, and I willed all my considerable resiliency to travel from my body into hers.

"Oh, Corie, you *have* grown up," she murmured into my hair. "No more secrets with Kent. And don't you dare go away yet. I've missed you too much."

Kent did not stay much longer after that. Before he left, he paused to hug Elisandra briefly and ruffle my hair. I scowled; Elisandra smiled. No wonder she was the one he loved.

Though that was a very strange thought and would take some getting used to.

Elisandra had agreed that we should take dinner in her room, which did not please Greta when she was told.

"Your first night back, you should be in your customary place of honor for all the castle to see," her mother said. "You should be reminding the wild young prince who his affianced bride is—"

"He knows very well who I am," Elisandra said. "I'll deal with Bryan tomorrow. Tonight I'm tired, and I want to see Corie."

Greta fought the decision bitterly but, in the end, Elisandra had her way. Daria and Cressida brought food from the kitchen and arranged it on a pretty table in the center of the room before quietly leaving. The two of us talked contentedly throughout the meal, catching up on the events of the intervening months. Gradually it occurred to me that Elisandra's news was more of the court and its visitors; she said very little about herself, her thoughts and her feelings. I was slowly beginning to realize that she never did.

Finally, abruptly, as she finished some light tale of a solstice mishap, I said bluntly, "So who's Borgan, and what did he say to you?"

She looked startled for a moment, then her face reverted to its usual composed demeanor. "He's Dirkson's son. Megan's brother. He gave me the shawl with the intimation that it was something he planned to give to his bride."

"But you're going to marry Bryan."

"And Borgan knows that."

"Then why—?"

She tilted her head to one side, regarding me. We had never discussed political intrigue; it had never before occurred to me that there might be any. Everything had, for so many years, seemed to me to be exactly as it appeared on the surface.

"Dirkson is ambitious," she said. "Tregonia is the largest of the eight provinces, and adjoins Auburn. He does not see why he should not have some stake in the royal house, being so near the crown. Also, he does not care for Bryan."

"Kent mentioned something of the sort," I said.

"Did he? Well, Dirkson is not the only one, but he is the most vocal. He has said publicly and quite often that he will not accept Bryan as his liege. He has also said that he would be more malleable if there were some connection between his house and the royal court. He thinks to marry his daughter to Bryan and his son to me."

"But *you're* going to marry Bryan," I said again.

She gave me a strange, unreadable look. "We are not married yet," she said.

I was bewildered and oddly panicked. "But—Elisandra—don't you want to marry Bryan? I mean—you have been betrothed to him forever—"

Again, the unreadable expression; her thoughts appeared to be turned inward. "What I want does not matter in the slightest," she said softly.

"Of course it does," I said impatiently. "If you love Bryan—"

Now she looked at me sharply. "If I love Bryan!" she repeated. "If I love anybody! My will is not consulted in these matters. I am a pawn, a bargaining chip. I am a possession to be laid on the dicing table. Matthew will do with me what he will."

Now I was the one to stupidly repeat phrases. "Lord *Matthew*—"

There had been a surge of passion in her voice a moment before, but now she spoke in a completely calm and colorless tone. "I have no estate of my own, and my mother very little. All of the Halsing lands are held in trust by Jaxon, but they will not go to me, or you, until we marry. And even then we must marry a man of Jaxon's choosing. Jaxon supplies our household expenses at Castle Auburn, but we are here, all of us—you and I and my mother—at Lord Matthew's sufferance, because I am betrothed to Bryan. If he decides the crown would gather more glory by being bestowed elsewhere, he has the right to break my engagement to Bryan. And then my position becomes even more precarious."

I felt my throat close, my lungs contract in a kind of fear. None of this had ever occurred to me; I had never considered her anything but cared for and safe. "But surely Bryan has something to say about all this," I said in a constricted voice. "Surely Bryan has always wanted to marry you——"

"Has he?" she said. "Who knows what Bryan wants?"

"And what do *you* want?" I asked desperately.

"I want——" She stopped abruptly, and then she gave a sweet but brittle laugh. "I want to talk about something happier," she said, almost gaily. "I want to talk about you and your visit here and how we have three long months together."

I was not yet ready to abandon the subject. "But if you did not marry Bryan—if you did not marry anyone—Jaxon would still provide for you," I said. "There would be a place for you at Halsing Manor."

"Maybe," she said. "I've never been sure." She gave me a quick, direct look. "I have always envied you, you know, because you have another life to go to. But if I do not marry to please the regent and my uncle, I do not know what will become of me."

"You'll come live with me," I said instantly, "in the cottage. I'll teach you all my spells, and you could be a witch as well."

She did smile at that. "I'd like that," she said. "A country witch."

I leaned over, putting my hand upon her wrist. "Elisandra," I said. "Do you *want* to marry Bryan?"

But she had done with secrets. She smiled and jumped to her feet. "I forgot! Your present! Come see how lovely it is."

She would not say another word on the subject that would trouble me for the rest of my stay at the castle. Instead, she ran to the closet and pulled out a large bundle wrapped in the softest paper. When I folded back the tissue, I found yards and yards of crimson silk shot through with glittering strands of gold.

"Isn't this lovely?" Elisandra murmured, holding a fold to her face. My fingers were lost in it; it was like stroking moonlight. "I'm sure we have enough time before the ball to have it made into a gown. It will look perfect with your dark hair and eyes."

It would have looked perfect with her own. It was a sumptuous gift. We rolled the yards of material into one long shawl and I threw it over my shoulders to go prance before the mirror. "My,

Lady Coriel, don't you look superb," Elisandra said, bowing low. "May I be so lucky as to have this first dance?"

We joined hands and did the first few steps of a minuet. "Nobody ever calls me 'lady,' " I said. "I'm not."

"It's how Matthew has been referring to you in the past few months," Elisandra said, dipping regally with the imagined music. "So the fashion has taken hold. My mother does not care for it, as you might guess, but the other day I heard her correct Angela for *not* calling you by the title, so she seems to have reconciled herself to your elevation."

"So Matthew wants to use me as a chip as well," I mused.

Elisandra dropped her hand, and the pretend music came to a sudden halt. "He always has," she said. "It is the reason my mother has spent so much time with you. Matthew has required it of her. He intends to see you advantageously placed."

I shrugged. "I think," I said grandly, "the regent might be disappointed."

Her laugh trilled out, so happy and so genuine that it made me smile as well. "I know," she said. "And that is such a source of satisfaction to me."

I grinned back. "You are not as dutiful as you seem," I said.

Her face settled into its more composed expression. She gave me a searching look. "You are joking," she said, "but that is really true." Before I could pursue that avenue any further, she turned brisk and efficient. "Come, let us put this carefully away. In the morning, we will have you measured and the seamstresses can begin on your gown. Do you have a style in mind? Something not too prim, not with that color—"

We sat side by side on her bed and looked through sketchbooks the castle tailors had put together, trying to decide on a fashion. We had not been doing this very long when I sensed a great weariness in Elisandra, a bone-deep exhaustion that made it hard for her even to hold the pattern cards in her hands.

"You look tired," I said. "I think it's time I left so you could sleep."

She smiled sadly. "I *am* tired, but these days I do not sleep well," she admitted. "Perhaps that is why I am so tired."

I jumped to my feet. "I'll be right back," I said, and ran from the room. I was back in a few minutes, my satchel in my hand. Elisandra had laid the sketchbooks aside, but otherwise had not moved from her place. I climbed up next to her again.

"Are you having trouble falling asleep, or do you wake up in the middle of the night?" I asked in my best professional voice. "If you cannot sleep through the night, are you wakened by dreams or bodily pains? When you waken in the morning, do you feel sluggish and stupid, or is your mind clear and active?"

She laughed at me, amused and a little impressed. "I cannot fall asleep, and I wake in the middle of the night and cannot sleep then, either," she said. "I have no physical pains, and my mind is very clear."

I nodded. "Good. I will give you an herbal powder, and you will mix one half of a teaspoon in a glass of water every night before you go to bed. It will rock you gently to sleep and help keep you in that state the whole night long."

"I would be glad if that were so," she said, "but I doubt it."

I was shaking out callywort into a shallow bowl she kept on her nightstand. "Try it and see," I retorted.

I could hear her lifting and shaking various vials from my satchel. "This looks interesting. And this one. Oh, and this is a pretty color of blue. What's it for?"

I turned to see what she was holding up to the candlelight. "That's halen root," I informed her. "It reduces pain. But you can only use a tiny amount of it, because too much will kill you."

She quickly replaced the vial in the bag, then continued to stare down at it dubiously. "Really? How much?"

I replaced my other jars of herbs after stoppering them tightly. "There's enough in this little jar to kill a dozen people," I said. "But it has a somewhat salty taste, so you couldn't really administer it in someone's wine or water."

"I thought your grandmother didn't teach you the blacker magics," she said dryly.

I grinned. "This isn't magic, it's herb lore. You can find halen root at any apothecary's shop from here to Faelyn Market, though it will cost you something once you get out of Cotteswold. You have to be careful with it, and always have the antidote on hand."

"The antidote? What's that?"

I picked up another vial. "Ginyese," I said. This powder was white and fine, so pale it was almost translucent. "Also to be found at any apothecary's shop."

She took it from me and held it up to the light. In her hands, it seemed to have a backlit, milky glow. "And does it taste salty, too?"

"No, no taste at all."

"And how much is necessary as an antidote?"

"If you swallowed a teaspoon of halen root, you'd need only a few grains of ginyese," I said. "Actually, ginyese is a wonderful antidote for most poisons, if you take it quickly enough after you've swallowed the toxin, because the body rejects it. So it rejects everything else in your system. Some people even use it for fevers, because they think it cleans the blood."

She laid the bottle back in my bag. "You do know the most interesting things," she said. She picked up another jar, a small clay pot with flowers inscribed on the sides. "What's in here?"

"Love potion," I said with a smile.

She looked at me. "Not really."

I nodded. "Really. I was dispensing some the other night, in fact."

"You were dispensing—and to whom? Did it work?"

Now I was grinning widely. "To a lovesick guardsman on duty at the castle gates. We fell into a conversation. I don't know yet if it's worked, but he seemed quite hopeful."

"And how much of *this* do you have to take to be successful? And is there an antidote?"

I laughed. "And why would you want an antidote for love?"

"If you changed your mind. If the man wasn't quite who you thought he was."

"In that case, I think the antidote would be to avoid him."

She pulled the cork out and sniffed at the contents. "Too late!" she said. "He already loves you. This smells like nothing at all."

"That's why it's so easy to slip into someone's food or drink.

Why would you not want someone to love you? Assuming he was not a total boor."

She replaced the stopper and laid the jar back in its place. "Sometimes it's simpler not to be loved," she said. "What about this jar? Oh, now this has an awful smell. You can't surprise anyone with *this* potion, I'll wager."

One by one, she went through every bottle and vial in my collection. I showed her the mixtures and dosages that would cure a cough, encourage conception, and enhance the memory. I showed her the draughts that would reduce fever and calm despair. I could not tell if she was genuinely interested in the drugs, or interested in learning more about me by examining the things I already knew. When we had been through the whole satchel, I insisted that she change into her nightclothes and drink down the brew I had mixed for her. It was strange, this night, to be the sister who tucked the other into bed, kissed her on the forehead, and bade her to sleep. She smiled up at me after I had blown out every candle but the one I held in my hand.

"I missed you, Corie," she said. "I'm glad you're here."

7

A few weeks later, the castle slowly began to fill with guests. I was of two minds about the summer ball that promised to be the greatest social event I had ever attended. On the one hand, it was exhilarating to witness each new arrival, to whisper with Marian and Angela about which handsome young nobleman might dance with us at the ball, and to vocally disparage the charms of all the other young women. Each dinner was more lavish than the last, and there were constant entertainments planned for the afternoons and the evenings. On the other hand, such commotion definitely changed the easy rhythms of normal court life. I rarely got to see Elisandra alone, or Kent, or even Marian and Angela. Even late at night, the hallways were alive with constant chatter and activity; the castle never seemed to sleep. I felt both caught up in the excitement and displaced from my element. Like Elisandra, I was finding it hard to sleep.

That may have been because I still had not given up my late-night rambles, though these days they did not last so long. I was finding it harder and harder to make the pilgrimage to the very top of the castle, to the room where the aliora lived. Each new highborn arrival brought a new aliora in his or her train, servant to that household; and each of those visiting aliora was housed in the attic

with those of Castle Auburn. The addition of each new frail body
to the score or so already on the premises had a strange, unsettling
effect. There was an aura radiating from that open room—like a
glow or a scent or a hum, though it was none of those things—a
sense of power building or strength coalescing. It was as if the aliora
drew courage from each other, reinforced each other, renewed each
other. It made me afraid to stand there, absorbing that odd, bitter
emanation; it made me hungry every night to feel that jolt of energy again.

As a direct antidote to this fey sensation, every night I hurried
downstairs to seek out the very human company of the guardsmen
at the gate. I had become firm friends with Cloate, Shorro, Clem, and
Estis; and I was closely following the progress of Cloate's romance. It
was proceeding somewhat slowly, to Shorro's disgust, but the pace
seemed to suit the more cautious Cloate.

"She comes to the yard and watches his practices, four days out
of five," Shorro told me. "Some days she'll stay and talk. Other days
she hurries back to the kitchens as if afraid he'll take her right there
in the mud."

"Shorro!" Cloate exclaimed. "You're speaking to a lady!"

"Really? She comes to watch him? I'd like to see this girl. Maybe
I'll come out one afternoon and watch you."

Shorro swept me a bow. He'd been practicing. Estis had informed
me that, with all the ladies' maids pouring into the castle with the
influx of visitors, Shorro was living in bliss. "Not getting two hours'
of sleep a night, but a happy boy," was the way the other guard
phrased it. Shorro had punched him in the arm, but I believed it
was true. Shorro was a flirt.

"We'd be happy to have you watch our poor efforts," the short
man said. "I would fight most fiercely for your favor."

"Shorro," all three of the others reproved him simultaneously,
but I giggled. I pulled off the trailing scarf I wore at my waist and
twirled it through the air in his direction.

"Fight, and make me proud," I said. "I'll be there tomorrow.
One of you will have to point out your girl to me," I said to Cloate.

*   *   *

THE NEXT DAY I showed up at the weapons yard, where I had spent very little time in the past weeks. I was surprised to see how many of the castle guardsmen were lined up in the yard, practicing their swings and battling against each other. Then I noticed that many of the watchers were the house guards of the visiting noblemen. Kritlin knew what he was doing. He was making a show of strength for the gentry.

In addition to the other soldiers leaning against the fence and watching the maneuvers, there was the usual assortment of castle servants and nobles gathered on the sidelines. I was surprised to see my sister's maid, Daria, standing near the fence, her gaze fixed intently upon the action on the field. I tried to guess which of the guardsmen she was following, but their helmets and practice vests made them hard to distinguish from each other. She was keenly interested in someone's fate, that much was clear from the expression on her face.

I spotted Shorro quickly enough, for he had tied my scarf high around his left arm, where anyone could see it. He was a deft swordsman, despite his lack of height, and he fought with a zest that made him both careless and hard to defeat. Today he was victorious in all three matches I observed before Kritlin called for a change of players.

Shorro came immediately to my side once he left the field. "That's her—the tall gangly one with the straight hair," he said, nodding in the direction of a plain, severely dressed woman. "She looks dull, don't she? But Cloate can't get enough of her."

I thought she looked serious and watchful, the kind of woman who did not easily exchange her virtue for pleasure. But I had a higher opinion of Cloate's fidelity than I did of Shorro's, and I thought he might have picked wisely.

"Are guardsmen allowed to marry?" I asked.

Shorro reared back as if I'd tossed him an insult. "Marry! Why would they want to?"

"I know *you* wouldn't," I said patiently. "But those that are interested. Are they allowed?"

Shorro nodded. "Yes, even encouraged. Kritlin thinks marriage steadies a man."

"I like her," I decided.

Shorro rolled his eyes. "Since you know her so well."

I grinned. "And you can tell Cloate I said so."

He stayed beside me for the next few minutes, idly talking, but I did not listen closely to what he said. My eyes had wandered back to Daria, standing so still at the corner of the yard. Only now she was not alone. She was gazing earnestly up at the face of a tall, lanky, freckle-faced guardsman whom I had not had a chance to talk to since my return to Castle Auburn.

"Well," I said aloud. My voice sounded harsh and sour.

Shorro stopped midsentence. "Well, what?"

I shook my head. "Nothing. Go on."

He resumed his prattle; I continued watching. Roderick appeared to be listening to Daria far more than replying. He nodded a couple of times, and shook his head once, but for the most part, he seemed to have little to say. At one point, I saw Daria reach her hand inside her bodice and pull out some small object—a note, I thought, folded as small as it would go. Roderick took it and slipped it inside his pocket without looking at it.

Lucky for him Kent taught him to read, I thought, my internal voice sounding nasty even to me. I was surprised at the depth of my sudden animosity. What did I care how many servant girls Roderick dallied with? It was just that he had not seemed like the type. It was just that I had thought him better than Shorro, more serious even than Cloate. Even Kent had spoken highly of Roderick. It was just that he had seemed special to me.

"Me again," Shorro said suddenly, responding to a shrill whistle from the field. He slipped his helmet back on, but managed to wink at me through the visor. "Watch for me."

I stayed awhile longer, but some of the pleasure was gone for me. This time I watched Roderick's lean, rangy body as he left the fence and headed back into the mock combat. He moved with a compact ease, disabled his opponents with economy, and was not struck down while I was there. When I glanced back to see how

Daria was impressed with his ability, I found she had already left the scene.

I ENCOUNTERED MY next somewhat tarnished idol the very next day. I had awoken quite late, since I had not returned to my rooms till nearly dawn, and I was strolling through the north gardens hoping to enjoy a few hours of sunlight. I didn't pay much attention when I heard a chorus of male voices rising from a nearby path—riders often chose to cut through the gardens on their way back from the stables—but suddenly I was in the middle of a group of young noblemen, all dressed for riding and smelling faintly of horse. One of the men was Bryan.

"Corie!" he exclaimed, bounding up to me and taking me in a fierce hug. I was both surprised and uncomfortable, for he held me much too tightly and no one behaved this way in the gardens—at any rate, not in the daylight and not with an audience. "Where have you been hiding yourself? I haven't seen you for a week."

"I've been here," I said, unobtrusively struggling to free myself. This didn't work. Keeping one arm around me, Bryan pulled me around to view his fellow riders. I recognized one or two of them, most of them young lords about Bryan's age, a few of them grinning at me, a couple looking bored or ill at ease.

"You know all these impressive scions of their respective noble houses, don't you?" Bryan cried, still in an overexcited voice that suited neither the hour nor the setting. "There's Max. There's Holden. That's Lester and Borgan and Hennessey—"

I tried to pick out Borgan of Tregonia, but no one was responding to the names Bryan was reeling off so fast. "And Jude is somewhere, but maybe he's ahead of us, because I don't see him at the moment—"

"Back at the stables," one of the young men interjected. "Worried his mount may have taken a pebble in the hoof. He'll be by any minute."

Bryan squeezed my shoulders and finally dropped his arm. "So, will I see you at the ball? Will you reserve a dance for me?" he demanded. "None of this pretending to be shy with me—you've known me your whole life, after all, or most of it."

"I'd be glad to dance with you, Bryan," I said. For it was still true that he remained the most beautiful man at the castle, and the thought of dancing with him made me a little breathless.

He swept his hand out to indicate the men of his riding party. "All of them will want to dance with you! Right—eh, Hennessey? For this is Elisandra's sister—Jaxon Halsing's niece, you know. You've heard my father talk of her."

The man called Hennessey gave a start of recognition and came forward. He was dark-skinned, dark-haired, with close-set eyes and a close-cropped beard. Older than Bryan by a decade at least—and not the sort of man I would have expected to enjoy an outing with the prince.

"Lady Coriel," he said, taking my hand and bowing over it. "Yes, Lord Matthew has spoken of you often. I had hoped to meet you before this."

"Back to the castle," Bryan called, "for luncheon is on the table!" The whole untidy party began to jostle back down the path. The whole party except Hennessey, who stood before me, blocking my path.

"I'm sorry," I said, as prettily as I could. "I did not catch your name. Lord—Hennessey?"

I had caught the name, of course, but I wasn't sure of his lineage. He obligingly gave me the details. "Hennessey of Mellidon. I'm Arthur's middle son."

Ah, yes. Hours of studying with Greta over the past three summers helped me fill in the rest of this story. Viceroy Arthur was old, sick, and feeble but not yet ready to relinquish his authority; his eldest son did most of the actual administrating and was known for his swift dispensation of justice. That son had married young, but his wife failed to produce the desired heir, so he had divorced her and married again two years ago. This new bride had also so far proved infertile, leading to some speculation about the man's virility. The youngest son, who hated his oldest brother, had married more successfully and had sired numerous offspring, two of them boys.

Hennessey, always allied with his older brother, was looking to find his own wife and, if possible, cut out the younger brother in the succession.

It seemed someone might have suggested me as a possible match.

"Of course," I said, offering my hand again and giving a formal curtsey. "You've come for the summer festivities, I take it? How do you like Auburn so far?"

He tucked my hand into the crook of his arm and proceeded to escort me slowly back to the castle. "Much better—now," he said. "I had heard that Elisandra's sister was her rival in all things, but I had not thought it possible. Until I laid eyes on you."

The heavy gallantry came awkwardly from his mouth. I could not imagine any set of circumstances that would induce me to relocate all the way to Mellidon. I smiled nonetheless. "How flattering. Tell me how you have spent your days—hunting, I take it? What's the hunting like in your part of the world?"

This, as I had suspected, was a topic he was quite comfortable with, so we passed the rest of the brief walk in a discussion of hawks and hounds. Once we stepped through the great doorway, I clapped my hands to my cheeks.

"Oh, no!" I exclaimed. "I'm late—I'm so sorry—you can finish your story some other time." And I dashed down the hall and up the first stairwell before he could ask about sitting with me at dinner that evening or dancing with me at the ball. A temporary reprieve only, and I knew it, but it made me gleeful nonetheless.

That evening, I waited in Elisandra's room as Daria fixed her hair, and I related some of the incidents in the garden. A flicker of distaste crossed Elisandra's face and was quickly gone.

"I do not care much for Hennessey myself," she said.

I teased, "Oh, then, I should not marry him just to please you?"

She met my eyes in the mirror. She was not laughing. "Do not marry to please anyone except yourself."

I tossed a sachet ball in the air. Greta wanted me to tuck it in my pocket, to create "a perfumed air of mystery" as I walked, but I hated its smell and refused to carry it. "I don't think I shall marry anyone," I said nonchalantly. "And I don't know that I will flirt with any of them, either. It's not as pleasant as I always thought it would be."

Now Elisandra permitted herself a small smile. "Perhaps you have not flirted with the right people."

I shook my head. "Even Bryan—it feels so odd when he takes my hand and says such things. He never did anything like that before. I can't believe how he's changed."

Now Elisandra's eyes were on her own reflection. "Bryan has not changed," she said in a low voice.

Am I the one who changed, then? I wondered. But perhaps that was not what she had meant. Daria gave Elisandra's hair a final pat and said, "Done, my lady."

Elisandra nodded gravely. "Thank you." She came to her feet, lovely in a silver-blue gown, and said to the maid, "You need not wait up for me tonight. I believe there's entertainment after the meal, and I don't want you to be up till all hours."

"Thank you, my lady," Daria said, dropping a small curtsey. I could not keep a quick resentful thought from crossing my mind: *With what attractive guardsman will you be spending your free hours?* But, of course, I did not ask the question aloud. It was too absurd.

Downstairs, the seating was more formal than usual, which I instantly knew spelled trouble for me. Indeed, the servants directed Elisandra to the head table, while I was placed at the second of the perpendicular tables—a fairly high honor, which I knew, and which I did not appreciate. For Hennessey of Mellidon was already seated in the chair next to mine, and he smiled as he watched me approach.

WE MADE IT through dinner amiably enough, though Hennessey's conversational abilities did not improve much with familiarity, and I made absolutely no replies to his attempts at gallantry, which he must have found discouraging. I managed to elude him as the guests all filed into the large salon for the evening's entertainment. I had no idea what this might be, so I caught up with Angela as people began to seat themselves in rows of chairs set up before a low dais.

"What's going on? Is someone performing?" I asked.

She grabbed my arm and led me to the row where Marian had already settled. *"Corie!* You were seated by Lord Hennessey! What an honor for you! There's talk that he might be the next viceroy, once his father dies and his brother proves impotent—"

"I thought he was a little boring," I said.

"It doesn't matter if he's boring! A husband doesn't have to be interesting to make you wealthy and powerful."

I wanted to get off this topic. "Well, you didn't fare so badly yourself," I said, for I'd noticed. This matchmaking game was new to me, but I was beginning to make out its intricacies and arabesques. "Wasn't that Lord Lester seated beside you?"

This she was just as happy to talk about. Then we discussed Marian's dinner partner as well, while the rest of the guests filed in and made themselves comfortable. I still had no idea who would be performing, so I was amazed to see a half dozen aliora enter the room and climb to the small stage. Three were creatures I had never seen before, a very old woman, a fair-haired young man, and a young woman with absolutely luminescent skin. With them were Andrew and two of the other aliora who lived at Castle Auburn.

"What is—are the aliora going to sing?" I asked, dumbfounded, for I had never witnessed such a thing.

Angela shook her head. "They don't sing, but they play music— it's unearthly beautiful. You've never heard them?"

"No."

"Actually, it's rare that they perform anymore. Those two—the old woman and the young one—apparently were part of some, I don't know, musical clan in Alora before they were captured. The old one lives in Tregonia and the young one in Mellidon, so they're rarely together. When they are, they always perform concerts. My mother said it was the best reason to invite Hennessey here." She giggled.

I was incapable of even the smallest smile. The image conjured up—aliora torn from their homes, separated, reunited in bondage and only then being able to enjoy one of their simple, essential pleasures—suddenly made me mute and horrified. How had such a thing happened? I knew the answer to that—I had almost been part of it, just three years ago. How could my uncle do such things? How could I have thought they were permissible? I could not fit my mind around the answers. I could not dream up an acceptable solution.

While I wrestled with guilt and anger, the aliora arranged themselves on the stage and took up their instruments. Three of them carried long, thin tubes that appeared to be hollowed-out tree limbs; but their own arms were so long and thin, and so carefully placed around the tubes, that at times it looked as though they held not one but three of the attenuated instruments. The two visiting women seated themselves and unfolded metal boxes in their laps. From where I sat, I could not tell if there were strings inside the boxes or some other device for creating music. Andrew idly juggled a handful of glass cylinders which made a loopy crystal chiming as they struck together.

The old woman addressed some question to her fellow musicians and they all grew still. Then, on some signal that I could not see, they all began playing simultaneously.

It was as if the trees in the forest suddenly sat down and began to speak; it was as if the river pursed its lacy lips to tell a tale. The aliora did not produce music as I was used to hearing it, but sounds, voices, the whispers of the woodland animals in a language suddenly ordered and comprehensible. Except that it was not comprehensible—there was no story—but there was the sense of communication, of mysteries made clear and universal truths unfolded. I sat there under the patter and sigh of their windsong and thought, *Yes, now I understand. Of course. Why did I not know before?* I was spellbound. I was ecstatic. I was ensorceled.

When the music abruptly halted, I literally gasped—as did half the humans in the room. I felt stupid and heavy, as if I had dragged myself from a woodland pool where I had lain all day letting the water take my weight. The room seemed to close in, the walls were too dense and the air was too thick with the scent of nearby bodies. Someone near me began to speak, but I could not understand her words.

Before I had time to panic, or even wonder, the music started again. Once more I was buoyed by its soothing explanatory rhythms. The world seemed huge, suffused with sparkling diaphanous lights; every single creature, every single object within it, swayed to its preordained melody. There were no lapses, nothing did not fit in. The castle, the surrounding countryside, the provinces stretching farther away than I could even imagine, seemed part of one harmonious whole, laid out in a pattern that was beautiful and complete. I lifted my hand, as if I could stroke the weave of the tapestry. Even the fact that there was nothing substantial to feel did not lessen my understanding of the canvas. Everything was brilliantly clear.

The music stopped again, and again I was disoriented and at a loss. I had enough clarity of mind to think, in that wretched interlude, *If everyone feels as I am feeling, why would they ever allow the aliora to play for men?* Then the music began again, and I did not care that without it I was forlorn and confused; I just wanted it to continue for the rest of the night.

I couldn't say exactly how long the concert continued in this fashion. It seemed like days that we were hypnotized by the aliora, but it might have been only an hour or two. And who knows how long they would have continued playing, if not for a sudden interruption at the back of the salon. The door was flung open and a loud voice cried, "This concert can go on all night! Because I've brought another one to join the orchestra."

And with that sudden, sickening cessation of sound, the aliora stopped playing. The human crowd produced equal numbers of protests and cries of astonishment. Some people leapt to their feet and pointed. I heard someone laugh. More distantly, I heard a soft, keening sound as if a child was crying. Slowly, because I knew what I would see, I turned in my chair.

To see my uncle Jaxon filling the doorway, his hands on his big hips, his smile breaking the dark riot of his beard. He was wearing travel-stained clothes and looked as if he had just this minute ridden in through the gate. Crouched beside him on the floor, scantily dressed and whimpering over the gold chains around her wrists, was an aliora girl who looked scarcely older than a child. She was so small, and so thin, that the strands of her long full hair seemed more robust than her arms and legs. I could have lifted her with one arm and cradled her against me, and still had room left in my arms to hug my sister.

The gentry around me were greeting this astonishing sight with low exclamations of delight. "Another aliora! Jaxon, you promised me first bid." "Look at how small she is! She'll be wonderful with children." "The greatest hunter of our generation." "Congratulations, Jaxon! Well done!"

I could not listen to them. I could not look at my uncle. Heedless of how I might appear to anyone who saw me, I struggled to my feet and hurried past the stage to the small servants' door nearby. I had not gotten very far down the hallway when I came to my knees and became sick right there in the corridor.

8

Later, of course, it was Angela who told the tale. It's possible I could have had it from Jaxon himself, except that there was no way I could have asked him the story. During the days following his arrival, I was not sure I would ever be able to speak to him again.

I don't know at what keyholes Angela listened to come by her information, but since it tallied with what I already knew, I believed her. Although I wished with all my heart that I did not.

According to Angela, Jaxon had spent two weeks in the forest by Faelyn River, hunting for aliora. He had been incredibly patient, making an almost nonexistent camp where he would lie for hours, night and day, unmoving on the forest floor. He became so familiar to the birds and wild creatures that lived in this part of the forest that they no longer feared him; they chattered in his ears and built their nests in his beard. The creeping ivy that twined around all the great oaks wrapped around one of his ankles with a slow and spiraling motion. Seeds took root in the creases and pockets of his clothes.

He stayed there so long that eventually even the aliora grew careless. Groups of three and four came wandering by, chattering as excitedly as the squirrels and the crows. He made no attempt to snare one of these travelers, but he had an idea: He would follow them back to their home and finally see the fabled boulevards of Alora.

He waited another three days until a party of five aliora passed through—a group so large, he reasoned, that they would travel slowly and not listen for sounds on the trail behind them. Indeed, this band of travelers included two very young aliora, so young they could scarcely walk on their spindly legs, and the adults evinced much merriment as the toddlers tripped and waddled down the paths. Jaxon rose stealthily from his hiding place and followed them through the forest.

They had not gone far before the aliora he was trailing disappeared.

Jaxon stood on the path and stared about him, wondering if he might have imagined the whole thing. He had eaten very little in the past week, after all, and the forest could induce hallucinations. But he had absolutely believed they had walked before him, laughing and gesturing. Perhaps they had crossed some invisible boundary. Perhaps they had stepped through a warded door.

So, he took a deep breath and continued in the same direction, stepping boldly where the aliora had stepped—and he felt a feathery tingle along his whole body as he crossed into wonderland.

This was not the forest he had traversed so many times and slept in for half a month. This was a place of glancing white light, open blue skies, fantastical dwellings in riotous colors, and streets cobbled in alabaster. He stood on the edge of paradise and stared. Aliora were everywhere, congregating at open doorways, spilling out of the fanciful windows, calling to each other across the white streets. He could not see to the edge of the city. He could not count the aliora.

As he stood there, gaping, he became aware of a soft, incessant noise—a humming or a buzzing or a rapping—it changed as he listened, changed in pitch, changed in quality. It was as if bees flew by, then birds caught the melody and changed it to a unison trill, and then hundreds of kittens overtook them with their rough and boisterous purring. It seemed to be communication of a sort, though he would not call it language.

He would learn, in the next few days, that it was the sound of the aliora. It was their collective voice, the harmonious reverberations of their subconscious, attuned to each other and playing back the mood of the whole.

He would say, later, that he stood there an hour watching the streets of Alora, incapable of moving forward or stepping back into the familiar emerald forest. But perhaps it was not that long; he would also learn that time, in Alora, was fluid and hard to segment. He might only have been standing there five minutes before a completely unexpected figure bounded up to him.

"Jaxon Halsing!" it exclaimed, and a few seconds later, Jaxon realized that it was a human and one that he recognized—a hunter named Jed Cortay. "I cannot believe my eyes!"

Neither could Jaxon, for this was a man he had known well. Jed Cortay had been a coarse, burly, damn-your-eyes woodsman who would take any pelt, whether or not it had value. The man who stood before him now had the same height and the same body, though considerably slimmed down, and a face with roughly the same features—yet he appeared transformed somehow. Almost how Jaxon imagined a man might look transmogrified by death and elevation to the realm of angels.

"Cortay," Jaxon named him, and they grasped hands with tremendous vigor. At one time, they had been great friends. "What are you—is it possible? All this time I thought you were dead."

Cortay laughed loudly, and the ubiquitous hum around them jumped with a surge of hilarity. "No! Living here—a changed man—a blessed man. Halsing, you don't know what you've stumbled onto."

Jaxon looked around again. "It's Alora," he said. "Or at least it matches my dreams of it."

Cortay took him by the arm. "Your dreams could never have been this miraculous," he assured Jaxon. "Let me show you. You will not believe it. It is too beautiful for words."

Indeed, at this point in Angela's recital of Jaxon's tale, the descriptions became sketchy and filled with superlatives. It was as if human speech could not re-create the marvels of Alora; there were no adjectives gorgeous enough to encompass the architecture, the music, the texture, the scent of that place. Jaxon and Cortay spent hours (perhaps minutes) wandering through that amazing city, until they at last came to the most splendid house of all. I could not visualize it from Angela's telling—"It had five stairways and no walls, except walls of ivory lace, and trees grew in the front rooms, and golden light spilled over everything"—but it was not hard to guess who lived here. The queen of the aliora, the woman who called herself Rowena.

He had seen her since that summer evening by the river when I had overheard their conversation, for his opening words to her were, "You look wearier than you did last fall." And she replied, "I have but recently come from searching the land of humans for something I lost. I find that whenever I cross out of the boundaries of Alora, I grow tired and feel my age, but when I am home again, I am renewed and fulfilled. In a day or so, you will not be able to make such an accusation."

"It was not an accusation," he said. "Merely, I noticed."

"And what I notice about you, Jaxon Halsing," she said, "is that you are standing in my home, where you have often been invited, and where I never thought to actually see you."

"I have decided to take you up on your offer of hospitality," he said, "and see just how generous the aliora can be."

She glanced at him out of her dark, slanted eyes as if assessing him—his motives or his nerve. "And are you not afraid?" she asked. "To be here—among my people and their sorcery—afraid of being held prisoner or seduced by beauty?"

"I fear nothing," he said brazenly. "You claim that no one is kept here under duress—I wish to prove it by my own experience. You say that no one who arrives ever wishes to leave—but I tell you now I will not stay. I have come to see you in your home and walk out again."

She extended one hand to him, so long and delicate and small that he was almost afraid to take it for fear of bruising the flawless skin. "Stay as long as you like and leave when you wish," she said. "All that I ask is that you enjoy yourself while you are here. For this is Alora, a place of wonders, and all who abide here are filled with joy."

He spent the next ten days in Alora. He lived in Rowena's lace-work house, and at her table he ate food that was even more impossible to describe than the city itself. He spent his days drinking some strange potent brew and reminiscing with old friends. For in Alora were five men he had once known very well—hunters who had vanished some years ago and been presumed dead or enslaved. But no, here they were, happy, healthy, delighted to have him among them, constantly praising the gentleness of the aliora and the sweetness of their life among their former prey. He spent his evenings flirting with the queen of the aliora, though Angela's story did not include many of the details of that pastime.

And one day, well-fed, content, welcomed and unwatched, he snatched up Rowena's niece and dove back out through the magical boundary, into the forest he knew. He ran for hours, the weeping child in his arms, and he did not stop running until he made it clear of the forest.

And then he came to Castle Auburn to show off his prize.

JAXON STAYED AT the castle for the next three days, urged by the regent to attend the summer ball. The only time I saw him in semiprivacy was one afternoon when he came up to visit Elisandra and me in my sister's sitting room.

"How are my favorite girls?" he demanded, giving each of us a fierce hug that carried us off our feet. "Corie! You look so much like your sister! Matthew says all the young men are circling around you like hawks on the hunt. I'll be hearing an interesting announcement any day now, I suppose. And Elisandra—such a beauty. Your father would be so proud of you."

I could not speak to him, the man I had always adored. But Elisandra took his arm with every evidence of affection, led him to her favorite sofa, and sat beside him. "I've missed you," she said. "Tell me about your travels."

He obliged, describing a recent visit to Faelyn Market as well as a journey farther afield, to Chillain. He made no mention of the successful hunting venture—but then, I reflected, he seldom did.

Those tales apparently were only for the ears of men, seasoned hunters and hardened warriors not affronted by tales of violence and
betrayal. I wondered again how Angela had gotten the story. Jaxon
reserved his more charming exploits for recitation to the ladies.

"And in Faelyn Market," he was saying, "I purchased gifts for
both of you." He slipped his hand into his pocket and came out
with slim packets wrapped in tissue and marked with our initials.
I had to come forward from the chair where I had taken up residence—across the room, as far from him as I could get—to gingerly
take my gift. "I think you'll be pleased," he said. "Only girls as
beautiful as you two could wear such things."

Elisandra opened hers and gave a soft cry of delight. My fingers
were clumsier but I managed to rip back the paper. Inside lay a
delicate gold chain strung with rubies. Elisandra's necklet was hung
with emeralds and onyx.

"Let me see you wear them," he asked next, and perforce I fastened the chain around my neck as Elisandra donned hers as well.
It was the perfect length, the largest central jewel coming to rest
in the hollow of my throat. We both went to the full-length mirror
in its dark oval stand to admire our newfound treasures.

"Uncle Jaxon, this is so lovely," Elisandra said, crossing the room
to his side. He had pulled himself to his feet and was smiling down
at us with great satisfaction. "Thank you so very much for thinking
of me." And she hugged him, then stretched up to kiss him on
the cheek.

I followed her more slowly and did not speak with quite as much
enthusiasm. "Yes—very beautiful. I can wear the necklace with my
new ballgown."

Jaxon laughed and swept me into an embrace that took no account of my reluctance. When he released me, he caught me by the
shoulders and peered shrewdly down at me. "You're not my usual
sunny Corie, but I know what ails you," he said. "Don't worry—
there are plenty of beaux out there if this one doesn't suit you. No
need to fear that you won't be wed."

At this, I could not help staring at him, possibly the first time
I had met his gaze since he arrived at the castle. My expression

amused him, for his laugh rolled out again and he gave me a final hug.

"I'll see you both at the ball," he promised. "Save a dance for me."

And he was finally gone.

I turned my stare on Elisandra. "He thinks I'm mooning over some *beau*?" I choked out. "What could he—why would—I don't know what to say to him, I don't know what to think—"

Elisandra had moved to the door behind Jaxon, and now she stood across the room, watching me from a distance. She knew something of what I was feeling, for I had wept in her arms the night after the young aliora was brought to the castle. But I had not told her Angela's story—I was not capable of repeating it.

"He asked me yesterday why you seemed so preoccupied," she said. "This is a man you have loved your whole life. You cannot expect him not to notice when you suddenly do not speak to him."

"And you said—?"

"I told him you were heartsick. Which is the truth. Although I knew he would misinterpret my words."

I shook my head and sank to the chair where I had taken refuge before. "I am he is I don't know that I can bear to be in the same room with him. That girl—that child—and he stole her from Alora—"

Elisandra crossed the room and came to a halt directly in front of me. My head was in my hands and I did not look up; I stared at her fine silk slippers through a haze of falling tears.

"He is the same man he always was," she said calmly. "He loves you as much as he ever did. He has hunted aliora for twenty years, and you loved him for seventeen of those years. What has changed? How is he different?"

"Perhaps *I* am different!" I cried, wrenching myself to my feet and beginning to pace. "Perhaps I didn't realize—and maybe I should have realized!—and now I do, and it's horrible. There's so much wretchedness and misery—and *he has caused it*! He has been cruel! And I cannot believe I did not see it before, and I cannot believe I could have loved him."

She turned to watch me as I paced, making no effort to stop me. "I despise his trading in the aliora," she said, still in that serene voice. "It makes me heartsick as well. Yet it is a profession that the world views as honorable. He has received praise and glory and monetary advantage for pursuing this career. What is to tell him that it is an evil thing to do?"

"His heart!"

She nodded. "You have hunted with a trained hawk on your wrist. Wasn't that once a wild creature? Didn't some hunter steal it from its native habitat, tear it from its mate and offspring, force it into a foreign way of life? And yet no one worries over the hawks in their cages or thinks they have been mistreated. How is it any different to capture an aliora?"

I had stopped in my striding; now, through puffy red eyes, I stared at her. "It is different," I whispered.

She nodded again. "It *is* different," she said. "But some men do not think so. How are they to learn that? Unless someone tells them. Unless they discover it for themselves."

"He will never discover it on his own!" I cried.

She appeared to consider. "I think he will," she said. "I think he already has. And he stole this child because—because he was afraid he did not have the heart to do it. He seems very proud of himself, but there is something in him. . . . I think that visit to Alora took more from him than even he has realized."

I shook my head violently. "How can you understand him? How can you forgive him? Such a cruel man, who has done such terrible things—"

Now her face changed, though the expression was hard to read. It went from her habitual tranquillity to a look that was even more remote. "I have known men much worse than Jaxon," she said quietly. "I will never call him cruel."

9

During the next two days, I recovered some of my equilibrium, though I still avoided Jaxon. I was beginning to regret my easy bargain with Cloate, which had resulted in my downing half a draught of that benighted potion. It had not opened my eyes to the charms of a lover, oh no; it had opened my eyes to the true natures of everyone else around me. I was wishing with some intensity to still have my eyes tight shut.

It was not only Jaxon I could not bear to see these two days, but also Hennessey of Mellidon, Angela, and even Bryan. To me everyone seemed either shallow or tainted, and I wished with all my heart to be back at my grandmother's cottage. There at least I understood the rivalries and the desires. Here, nothing was simple and everything was suspect.

So, again, I slept late and avoided the communal breakfasts, slipping out of the castle sometime around noon. Both of these days I went on long, solitary rides, which I broke with vigorous walks while my poor horse rested. The day of the ball I rode so far, and walked so long, that the afternoon sun was seriously thinking about setting before I was on my way back to the castle. I had much to do before the dinner that night—bathe, wash my hair, dress my hair, step into the gorgeous folds of the red silk dress that had been designed for me. . . . I urged my horse forward faster.

I had traveled about half an hour on my homeward route when a rider came in sight in the distance. It was not long before I could make out his black-and-gold livery, the colors of Auburn. Soon enough he resolved himself into Roderick.

Who appeared to be looking for me.

He sent his horse in a wide circle and drew up beside me as I continued toward the castle. I was disproportionately glad to see him. "Roderick!" I exclaimed as he jogged up. "Are you out hunting for game?"

He sat on his mount with his usual air of relaxed negligence. He looked fairer, taller, and thicker in the bones. A man. He had still been almost a boy when I first met him three years earlier. "Hunting for you," he said. "Your sister was worried."

"But I'm fine. I always go out riding by myself."

He glanced at the sky, gauging time by the angle of the sun. "I guess she thought you'd be back by now. A lot of activity going on at the castle tonight."

I nodded gloomily. "The ball."

He glanced my way with a small grin. "You don't sound too excited about it."

I sighed, laughed, and ran a hand through my unbound hair. It was a knotted mess. It would take forever to brush and clean and curl. "I don't think I'm cut out for court life," I said. "I am not enjoying this season, that's for sure."

He seemed to listen with more attention than he usually gave me. "So, you think you'd be happy back in your grandmother's village, never seeing the fancy nobles of Castle Auburn again?"

"If not for Elisandra," I said.

"If not for Elisandra," he repeated.

"Yes. Oh, yes. I'm not fancy myself. The more I'm here—this year, anyway—the less I want to stay."

He gave that small, quick smile that lightened his wide features and was gone. "I have to say that life at Castle Auburn is not exactly what I thought it would be, either."

I looked at him curiously. "But you were mad to come. Didn't you say so once? You couldn't wait to leave your father's farm and journey to the prince's court."

He nodded. "Yes. The honor and excitement of being a king's guardsman. There was nothing that could have held me back from tasting that life."

"And now?"

"Now?" He seemed to consider the landscape before him, as if its green contours were engraved with the answers he wanted. "Like you, I have a compelling reason to stay. But it is not the reason I expected when I came here. And if it did not exist—yes, I think I could go back to my father's farm and be happy. I know I could. I could buy my own land, raise my own cattle, be a simple man again." He glanced at me, a trace of humor in his hazel eyes. "I'm not a fancy man, either, as it turns out."

I had fastened my attention on his earlier remark—that he had a compelling reason to stay put. "I've seen you with her," I said before I could think. "I was surprised at first but—but she's a good enough girl, I suppose."

Now the look he turned on me was both narrowed and watchful. "Who have you seen me with?" he said.

I gestured ineffectively. "Daria. My sister's maid. She came to the weapons yard to watch you practice."

His eyes didn't waver from my face. No more looking to the landscape for answers. "Daria is not the reason I am staying."

Now I was astonished. I had been convinced. "But you said there was a woman—"

He shook his head. "That's not what I said. I said there was a reason. I did not say who or what the reason was."

"But I—" Now I was embarrassed. And if he was not in love with Daria . . . but he still had no reason to favor me. I felt awkward and stupid. "I'm sorry, then, I guess I assumed—"

Now he was grinning again. He shifted in the saddle to face forward once more. "Although she *is* a good girl, as you say, and a pretty thing. But my heart is not free."

"I have no interest in your heart," I said crossly.

He laughed aloud and gave me a sideways glance. "No, and I have no interest in yours," he said. "Shall we be friends, then?"

"It's not much of a friendship when one of you never makes any effort to see the other of you and then only teases you or scolds you when he does see you," I said very rapidly and childishly.

Roderick was even more amused. "I don't tease you. And I've only ever scolded you when you were foolish. But you might notice that it's not my place to do either of those things—Lady Coriel."

"Well, you do avoid me," I said. "This is the first time you've talked to me this summer."

His voice gentled. "How can I seek you out, living in the Halsing suites as you do? Every time I have seen you from a distance, you have been talking to some lord or off on some errand. Guardsmen are not at liberty to claim the attention of a lady such as yourself."

"Well, then—well, then," I said, both elated and a little nervous. "What do your duties allow? Can you ride with me?"

"My mornings are bespoken and most of my evenings. There are two afternoons a week I am free."

"Then—perhaps on those afternoons—at least once a week—"

"I would like that," he said.

I frowned a little. "Although—I suppose someone might notice if I went off riding with you that frequently. You would never believe how these people gossip. I should bring someone along with me, from time to time, so it does not look so particular."

He gave that lazy smile. "Your sister's maid."

I laughed. "Or my sister! She needs to escape from the scheming at the castle now and then. I don't think she is very happy this summer, either."

"I'm sorry to hear that," he said politely.

We had by this time made it to the castle gates. I waved at the guards, for I knew them through Shorro, and they waved back at me instead of giving me the traditional salute. Roderick gave me another sideways glance.

"Although I do not think you should worry so much about how

odd it might seem to have a friendship with me," he said in a dry voice. "Since you seem to make friendships everywhere."

I laughed again. I was feeling remarkably cheerful. For perhaps the first time this summer. "I did them some favors," I said carelessly. "So now we're friends."

"Gave them salve for their wounds, as you did for me?"

"And salve for their hearts. And other remedies."

"You must be popular indeed," he said.

I would have ridden straight through to the stables, but Roderick edged me across the cobblestones toward the castle doors. "It's late, and your sister's worried," he said. "I'll take your mount back to the stables."

Indeed, it was even later than I had realized, so I was happy to fall in with this plan. We pulled up before the grand stairway leading to the castle, and I hopped from the saddle before Roderick could think of dismounting to help me. He leaned down to take my reins.

"Three days from this one, I am free," he said in a low voice.

"I'll come to the stables," I said. I could not help giving him a wide smile, and his own quick, easy one came in return. I whirled around and fled up the castle stairs—

To find Kent awaiting me at the very top.

"And exactly where have you been all day?" was his greeting. He took me by the wrist and pulled me through the doors, none too gently. The two guards touched their fists to their foreheads for Kent's benefit, but grinned at me when he could not see. "Your sister is sitting at the window watching for your return, and Greta is shrieking at all the servants that they must keep better track of you. I sent Roderick out searching for you, and I'm glad to see he found you, but I can't believe you would be so inconsiderate as to be gone all afternoon, this day of all days—"

I twisted my hand free but hurried beside him through the corridors. "I don't know why everyone's so worried. I always go off by myself, and I'm always back in time for whatever I've promised to do."

"It's just that you're so careless!" he exclaimed. "And it's not like you haven't gotten hurt before on one of your rides—"

"Three years ago," I reminded him. I was breathless. "Could we slow down a little?"

"And where do you go off to all the time, anyway? No one can ever find you when they're looking for you."

"Who's looking for me?"

"Well—your sister, of course, and then Bryan asked where you were, and that stupid Mellidon lordling—"

"Hennessey? What did he want?"

"A little of your time, apparently! As did everyone!"

I found this brand of annoyance completely out of character and irritating in the extreme. Kent was always the one who had found my exploits amusing when I was a child. Now he seemed to think I should suddenly alter my ways to suit his notion—the court's notion—of how a lady should behave. I came to a dead halt in the middle of the corridor. Kent strode on for a few more paces, still ranting, before he realized I was no longer beside him. He spun around and stalked back.

"What do—" he began.

I interrupted. "Thank you for your escort from the front doors, but I know my way to my own chamber," I said sweetly. "I shall find my way from here, Lord Kentley."

He had opened his mouth as if to interrupt me in turn, but now he shut it abruptly. Suddenly he looked embarrassed. He struggled with the remnants of his anger and a wish to apologize; I could read the conflict in his face. "I suppose I've reacted a bit strongly," he said in a more subdued voice. "I'm sorry, Corie. It's just that you were gone so long, and Elisandra was so worried—and no one ever knows where you are these days—"

I held up my hand for peace. "I'm here, I'm safe, don't worry about me," I said. "But I have to go get ready or I really will be late for dinner."

"And the ball," he added. He looked as if he wanted to take my hand, to extend the apology, but decided against it. "You will save me a dance, won't you? You won't give them all to Hennessey and Bryan?"

"I'd like to give *all* of Hennessey's dances to you," I said truthfully. "I'll promise to dance with you as often as you like, if you'll make me a promise in return. Every time you see me with Hennessey of Mellidon, you must abandon whichever girl you're flirting with at the moment, and come rescue me."

He was smiling. "I don't flirt."

I gathered my skirts in both hands. "That wasn't the answer I was looking for."

He pivoted to watch me move away. "I promise. You shouldn't flirt, either."

I laughed aloud, lifted my hems higher, and ran down the hallway. Up the stairs, down the next hall, I arrived breathlessly at Elisandra's door. After a perfunctory knock, I turned the handle and stepped in.

"I'm sorry you were so—" I began, then choked off my words, because the chamber was completely dark. The curtains were drawn, no candles were lit, and no one appeared to be in the room.

Until a shape stirred on the bed, and Elisandra's voice came lightly across the room. "Corie? What's wrong?"

I hurried to her side, filled with remorse. "I'm sorry! Were you sleeping? I didn't mean to wake you."

She held up a hand, which I could barely see, to draw me down beside her. I sat on the edge of the bed. "What time is it?"

"Just about sunset. I'm so sorry to wake you."

She smothered a yawn and pushed herself to a sitting position. "I wasn't sleeping, I was just resting. Have you had a nice day?"

I nodded in the dark. "Yes. But I'm sorry I was gone so long. I didn't mean to worry you."

She yawned again. "I wasn't worried. You're always off by yourself. I knew you'd be back in time."

I stared at her, what little of her face I could see. "Then—" I shut my mouth. "I've got to go bathe, or I'll never be ready in time," I said. "Can I come in while you're getting your hair done?"

"Of course. Come in sooner, and Daria will do yours as well."

I rose to my feet. "I'll just braid it back. I know how I like it. I'll see you in an hour or so."

I slid out of her chamber, down the hall and into my own room, where I stood for a long time with my back against the door. If not Elisandra, then who had been so worried about me all afternoon that riders had to be sent in search of me and escorts awaited me on the castle steps? Earlier in the week, I had cursed my newfound gift of true seeing, but now everything was more confused than before. I shook my head, as if that would clear it, and went to call Cressida for a bath.

DINNER THAT NIGHT was the most extravagant I had seen at Castle Auburn. Close to two hundred sat down at the ten tables set up in the great dining hall, and their array of shimmering silk and flashing jewels made a tapestry of color under the mellow gold light of a thousand candles. Fantastic centerpieces graced each table, topiary in the shapes of animals, wood carved to resemble gargoyles, stone chiseled in the flowing shapes of men and women circling in a dance, all of them plumed with fountaining water. Every woman was dressed to catch the eye of the prince; every man was dressed to distract the women. Opulence lay across us all like an opiate perfume.

The servants brought course after course of food: honeyed fruits, glazed vegetables, stuffed fowl, braised beef, creamed potatoes, herbed bread, dips, sauces, spices, garnishments. Then the sweets came around: caramels, pastries, cakes, candies. It hurt to eat. I could not imagine summoning the energy, after this, to twirl around the dance floor in a waltz.

There was so much food, and everyone ate it so greedily, that there was almost no conversation during the entire course of the meal. Therefore it did not matter much to me that Hennessey of Mellidon sat on my right and Holden of Veledore on my left. I exchanged the merest of pleasantries with them between spooning up my soup and biting into another biscuit.

When the last guest had refused the last piece of pie, Lord Matthew rose to his feet. He, of course, sat just to the left of Bryan at the head table; with them sat Kent, Elisandra, Greta, Dirkson, and a ravishingly beautiful woman named Thessala of Wirsten. When he stood, the slight murmur of conversation that the overstuffed gourmands had managed to produce fell instantly silent.

Lord Matthew surveyed the crowd. "Thank you all for coming," he said in serious, measured tones. "We are pleased to extend our hospitality to such an illustrious collection of friends. And I hope that you all will join me now in the traditional double toast of Auburn, to the health of the prince and the prosperity of the realm."

He paused to pick up two glasses—water in his left hand, wine in his right. Everyone at all ten tables hastily checked or refilled their own glasses from the bottles and carafes before them. I had drained my water glass three times but barely touched my wine, so I quickly poured a mouthful of water into my lefthand goblet.

The regent raised his water glass, and everyone else in the room followed suit. "To the prince," Matthew said. The crowd roared back, "To the prince!" We all sipped from our glasses. Matthew raised his other hand. "To the realm," he said. It was not my imagination that the reply this time was a little more heartfelt: *"To the realm!"* We all tossed back our wine. Bryan came to his feet and made a fluid bow, and a ragged cheer went up from most of the men and women gathered in the hall. Some, I noticed—mostly men—remained silent during this spontaneous show of approval; but all of the women were applauding madly.

"True in water." Matthew intoned the customary benediction. Those familiar with the blessing responded, "True in wine."

Bryan sat, but Matthew still stood, his glasses restored to the table and his arms flung out for silence. "It is important," he said, his strong voice carrying easily across the room, overriding even the trailing murmurs of conversation, "that we all realize why we are gathered together this day. To celebrate another successful year, yes. To renew our bonds of fealty and affection, yes. To enjoy the hospitality of the prince in a great festival of music and wine—that also."

Matthew permitted himself a small smile. The crowd laughed with disproportionate amusement. Matthew's smile disappeared.

"But we are all truly here together for another, more crucial reason," he resumed. "We are here to remind ourselves that we are indeed a kingdom—not eight provinces linked by a common language, a favorable trade exchange, and advantageous marriages over the past two centuries. We are a kingdom, with one head and many limbs, one heart and many organs, one center, one soul. One year from now, my nephew will take his crown. We all will gather again to witness that spectacular event. Let us plan now to make ourselves stronger, richer, more faithful and more loyal in the months ahead. We are united now under a regent. We will be seamless then under the hand of the king."

He raised his empty hands, and again the crowd clamored out its approval. But to my ears, the shouting sounded a little perfunctory, not passionate or convinced. Kent had told me that some of the lords were reluctant to take a boy as their king, and in the faces around me I clearly perceived that reluctance—and a certain calculation. Matthew could not have said more clearly that he expected complete compliance and fealty as the power in the realm changed over; but I could tell that his open warning had not impressed everyone. It was odd to sit there amid the glitter and the ceremony, hearing the calls and clapping all around me, and know that some of the nobles were debating their options. The world was not so simple and harmonious as it had always seemed.

After that, Dirkson of Tregonia got up to make a speech, and then Goff of Chillain. Bryan said a few words, mostly pretty diplomatic expressions of pleasure at the large numbers of nobles in attendance. After that, three men I didn't recognize rose to their feet and made long, solemn testaments to the strength of the realm, and I could feel myself begin to grow sleepy. All that wine, all that food, all that talk. I squirmed in my crimson dress and forced my eyes wide open.

Finally all the posturing was over, and Matthew was on his feet again. "To the ballroom!" he announced. "Let us celebrate all night!"

This pronouncement revived everyone, and I jumped gladly to

my feet. Suddenly the disadvantages of sitting next to Hennessey became clearer. "Let me be your escort to the ballroom, Lady Coriel," he begged me, taking my arm in a tight hold. "And dance at least the first number with me. That will make my evening complete."

"Certainly," I said with the false smile I had begun to cultivate in the past few weeks. "I will be happy to dance with you."

Despite that unpromising beginning, it really was a wonderful evening. Hennessey, though not a naturally graceful man, had made some effort to learn the common dances, and we managed to get through the first two pieces with actual pleasure. He relinquished me to the first noble who asked for my hand, and I only saw him once or twice after that. I did notice that he danced with Marian a couple of times, and she looked quite giddy at his attention. I thought that she would find Mellidon a lovely place. I hoped she got a chance to visit it soon.

As for me, I didn't much care who else asked to be my partner— I simply loved the opportunity to dance at all. I had never been quite this popular before, and I realized that Kent had told me even more truths that first morning I was back. I had been put forward as a prize worth winning, and more than a handful of nobles were making it clear that they considered my lineage acceptable, if colorful. I scarcely sat down all night.

My most memorable moment, of course, came when Bryan claimed his promised waltz. I had been making a flirtatious curtsey to my most recent partner when Bryan swept up behind me and caught me in his arms. I could not repress a little shriek, for he swung me around, quite lifting me off my feet, before setting me down and dropping into a magnificent bow.

"My dance, lady, I believe," he said, and closed his arms around me the instant the music started playing. I was breathless from his embrace even before we started romping around the room, and the expression on his face made it even harder to breathe. He was watching me intently, paying no attention to the couples on the floor around us, and a small smile flickered around his lips. He seemed to be appraising me, the texture of my skin, the shape of my eyes, the modeling of my cheekbones, the promise of my smile. He was seductive; he was mesmerizing. I could not look away, though I felt the heat slowly rise across every surface of my face.

"Yes," he said at last, in a slow, drawling voice, "I think you would be worth just about any coin. It's a shame you are exactly who you are, or I might pay the fortune to find out if I was right."

I was not entirely sure what this meant, though I could hazard a guess, and I felt my blush grow even hotter. "You're holding me too close, Bryan," was all I said in reply. "I can hardly breathe."

He laughed at that, squeezed me even tighter, then relaxed his hold. "I cannot imagine I am the only man tonight who has been so bold," he said.

"No, everyone has been most well behaved," I said demurely.

He laughed even more loudly at that. "Not for long, I wager," he said. "If you were to take a little walk—out to the balcony, for instance, or even farther, to the gardens, I think you might be surprised at just how ungentle a gentleman might be."

I opened my eyes wide. "But I don't want to go to the gardens," I said. "I want to stay here and dance." This made him smile again.

We had danced so long in charged silence that now the music was drawing to a close. Bryan twirled me around and around until I was almost too dizzy to stand, and then he released me to make his final bow. I dropped clumsily into my own curtsey, thinking perhaps I might just tumble forward onto the floor. For the first time, I wished I might take a few moments and sit down to recover.

This wish was not to be granted. Someone took my arm just as I was straightening to my full height, and I was pulled back into the next set before I even recognized my partner.

It proved to be Jaxon.

I stiffened in his hold, but he did not seem to notice. He was smiling down at me with a great deal of energy and fondness. "First all the petty nobles, then the prince, and now Lord Halsing himself," he greeted me. "Lady Coriel has made quite a series of conquests tonight."

A ballroom was not the place for serious conversation; you did not accuse a man of slavery and brutality in a glittering sea of fashion and music. I forced myself to smile. This was such an easy game to play I could not believe I had not learned it sooner. "And, of course, my best partner is my current partner," I said. "I endured all the rest of them merely to have this moment with you."

He laughed and then patted my back. "You do me proud, you and your sister," he said. He sounded more sincere than I had. "Your father would have adored both of you. So, it's up to me to do it in his place."

Maybe it was the woeful timbre of the violins—attempting though they were to make gay music—that made his voice sound, to me, unexpectedly sad. I tried to peer through the riotous curl of beard, through the ruddy layer of skin, to the soul beneath. Who was this man who could love me, love my sister, then turn around and wantonly destroy a stranger?

"Are you enjoying yourself?" I asked at random, just to hear him speak again.

"Oh, it's a grand party!" he said carelessly. "Trust Matthew to do it up right. I couldn't spend more than a week in such a place with such people—give me freedom and the open skies!—but I enjoy the talk and the music and the pretty ladies." He patted my shoulder again.

I had been right the first time. His sonorous voice echoed through a hollow place of sorrow, catching its reverberations from those ragged walls. His gaiety masked a deep well of loneliness; he was a bright outward shape wrapped around shadows. It frightened me to see this so clearly, as if I suddenly found I was waltzing with a ghost through the multicolored fantasy of a dream. All my love rushed back for him, complicated and partisan.

"Uncle Jaxon—" I said, my tone warm and urgent.

He laughed and gave me a little shake. "So, tell me about your triumphs tonight, Corie! Who do you like? That Hennessey? He's a good match, but you might do better. And the viceroy's castle is so far from Auburn. You need someone closer, in Tregonia perhaps, or maybe even Auburn itself. The Halsing estates are at the Tregonia border—maybe we should look near there for your proper husband."

"I don't care about husbands," I said. "Uncle Jaxon—"

"Well, you should care, but that's all right. Greta and I will care for you," he said, smiling again.

Impossible to change the subject; impossible to introduce a serious one. I gave up, and let him reel off for me the names of acceptable matches. But I watched him, and I grew more convinced. Something was seriously wrong with my uncle Jaxon, and I cared more than I had believed possible that there should be a way to fix it.

After my dance with Jaxon ended, I was claimed by a Chillain noble, and, later, some lordling whose name I never did catch. As this dance ended, I managed to slip away from the dance floor and behind one of the white columns that ringed the room. There I stood for a few moments, my eyes closed and my back against the smooth marble. It felt cool and refreshing through the silk of my dress, which was just slightly wet from sweat. I was hot; I was thirsty; I wanted just twenty minutes to be invisible, and then I would dance again.

"I cannot believe it," said a voice to one side of me, "Lady Coriel has excused herself from a dance."

I opened my eyes, though I had recognized the speaker's voice: It was Kent, and he stood before me, regarding me with amusement. He was also holding two glasses filled to the brim with amber liquid. "I have attended balls at Castle Auburn before," I said. "I don't recall being quite so sought after."

He grinned and handed me one of the glasses. "I'm assuming all your exertions have made you thirsty," he said.

I sniffed the contents. "I don't think I can drink another glass of wine."

Kent shook his head. "Apple juice. I have a few of the servants bring it in especially for me. It looks like wine, so no one can tell I have no head for liquor."

Gratefully I sipped the sweet drink, which tasted better than dayig fruit at this particular moment. "How strange," I said. "I always thought you excelled at every nobleman's skill."

He grimaced. "There's more than one that I lack, as my father would happily tell you. But to my way of thinking, drinking is hardly an accomplishment, though an ability to keep a clear head comes in handy if you do happen to be imbibing. Bryan thinks it's funny that I don't like wine."

I savored each mouthful of juice because I knew I would still be thirsty when this small amount was gone. "But then, sometimes Bryan's sense of humor seems misplaced," I said. "What other skills do you lack?"

"What other—" I had caught him off guard, though he recovered quickly. He smiled. "I am not the diplomat my father is. I enjoy neither the wrangling nor the bullying that is required, one after the other, to get my way. The polite lying comes easier, but not much."

I took another sip. "And?"

"And? You mean, what are my other flaws?"

"Yes."

He considered. "Sometimes I see the other man's point of view. This makes me a little less ruthless than he would like."

"Your father can be a little insensitive at times."

"Yes, that's been my experience," he said coolly. "A fair man, but not particularly warmhearted."

"Which makes me wonder how you turned out the way you did."

"What way exactly would that be?"

"Fair. Tolerant. Honest. Willing to listen." I took another small sip. "Warmhearted."

He shrugged and settled himself on the edge of a huge potted plant. "Sometimes we become what we see," he said. "Sometimes we take what we see and make it the model for what we refuse to become. Sometimes we do a little of both."

"Does that mean you are like your father in some ways?"

"Oh, yes. My father will not tell a lie. Even to win a political edge, he won't do it. And he opposes violence in every instance except the most extreme. And he values intelligent people. He listens to them. That's where I developed the habit."

"You're intelligent. Does he value you?"

Kent looked surprised that I had asked the question. "Most of the time," he said cautiously. "Until he comes up against one of my perceived flaws."

I smiled. "The lack of diplomacy. The lack of ruthlessness."

He smiled back. "And no skill at flirting with the ladies."

I opened my eyes wide. "Not something he's very good at himself!"

Kent laughed. "He's already married and produced an heir. He doesn't have to win a bride."

"I wouldn't think there would be much 'winning' to do on your part," I said thoughtfully. "If I'm considered a match worth making, just by virtue of my Halsing blood, think how much more impressive you must be. One step away from the throne, after all."

"It's a big step."

"Close enough to make you a prize." I frowned. "And don't tell me you aren't successful with women, because I've seen Megan of Tregonia and Liza of Veledore—yes, and Doreen and Marian and Angela, too—fawn over you like you were Bryan himself."

He smiled at the comparison, but when he spoke, his tone of voice was serious and deliberate. "I suppose I should have said, my father is unhappy that I care so little about making such a connection," he said. "He wishes I had chosen a bride long before this."

"And why haven't you?"

For a moment I thought he would not answer. Which was strange because, odd though this conversation was, I had never before known Kent not to tell me anything I asked. "Why haven't you?" I repeated.

He looked down at his empty glass. "One of the other ways in which I am different from my father," he said. "I am not interested in marrying where I do not love."

I spoke in a jesting voice. "And of all the women in the eight provinces, you have not been able to find one you could love?"

Now he looked at me again, and his face was completely serious. "That's the problem," he said. "There is one."

I remembered, suddenly, how he had watched Elisandra pace through her room the day she returned from Tregonia. I remembered how, this very day, he had—on her behalf—sent riders out to search for me. I remembered how much of the time I had spent in my sister's company had also been spent in Kent's. "And I think I know who she might be," I said softly.

His expression changed to something I almost could not decipher—I finally decided it was sardonic disbelief, which seemed strange. "I doubt that very much," he said.

I straightened from my pose against the column, somewhat in a huff. "I have eyes," I said. "And I have drunk serums that enhance my ability to see the truth."

His voice was dry. "Not lately."

"Then tell me who it is you are so fond of, and you will see that I am right."

Now he had lost his cutting edge; he was laughing. "You tell me the name of the lady for whom you think I pine."

"My sister."

Slowly, deliberately, so I could not miss the motion, he shook his head. "No," he said. "It is not Elisandra I love."

"Why, Kentley," I said in a mocking voice, "I believe this is the first time you have lied to me."

A smile brushed his lips, was repressed, then peeked out again. "Lady Coriel," he said, "I never lie."

"I do not believe you."

He stood up and offered me his crooked arm. "Then I guess I will just have to live with the knowledge of your suspicion," he said. "May I escort you back to the dance floor?"

I was annoyed; up until this point, the conversation had been intriguing, even a little heady, and now he had ruined it all by laughing at me. I could not remember any time until this summer that Kent and I had gotten along so poorly. But I did not want to flounce away from him. Tonight, at least, I had more dignity than that. I lay my hand on top of his. "Certainly you may."

"And have the next dance?"

"If you like."

He smiled. "It will please my father," he explained. "For me to dance with the most sought-after woman of the evening."

I had to give him a swift, minatory look for that comment, but when he laughed, I could not help laughing back. I enjoyed this dance perhaps more than all the others: because I knew Kent so well; because I did not have to flirt with him or try to discourage him from flirting with me; because I had danced with him my whole life and did not have to worry that he would endanger my toes or fling me off balance; because the orchestra played one of my favorite pieces. For all those reasons.

It was clear, as the music ended, that he was guiding me across the floor to some specific point, so I allowed him to lead me where he would. We ended up beside Elisandra and her partner of the moment, Dirkson of Tregonia. He was paying her an exceptionally fulsome compliment as we twirled up beside them.

Elisandra answered with her usual composure. "Indeed, thank you, my lord. You do me too much honor."

Dirkson looked annoyed when Kent and I stopped beside them and Kent instantly took Elisandra's hand. "I've scarcely seen you all evening," he said. "You've been even more popular than your sister."

Dirkson actually scowled, an unattractive expression for a man well into his fifties. "I had hoped to persuade Elisandra to take another turn on the floor with me," he said.

"If she accepts anyone, it should be me," Kent said. "For I have not had one dance with her all evening, and you have had three or four."

I thought it was significant that Kent had been counting Elisandra's partners. Dirkson continued to sulk. "Yet you have many more opportunities to invite the lovely lady than I have, living as you do in the same castle," Dirkson said with clumsy gallantry.

"This is the night and the dance I want," Kent said. "But Corie would be charmed to take her sister's place."

Not at all, but I smiled at the viceroy anyway. He gave me one quick glare, then bowed in Elisandra's direction. "With you or no one," he said.

Elisandra said, "I thank you so much, but I am not interested in dancing with anyone right now. Someone stepped on my toe a while back and it is really quite painful. I beg you to excuse me this time."

There was a moment's sullen silence, then Dirkson bowed to her again. "As you wish. Ladies. Lord Kentley." He turned on his heel and was gone.

Kent looked after him, a small smile on his lips but a slight crease in his forehead. He was both puzzled and amused. "That was rude," he said. "And so unexpected! I did not think anyone could refuse Corie this night."

Elisandra looked over at me with a smile. "Yes, you have been quite besieged," she said. "Have you enjoyed yourself?"

"Oh, so much! Although it's somewhat disconcerting to think that people only like you because of your uncle's extensive farmland and his hints of an inheritance."

"Nonsense, they like you because of your red dress—and the way you wear it," Kent said outrageously.

I flashed him an indignant look; Elisandra sent him a reproving one. She reached out to touch my cheek with one finger. "They like you for your fresh prettiness and your marvelous smile," she said. "Everyone wants to be around someone who's happy. You look happy."

"I feel exhausted," I said on a long sigh. "But I did have fun."

"Unlike your sister," Kent said. He was watching Elisandra again. How could he say he did not love her? Concern was written all over his face.

Elisandra's face, on the other hand, as usual gave nothing away. "My evening was interesting," she said calmly. "As you say, I was almost as popular as Corie."

"Did Bryan dance with you?" Kent wanted to know.

"Oh, yes. Twice."

"That's good, then."

"And Borgan of Tregonia, three times. And Goff of Chillain, also three times. Would you like the complete list?"

Kent shook his head. "So, it means they consider the situation fluid," he said, his voice very low. "That makes me very uneasy."

"Really?" she said. Her voice was idle, almost absentminded, but I sensed a wealth of locked emotion behind it. I frowned, watching her. I was not entirely certain what they were talking about. "I think it would be a relief, actually," she said.

"It makes every alliance renegotiable," Kent said. "If he marries elsewhere, it completely changes the power structure."

Elisandra still spoke in that lazy, disinterested voice. "That would be completely acceptable to me," she said.

"And if nothing changes? If everything goes forward as planned?"

Her face, if possible, grew more masklike; she still smiled, but there was even less to read in her eyes. "Then I shall endure that as well," she said. "I am very adaptable."

He was still watching her with that analytical intentness, as if he could decipher secrets in her face that were invisible to me. He shook his head slightly. "I don't even know what to wish for," he said. "The safety of the realm, or yours."

"I'll be fine," Elisandra said negligently. "I always am. Corie, let's make Kent fetch us some refreshment, shall we, while we stay here and gossip? Would you mind sitting out just one dance with me?"

"Oh, no! My feet hurt, too," I said. I was bewildered and uneasy at their conversation. I had no illusions that she would confide in me now, but it was clear that she needed a moment to collect herself, and I was not likely to turn her down. I gave Kent a quick smile. "If you could find more of that apple juice—" I said.

He nodded. "For both of you. I'll be right back."

He left, and my sister and I sat in two elegant high-backed chairs and whispered about the dancers still on the floor. She seemed completely relaxed and at ease, but I could not shake my disquietude. Had they been talking about her betrothal to Bryan? Was that what she would be happy to see challenged? She had never seemed particularly fond of Bryan—but then, Elisandra never showed much fondness to anyone except me. What was going on behind that cool, still facade? How could even Kent tell what she was thinking?

He returned with our drinks, and before I had even finished mine, Hennessey of Mellidon came up to ask for the favor of a dance. Elisandra smiled and waved me on, so I jumped to my feet and returned to the floor. I danced for the rest of the night, though I tried to keep track of Elisandra from this point on. I saw her pass from the hand of one lord to another, protestations of a bruised toe forgotten, but I did not see her in Bryan's arms again. Once again, I wondered; but no one was being forthcoming with the answers.

10

The days following the summer ball were flat and dull. The castle quickly emptied of grand company and we were left with what seemed like a small, unimaginative circle of constant companions. I took up my earlier nocturnal habits and renewed my friendship with the night guards. Cloate (I learned from Shorro) had stolen a kiss from his reserved young kitchen maid, and she had neither slapped his face nor refused to meet him again the next afternoon. He was thrown into transports by this mark of favor.

I also had a chance to go riding with Roderick several times over the next couple of weeks. After that last edgy, interesting conversation, our time together had become strangely companionable. He told me more about the country where he grew up, and I responded with tales of my grandmother and Milette. He laughed at my description of the village girl.

"I don't think she's quite as vile as you've painted her," he said. "Probably comes from a family of five or eight—no hope of a quiet hour there—and no dowry that might interest a farm boy. Has to be looking out for herself any way she can, and loring's the best for that."

"Loring?" I repeated.

"Knowing herb lore. That's what it's called in Veledore."

"Well, I hate her anyway," I said mulishly.

He smiled. "Hate her all you like, but try not to be unkind to her. She's just trying to make her way in the world."

Privately I knew he was right, but I would not admit it aloud, and soon enough I changed the subject. The next time we went riding, Elisandra came with us, and so Roderick rode behind us and scarcely spoke a word. It was a comfort to have him along, nevertheless, and I was pleased that we had managed to forge a relaxed friendship.

My other wanderings took me in darker directions. One night, standing outside the open door to the room of the aliora, I heard the low hum of companionship sharply broken by a series of hopeless, bitter cries. I would have started through the curtained doorway except that it was clear others—more capable of giving solace— were already at the side of the sufferer, offering soothing words and expressions of hope. I could not be sure, of course, but I thought the one weeping was the youngest girl, brought here by Jaxon, and I almost could not endure the knowledge.

The next day, as Cressida came to help me with my bath, I questioned her.

"That new aliora," I said, as casually as I could. "What's to become of her? Is she to stay at Castle Auburn?"

Cressida dribbled fragrant salts into the water and tested the temperature with her slender fingers. Kneeling over the tub, all thin arms and folded legs, she looked like a shrub crouched over a streambed, wispy and fey and still. "She'll stay for a while at least," Cressida said in a soft, careful voice that seemed to screen back emotion. "She's too young to go to a household on her own."

"Did someone want her?"

"Oh, yes. Your uncle Jaxon had a dozen offers. But Andrew convinced him that she needed time."

"How much time?"

Cressida shook another handful of crystals into the water and appeared to watch them dissolve. "Longer than Jaxon thinks," she said on a sigh.

I felt my heart squeeze in protest. "Is she—but she'll be—I mean, in time, she'll be fine, won't she?"

Cressida turned her head to gaze at me, a weight of sorrow in her face. I felt centuries of despair in that gaze, eons of longing. "She has been torn from her family and her life and will be sold into slavery," the aliora said in a low voice. "Imagine yourself in her place and answer your own question."

Shock ran through me with a physical jolt; I felt my veins crisp and the hammering of my heart turn feeble. It was not as if I had not considered any of this before. It was just that Cressida, Andrew, the others had not seemed so wretched in their captivity.

"But I—" I whispered. I shook my head. "I—"

She nodded and returned her attention to the bath. "I know," she said. "And it is not like you are free, either."

Freer than many others, I thought, and slid into the steaming tub. "I have some herbs that may help her," I said to Cressida as she shampooed my hair. "Some callywort and stiffelbane. They will soothe her. If you think that would be a comfort."

"Callywort? Yes, it's something we use in Alora all the time," she replied. "I'm not familiar with stiffelbane."

"Very effective," I murmured, hypnotized by the feel of her fingers on my scalp. "I'll bring some up."

"Thank you."

Her hands in my hair were so careful, so gentle. How could she resist the urge to push me beneath the water and hold me under till I drowned? It was not fear of reprisals that kept me safe from her, I knew; she did not have violence in her. None of the aliora did. Their great personal grief was matched by their enormous capacity for love. If I was threatened, Cressida would try to save me; if I was ill, she would nurse me; if I died, she would mourn. I could not have summoned that kind of love for a captor.

I did not understand her. Understand any of them.

LATE THAT AFTERNOON, after I returned from my ride and before I dressed for dinner, I climbed the stairs to the top of the castle, and passed the golden key to enter the domain of the aliora. It was a busy time of day for them, for their mistresses and masters were all in the process of changing from daywear to evening dress. But Cressida was there, because Elisandra relied on Daria for this duty—and so was Andrew.

"Where's Bryan?" I asked Andrew as soon as I saw him. "Shouldn't you be with him?"

"He has not come back from the hunt yet. I'm watching." The largest window in the garret looked out over the stables; Andrew would easily be able to mark the prince's return.

I hefted my satchel for them to see. "I've brought my medicines. Where is—What is her name? I haven't heard it."

Andrew and Cressida exchanged quick glances. "We have not yet given her a name you can pronounce," Andrew said.

His eyes turned toward a bed across the room, which was the first time I noticed the young aliora, sleeping. She lay on top of a thin white sheet, and was so thin herself that she looked like a collection of kindling piled before the pillow. Her long brown hair was spread around her and fell to the floor in silken pools. Her skin was so white it seemed to melt into the weave of the sheets.

"Call her Phyllery," I said softly. Andrew looked puzzled, but Cressida gave me one quick, sharp look.

"That's not a name I know," Andrew said.

"It's a plant," Cressida said in a subdued voice. "It has some minor healing powers."

I went closer to the bed, drawn by the girl's helpless, broken presence. "It has a rare, beautiful blossom that blooms for a day, then falls," I said. "Anyone lucky enough to see it in the wild feels blessed for a lifetime."

"That seems fitting enough," Andrew said.

I stopped a foot away from the sleeping girl. Even by aliora standards, she looked fragile; the pale skin looked ready to dissolve away from the bones beneath. Her fingers looked too long for her hands. Her fabulous hair looked dusty and unused.

"She hasn't been eating, has she?" I asked abruptly.

Cressida came to my side. "She tries. Food will not stay in her body."

"I don't want her to starve," I said.

"Neither do I."

I watched her awhile longer, then abruptly turned on my heel. Seating myself on one of the empty beds, I opened my satchel and began pulling out packets. "Stiffelbane. It'll calm her when she weeps in the night. Orklewood. It will soothe her stomach and help her retain her food. Callywort. It will help her sleep, but don't give it to her unless she's wakeful."

Cressida took the herbs from me without speaking, but Andrew said, "How do you know she weeps in the night?"

I fastened my satchel and came to my feet. I felt older than my sister at this moment, older than my grandmother, older than the world. "I would," I said.

Cressida looked at the packets in her hand. "And are these safe to give her?" she asked. "We aliora are not formed as you are."

Andrew took a sample from Cressida's hand. "I'll try them myself first."

"That might be a good idea," she said.

I hesitated a moment, for I didn't want to go; but I had no other business there, and it was hard to stay. "Let me know how she does," I said at last, and left the room.

That night I did not return, and for three nights running could not bring myself to steal up to the loft and spy on the aliora. It was left to Cressida to tell me—in her soft voice, keeping her emotions rigidly in check—that Phyllery had passed three straight peaceful nights and managed to eat every meal. I nodded solemnly, and we spoke no more about it.

I did not charge for this healing service, but I felt even more professional at this success; and yet I could not say I was proud of myself, either. Better, perhaps, to have given her halen root—not just enough to ease her hurt heart, but enough to gently halt its frantic beating. Better, perhaps, to have let her quietly die.

As it turned out, not a week later I was given a chance to use some of my halen root, though this time for its intended purpose: to ease pain. I hadn't expected to face this particular professional crisis, either, and I was no happier with what I learned on that call.

It was night again, the time this summer when all of the events of my life seemed to unfold. I was wandering through the servants' quarters, usually the most silent part of the castle, when I caught the urgent, miserable sound of someone shrieking. My first instinct was to freeze where I stood. My second was to follow the sound of anguish as quickly as I could.

The trail led me to a closed door far down in the servants' wing, where the younger women had their quarters. This close, I could catch not only the intermittent wail of agony but the undertone of women's voices gathered in discussion. I stood outside the door and listened, trying to determine who was inside and what the trouble was. I caught Giselda's voice, sharp and certain, and a young girl's reply. Then the screaming started again.

I hesitated a moment, then pushed open the door and went in.

A few quick seconds gave me the whole scenario: a pregnant young woman sprawled on the bed, sobbing and shouting; Giselda bent over her belly, checking for movement and progress; two other young servant girls nearby, boiling water and looking frightened. One was Giselda's apprentice, and she should have been more use than this, I thought with a flare of contempt. The other was a girl I did not recognize—a kitchen maid, perhaps.

Giselda looked up sharply at my entrance. "Lady Coriel! What are you doing—!"

I waved a hand to silence her. "I couldn't sleep. And I heard sounds—this woman crying—"

Giselda's hand put light pressure on the girl's body, and she screamed again. "The baby's breech and I can't turn him. I need to cut her open, but I can't calm her enough. I tried to tie her down, but she's already broken one cord. I may lose them both."

"Let me help," I said. "I've attended a hundred birthings."

"If Lady Greta knew where you were—"

"She won't know. I'll be back in ten minutes. I need to get my medicines."

Giselda protested again, but halfheartedly. Even she knew she could use assistance. I flew back to my room, snatched up my satchel, and ran down the hallways again. I was breathless as I skidded back into the servant's room, where fresh howls of pain could be heard all the way down the hallway.

"I have halen root," I announced the instant I darted through the door. "Let's start with that."

It was a wretched night for all of us gathered in that room—for the writhing, suffering girl; for the weary old apothecary; for the assistants; for me. I had, as I said, been to a hundred birthings, but none of them as bloody as this one. We kept feeding halen root to the mother, more and more of it because she showed no reaction, still sobbing and cursing with the same demented energy. And then, suddenly, between one cry and the next, she went limp and silent in the bed.

"No—too much—oh, dear heaven—" Giselda muttered.

"I've got ginyese," I said briskly, already measuring it out. "I'll revive her."

Eventually I found the proper mix of drugs while Giselda and her assistants labored over the woman's distended body. The patient had finally grown quiet, childlike, giving out hiccuping little whimpers from time to time but no more of those bloodcurdling shrieks. Still, it was nearly dawn by the time Giselda delivered the child, a puny, angry, squalling boy covered with blood and mucus.

"Quickly—the towels—" Giselda commanded, and her assistants cleaned the child while Giselda finished her business with the mother. I was aiding Giselda, so at first I had no attention to spare for the baby. Giselda had not forgotten him; while she tended the mother and wiped away the blood, she called out questions about his toes and fingers and the color of his skin. All the answers seemed to be satisfactory, and we could all tell by his unabated crying that his lungs, at least, were perfectly healthy.

Once most of the mess was cleared away, Giselda went to the mother's head and patted her sharply on the cheeks. "Tiatza! Can you hear me? Tiatza, you have a nice strong boy."

Tiatza? Where had I heard that name before?

The mother did not answer, just moaned and turned her head aside from Giselda's insistent hands. "Can you hear me, girl? A boy, and he looks fine and strong."

Tiatza said something incomprehensible, then burst into tears. "Not at all," Giselda said calmly. "You'll have to be a good girl now and do what you're told."

Whatever that meant. I left Giselda to her ministrations and went to join the assistants, who were wrapping the newborn in lengths of white cotton. For the moment, he had ceased his wailing, so I thought I might be willing to hold him. "Can I see him?" I asked, peering over the unknown maid's shoulder.

"He'll look like his daddy, this one," she said, and handed the baby to me.

At first, all I noticed was that his eyes were open, and that he appeared to be staring at something over my shoulder. The next thing I saw was that his head was covered with the finest, sleekest red curls I'd ever seen.

"Look like his daddy—?" I said stupidly, automatically rocking the little form against my chest. "And who's that?"

Nobody answered me, though both the assistants gave me long, significant looks and even Giselda glanced over at me from the bedside. It was all coming together for me now. The red-haired boy, child of a red-haired man. Tiatza, about whom Elisandra had inquired on her first day back from Mellidon.

In my arms I was holding the illegitimate son of the prince of Auburn.

I STAYED IN Tiatza's room another half an hour, helping Giselda clean her up and monitoring the drugs I had administered. Tiatza was sleeping now, exhausted by her labors and her screaming, but her breathing seemed normal and untroubled; I did not worry about the side effects of the halen root.

"I can leave some behind, in case she is in pain later," I offered to Giselda as I packed my satchel.

The old woman shook her head. "I've got less tricky medicines to dose her with if she needs them. Thank you for your help, though. I don't know how much longer we could have stood her shrieking."

"If you ever need me—"

"Lady Greta would not be pleased to know you have been midwifing servant girls," Giselda said firmly.

I smiled. "Just let me know," I finished.

Eventually I was out of the close, fetid room, but even the quiet hallways did not seem open and clean enough for me. I hurried down the corridors, down the stairs, and out into the fresh, limitless night. The stars were receding into the face of oncoming dawn, but I judged there to be an hour or more before the sun edged above the horizon. I was exhausted, but too tense to sleep. I felt hot and filthy and sick and old.

Hot and filthy I could do something about. I headed directly for the great fountain, murmuring with its constant waterfall, and paused only to take off my shoes and drop my satchel. Then I vaulted over the rim and straight into the cold bubbling water. I sank to my knees, then extended myself facedown, under the surface of the water. I wondered if I could float there forever, a water nymph, indistinguishable from the sprays of the fountain itself, quiet, calm, undisturbed.

I surfaced noisily, gasping for air and spewing water everywhere, then I ducked below the surface again. The night air was so warm that even the chill of the water was not enough to cool my skin. I wished I had soap and brushes so I could scrub myself thoroughly, scrape away the top tainted layers of flesh and hollow out the bones themselves. Giselda had done more of the bloody work than I had; I could not understand why I felt so unclean.

Twice more I came up for air, then settled into the water again. The fountain was so big that even its curve did not distort my body; I could lie in it almost supine. My hair drifted above me, curling and uncurling with its own wayward motion; my blouse and my skirts billowed about me where they had trapped air in their folds. If I could sink to the bottom of the fountain and find some handhold, a gargoyle's face, perhaps, or an iron ring embedded into the stone, I could stay underwater forever, invisible and serene. . . .

The next time I surfaced, Kent was standing beside the fountain, watching me.

I gave a little shriek and fell clumsily back into the pouring spray before righting myself and trying to muster my dignity. In the graying light, his face looked serious and unsurprised.

"I saw you come up twice before, so I knew you had not drowned," he said in a solemn voice, "but this time I was beginning to wonder if you were willing to make the effort."

I put my hands up to my sopping hair and began to wring out the water. "What are you doing out here?" I asked.

He lifted his eyebrows. "That's a question I imagine might be more profitably directed at you," he said politely.

I flushed. "I often roam the castle grounds at night."

"So I hear."

"Who tells you such things?"

He shrugged. "Servants. Guards. People who have seen you. It explains your morning absences—though nothing, as far as I know, has quite explained your midnight ramblings."

Now I was the one to shrug. "I grew accustomed to these hours last winter in the village. I've discovered that some of the most interesting events occur when everyone else is asleep."

"For a while, I thought you might be slipping off to meet some ineligible suitor by moonlight," he said in a level voice.

I was instantly irritated. "And who might that lucky man be?"

He smiled slightly. "But since you seem to have such a low opinion of men—"

"Lower these days than most," I said.

He held out his hand as if to help me from the water. I hesitated, and he dropped his hand. "And why would that be?"

I waded forward in the water and he extended his hand again. Carefully holding on to his fingers, I climbed from the fountain with as much grace as I could manage. This was not much, considering how the wet clothes dragged me back. Once I was free of the water, my blouse and skirts clung to my skin. I was suddenly embarrassed at how much of my body they revealed.

"Are you cold?" Kent asked suddenly, releasing my hand as soon as I had found dry footing.

"Oh—not really," I said, but he stripped off his jacket anyway.

It was a plain cotton garment, well-worn and a little small for him; it must be like my ragged gray dress that I wore most of the time around my grandmother's cottage. I was grateful when he put it around my shoulders. It was kind of him to make the gesture. "Thank you."

He took my hand and proceeded to walk me, slowly and with complete unself-consciousness, around the perimeter of the fountain. "Why do you hate men more than usual these days?" he asked again.

I sighed quietly. "I have just—by chance—attended the birth of Bryan's son to some servant girl named Tiatza," I said. "I believe you are familiar with her situation?"

He peered at me in the dark. "A boy, you say? That is bad news."

"And why? Why any worse news than the birth of a girl?"

He made an inconclusive gesture with his free hand. "Because bastard girls are not likely, when they are twenty years old, to try to win support for a bid for the throne. Bastard girls disappear to some country farmhouse with their mothers, or get married off to minor lordlings, or get raised by some priestess in Chillain. Bastard boys are much more troublesome."

I withdrew my hand and stood stock-still beside him. It was growing light enough for me to see his face, and it was clear he had no idea what he had just said to me. "Some bastard girls don't care for any of those choices," I said quietly. "And they didn't realize that was the category into which they were blindly thrown."

Now he flushed and snatched at my arm. "Corie—I'm so sorry, forgive me. Corie—"

I jerked my arm from his hold and stalked a few paces away, but he instantly caught up and grabbed my arm a little more forcefully. "Corie, I'm sorry," he said, pulling me around to face him. "That was a dreadful thing to say."

"True, though."

"Which makes it even more dreadful."

I stared up at him. Through the thick cloth of his jacket, through the thin wet layer of my dress, I felt the heat of his hands; his face, as he stared back down at me, seemed so sincere and so sad. "What makes you think," I said slowly, "that I will do any of the things you and your father have decided I should do? I am not willing to marry to oblige you. There is no reason in this world that I should."

"My father would say," he replied carefully, "that there is every reason. That you have been fed, housed, dressed, and educated at his expense for the very purpose of serving his ends at some future date. He made you an eligible bride, and he expects some repayment for his effort."

"I was not brought to Castle Auburn to be groomed for such a part. I was brought here at my uncle Jaxon's insistence—to get to know my sister, to be included in the life that was half mine by rights."

"Your uncle Jaxon is a politician as savvy as my father. He may have loved you, and he may have wanted you to love Elisandra, but that is not why he brought you, year after year, to Castle Auburn. He will inherit some lands when your marriage settlement is decided—and Greta herself will receive a handsome fee for her part in the transaction. Your life here has not been free, Corie. It was your own innocence that protected you from realizing that."

I could not tear my gaze away from his face. I felt like Tiatza— I wanted to shriek in rage and pain. His own emotions had been exorcised from his stark expression; his eyes gave nothing back but my reflection. "Is that what you expected of me, Kent?" I asked softly, no longer able to talk in circles. "To pay for my existence with my freedom? Were you in the room with your father and my uncle, plotting which noble I should wed?"

Now his face seemed to crumple, as if the emotions could no longer be kept in check; he looked away quickly so I could not see. "No," he whispered. "Like you, for a long time I did not realize why you were allowed to run here like some kind of tame pet. That is not my father's usual way—certainly not Greta's. I was stupid. I did not realize how they planned to use you. Until recently. This summer."

I remembered our first breakfast meeting, his oblique comments and watchful eyes. He had warned me as best he could, but I had not been taking too many hints just then. "And did you think those arrangements were good ones?" I asked. "Did you think that was an excellent way to dispose of me?"

He watched me closely, his expression now closed and bleak. "No," he said. "That is not what I would have planned for you, had the issue been mine to decide."

I shook myself free of him, and he let his hands fall helplessly to his sides. I resumed my measured pacing around the fountain, and he matched me step for step. "Just what power *do* you have, Kent Ouvrelet of Auburn?" I asked presently. "You seem decisive and self-assured. You're an intelligent man with an impressive lineage. It would seem you could do whatever you chose. And yet, from the things you have said—"

"To some extent, I, too, am at the mercy of the court maneuverings," he admitted in a low voice. "But if I chose, I could be entirely my own man. I have estates that I inherited when I turned twenty-one last year. Estates that only the king's or the regent's command could take away from me. I could retire to them tomorrow, run them with my whole heart, and never partake in the politics at Castle Auburn again. I could do that. I have considered it."

"And why don't you?"

"Because I was raised to believe that every man has a responsibility, and the strongest man has the heaviest responsibilities. I believe Bryan will be a troublesome and erratic king. And I believe that if I am here at Auburn, I might be able to exert some influence over him. Although I believe that less and less these days."

"What influence do you have over him now?"

He laughed shortly. "I have actually kept him from a rash pursuit now and then. I convinced him not to be rude to Goff of Chillain when he arrived for the ball. I convinced him to invite Thessala of Wirsten to attend the festivities. And he does ask for my advice now and then, on matters he does not dare discuss with my father. My hope is that if he likes me, he will trust me, and may once in a while—when it matters—be guided by me."

I abruptly halted one more time and stared up at him. "You hate Bryan," I said slowly.

He nodded. "I always have."

"Then—but—there are things I am only just learning about him, but when he was young—when he was a boy—he was sweeter then—"

Kent shook his head. "You asked me once if I was jealous of him."

"I did not!"

"Not in so many words. But that's what you meant. I've thought about it often ever since. Perhaps I am. Could I rule in Bryan's place, better than he could? I believe that with all my heart. But almost any man could. Bryan is vain. He is cruel. He is selfish— and he is dangerous. And he has been these things since he was a child. Because he was beautiful, a lot of people did not realize how unattractive he could be. I can't change him. I can't depose him. But if, in the smallest way, I can control him, then my place is here amid the politics that go on at court. I may still hate what happens. But I may hate it less."

I took a deep breath and released it. "Elisandra," I said.

He nodded. "Precisely."

"You don't want her to marry Bryan."

"If she doesn't, the whole realm is in jeopardy. The alliances shift and the power base grows unstable. More unstable than it already is."

I repeated, "You don't want her to marry Bryan."

"If she does, she will be so unhappy she will die."

"You love her," I said, as I had that night at the ball. "You always have."

He looked down at me. "We have been each other's only friends for so long. It's true that's a kind of love. I don't know what to do to save her."

"From Bryan?"

He gestured. "From any of her choices. I don't know that there is any way to make Elisandra safe."

Now, suddenly, though the sun had risen and my dress had started to dry, I was cold to my bones. She had known of Tiatza's condition; she had known, I was sure, of Bryan's petty flirtations and perhaps his more serious ones over the past several years. She had never said, in all the years I had been coming to Castle Auburn, that she loved Bryan. I had always assumed she had, because I had assumed that everyone did.

But she did not love him, and she did not want to marry him, and unlike me, she had no choices.

"You could marry her," I said suddenly. "That would keep her safe."

He smiled bitterly. "It would enrage Bryan—and my father— and half the lords of Auburn, who have no marriageable daughters to offer in her place. It would cause a furor like nothing you have ever seen."

I shrugged. "Don't stay to see it. Take her back to those estates of yours."

He considered me. "And leave the realm in turmoil?"

"If it will keep Elisandra happy."

"Is the happiness of one person worth the chaos of the kingdom?"

"*I* think so."

He shook his head. "I have to think in larger scales."

I flounced away from him. "Then I have no use for you."

"Corie—"

I skipped ahead and would not turn back to talk to him. No more promenading around the fountain for me, either; catching up my satchel and shoes, I ran toward the broad steps of the castle. He caught up with me, still talking earnestly, but I would not listen. I stripped off his jacket as I strode along, and nearly flung it at him over my shoulder.

Abruptly at the foot of the grand stairwell, and heedless of the alert guards at the top of the steps who could hear every word, I stopped and addressed him.

"I will counsel her to do whatever it takes to be free of you and this place—to find happiness," I said. "As for me—do not for a minute think I will do what I am told. Your stupid father guessed wrong about me. Yes—and you did, too."

With that, I picked up my damp skirts, ran up the stairs, and fled into the castle.

*   *   *

I SPENT THE whole day sleeping, and had a tray sent up for dinner. The result was that Elisandra came looking for me after the meal. She was dressed in her dinner clothes, all black and silver, and she looked like the spirit of the night come down to earth to visit with mortals.

"Are you unwell?" she asked, sitting beside me on the bed. I was spooning up the last of my strawberries and reading a romance. The day had been in such marked contrast to my efforts and arguments of the night before that I actually felt rested and happy.

"No," I said. "Just wanting to be alone for a while."

"I'll go, then."

"Not alone from *you*," I said, stretching out a hand to keep her in place. "I have not seen you all day."

She settled back on the bed. "You've been sleeping all day."

"So, did anything interesting happen while I was in bed?"

"I had a long talk with Kent. That was interesting enough."

"And he told you about Tiatza?"

She nodded. "Among other things."

"You knew about her. About the baby."

"A lot of people did. Matthew was furious. But you cannot stop a baby from coming."

I could, for I knew the poisons that would react against conception, but I did not say so. "What happens to her now? And the child?"

"She'll be sent off to one of Matthew's estates. The boy will go with her. I imagine they'll monitor him pretty closely as he grows up. It's really up to Bryan what becomes of him in the future. Maybe he'll call the boy to court, give him a title. Maybe not."

I said fiercely, "I hate him for this. I hate Bryan."

Elisandra gazed at me sadly. "It is common for kings and princes to sire bastards."

"And not only royalty."

Like Kent, she looked as if she had forgotten, for a moment, what I was. "True."

I narrowed my eyes, watching her. "You must hate him, too."

She gestured helplessly. "Not for this."

"There are enough other reasons."

"I cannot afford to hate him."

I reached out a hand to place on her arm. "There must be some way for you to escape this trap—"

She laughed and covered my hand with hers. "Corie, do not be so dramatic. I'll be fine. I know exactly what to expect and what to do. I can take care of myself."

"But I—"

She patted my hand and then stood up. "There's no change that comes by discussing it," she said gently. "Now, *I* need sleep even though *you* do not. And maybe you'll be awake some part of tomorrow. We could go riding."

"That sounds like fun," I said in a hollow voice, as I watched her leave. Soon I tried to sleep, but could not. I spent the next day worried, perplexed, and on edge. Not until we went riding late in the afternoon did I cheer up, and then only for a few hours.

THE NEXT FEW weeks flew by, golden summer days growing shorter and brisker as the season advanced. I spent my time much as I already had up to this point, with one exception: I was more in demand as a witch and healer, for word had gotten out about my ministrations to Tiatza. I did not mind this at all, of course, though I was surprised at some of my clients: Greta needed a tisane to cure a headache, Daria wanted a draught to help her sleep, Marian's mother was looking for a potion to ease a recurring cramp in her left leg. I charged everyone a small fee and gloated at my superiority to Milette, who was still stirring stews and tonics over my grandmother's fire.

Jaxon returned to the castle for a few days, looking as gaunt and abstracted as a burly man could look. Elisandra invited him up to her sitting room two afternoons in a row, where she fed him kitchen delicacies and made him promise to watch his health. Her sober concern made him smile and tease her, but it was not his old, hearty style; I did not hear him laugh once during his whole visit. I took care to wear my ruby necklet at the dinners he attended. He smiled painfully when he saw me and told me how beautiful I looked, but he did not seem to care how any of my own courtships were progressing. He asked me no questions and set up no more introductions, at least from what I was able to determine. This pleased me well enough, but I had to admit to some concern for him.

Though I was happy if it was his own black history that was causing him wretched nights. At any rate, he did not mention any more forays into the forest to hunt for prey, and I wondered if his conscience was troubling him after his last wild abduction.

He had planned to stay a full week, but he left two days early after a bitter argument with Matthew. Angela supplied me with that news, and was even able to conjecture as to the cause.

"I think they might have quarreled over the baby," she whispered. We were in her room, and not even Marian was nearby, but both of us felt compelled to keep our voices low.

"What—Tiatza's baby?" I whispered back.

She nodded. "The regent wanted Jaxon to take her—and the boy—to Halsing Manor, but Jaxon wouldn't do it. Said he didn't have enough men on his property to keep the boy safe." She sent her blue gaze glancing around the room again, and spoke in even softer tones. "As if he thought someone might try to steal the bastard away."

"So, then—what becomes of him? Of her?"

Angela shrugged. "I guess they'll be sent somewhere else."

And indeed, not three days later, a small caravan set out from the castle for the Ouvrelet estates on the western edge of the Auburn province, and Tiatza and her son were in one of the carriages. Half the inhabitants of the castle, or so it seemed, turned out to see the caravan pull away; all of them pretended to have some other urgent business in the forecourt. I did not see Bryan or Matthew or Kent or Elisandra among the gawkers, but Doreen and Angela and Marian were there, pretending to take in the air. I spotted a handful of other noble ladies in the crowd, too. There were more than a dozen guards loitering near the gates, and twenty or thirty servants had found excuses to sweep the stairs or drain the fountain or trim the hedges on the main walkways. The servants clearly had the greatest interest in and sympathy for the woman being sent so far away. She was one of theirs; her fate could so easily be their own.

Tiatza herself did not make goodbyes to anyone, just hurried down the stairs and into the coach, cradling her son in her arms. I had only seen her that one night—clearly not at her best—and I wondered now what she was thinking, if she was afraid, if she was plotting. She seemed too young and frightened to be planning coups on behalf of her infant son.

The outriders shouted the order to begin, and soon the whole little group was under way and out the gates. The crowd in the courtyard began slowly to disperse, though the sense of anticlimax was strong and everyone seemed reluctant to leave. I headed toward the guardsmen at the gate to see if any of my friends were on duty.

I quickly detoured back around the fountain and plunged my hands into the falling water as if that had been my intention all along. Roderick was among the guards, but standing slightly apart from them, and engaged in close conversation with the maid Daria. She was gazing up at him with that same familiar, intense expression I had seen on her face the last time I had spied them together. It didn't take any special intelligence to guess that they had met many times since then. As I watched, she handed him a small packet; his hand closed over hers for a moment, and I imagined the fierceness of his grip. Then he let her hand fall, as he slipped the treasure into his breast pocket.

I leaned over the fountain and splashed my face once, twice, three times. I was too hot to cool down. It was none of my affair if he loved the sturdy little western girl, but he had told me he did not. Perhaps that was my fault; I should not have asked if I did not want to be lied to. Perhaps, in his situation, I would have lied as well. But it made me angry, and I knew that it should not. So I threw more water on my face to remind myself that I had no one to be angry with but myself.

It was not to be the last shock of the day, though the final one came very late, after a formal dinner that lasted too long and left me stuffed and sleepy. I went to my room alone, leaving Greta and Elisandra behind continuing to make polite conversation. Cressida had been in my room to light candles and leave fresh water—and someone else had been there, too.

Spread on the coverlet were the contents of my satchel, powders, packets, and vials all tumbled together in one colorful, aromatic mess. I exclaimed aloud and hurried over to sort through the disarray, trying to determine what was missing and what could still be salvaged. None of the bottles or jars had been broken, though a few of them stood uncorked on a nearby table. Everything had been opened. Everything had been touched.

I retied bags of dried herbs and restoppered the bottles, thinking quickly. There had been a parade of people to my rooms the past few weeks, and more than one had asked me to describe the effects of my various potions. If I had to guess, I would think that the desperate intruder was one of the silly moonstruck girls who had wanted an elixir of love. I had told them there was no such thing, but plainly they had not believed me.

Indeed, the packet of pansy pat was missing, and the vial of jerron ("which heightens attractiveness," as I had phrased it to one visitor) appeared to have been emptied into some other container. I could not help but be annoyed. It had taken me some effort to gather, dry, and mix these herbs myself, and I would have to replace the stolen ones. Not only that: As my grandmother had repeatedly told me, herbal magic was not something to play with, certainly not for amateurs. There were too many things that could go wrong.

I would have to start locking my satchel away when I was gone from the room, which was a bother. But I was a responsible woman, and I could not allow such thefts to continue.

It was only later, as I was lying in bed attempting to fall asleep, that I remembered the scene I had witnessed earlier in the courtyard. Daria gazing soulfully at Roderick; Daria passing Roderick a thin packet of—something. I had assumed it was a folded note, but it could as easily have been an envelope of dried herbs. I could not imagine what she might have told him to convince him to sprinkle the mixture in his food—but then, I had never attempted to come up with creative lies in order to dose the object of my affection. She was a resourceful girl; no doubt she had sounded very plausible.

I considered confronting her, if not that very night, the next day; I considered telling Elisandra. But I had no proof. So many people had access to my room. So many people had reasons to dabble in witchcraft. So many of them thought those reasons were good.

I turned on my side and willed myself to dissipate my anger, to relax and fall asleep. But I was still awake an hour later when I heard the echoes of Elisandra's voice answering her mother as they came down the hall. It was a long time before I was able to sleep that night; and even longer before I was able to release my anger.

11

And then the summer was over and it was time for me to return to my grandmother's.

Elisandra, as usual, loaded me down with gifts she had hoarded all during the summer—books and gloves and lace shawls and earrings. Angela actually cried and promised to write me weekly while I was gone. During my last formal dinner at the castle, Matthew offered me a farewell toast ("to our dear lady Coriel, friend in water, friend in wine"). I was embarrassed beyond measure and could scarcely choke back my tears. Bryan, of course, refused the drink of water, but gazed directly at me as he downed his entire glass of wine. Kent came up to me afterward, straight into the crowd of well-wishers who had gathered to say goodbye, and took my hand in a strong grip.

"We'll all miss you, Corie," he said, not releasing me. "The winter will seem even longer because you're not here to brighten the days."

I laughed self-consciously, and the women standing nearby cooed. "It will be spring again soon enough," I said.

"When do you leave, Corie?" someone in the circle asked.

I answered awkwardly over my shoulder, for Kent still had hold of my hand. "Very early. Otherwise we'll be four days on the road to Southey. If we travel early and long, we'll make it in three."

"My father has arranged for an escort of guards," Kent said.

I nodded at him soberly. Normally, of course, Jaxon would have come to the castle to take me home, but he and Matthew still had not repaired their breach. "I've taken my luggage down to the stables. I'm ready to leave in the morning."

"We'll miss you," Kent said again. Then he surprised me (and everyone still watching) by bending over and kissing my hand. His lips against my skin felt serious, but when he straightened, he was laughing. "Just so you don't forget," he said, "what it is to flirt with a lord."

From this scene I escaped as soon as possible. I spent the rest of the evening in Elisandra's room, talking over insignificant, silly things, watching Daria move around the room and neaten everything with small, possessive touches. I wished I could find it in me to really hate her or to give in and like her. She was too much like Milette—she had something I could not have, and so I resented her—but I realized the fault was mine and not hers.

I sighed, and finally pushed myself to my feet. "Don't get up in the morning," I said into Elisandra's ear as I hugged her goodbye. "Sleep away my leavetaking."

"You'll be sad if I'm not there to wave goodbye," she said.

"I'll be sad anyway."

"And I am already," she said.

I SLEPT POORLY, rose early, threw a last few items into a small bag, and crept down the empty hallway. There was no noise from Elisandra's room, so I hoped she still lay sleeping in her bed. The more levels I descended in the castle, the more activity I encountered, and at the ground level, all sorts of people were already bustling about. I ate a quick breakfast in the small dining room, where I said farewells again to Angela's parents and Doreen. Then I made my way out the grand hallway and down the front steps. There was a contingent of four guards awaiting me and a small carriage drawn up to convey me. I hurried forward so as to keep my escorts waiting no longer.

I had only taken a few running steps when I heard my name called from some distance away. "Corie! Corie!" I swung around to see Elisandra and Daria hanging out the window of Elisandra's room, waving madly. Elisandra was blowing kisses. Her unbound hair streamed out the window like a banner; she looked as if she had just that minute tumbled out of bed. I laughed and waved and sent back airborne kisses of my own.

Then I scurried on up to the coach and threw my bag and satchel inside.

"You have everything you need?" asked a voice behind me. I turned in surprise and delight.

"Roderick! Are you in my escort detail?"

He gave me a slight smile and nodded. "Not a duty I requested, let me say to your face, but Lord Matthew said you were precious cargo and needed to be guarded closely. So, Kritlin gave me the assignment."

He helped me into the carriage and instantly released my hand. "But this is wonderful!" I exclaimed. "Now you can meet Milette!"

He laughed and shut the door with emphatic force. "I look forward to it."

I leaned out the window, to see Elisandra and Daria still watching from above. "Goodbye!" I called, waving even more wildly. "Write me!"

Roderick turned to see whom I was addressing, then raised his hand to offer a quick salute, fist to forehead. Elisandra and Daria both waved back, as if they could distinguish from this distance just which guardsman was assisting me. Or perhaps they could. Perhaps Daria had known all along who would be riding with me to my grandmother's village, and that's why she had come to the window at all.

Not that it mattered to me.

Within minutes, we were under way. The carriage was small but well-sprung, and I thought I might like this mode of travel. With Jaxon, I usually had no choice but to ride, which I enjoyed for the first few hours of the day. It did grow tiresome after a while. But in my carriage I could read, daydream, or sleep; and I proceeded to pass the first few hours in the last pursuit.

WE MADE GOOD time on that trip and I, true to form, made friends with all the members of my escort. We had two extra horses in our train, and I elected to ride for part of every day. Roderick was by no means inclined to monopolize my attention, so I had a chance to get to know the other three who had drawn this duty. One of them, young and lively, reminded me of Shorro; the other two were quieter but kind. I liked them all.

My most interesting conversation came late the afternoon of the second day, when Roderick brought his horse up alongside mine. We talked idly of our inn the night before and our probable accommodations this evening. Then I asked where he would go once he had left me at my grandmother's.

"Back to the castle, of course," he said, looking surprised. "Where else?"

"You're not far from Veledore," I pointed out. "I thought you might want to take a quick detour home."

"I thought of that," he admitted. "But it's almost harvest time, and the fields will be rich with grain, and there will be cider festivals every night—"

"That sounds delightful!" I exclaimed. "Go!"

He gave me a quick sideways glance. "So wonderful," he said, "that I'm afraid I wouldn't be able to make myself return to Auburn."

I considered that a moment in silence. "Are you thinking about leaving the guardsmen?" I asked.

"I think about it," he said. "My father has said bluntly he would be glad to see me home. So many of the things I wanted to escape from I find are the very things I miss."

"But you said— What about that girl? The one who keeps you at the castle?"

"I never said there was a girl."

"Well, that's what you meant, no matter what you said," I replied impatiently. "What about her? I thought she was the reason you were staying."

He was quiet a moment. "An ill reason to run my life," he said lightly at last. "There's no hope there."

I found my heart suddenly scrambling to get outside my ribs. "Then—this might be the last time I see you? You might not be there next summer when I return?"

He gave me that sideways glance again, complete with a small grin. "Oh, next summer. I'll wait that long. To see the prince married, after all—that's something to witness, no matter how a man feels about the prince."

I digested that. "You're not fond of Bryan," I said.

"That would be the mild way to put it."

"And that would be the real reason you would return to your father's home."

He nodded. "If you take a man's dollar, you ought to respect the man. If you don't, you shouldn't scorn him behind his back. It's getting harder for me to behave as I ought. So, it's time for me to leave."

"What has he done," I asked, "to make you hate him?" I could think of a dozen reasons myself, but how many of those did Roderick know?

"He's a weak man, and a cruel one," Roderick said without hesitation. "He'll wound an animal on a hunt, then make no effort to find it to end its suffering. And he cannot be reasoned with. And he's stupid."

I opened my eyes wide, because this was a strong speech coming from someone whose station was so far below the prince's. "I hope this is not how you've been talking in the barracks."

He laughed softly. "No. I've never said it to anyone before. I could lose my head, not just my career. But you're safe enough. You don't like him, either."

"I used to," I said slowly. "Until this summer."

"Why did it take you so long?"

"Because he's so beautiful, I guess. So alive. Because I got in the habit of adoring him. But everyone seems to be falling out of that habit these days. Kent has said things—" I stopped and shrugged.

"What has Kent said?"

"I don't think Bryan is popular with the viceroys," I said somewhat lamely.

Roderick nodded. "Even less than you realize. During that summer festival, all the viceroys brought their own guards in train. Men talk when they're playing dice at night, and they talk in their masters' words. Not one of them spoke highly of the prince."

"Then—" I started, but could not imagine what question to ask next.

Roderick glanced down at me and seemed to suffer a change of mood. "Ah, don't worry over it," he said lightly. "All that will change when your sister becomes his bride. She's a well-liked girl with considerable charm. The lords think she'll keep him in hand."

"If she marries him," I said, my voice very low.

"They'll marry. They're too far down that road to turn back. They'll marry, I'll stay to see, and then—then perhaps back to the farm for me. Who knows what the next year or two will bring?"

Even less happiness than I thought, I said to myself, but did not speak the words aloud. The future looked drearier every time I looked into it.

THE FOLLOWING AFTERNOON, just before sunset, we arrived at my grandmother's cottage. Naturally the first person I had to see was Milette, out front tending the garden. She stopped her work and stared at us as the cavalcade pulled up. I supposed she had never seen a sight quite so fine as a royal equipage guarded by four liveried men. I was pleased to note that she was wearing her very oldest gown, had dirt on her face, and her hair was tied back in the most unbecoming fashion imaginable.

"Once again, back with my best friend," I murmured to Roderick as he lifted me down from the coach. He laughed and set me on my feet.

Milette seemed quite unself-conscious as she hurried forward to greet me. "Corie! I didn't realize you were coming back so soon! I thought you wouldn't be here for another month at least."

I was instantly annoyed. "No, here I am—summer's end—the time I always return home. I wrote grandmother to expect me."

"I guess she forgot to mention it."

I looked expressively at Roderick, whose face was completely wooden. "Where would you like me to carry your luggage, my lady?" he asked in the most formal, respectful tones I had ever heard from him. For a moment I was astonished; then I realized he was doing his best to impress Milette on my behalf, and I was grateful.

"My room is inside. Let me show you."

I led him through the small, untidy house. Milette followed us, talking while Roderick settled my trunk in the room. "Your grandmother's in the village for the evening. That Clancy girl is having her baby tonight, or maybe tomorrow. I didn't make enough dinner for two."

"Then I'll have to feed myself," I said pleasantly. "Excuse me, Milette, I just want to check the carriage one more time and make sure I didn't leave anything behind."

She trailed behind us back outside, too, though I had hoped for a private goodbye to my friend. "And your room hasn't been cleaned for ages. I just know it's full of dust."

This time I did not bother to reply. Ducking my head inside the coach, I took one quick look around. "No, I've got it all," I said. I took a regal stance before Roderick and gave him a queenly nod. "Thank you for your escort. I'll tell Lord Matthew I was pleased with your services."

Not betraying the smallest ounce of amusement, he put his fist to his forehead and bowed so low his hair brushed the dirt. "It was an honor," he said. "My lady."

He swung back into the saddle, saluted me again, and gave the order to ride out. Though I wanted to watch him till he disappeared, I forced myself to turn back to Milette. Who was staring.

"He sure treated you like a grand lady," she said. I thought I detected a trace of envy in her voice.

"It means nothing," I said airily. "That's how all the servants address nobility at the castle."

"But you're not——" she said, and then abruptly shut her mouth.

"I'm not going to waste any more time talking in the road," I said, heading for the door. "I'm hungry. I'm going to make myself something to eat."

THE NEXT FEW weeks were fairly miserable, as I tried to resume the rhythms of village life and figure out exactly how far Milette had outdistanced me in our studies. I think both she and my grandmother were surprised at how determined I was to make up for lost time, for I stayed up late many nights, reading through the crumbling texts and stirring up concoctions over the small fire in my room. Only I knew why I was so doggedly intent upon learning everything I needed to know to become a wise woman and a healer; I had no intention of becoming a prize for the furtherance of the regent's goals.

Still, I missed my sister and my friends, and Milette's constant self-satisfied presence did not contribute to my contentment here in what I considered my real home. My grandmother seemed happy enough to have me back—as happy as she ever was—and I certainly did not feel unwelcome. But my place seemed less certain than ever. I was beginning to think I did not belong anywhere.

As summer reddened into autumn, everyone in that cottage grew more accustomed to my presence and life became more pleasurable again. I joined my grandmother and Milette at the harvest festival held every fall in the village, and we had a wonderful time. There were costumes, contests, concerts, dances, hay rides, prayer breakfasts, moonlight feasts—an ongoing cornucopia of events.

Several of the young men I only vaguely recalled as farmer's sons showed up at these gatherings dressed in their finest lawn shirts and leather breeches, looking freshly washed, clean shaven and handsomer than I remembered. I wore my red silk dress to one of the starlit dances and made, if I may say so, a very definite impression. It heartened me greatly to know that I did not require the whispered

promise of a royal dowry to be the reigning belle of an im-
promptu ball.

Milette had her own circle of admirers at this event and—though
I did not begrudge her a single one of them—I had to wonder if
she had not resorted to magic to enhance her charms just a trifle.
For she was by no means an extraordinary girl, just moderately
attractive and not exceptionally bright. Then again, neither were
her swains.

Then again, neither were mine, but they were puppy-dog friendly
and boyishly happy, and I did not have to wonder if every word
they uttered masked a torturous thought. I relaxed into their banter
as I relaxed into their embraces when we undertook the energetic
country dances, and I enjoyed myself more than I ever had at Castle Auburn.

I could live here the rest of my life. Here, or somewhere very
like it. I would not let myself be coerced into accepting any groom
of Lord Matthew's choosing.

ELISANDRA WROTE FAITHFULLY to tell me of events transpiring at
court. Dirkson and Megan were at the castle for a visit, but it was
Kent whom Megan seemed interested in this time. Hennessey of
Mellidon came to Auburn for a week, and asked after me more than
once. Bryan spent a month in Faelyn and came back looking thin
and wicked.

*I think from having sampled too many of the pleasures of Faelyn Market,
which he does not get much opportunity to indulge in under Matthew's
watchful eye,* Elisandra wrote in her perfectly even hand. *Kent's comment
was that the next time Bryan went traveling, he should go along as escort,
and Matthew seems agreeable to that. Although he plans to travel to Ouvrelet
House for the winter holidays, and there seems to be no reason to guard him
there, so Kent is coming with me instead.*

Elisandra was to spend the solstice holidays at Halsing Manor,
as she did every year. I was always invited, but I had always refused
in the past, because I thought my grandmother would resent this
defection even more bitterly than my summer absence. This year, I

had an additional reason for not going: to avoid Hennessey of Mellidon, who had also been invited to share the holidays with my uncle. Not a chance I would join him there.

Our own winter solstice passed quietly enough, although, since this was my grandmother's favorite holiday, we spent a great deal of time baking and lighting candles and reciting blessings on the slumbering spirits of the world. On the night of the solstice itself, we did not sleep at all, but stayed awake with fires at the four corners of the house to drive away the darkness of winter. Then we ate a huge breakfast when the sun came up, wished each other luck and good fortune in the following year, and slept the whole day away.

The next news I got from Castle Auburn came from Angela.

Not until recently had we become correspondents—the year before I had gotten my first intermittent letters from her full of gossip and idle speculation. She was a terrible writer but a wonderful source of information, and I wrote her back often just to encourage her. I had less to tell, of course, but at least I could put words together in an entertaining fashion.

This letter began simply enough in her usual, rambling style. The solstice holidays had been dull; there was no one at the castle to talk to, for even Doreen was gone. She was looking forward to Elisandra's return, and Bryan's, of course, though there was very sad news out of Ouvrelet House, where Bryan had spent the solstice.

For that's where Matthew had sent that awful girl—Tiatza, you remember her? Apparently she tried to see Bryan while he was there, but, of course, he didn't want to—I mean, we all know he shouldn't have done what he did, but, of course, he wouldn't want to see her now after all that happened and even though she's a silly girl, you'd think she'd understand that. And she must have gotten very upset when he wouldn't talk to her because the day before he left she took that little baby and the two of them jumped off the top of the manor house and died. It was the middle of the night and no one found them till the next day, and so they were all broken and horrible and then it had snowed, too, right on top of them. I thought it was just the saddest story. They say Bryan won't talk about it at all.

Did I tell you about the new dress I'm having made? All in green and blue because, of course, those are the Faelyn colors, not that I have any real hopes in that direction, but Lester will be here in a couple of months. . . .

The letter went on for another two pages, but my mind had stopped processing the words. Image after image flashed through my mind, complete with appropriate sounds: Tiatza screaming and writhing upon her birthing bed; Bryan twirling me around and around on the dance floor; Kent telling me, "Bastard girls are not likely, when they are twenty years old, to try to win support for a bid for the throne. . . . Bastard boys are much more troublesome."

It was barely possible that that wretched girl had chosen to fling herself off the roof of Ouvrelet House, her luckless child in her arms. But I could think of other scenarios, more horrifying, more violent— more practical, if you were an ambitious man whose future was looking a bit questionable anyway.

I put the letter down without finishing it, and went out into the weak winter sunlight to absorb what warmth I could.

A WEEK LATER, Hennessey of Mellidon showed up at my grandmother's house.

The three of us were in the kitchen, preparing a poultice for a sick child, when we heard the knock. I was counting out a complicated series of measurements, so Milette went to answer the door. She returned three minutes later, looking dazed and uncertain.

"Someone's here to see you," she told me.

My grandmother looked over at me sharply. "Some of your fine castle friends?" she asked. "Be sure and invite them to dinner."

I finished counting the seventh teaspoon of tiselbane and pointed to my place on the recipe page. "These are the ingredients I've already added," I told Milette. "I'll be back in a few minutes."

Then I went to the door and saw Hennessey there, and felt my whole body grow tense with dread.

"Lady Coriel," he said, bowing with his usual, imperfect style. Milette had left the door wide open and he stood awkwardly inside it, one foot on the stair outside, one foot on the threshold. He was dressed in travel woolens and was no fashion plate at the best of times, but in this plain place he looked gorgeous enough to be dazzling. I smoothed down the folds of my brown dress and was glad it had been clean when I put it on that morning.

"Lord Hennessey," was my witty response.

He straightened and looked swiftly around the room. "I did not think—I understood that you lived with your grandmother, but I did not realize— Forgive me for staring."

I almost felt sorry for him, but I have to admit my heart was beginning a tentative jig. He was not as proud as, say, Bryan, or even as well connected as Kent, but he knew what honor was due his family, and none of it could be found in this cottage. Perhaps he would not offer for me after all.

"Yes, we lead a simple life here," I said easily, as if I did not realize how shocked he was. I did not want to embarrass him further by showing outrage or mortification myself. "Have you traveled far? Could I invite you in for refreshment? My grandmother and her apprentice are busy in the kitchen or I would introduce them to you."

"No, I—well, yes, if refreshment is available," he said, seeming to gather his courage in one determined clutch. "Do you have— cider, perhaps, or ale?"

I smiled. "The best cider in the eight provinces," I said. "Do come inside."

As I closed the door, I glanced out to see a cortege of perhaps ten men clustered on the road leading to the cottage. Good, he had an escort; he would not want to keep them waiting long.

"Have a seat," I said, gesturing to a rather dilapidated chair. "I'll be back in a moment."

I hurried to the kitchen and there, under Milette's astonished eyes, poured out two goblets of cider for my guest and myself. My grandmother watched with a cynical smile.

"Not what he's used to in Auburn, I take it," she said.

"Far better, in fact," I said, and returned to the parlor.

Hennessey had seated himself gingerly on the old ladderback chair; I handed him a glass and took my own place in the rocker. "Have you traveled far?" I asked again.

"Thirty miles today. More than a hundred since I left Auburn," he said, sipping at the cider. His expression changed to admiration. "This is excellent!" He took a bigger swallow.

"Made here in the village. It's famous all over Cotteswold. I can send a bottle with you, if you like."

"Or perhaps I'll stop in the village and buy some for myself."

"A good idea. Stop at Darbwin's tavern. The building is white and red—you'll see it as soon as you ride in."

"I'll certainly do that."

"So, you were in Auburn for the holidays?" I asked. "What brings you this far south?"

As soon as I asked the question, I knew it was a mistake, for he took the opportunity to answer baldly, "You do."

Into the strained silence that followed I said faintly, "That's flattering."

He set down his empty glass and leaned forward, but I was not quite close enough for him to take my hand. "Lady Coriel, I have never so greatly enjoyed any woman's company as I have yours. I have missed you since I returned to Mellidon—I have thought about you often. I hoped you would be at your uncle Jaxon's for the holidays, but you were not. And I had to see you."

"Lord Hennessey—" I said gently.

He would not be interrupted. "I know you are young. I know I am not romantic. But I'm a good man with good property, and my brother will be viceroy in a few years' time. That makes me a good match for any woman—and I wish you would be that woman. I would like to ask your uncle Jaxon to let you be my bride."

I have to say, I had never liked the man so well as when he offered this unpolished, rather businesslike proposal that managed to be completely uninsulting. I would not have thought he would have been able to pull off such a thing. But even that feat made me no more eager to marry him.

"Lord Hennessey," I said even more gently. "I'm honored. And I know that my uncle and the regent would both be pleased to see me make such a match. But I am not anxious to marry anybody right now. I am not overfond of court life—either in Auburn or in

Mellidon, where I assume things are much the same. I believe you are a good man, I truly do. But I don't think you're the man for me."

He sat back in his chair, looking more disconsolate than angry, and I liked him even more. "Mellidon has far less pomp than Auburn, if that means anything to you," he said. "We go whole seasons without seeing a soul outside the immediate family."

"That does sound attractive," I said with only the faintest trace of irony.

"You could do what you wanted. Spend months with your sister, months with your—your grandmother here. I wouldn't interfere much with your life."

"Lord Hennessey," I said in a kind voice. "I do not wish to marry you."

He gazed at me a long moment in silence. His close-set eyes looked unhappy enough to make my heart feel a little pain; I would have done anything to have this interview at an end.

"And is that your final word?" he asked at last.

I came to my feet, laying aside my goblet and holding out my hand. He rose reluctantly and took my hand in his. "No," I said. "My final word is that I wish we could always be friends. If that is not too much to ask of you."

"I doubt I'll be seeing much of you," he said with a shrug. "I don't get to Auburn often."

I struggled not to laugh at this ungracious reply, though I still felt sorry for him. "Well, then, I'd like to know you did not think harshly of me for this day's work," I said.

"I'll be sad, I think," he said. "You can't change that."

"I would if I could," I said.

He dropped my hand. "I must be going," he said. "I don't believe I'll stop in the village after all."

"Then allow me to do this one last favor for you," I said. "We have two kegs of cider out back. Let me fill a jug for you to take on your way as a parting gift." He hesitated, clearly wanting to refuse. I added, "So that I can be sure you are not angry with me."

"Very well," he said. "And then I must leave."

I hurried back to the kitchen, pulled down one of the empty

jugs that lined the shelves, and filled it almost to the brim with cider. Then I rummaged through the dried herbs on the pantry shelves till I found a bottle of rue-bane. I shook a handful of this into the jug before stoppering it. Finally I shook the container vigorously to mix the ingredients.

Grandmother and Milette watched me without speaking.

"A gift for my friend to take on the road," I explained with a half smile. "A sort of remembrance."

"Not with rue-bane," my grandmother retorted. "That's for forgetting."

"I know," I said. "That's the point."

Hennessey was already at the door, impatiently waiting, when I returned to the parlor. He crooked his finger through the loop at the bottle's neck and thanked me gravely for the gift.

"Travel safely," I said. "I wish you well."

He nodded, gave me one last hopeless stare, then turned and strode to his horse. I watched the whole cavalcade ride away, and I was depressed for the remainder of the day.

THE NEXT NEWS I received from Castle Auburn was even worse.

It was a letter that came from Elisandra three weeks later, which, as was my habit, I ripped open as soon as it fell into my hands. The first few sentences expressed an interest in my health and a response to some minor observations I had made in my own last letter. In the second paragraph, she mentioned how she and Daria had detoured to Faelyn Market for a few days on their way back from Halsing Manor, and how they had done nothing but shop, *to my infinite delight and weariness.*

The third paragraph was what made me stand stock-still in the middle of the parlor and devour the rest of the words on the page.

After considering the matter carefully, and having some long, secret meeting with Uncle Jaxon, Lord Matthew has decided that my marriage to Bryan should go forward as planned this summer. He has waited so long to make the announcement, I think, because of protracted negotiations with Dirkson of Tregonia, which have somehow fallen through. Even Kent was not too specific on what went sour in the arrangement with Dirkson, but Matthew returned from there in a rage not three days ago. And yesterday he made the announcement about my wedding.

Everyone here is in a flutter, because he has set the day for the summer solstice, which only gives us a few months to prepare. And every bride knows that that is scarcely enough time to pull together a wedding! Fortunately, Matthew himself is taking responsibility for the guest list. All I have to worry about is my gown. My mother has some plans for teas and breakfasts and balls to accompany the event, but I will leave that to her. She is in transports, of course; this is the day she has dreamed of for so long.

I have told Bryan that I would like the ceremony to be as simple as possible, and he has agreed that we should each have two attendants apiece. He has chosen Kent and Holden of Veledore. I, of course, want only you by my side, but I have decided that your friend Angela should be my second bridesmaid since I must have two.

There has been other news here which I am sure you will be interested in hearing. While he was traveling back from Ouvrelet House, Bryan apparently had some trouble on the road—bandits who attempted to hold him up, not realizing what an august personage he was. He was never in any real danger, since he travels with an escort of twenty men, but the guardsman Roderick (whom I am sure you remember) distinguished himself well in defending the prince. So, now Bryan has named Roderick his personal guard, to attend him at all times. It is a great honor, as you might imagine, though I have not had a chance to ask the Personal Guard how pleased he is with his new appointment.

One final note, and then I really must send this on its way. Hennessey of Mellidon came by Auburn a week or so ago on his way back home after a tour through the southern provinces. Kent told me afterward that his father was very puzzled by the man's attitude, for you must know that Arthur of Mellidon has been practically insisting upon an alliance with the castle for the past year, and you were the alliance they had settled on. But—according to Kent—Hennessey told Matthew that he had decided to look elsewhere for a bride, and that he realized this upset their negotiations and that he was willing to make some concessions because of it. Kent told me that his father had been afraid you would refuse Hennessey, and had been considering how to coerce you to the match, so this left poor Matthew completely nonplussed.

Kent and I speculated that Hennessey came to see you in the village and was so taken aback at your lifestyle there that he could not bring himself to make the offer. I would commiserate with you, except I know this was not an offer you were hoping for—and I tell you this now merely to relieve your mind. But do not think Matthew has forgotten you! I'm sure he is already scheming to marry you off to some other political ally, so expect to be inundated with suitors at my wedding.

Oh, Corie, I miss you most dreadfully. I count the months and weeks and days until I shall see you again. All my love, Elisandra.

I read this letter three times. So much in it to make me ponder, worry, and shiver! Elisandra to marry Bryan after all—what havoc would that wreak in her life, or would she, like Kent, be able to exert some influence over the wayward prince? Roderick to be Bryan's personal guard—how galling that news must have been to the homesick soldier who had told me plainly how much he hated the prince.

The only cheer the letter held for me was the news about Hennessey. It was good to know, in this calamitous world, that there was one soul that was not troubled and under siege—and that I had been the one to buy him peace. A small comfort, perhaps, but better these days than none.

FOUR MONTHS LATER I was on my way to Castle Auburn, to spend the summer at the royal court and witness my sister's marriage to the prince.

PART THREE

Weddings

12

At Castle Auburn, everything was mayhem.

The suites that Elisandra shared with her mother, her maid, and (sometimes) me were filled—every room, every corner—with the items of her trousseau. Formal gowns, casual dresses, petticoats, chemises, shoes, slippers, cloaks, shawls, gloves, hats, bed linens, nightclothes, jewelry boxes, perfume bottles, hair combs, trinkets, vases, books—everything old and new that Elisandra planned to take with her to her new quarters across the castle was laid in piles and mounds and trunks around the rooms. Nothing could ever be found. Daria and I spent one whole day looking for a missing glove, which we never located, which required Elisandra to revise the ensemble she had planned to wear to a formal dinner that night—which required us to spend another two hours searching for the shoes that matched the new dress.

Greta was in a perpetual tizzy, constantly issuing orders to Daria, Cressida, and me, then remanding those orders with her next breath. She looked as if she never slept, spending the night hours instead planning table arrangements, counting guest lists and reviewing all the things that could go wrong at the wedding. It was a real pleasure to me to see her go an entire day with her hair imperfectly combed and her earrings mismatched, and one day the back of her dress was

unbuttoned till noon at least before someone mentioned it. That day
my happiness was almost unbounded.

Nonetheless, I spent most of these days in a state of low-grade
worry, watching Elisandra and wondering what she was thinking.
As always, that was impossible to tell. Upon my arrival at the castle,
I had taken our first solitary moment together to ask how she was
faring and if she was dreading this marriage to Bryan. She had
laughed, squeezed my hands, and said, "Don't be silly. I have prepared for this for years." She even met my gaze, calm and composed
as ever.

I could not help but doubt her.

The wedding was set for the morning following the summer
solstice, which meant we would have the longest day of the year to
pass in revels to celebrate the event. There was to be an entire week
of festivities preceding the actual ceremony, including formal balls,
hunts, dinners, contests, and fairs. Representatives from each of the
eight provinces were to be present; this was to be a show of unity
such as the country had not seen since the funeral marking the death
of Bryan's father.

In the weeks leading up to the ceremony I divided my time
between helping Elisandra as much as I could, and renewing my old
friendships at the castle.

I was not staying out quite as late as I had during my previous
visit, but I did manage to spend a couple of convivial evenings at
the main gates swapping stories with Shorro and Cloate. The two
of them were proud to inform me that they had been assigned night
gate duty for a second year in a row—a high honor, they said,
though I asked innocently if perhaps it was Kritlin's way to avoid
seeing their unprepossessing faces by the light of day? I had also
asked, the very first time I saw them, how Cloate's romance was
progressing, and was thrilled beyond measure to learn that he was
planning to marry that very summer.

"Because she's accepted me, Kritlin's already given me an apart-
ment in the family barracks. We've decided on the day a week before
the prince's marriage. It seeming a very good season for weddings,"
Cloate said. He was beaming. I had never seen the dour man so

elated, and it gave me a little hope. Some folks, it seemed, could still marry for love—and even if that love had been assisted by magic, it still seemed a positive omen.

"Let me know when *you*'re ready to settle down," I told Shorro. "I'll mix up a special potion just for you."

"Not till the moon falls," he said with a grin. "Not till the world ends."

I did not go by the aliora quarters at night anymore, though I dropped by during the afternoon hours more than once. Andrew had formally introduced me to the young girl named Phyllery, who was so changed I almost would not have known her. She was shy but smiling, and she sidled forward to meet me, giggling behind her hand. Someone had plaited her hair back with flowers and ribbon, and she was dressed in a pretty pink gown hung with all sorts of lace and bows. She looked—arms and braids and sashes all aflutter— like so many banners dancing in the wind; she was nothing but long thin streamers of color. Still laughing behind one palm, she laid her free hand in mine, and I felt that shock of delight that the touch of an aliora so often brings.

"She seems to have recovered nicely," I said to Andrew.

"In most ways," he said.

"How are you? How do you like living in the castle?" I asked the girl. She just blushed, giggled again, and pulled her hand away.

"She doesn't talk," Andrew said.

"She hasn't learned human speech?" I asked.

"She doesn't talk at all."

I looked at him sharply. "Could she talk before? In Alora?"

He nodded. "Oh yes. And when she arrived here, she told us— many things. But since then—" He shrugged. "We are grateful for the smiles, at least. And Angela talks enough for three, so there is no reason Phyllery should need to speak."

So, this little bashful child had been sold into Angela's service. That was good news, at least; Angela's only spite was verbal, and even then, there was no real malice in her. She was always carelessly kind to her servants. This child would fare well enough at her new mistress's hands.

Nonetheless, I sighed, and Andrew gave me a sympathetic smile. "You seem sad, Coriel."

I nodded. "The world makes me sad these days. Things I would not have noticed a year ago seem dreadful to me now. Is that a function of growing older? And will everything seem more dreadful every year, from now until I die?"

Andrew smiled again and held out his hand to me. I let him draw me into his embrace, and rested my head against his flat, warm chest. His arms came around me, straw-thin and weightless as reeds. It was like being hugged by cattails and bird feathers, and yet it was incredibly comforting. I could not remember the last time I had received solace in Andrew's arms. I closed my eyes and allowed the sweet scent of his skin to lull me to calm.

"Aren't you very young to be seeing the world as such a bleak place?" he asked in a soft, chiding voice. "What has happened to make you so fretful and unhappy?"

"Everything," I said, my voice muffled against his shirt. "Phyllery. Elisandra. Yes, and Roderick and Hennessey and everybody else, too. What's to become of any of them?"

"I can't imagine what their troubles are," he began, his voice warm and amused, "but I think—"

"Andrew! Coriel! Stop that!" The sharp voice broke us apart in astonishment, and I whirled around to face a sight I had never seen: Cressida in a rage. She strode forward and actually grabbed my arm, and her grip hurt.

"Cressida! What—"

She yanked me from Andrew's side and glared at us both impartially. "Bad enough that the human girl comes up here to consort with aliora—bad enough when she was a child that she would go to you for comfort. But now—" She pulled her implacable gaze from Andrew's face and frowned at me instead. "And you, Corie. You're an adult, you know better than to lounge in the arms of men—"

"I was just—"

"Don't tell me your innocence! You're a noblewoman in the royal castle, and you know how every gesture is watched! To stand embraced like that with someone who is no better than a servant—if Lady Greta should see you, or the lord regent—"

"Neither of whom has ever climbed these stairs," Andrew murmured.

"Or *anyone*," she added, ignoring him. "You've your own reputation to think about, that should be foremost in your mind, but you jeopardize Andrew, too. What do you suppose happens to servants caught loitering with the castle gentry?"

"They get thrown off of mansion tops," I said in a low voice, thinking of Tiatza. "But I did not think—I was just—"

Cressida's voice softened as her face lost its harsh mask of rage. She dropped my arm. "You have to start thinking, Corie. All the time. You cannot make foolish mistakes."

I spread my hands. "I'm sorry. I won't come up here anymore."

"That would be best," she said.

I had not meant it; it had just been a conciliatory gesture. "But I—" I began.

She nodded. "I know. But the prince becomes king this year, and the whole world changes. Now be good. Go back to your room. I'll see you when I come to dress you for dinner."

And like that, my best refuge was taken away from me. I did not really believe that I was jeopardizing the aliora by spontaneous displays of affection—I had often seen Elisandra hug Cressida and Bryan would sometimes hang upon Andrew's arm—but Cressida was right; I was no longer a child. If I wanted to keep a sterling reputation at the castle, I had to guard my actions carefully from here on out.

But *did* I want to keep that reputation—?

I went back to my room and, not for the first time, pondered what might become of me.

THE OTHER FRIENDSHIPS were easier to maintain. Angela shrieked with delight the first time she saw me, and insisted on drawing me back to her room to tell me everything that had happened in the past nine months. Kent made a point of taking me riding three times in my first two weeks back, merely, it seemed, for the pleasure of my company; he did not once say he had missed me. He seemed relaxed and amiable as ever, but a little withdrawn, as if cares that he could not discuss lay heavily on his mind. This miffed me a little, for once or twice last year it had seemed that he had chosen me for a confidante. I, at least, had thought we were closer than his remoteness suggested.

But I did not question him about his silence.

It was harder to get a chance to speak with Roderick, though I saw him continually. As Bryan's personal guard, he accompanied the prince everywhere when Bryan left the castle confines. During formal dinners and dances, when there were many strangers present, Roderick also followed Bryan indoors from room to room. During dinner, the guard would stand at alert attention just behind Damien's chair, watching the servants, the visitors, and the prince. I tried to catch his eye from time to time, and occasionally he would give me an infinitesimal nod, but he never once smiled.

I could not imagine that he felt much like smiling. I could not imagine that he enjoyed his new position. For his sake, I was glad the wedding was drawing so close, because I knew he planned to leave Bryan's service once the prince was married. For my own sake, I would be sorry to see Roderick go—and, of course, for Elisandra's sake, I wished the wedding day would never dawn.

As it turned out, there were other weddings to celebrate first— a strange wedding, a strange celebration, and the beginning of more changes than I could count.

THREE WEEKS BEFORE the solstice, I was in the breakfast room much earlier than my wont, with the result that I had the opportunity to share that meal with Bryan and his uncle. I had not slept well the night before and had decided, when dawn came unforgivingly in, that I may as well get up. The day itself might have more to offer than the restless night.

The first offering was Bryan, turning away from the sideboard with a full plate in his hands. "Corie!" he exclaimed. He instantly laid his plate on the table in front of Damien, and bounded across the room to kiss me noisily on the cheek. This had been his method of address since I arrived at the castle at the beginning of the summer, and it still made me nervous. He had changed so much in such a short time. His fair skin seemed ruddier, coarser, the skin of a man much older; his red hair seemed too bright to match his own flesh tones. His quick, familiar hug always felt shockingly intimate, and the expression on his face—well, it was hard to describe. My grandmother would say he looked to be full of mischief, but it seemed worse than that to me. He looked feverish, at times. Overexcited. Unrestrained.

On this morning, I took the kiss and turned instantly to greet the regent, sitting over his own plate at the table. "Bryan. Lord Matthew. Damien. Good morning."

Damien, of course, said nothing, merely bobbed his head in a silent greeting. Matthew spared me one quick look from his narrowed eyes. He was a smooth and calculating man, who had always seemed, to me at least, completely unemotional. Was this how Kent would turn out? Was his coolness this summer just a portent?

"Good morning, Lady Coriel," Matthew said formally. "It's rare to have the pleasure of your company so early in the morning."

"But delightful," Bryan amended. "Here, sit by me. Damien will make room."

"Let me get some food first," I said to Bryan. "Well, I woke early, so I thought I'd rise early," I replied to Matthew as I filled my plate. "I admit, it is a rare hour for me."

"We're happy to see you," the regent said as I settled at the table, next to Bryan and across from Matthew. "I have learned today that interesting guests will be arriving soon. Ordinal of Wirsten will be attending your sister's wedding as part of the viceroy's train. He's an intelligent, sober man with good property. I think you'll enjoy meeting him."

"I'm sure I will," I said politely.

Bryan snorted. "He's a pompous old man who can scarcely see to shoot a crossbow."

"He's a seasoned and thoughtful veteran," Matthew corrected him in measured tones.

"Well, he may know old war stories but he's forgotten all the skills," Bryan sneered. "Give me a dagger to his sword, and I'd dismember him every time."

"No doubt. However, we do not want you to dismember him," Matthew said dryly. "You must save that pastime for some less desirable party."

Bryan laughed, as if Matthew had intended humor. "I look forward to meeting him," I said.

"Your uncle also will be arriving in a day or two," Matthew pursued. "In his last letter, he hinted at changes he plans to make in his lifestyle. Naturally I am most curious to learn what these are. No doubt you will wish to visit with him as well."

"Oh, always," I said, still in my polite voice, but my heart had quickened. Changes? Jaxon? I had last heard from him in early winter, shortly after the solstice, once Elisandra had returned home. He had sent a brief note, expressing his regret that he would not be able to escort me back to the castle for my summer visit, but promising to see me sometime during the season. Even at the time, his note had made me wonder.

Matthew touched his napkin to his lips. "And soon, as you know, the castle will be quite filled with other guests. These are splendid times for Auburn."

Bryan took his juice glass from Damien's hand and raised it in a mock salute. "Splendid," he echoed. "A glorious summer indeed."

THE FIRST CHANCE I got, I asked Kent and Elisandra what Matthew had meant. I had not planned to pose the question to Kent as well; he just happened to be in my sister's sitting room that afternoon when I came in after my ride. The two of them appeared to be in deep conversation, which they broke off the instant I entered.

"Elisandra, did you—oh. Good afternoon, Kent. Daria didn't tell me you were in here."

He touched his fist to his forehead in light mockery. "Yes, Lady Coriel, and I am thrilled to see you, too."

I settled myself next to my sister on her sofa, and she smiled at me. "Did I what?" she asked.

I had to think back to what I had been saying as I walked in. "Did you—oh! Did you notice anything odd about Uncle Jaxon over the winter? Lord Matthew was hinting at something over breakfast."

"If you had breakfast with my father, you must have been up the entire night," Kent commented. "I'm surprised you're awake now."

Elisandra's perfect features drew into a slight frown. "Odd? He seemed a little distracted, that's true. He met with his estate managers for three whole days, but I assumed that he was discussing normal affairs of the property. He didn't mention anything amiss."

Kent's face had dropped the teasing look; he now wore his new serious expression. I leveled a stare of accusation in his direction.

"You know something," I said. "What's going on?"

"My father seems to think," Kent said carefully, "that your uncle is planning to marry."

"Marry!" Elisandra and I exclaimed in unison. She added, "Marry who? He never mentioned any woman."

"He always swore he would never marry," I said.

Kent shrugged. "I think my father is guessing. It seems Jaxon has asked for copies of his brother's will, and one of the clauses in it concerns the disposition of the Halsing estates if Jaxon marries and has heirs."

"And what exactly is that disposition?" I wanted to know.

"Strange," Kent admitted. "As it stands now, Halsing Manor is Jaxon's for his lifetime. After he dies, it goes to Elisandra's second-oldest son."

"Second-oldest?" I asked.

"Because my oldest will become king," Elisandra said.

"But if Elisandra did not marry Bryan—" I began.

Kent nodded. "Then she and her husband would inherit the estate upon her marriage. She cannot inherit the property herself," Kent added, "for the will was written on the principles of primogeniture."

"And if Jaxon marries and has heirs?" I asked.

"His heirs receive the property, but an annuity is paid out to Elisandra for the rest of her life. And a smaller one falls to you, I might add, but only until you marry."

I sat up straight at this news. "How much of an annuity? I might never marry if the amount is good enough."

"Jaxon would have to die before you would receive it," Elisandra reminded me.

"He's an old man. He lives a dangerous life," I said outrageously. "I can be patient for a while longer."

"Corie!" She was shocked, but Kent was laughing.

"Indeed, my father always said he had expected Jaxon to die before he wed," Kent observed. "And I'm not sure he's pleased at the news."

"Why not?" I demanded.

Kent shrugged. "Because if Jaxon was going to marry at all, he might as well marry to oblige the throne. My father long ago gave up trying to rope Jaxon into a political alliance. You can see where this might—annoy him a little."

"But you don't even know for sure that marriage is what he has planned," Elisandra said.

"True. It could be some other mysterious 'change' that requires the rewriting of the entire Halsing endowment schedule."

Elisandra silenced him with a glance. I left the room shortly afterward, looking for information from other sources. But Angela was surprisingly little help, though we spent at least an hour remembering the names of all the women of marriageable age whom Jaxon could have met in recent visits to the castle.

"Because I *don't* think he goes into society much when he's not here, except locally, and there are no brides to choose from near Halsing Manor," Angela said positively. "Did he travel much last winter, do you know? Did he visit Tregonia or Chillain? Though I still say Megan is too young for him, despite the tendency older men have to believe young ladies prefer them."

"He didn't mention any trips. He doesn't write me that often. I think it has to be someone near Halsing Manor."

Angela's eyes grew big with illicit speculations. "Could it be—

one of the *servant* women? Or—perhaps not quite that bad—a seamstress from one of the nearby towns? A lowborn woman? Perhaps someone who works in a tavern—"

That would certainly explain the secrecy, and I had to admit I could picture Jaxon enjoying the company of a woman not quite so well-bred as the ladies he might find at the castle. But—to marry one? Jaxon had never liked anyone's company enough to seek it out for more than a week or two at a time. It was hard to picture him choosing a partner for life.

Two days later, he arrived with the most unexpected companion in tow.

It was shortly after dinner, and all of us had withdrawn to the salon to hear some of the musical selections Greta and Elisandra had chosen for the wedding ceremony. When I say "all of us," I mean the fifteen or so people most nearly involved in the event: the bride, her mother, Bryan, Matthew, Kent, me, Angela and her mother, Cressida, Andrew, the four musicians, and the prince's personal guard. Matthew, Greta, and the bridal couple stood up near the musician's dais, critically listening to the musicians, while Angela's mother and Cressida discussed seating arrangements. Angela and I amused ourselves by parading up and down the narrow aisles between the chairs, dancing more energetically than the music would suggest. Kent came over twice to tell us to be quiet, but we ignored him. Roderick stood with his back against the wall and kept his eyes fixed on Bryan.

Into this domestic scene came Jaxon, strolling in with the queen of the aliora on his arm.

I'm sure there was not instant silence, for it took a while to catch Matthew's attention, and the musicians played a few more bars before they realized there was something odd about the quality of the silence in the room. But to me it seemed like all the noise in the world came to an abrupt halt the minute I saw Rowena of Alora step inside the door. Maybe it was the absolute stillness of Andrew and Cressida that seemed to shout silence in my ears; maybe my own astonishment erased all sound from the room. But I looked up and saw her, and everything else disappeared.

She looked exactly as she had that night four years ago in the wood by Faelyn River. Her skin was so white that, even in this candlelit room, it glowed with its own radiance; her thick black hair fell about her shoulders like a shawl. The air shimmered with her luminosity, waves of light so visible they reverberated off the walls and broke in shattered reflections over her dark head. As before, she was dressed in some opalescent gown that seemed to drape her in glitter. Her narrow, insubstantial hand rested on Jaxon's so lightly that she appeared merely to brush the fabric of his coat; her feet did not touch the floor.

Everyone in the room was staring at her, and no one said a word.

Jaxon glanced around at the lot of us, openmouthed and stupid, and burst into laughter. "I didn't know the sight of me would actually turn you all to stone," he said. "You've seen me walk in here before with an aliora on my arm."

"None quite so fair, though, I believe," said Matthew, the first to recover use of his voice. "All of us have heard reports of this one."

"No doubt you have," Jaxon said, and put his free hand over the queen's where it rested on his arm. "For she is the gift and royal treasure of Alora."

He spoke proudly—dotingly—as a man besotted. All the conversations of the previous days rushed back through my head. He had taken the queen of Alora prisoner—or perhaps she had ensorceled him. Who had bewitched whom? Why was she here? Was she the author of the changes that had been hinted at for months? I could not think how to frame the questions.

Matthew took a step nearer the new arrivals, though everyone else seemed rooted to the spot. Indeed, Cressida and Andrew, on opposite sides of the room, had fallen to their knees and had fixed their eyes on Rowena. They looked amazed, uncertain, terrified. Even less than I did they know what her presence signified.

"May I be permitted to know her name?" Matthew asked. "And why you have brought her here?"

"Her name is too strange and beautiful for you to pronounce," Jaxon said, still in that proud, elated voice, "but among humans, she is called Rowena."

"Rowena, queen of Alora," Matthew said. He had come close enough to extend his arm as if to touch the new arrival. "Will you take my hand?"

Jaxon gently but unmistakably pulled the aliora a step backward. "Strip away your rings," my uncle said. "The touch of metal pains her."

Out of the corner of my eye, I saw Cressida start and Andrew scramble up from his kneeling position. They had thought she had come here in shackles, as they had; but she was here of her own free will.

Matthew did not demur. He pulled his three heavy rings from his fingers and dropped them in a vest pocket. This time, when he extended his hand, Rowena laid her own in his palm. An indescribable look crossed the regent's face, and I knew exactly what he was feeling—that jolt of magic and longing that emanated from the skin of the untamed aliora.

"Welcome to Castle Auburn," Matthew said, bowing over her hand. "Do you stay long?"

Everyone in the room stopped breathing in order to hear her speak. "The length of our stay depends upon Jaxon's wishes," she replied, her speech formal yet lilting, mannered and yet somehow wild, as if she spoke with the river's voice, or the rainstorm's. "He is my guide for this portion of my journey."

"We have come for my niece's wedding," Jaxon said. "Though we may not stay for the ceremony itself. Great crowds of people do not make for easy company for my bride."

"Your *bride*," someone yelped (I thought it was Greta), and then there was silence no longer. Everyone was speaking. Everyone pressed closer to the newlywed couple though no one came close enough to touch. I saw Andrew and Cressida stare at each other across the room, doubt, hope, and horror in their faces. I did not move, did not speak, could not think. Stupefaction had rendered me immobile.

Matthew held his hands out for silence, and there was quiet, more or less, in the room. "This is most unexpected news," the regent said, and for the life of him he could not sound entirely happy. "I had never expected to see Jaxon Halsing wed."

My uncle gave his usual, sonorous laugh. "No, and neither did Jaxon Halsing! We have performed only one of the ceremonies that will bind us together till death, for we stopped on our way at a chapel in Tregonia. We must go to Alora to speak a second set of vows." He laughed again and pointed at Elisandra, who had circled through the crowd to come stand on his right. "A tedious business, all this swearing and promising, as you're about to find out, my girl. But I discovered I did not mind it so much once the day actually dawned. I spoke the words, every one, and not a single syllable choked me coming out."

A few people laughed at this sally. Elisandra merely smiled, but she put her arms around Jaxon's neck. "I am so glad for you," she said against his cheek. "May the happiness of the world pour over your soul."

He kissed her soundly and held her against him in a ferocious hug. When she pulled away, she was smiling, and she was tugging her rings and bracelets from her hands.

"Hold these," she said to Kent, who stood directly behind her, and then she placed her arms with infinite care around Rowena's frail shoulders. I saw my sister close her eyes and sway forward, struck by the same violent gorgeousness that had taken Matthew by surprise, and then she released the aliora and stepped back. "I am Elisandra," she said.

"You are as beautiful as your uncle has told me," Rowena said. "May your own marriage make you as happy as mine has made me."

Kent came forward next, his jewels already pocketed, his greeting formal. One by one the others made their obeisances to the aliora queen, all of them quickly laying their jewelry aside and making awkward curtseys to the new bride. She was unfailingly gracious, though she made only polite, meaningless conversation, and I sensed in her a terrific sense of strain. This was an alien place to her, and rife with hazards. Every room in the castle held metal of some sort—armor, furnishings, cutlery, sculpture—and that in itself could unsettle and even harm her. But there was more. Her own people were here enslaved; anyone in the castle might form the desire of capturing her for personal gain; and she had just tied herself for life to the man who had caused her folk their most severe suffering. I was not surprised to see that her chest rapidly rose and fell in a troubled, half-panicked motion; I was more surprised she was able to breathe at all.

Bryan was one of the last to greet her. It seemed to me he would have avoided the gesture altogether except that Matthew urged him forward. He did not bother to remove all his jewelry, as the others had, just took off the ring on his right hand and held it carelessly in his left. "Welcome, of course," he said, and dropped her hand immediately and stalked away. Kent and Matthew looked after him. No one else appeared to notice.

I was the very last human to offer my congratulations to my uncle and his new bride. I seldom wore more jewelry than the gold necklace Elisandra had given me, so I did not have much to worry about as I stepped up to the queen of the aliora and made a little curtsey. But I did not reach out my hand right away; I took a moment to study her face. She had a fey, shifting beauty that made it hard to chart the curves and angles of her cheekbones. Her eyes were deep and changing, even while I watched, darkening to black and lightening to gray. I knew once I touched her I would not be able to form a coherent sentence. I spoke before I could think the words over too many times.

"I'm not sure I understand why you married my uncle," I said. "For he has caused you a great deal of grief."

Then she smiled, the first time that particular light had broken over Castle Auburn, and everyone in the room gasped at the luster that bathed her face. "And you must be Corie," she said. "You, too, have been described to me."

"Why did you marry him?" I asked again.

I heard Matthew's admonishing voice speak my name, and someone (Kent, I thought) laid a hand upon my arm. I shook him off. Rowena was still smiling; the room was so bright we all had to squint to keep staring at her.

"We struck a bargain," she said. "I would marry him, and he would never sell another aliora into slavery. It was a bargain I was happy to make."

"You should never marry," I said, "except for love."

Now she laughed, and the world rocked back; the silver echoes drifted around our heads for the next few minutes. She reached out a spidery hand to brush my cheek and I felt the shock lance through me, bone to bone. "You should never marry without good reason," she amended. "Love is only one of those reasons."

But she had touched me and now I could not answer; I could not speak; I could not think. I wanted desperately to follow her from the room, down the great stone stairs that led out of the castle, through the guarded gates, and down the long, weary road to the edge of Alora itself. I could feel the green touch of the oak leaves against my skin, I could hear the indecipherable music of the river in my head. All around me were forest scents, earth aromas, the rustle and call of leaf and bird and wild cat. All I could see was Rowena's face.

"My wish for you is that you marry for love or not at all," she said, and though she spoke in a perfectly reasonable voice, I knew without question that I was the only one who could hear her. "But I do not have the power of bestowing that happiness upon you. One gift I can offer you, however."

I found, unexpectedly, that I could reply. "What is that?"

"A chance to visit Alora. I would be happy to have you come as my guest."

My own smile came, less luminous than hers, but genuine nonetheless. "And never leave again? I have heard stories of your hospitality."

"Sample it before you refuse me out of hand."

"Perhaps I will someday. When there is nothing left in my own world that pleases me."

"Then you will never visit, for you are a girl who will always find pleasure in something."

That comment gratified me more than anything else she could have said. I felt like I had been dealt a golden blessing, that I would henceforth walk the earth with a faint, ineradicable glow. "I wish I could give you something," I heard myself say.

"There is nothing I lack," she said. "But I would not scorn the good wishes of a wise woman and a friend."

"Then you have those," I said.

She leaned forward and kissed me on the cheek. For a moment, my mind blanked completely; it was as if a thunderclap had, for that second, obliterated the room. Then she stepped back and everything readjusted in one quick, somewhat sickening jerk of reality. The room seemed dim and ordinary, and my balance was precarious; I stumbled a little as I stepped away.

Matthew clapped his hands, and the whole room snapped to attention. "Very well! We are done here for the evening. Bryan, you and Kent will attend me in my study—we have much to discuss with Jaxon. Cressida, you will make the queen comfortable in Jaxon's quarters. Greta, tomorrow morning we will meet to go over the final lists. Thank all of you for your time."

And with these peremptory directions, we were all dismissed. Angela had caught my arm and was literally towing me from the room, but I hung back as much as I dared, wanting to witness the reunion of Cressida and Andrew with their beloved queen. I got a chance to see very little. They had crossed the room to her side, and she had put out a hand to each of them, and they stood that way, unmoving and mute, for as long as I was able to watch. But the expressions on the faces of the aliora I knew were a cross between rapture and terror, and I knew that her touch was undoing them as it had undone me. What gifts was she offering them, I wondered, what seductive promises, what messages of hope?

She had made it clear why she had married Jaxon, but there had been no need to ask him the question in turn. He adored her; she had bewitched him. He would not, till the day he died, regret his bargain.

13

The queen of Alora stayed for three days at Castle Auburn and caused a silver disruption wherever she went. She could not walk into a room or sit down at a table or even make the smallest gesture with her hand that did not cause the air around her to ripple with an invisible heat. Wherever she was, people stared at her; they tried, in transparently nonchalant ways, to edge closer to her, brush against her, find some excuse for addressing her with the most banal comment. She was unfailingly courteous, eternally smiling, a thing of seduction and beauty, and more than once I wondered how many denizens of the castle would be discovered missing once her visit had ended. She engendered in everyone she met a fierce, impossible desire to journey to Alora, there to stay till the end of the world.

I tried without success to learn what the castle aliora thought of Rowena's appearance here. Andrew would not even let me cross the threshold into the aliora quarters. ("We are all confused and unnerved here, Corie. Let us be.") Cressida, who still appeared every morning to help me with my toilette, had grown ferociously silent, but the strain of some difficult emotion was making her very bones seem shrunken and brittle under her flesh.

"So, what does this mean? What do you think?" I asked her for the hundredth time the morning of Rowena's third day in the castle.

"Is this a good thing for the aliora? If Uncle Jaxon no longer hunts them—"

"Your uncle is a difficult man for the aliora to trust," Cressida said quietly. "Who knows if he will keep his word?"

"He will. He loves her."

"Love fades."

"Then Alora itself will win him over. They say it is a magical place."

"He has been to Alora before and not been gentled."

I tried to catch a glimpse of her face in the mirror, but she had her head down, and her thin hair fell across her cheekbones. "He is a good man in so many ways," I said. "He will be kind to her."

"Perhaps that is what he intends."

"You are afraid for her," I said.

"I am afraid for all of us," she said on a long, shivering sigh so breathy that I almost could not make out the words. "If the queen succumbs to men, what hope is there for any of us to be free?"

I turned in my chair to face her. Long strands of my hair, which she had been braiding, slipped out of her hands. "But if she has given herself to him to save the rest of her people, isn't that cause enough for hope?"

She placed her hands on either side of my face and turned me back toward the mirror. "There is still slavery. There is still grief, and the world still goes on," she said sadly. "You are too young to understand that the promises of the future cannot undo the harm of the past."

Only then did I realize that she—that they—that all aliora had somehow believed that while Rowena was queen, they had some hope. They had believed that she would find a way, through seduction or magic, to release them. The bargain she had struck might protect those still living in Alora, but it did nothing to redeem the souls already in captivity. There were no retroactive contracts.

"Cressida—" I said, but I could not complete a sentence of comfort. Her hands came around and pressed over my mouth, shutting out the words I could not summon anyway. What flaw was it in my own heart that made me react to that touch as I always did, drawing strength and solace from the one who needed it even more from me?

THAT EVENING WAS to be a formal celebration of Jaxon's wedding. It had taken Matthew three days to put together a suitable guest list so close to the major event of the summer, but he had invited the highest nobles of Auburn to dine at the castle and extend their respects to the newest member of the Halsing clan. It was not a royal wedding, after all; it did not require the attendance of all the viceroys and their families. It was an Auburn event, and Auburn would observe the honors.

Naturally the evening started with a fabulous feast, course after course of the finest local food. I was amazed to see that one of the dishes offered was a fruit compote laced with dayig. I was sure Jaxon had requested it, but I was impressed that Matthew had had the resources, in such a short time, to harvest enough for a serving and find someone who knew how to cook it. Still, it was a foreign dish at the castle table, and several of the diners looked at it askance. Not me. I ate every bite and then took a second helping.

I assumed, of course, that all the seeds and poisons had been filtered out. But since my grandmother had scoffed at the hazards offered by the dayig, I was not too worried. Surreptitiously I watched the head table. Kent, too, had double portions of the fruit dish; but neither Damien nor Bryan took a single bite.

After the meal, there were interminable toasts and speeches by Matthew and a few of the Auburn nobles. Jaxon, when called upon to say something, rose to his feet and gave the whole room a wicked grin.

"I've snared the greatest prize in the eight provinces, and I am a happy man," he announced, raising a goblet in each hand. "And *that's* something you can drink to in water and in wine!"

"True in water, true in wine!" the crowd chanted back, and we all took a gulp from each glass before us.

Except Bryan. As he had for several years now, he left his water glass untouched and merely sipped his wine at Jaxon's toast. I happened to be sitting across the table from Angela, and I caught her eye at this flagrant breech of manners. Most often the water-and-wine toasts had been in Bryan's own honor, so there was no insult in his refusal to drink. But to decline to accept the sweet water of Auburn on behalf of another man . . . Angela raised her eyebrows high and shook her head very slightly. No doubt Matthew would have something to say about this in a more private setting.

After the meal we were all herded into the music room, which was large enough to contain a small crowd but smaller than the massive ballroom. The dais was set up with a row of stately looking chairs which left no room for the musicians, so the three of them sat in a corner playing soft melodies. As I watched, Matthew ushered Rowena to the middle chair on the dais, and he and Jaxon took their places on either side of the queen. There was to be a receiving line, and all of noble Auburn would have a chance this night to offer respects to Rowena Halsing.

Just to show the rest of us how these things were done, Kent was the first in line to pay court to the aliora queen. He approached the stage, then bent so one knee rested on the platform itself—not the completely prostrate bow one would make to a human royal, but a mark of deep reverence nonetheless. He took her hand and held it to his forehead, speaking some indistinguishable phrase of praise or approval, and then he straightened to his full height. She said something and gave him her brilliant smile, and they exchanged a few more agreeable observations. By this time, the line behind Kent was ten deep and continuing to grow. He dropped her hand and moved away. The next man stepped forward and made his bow to the queen.

"This could take the entire night," Angela said in my ear. "Do you think we're expected to curtsey to her again? We've been running into her in the halls anytime these past three days."

"If Kent did it, I think we're supposed to do it," I whispered back. Andrew was passing through the crowd, carrying a tray of wineglasses, and I snagged one from his hands. I smiled at him but he merely nodded; like Cressida, he seemed tense and unhappy at Rowena's continued presence at Castle Auburn.

Angela also took a glass from Andrew and seemed to meditate as she sipped from it. "Well, if Elisandra does it, I'll do it," she decided. "Or—no—if *Greta* kisses her hand again, then I'll know what's expected of us."

I giggled. "Fair enough."

But Greta, that court intriguer, was already in line behind two young women of the Auburn nobility. I gave Angela a smirk and together we made our way across the room to join the parade of well-wishers. Behind me, faintly, I heard male voices arguing. I looked around to discover the source. At first, I couldn't see anyone locked in disagreement, but I did catch sight of Roderick standing stiffly with his back flat against the wall. His gaze was fixed at a point across the room, so I turned to look in that direction.

Kent and Bryan were standing as far from the crowd as they could manage, facing each other, expressions angry, gestures short and sharp. What in the world could they be discussing so heatedly at such a time and place? Kent lifted his hand as if to make a point and Bryan batted it down. Kent's other hand lashed out to shove Bryan on the shoulder, giving the prince a push so hard that he actually stepped back a pace. Now Bryan looked furious. He raised both fists as if to strike Kent, but the older man caught the younger about the wrists and shook him, hard. I glanced around to see if anyone (except Roderick and me) was witnessing this, but no one else seemed to have eyes for anyone except the aliora.

When I looked back, Bryan had broken free of Kent's hold and was stalking across the floor in the direction of the dais. I realized then that Kent had been insisting that Bryan pay his respects to Rowena again, and the prince had been savagely refusing. Something Kent said had convinced him, and now Bryan was knocking through the disorganized crowd to insert himself at the head of the line.

Angela and I edged to one side to see.

Bryan made a bow so deep his red hair brushed the floor before the stage. There was so much drama in his gesture that the mockery was impossible to overlook. "Ah, the queen of Alora!" he exclaimed as he swept himself upright. "For how long do you intend to grace our court with your superior presence?"

Rowena regarded him warily; the men on either side of her were frowning. "For as long as my husband wishes that we remain here."

"Excellent! I hope it is for a good long while now! I think it is important that you grow accustomed to the ways and the touch of your human cousins."

And, putting a hand on either side of her face, he bent in to kiss her on the mouth.

And she shrieked and tore herself away from the gold on his hands.

Instantly Jaxon leapt up, bellowing rage; Matthew was on his feet, calling out commands. In a blur of motion, Jaxon flung himself on the young prince, throwing him to the ground. There was the sound of Bryan's head hitting the hard stone of the floor, and then there was no possibility of distinguishing one noise from the next, for the whole room exploded into sound and motion. The queen was still shrieking in pain; the crowd was shouting; an Auburn lord was attempting to pull Jaxon away from Bryan. Jaxon lashed out at this unfortunate noble, sending him sprawling across the room, and lifted his fist to pummel Bryan once more in the face.

Then the room blurred again and suddenly Roderick was at Bryan's side, punching Jaxon in the head, grabbing his shoulders in a powerful hold, and hauling him away from the battered prince. Jaxon cursed and fought in Roderick's grip, but the guardsman had reinforcements, as Kent and three other nobles regrouped to drag the furious husband away from the prince.

Matthew knelt on the floor beside Bryan, and Elisandra dashed onto the stage to see to Rowena. Moments later, Cressida appeared beside the aliora queen, pushing Rowena's hands away from her face and inspecting whatever damage had been done. The queen had grown quieter but was still sobbing, and even from this distance I could see the welts forming across each cheek. I stared at her, and then stared at the cruel man who had harmed her so—who was even now stumbling to his feet with his uncle's aid.

Just as Bryan achieved a standing position, one hand to his head and the other on Matthew's arm, Andrew approached him with a restorative bottle of wine. As I watched, Andrew lifted the bottle in one grand, simple arc, and brought it down with all his force on top of Bryan's head.

Guards poured in from every door. I was jostled against the wall, like everyone else, shouting out and craning my neck to see. I could not push enough onlookers aside. Huddles of people were escaping out the servants' entrance—the prince, the queen, Elisandra, others I could not make out. Someone elbowed me in the ribs, and I struck back with the intent to do damage. Everyone around me was similarly scratching and clawing and arguing with their neighbors. "What's happened to the prince?" a male voice shouted out. That cry was taken up, and no one answered. Someone behind me began weeping softly. It was almost more than I could do to keep from turning around and slapping her into silence.

Finally, probably no more than twenty minutes later, an exhausted Kent climbed the two steps to the stage.

"The prince is hurt and bleeding, but he will be well enough," Kent called out over the insistent clamor of the crowd. He held up his arms to ask for silence, but no one bothered to grant it. Kent raised his voice. "Rowena Halsing will also be well. We thank you so much for your attendance here tonight and apologize for this unpleasant scene. The servants will see you to your quarters or your carriages, depending on how you plan to pass the night. Thank you again for coming."

And, with this unsatisfactory speech, he climbed back down and disappeared. The crowd milled and muttered a few minutes longer, but clearly there were going to be no more explanations offered this evening. I pushed my way toward the door, determined to find Elisandra or Cressida or even Greta and demand more information. Someone clutched my arm and I jabbed my elbow back in automatic response, but Angela's voice caught my attention.

"Corie, it's *me*," she said. We pulled each other against the nearest wall, out of the unsteady flow of traffic. And we stared at each other.

"What *happened*?" she demanded. "Did Bryan do that on purpose?"

"*Why* did he do that?"

"I thought Jaxon was going to kill him!"

"Will she be all right, do you think?"

"I don't know! And Bryan! His face——!"

A few more sentences like this, and then, almost at the same time, we remembered the last participant in that little drama. Our eyes grew bigger and our hearts grew smaller.

"Andrew," I whispered.

"Bryan will kill him," she whispered back. We fell into each other's arms and cried like schoolgirls. The room emptied around us, and we paid no attention.

Jaxon seemed safe enough, though even that was debatable. But no servant could assault a member of the royal house and survive.

I HAD FALLEN asleep on Elisandra's bed by the time she returned, sometime past midnight. I had dismissed Daria as soon as I entered and then settled in for a long wait. It had not occurred to me that I would actually be able to sleep this night, so it was with a shock of disorientation that I came awake to see Elisandra seating herself before her dressing table.

"Oh. Sorry. I didn't want to disturb you," she said when she saw me sit up groggily. She was pulling pins from her hair and the long, thick locks were falling like so much abandoned night down her back. It did not seem to occur to her to be surprised to find me there.

"What *happened*?" I demanded, hugging my knees to my chest. "Will Bryan be all right? Will Rowena? What did Jaxon say? What did Matthew do? What——"

She shook her hair back, picked up her brush, and began to untangle the curls. "Bryan's bruised from Jaxon's attack and bleeding from Andrew's, but he doesn't seem to be in any danger. Matthew put him in his room, and sent Giselda up to him. I believe Kent will spend the night with him. He's furious, of course, but a little too stunned to do more than mutter. I think he'll be fine."

"But he—Elisandra, he did it on purpose. He tried to hurt her——"

Three more brushstrokes before she answered. "I know. He's a very jealous man, is Bryan. He did not like so much attention being diverted to—to someone he does not even respect. An aliora. A woman."

"Jaxon's *wife*."

"I know," she said again.

"And Jaxon! What will happen to him? Surely he had cause—surely the regent will not put him on trial or—or punish him—"

"He's gone," Elisandra said. "He and the queen. As soon as Cressida had tended to Rowena's face, Jaxon had his carriage brought around. Matthew made no move to stop him, so I cannot think there will be a trial ahead."

"Bryan will never forgive him," I said.

Elisandra brushed her hair five more times. "Jaxon will never forgive Bryan," she said. "I don't think we'll ever see him again at Castle Auburn."

I nodded, my throat closing against grief and assorted terrors. I had an even more awful question to ask. "And Andrew? What will happen to him?"

Elisandra laid her brush aside and rose to her feet. Moving slowly around the room, she snuffed out the half dozen candles that flickered along the walls, leaving only the one on the bedside table. She climbed into bed beside me and I blew out the last candle. Instantly the room was full of hulking shadows, pitch black against the filmy gray of the walls. Moonlight made a halfhearted effort to filter in through the heavy shutter, but mostly stayed in a small dispirited pool on the floor beneath the window.

"Andrew," Elisandra whispered in the dark, "cannot be found. They searched the castle for him, Roderick and all the other guards. They were still looking when I came up to bed."

I whispered back, using Angela's words, "Bryan will kill him."

"Matthew is afraid that, if they don't find him, Andrew will kill the prince," Elisandra answered.

"I don't think he has the strength," I said.

"I don't, either. But because of this fear, Andrew has been put under a sentence of death."

I could not keep the whimper from escaping, though I covered my mouth and tried to force it back in. I heard Elisandra's freshly brushed hair move against the pillow as she nodded. "I know," she said, and laid an arm across my shoulders to comfort me. "I know."

The next morning, we learned that Andrew had escaped in the night. Matthew suspected that he had climbed over one of the garden walls, for the roped ivy had been torn partway from the brick as if someone had used it to support his weight. And the soft ground on the other side of the wall showed the faint marks of footprints— and palm prints, as if the man had landed clumsily and had had to break his fall. None of the guards had seen anything.

"But he won't get far," Kent told us, buckling on his leather fencing vest and checking the fit of his gauntlets. He had stopped briefly in Elisandra's room to give us the news, showing absolutely no surprise that I was there, still in my nightclothes. Daria had refused to let him any farther than the sitting room, but we had quickly emerged from the bedroom, dressed as we were.

"Why not?" Elisandra asked.

Kent glanced over at her, his face extremely grave. "The shackles," he said. "He'll be able to run, but he won't be able to hunt, or swim, or even fend for himself. And Roderick thinks he may have hurt Andrew last night, when he pulled him away from Bryan."

"He would be safe," I said, almost to myself, "if he could make it to Alora."

Now Kent redirected his serious look to me. "He won't make it that far," he said. "I doubt he'll make it to the forest."

"Who rides with you?" Elisandra asked.

"Kritlin and Roderick and a half dozen guards. And, of course, Bryan leads the hunt."

"Bryan!" she exclaimed. "He's not well enough to ride!"

"He says he is. And he looks strong enough this morning. Just a few cuts and bruises. And I'd say," Kent added grimly, "that he's looking forward to the expedition. He's as excited as a little boy."

Elisandra shook her head—her whole body seemed to shudder. She drew her bedclothes tightly about her as if seeking extra warmth. "Kent, this is dreadful," she said.

"I know," he answered somberly. "I do not see how it can be made right."

She made one small, hopeless gesture with her hand. "If you—do what you can to keep him safe," she said.

"I will." He crossed the room in three strides and took her in a close embrace. Elisandra, who never sought comfort from anyone, dropped her dark head against the leather of his vest and let her hair fall in curtains around her face. I saw Kent kiss the top of her head. He saw me watching him, and, keeping his gaze upon my face, kissed her again.

Elisandra was the one to pull away. "Come to me when you return," she said, and hurried through the door back to the bedroom.

I was left staring at Kent across the room. He made no move to leave. "Which one of them are you going to try to keep safe," I asked, "Bryan or Andrew?"

His eyes were guarded; his face gave nothing back. "Which one do you think?" he said.

"Andrew does not deserve to die," I said.

"I agree," he said.

"But Bryan is your prince. He will be your king. You have to protect him."

Kent turned toward the door. "I know which one you would save," he said, pulling on the handle and stepping into the hall. "I wonder if you know me as well."

And he was gone.

THAT DAY WAS, without exception, the longest of my life. I only left Elisandra's room to go to my own and dress. There was no sign of Cressida; I did not expect there to be. I supposed none of the aliora would be fit for human company this day, but as it turned out, there was another reason I did not see her: Matthew had ordered all the aliora confined to their quarters. He did not want the events of the night before—and today—to lead to unrest and dissatisfaction.

I wondered if he had thought the aliora ever felt rest and satisfaction under his roof.

We got the news of the incarceration of all of the aliora from Daria, who brought us food and tiptoed around the room and left, sensing our desire for privacy. Elisandra and I spoke very little that day, but we could not bear to be apart from each other. It did not have to be said. We could not stand to be alone, and no other company was endurable.

For a while, she sewed and I attempted to read a book. Later, we played board games for more than two hours. She set up an easel and made a sketch of me as I wrote a letter to my grandmother. I did not have much to tell her and the ubiquitous Milette. Finally Elisandra read while I tried my hand at embroidering a pillowcase that she lent me. The results were execrable. I had no skill with a needle, and no desire to learn, either.

"I wouldn't shame a dog by laying this upon his bed," I remarked, showing Elisandra my efforts. She actually smiled.

"I like it," she said. "I'll put it on one of my pillows."

"Bryan won't let you sleep in the same bed with him if you bring this as your dowry," I said with an attempt at humor.

She bent her head back over her book. "Then stitch me another."

I had to wonder at that: make her another pillowcase, better than the first, so she would not be ashamed of my handiwork; or make her another just as bad as this one, to make sure Bryan would not allow her near?

I did not ask. Some questions Elisandra would not answer.

The afternoon stretched out more and more slowly until its gold became so thin it had to break reluctantly into crimson evening. Daria brought us trays of food for our evening meal.

"No one's eating in the dining room tonight," the maid observed. "Everyone's having a tray brought up."

"Where's my mother?" Elisandra asked, for Greta had not been in once this entire day.

Daria tried not to sniff, but she and Greta had no love for each other and never bothered to hide it. "With the other ladies of the castle in Lady Sasha's suite," she said. Lady Sasha was Angela's mother, even more adept at scenting scandal than her daughter. "They've all spent the day there gossiping." Elisandra gave her a level look, and Daria amended, "Talking amongst themselves."

"I suppose there's no news?" Elisandra asked.

Daria shook her head. "Nothing."

"Thank you. You needn't wait," Elisandra said. Daria curtseyed and left the room.

We picked at our food. Neither of us had an appetite, but eating was at least a diversion. We had each eaten a forkful of dessert when we heard shouting outside below us. We exchanged glances, then scrambled to our feet, running for the window.

There was just enough rosy twilight left to make out the caval-cade riding through the castle gates. Two liveried guardsmen were in the lead, followed by Kent, followed by Bryan. There was a strange gap between Bryan and the next several riders, all of them guardsmen; Roderick, bringing up the rear, was a few more paces back.

Elisandra and I stuck our heads out the window as far as they would go, clinging to the stone windowsill to keep from pitching forward. "There's Kent—there's Bryan—I don't see Andrew. Where's Andrew?" Elisandra asked.

I couldn't see any prisoner, either. "Do you suppose they couldn't find him?" I asked.

"I don't think they'd have come back without him. Not so soon," she said.

"They've been gone all day."

"They would have ridden into the forest, looking for him, don't you think? They wouldn't have given up until they couldn't find another track. But I don't see him. Maybe they didn't—"

Just then, Bryan stood up in his stirrups and loosed a *whoop* of triumph. He raised both fists in the air, prince victorious, and his horse shied nervously as Bryan kicked its ribs. Someone in the court-yard cried back a welcome or a congratulations. Elisandra leaned out even more perilously to see.

"Wait—I see something—what's that tied to the back of—" Her voice trailed off. She didn't need to ask; she knew. I knew. We had both seen it.

Tied behind Bryan's horse was a body, head and shoulders drag-ging along the ground, heels up in the air where the rope lifted to the saddle. In this light, and covered with dirt as it was, the corpse was impossible to identify, but we did not need to see face and features to know who had been hauled brutally back down the trail. All we could hope was that the creature's suffering had been short— that some friendly rock had smashed in his skull not half a mile from the point of capture, or that the own natural anodynes of the body had caused him to lose consciousness almost as soon as the return journey began. I could not really see that well in the fading light, but I was sure I could make out the shackles still on the aliora's hands. He could not have put up much resistance at all.

Abruptly Elisandra pulled her head in from the window and ran across the room. I heard her retching in the chamber pot, but I did not go to her. I had no comfort to give her. I was more miserable than I had ever been in my life.

LATE THAT NIGHT, Kent came to Elisandra's door. I was still there, of course; I had begun to think I might never leave. Again, we had sent Daria away, and Elisandra was lying in bed, sick with a fever, so I was the one to admit him.

"I knew you would be here," were the first words he spoke. "How is she?"

At least I was not wearing my nightgown this time. "How are any of us?" I said, closing the door behind him. "How are you? That must have been a nightmare journey."

Elisandra had heard Kent's voice and dragged herself in from the other room. Her skin was as white as her ivory-lace shift; the braids I had put in her hair made her look frail and childlike. She leaned against the doorframe that separated the two rooms and appeared ready to topple over.

"Is he dead?" she asked. "We saw him from the window, tied to Bryan's horse. Please tell me he's dead."

Kent nodded. "Dragging him back was Bryan's idea. I said what I could to change his mind, but . . . So, we tethered him to the horse and started back, as fast as Bryan could go. We went that way for maybe a mile. Andrew—I don't want to describe it. I forced Bryan to a halt, to argue another five minutes." Kent took a deep breath. "And while we were quarreling, Roderick slipped off his horse and cut Andrew's throat."

Elisandra's lips moved in a silent prayer of gratitude. Color actually washed across her face. That was bad; that was actually terrible; but there had been a hero, nonetheless, some mercy shown, and that made the story more bearable. Her hand tightened on the doorframe and she swayed forward. Kent had crossed the room before I had time to think and caught her in his arms.

"You're burning up," he said.

She nodded, her hair dark against his dark vest. "Corie gave me something for the fever. I'll be fine. I just need sleep."

"I'll put you in bed," he said, and carried her into the next room.

I stayed standing where I was, feeling small, invisible, and strange. Did they want to be alone, to tell secrets and take consolation? Should I leave now? Greta would tell me absolutely not; I was chaperone, of a sorts, for a rendezvous that should not even be taking place. No man entered a single woman's room this late at night, whether or not her relatives were strewn about to protect her. And certainly no man entered the bedroom of the woman betrothed to the man who would soon be king. . . .

But he did not stay there long. Moments later he emerged, closing the door behind him.

"Will she sleep?" he asked me. "Because of whatever drug you gave her?"

I nodded. "I'm surprised she's still awake."

"And the fever?"

"I'll watch it," I said. "I think it's just unhappiness."

Standing across the room, he inspected me. "You seem calmer than she does. Are you all right?"

"Sad," I said. "Horrified. But it is worse for Elisandra than for any of us."

He moved slowly across the room, heading in the direction of the outer door, but his eyes never turned from my face. "Because she is to marry Bryan."

"You could help her," I said. "Take her away from here. Hide her somewhere on your own estates. Marry her."

"She won't marry me."

"How do you know? Have you asked her?"

"She doesn't love me."

"She doesn't love Bryan, and she'll marry him in a couple of weeks!"

He stopped at the door, his hand on the knob. He was still watching me. "Things are not as simple as you seem to think, Corie. It is not so easy for her to walk away from the life that has been laid out for her. Elisandra does not believe she has the right to marry anyone else while Bryan wants her to be his bride."

I was so angry with him. What Elisandra did not believe was that she had any options. "You're just afraid," I flung at him. "Of what would happen to *you* and your life at court if you were to carry Elisandra away. Of what your father would say. Of what Bryan would do to you."

Now he, too, looked angry. "I am afraid of many things, but those are not the fears that keep me from action," he said.

I turned my back on him. "Then I don't understand you," I said.

I heard the door open. "No," he said, "and you never have." I heard him step into the hall and close the door with a little unnecessary force. I listened to his footsteps striding away down the hall. Then I listened awhile to the silence.

THE NEXT DAY, Elisandra was better and I was heartily sick of her two rooms. I left Elisandra in Daria's hands and headed to my own room to bathe and dress. To my surprise, the aliora was there waiting for me.

"Cressida!" I exclaimed, and hurried forward. I would have taken her in a hug, but she stepped back from me. She looked so wan and so delicate that she could have been a doll made from twigs of birch and alder; her face was so set it could indeed have been carved from wood.

"Lady Coriel," she said formally.

I came to a stumbling halt a few feet away. "But—are you all right? Have you—I'm so sorry about Andrew, so sorry. Is there anything I can do? For you—for the others?"

She held up both of those painfully thin hands to request my silence. Light made a playful halo around each shackle and seemed to pour through the translucent skin. "Don't ask. Don't talk," she said, and that lovely voice was reedy and wasted. "There is nothing to say."

"There has to be something to say," I whispered.

"I've drawn your bathwater," she said, turning away from me. "What would you like to wear today?"

I chose a dress at random and stripped down for my bath. Did it soothe her a little to reenter the familiar old routines, reassure her that there was sanity and structure to the world? Or did it gall her, one more murderous human to shield and succor, one more helpless girl to hate with all her heart? Cressida did not hate me— until Andrew's outburst the other day, I would have said the aliora were incapable of hate—but I did not understand how she could love me. Until this summer, I had always accepted the love of the aliora as a matter of course.

I bathed in silence and dressed in silence, while she handed me soap and perfume and undergarments. As I stood before the mirror, pushing my hair rather carelessly in place, I made her look at me in the glass.

"Tell me one thing," I said. "If he had made it to Alora, would he have been all right?"

For a moment I thought she would not answer, but I held her gaze with mine and would not let it go. "He would not have made it to Alora with the chains around his wrists," she said at last.

"And if the chains had been gone? Would he have remembered the way?"

She nodded. "The aliora always know the way home."

"And the queen? She will recover from—from Bryan's touch?"

"She will bear scars on her face for her lifetime. And she will fear men even more than she does now."

I turned to face Cressida. "She must hate my uncle."

"She wanted to," Cressida said.

She did not amplify and I did not ask any more questions. I thanked her for her aid, and went slowly downstairs to the breakfast room.

That day, and the next three, passed in the slow, cautious ways that days pass when you are recuperating from a serious illness. Except the whole court seemed to be experiencing the same disorientation and fearful sense of dizziness. Everyone moved slowly, as if their joints still ached, and talked in low voices as if to keep from waking feverish children. Mealtimes were subdued. Activities were kept to a minimum. Conversations were short, trivial, and inconclusive.

Only Bryan seemed immune from the pervasive malaise. He strode into rooms with his usual boisterous vigor; his laugh could be heard from three hallways away. He and Roderick went riding every morning, hunting most afternoons, and often practiced swordplay in the weapons yard. He drank a great deal of wine every night over dinner and looked about as happy as I could ever remember seeing him.

Kent did not talk to me at all during these three days.

And Elisandra's wedding was just one week away.

14

That night I went to Cloate's wedding, which had been deliberately scheduled for a sennight before the prince's. I don't think he expected me to attend, even though he had issued the invitation, but I would not have missed this for all the gold in Castle Auburn—the culmination of my first successful professional spell.

I wore a green dress that was pretty, though not particularly fancy, as I did not want to appear grander than the bride or her attendants. But I found, as I entered the servants' dining hall on the back side of the castle and facing the stables, that the abigails and kitchen maids and valets and groomsmen could do themselves up fairly fine when they had a special occasion.

The low-ceilinged room, badly lit by cheap candles, was lined with simple wooden pews and nearly filled with people. The cleric standing at the makeshift pulpit was the same man who preached to the gentry once a week, though I had to admit he looked a little less severe than I was used to seeing him. Perhaps he thought the members of the nobility needed more meditation on their vices and possible punishments; he looked quite affable and approving tonight.

I slipped into the very last pew and listened to the ceremony, which was brief and fairly joyous. "Love your god—love each other—love your fellow creatures" was the way it ended up. The crowd exploded into cheers of goodwill and speculation as the bridal couple kissed. I smiled and applauded with everyone else, and felt, for a moment at least, some of the bleakness melt from around my heart. Here and there, individuals might find happiness, or so it seemed; perhaps there was no need to despair entirely.

After the religious part of the ceremony was concluded, the newlyweds made the traditional parade up one side aisle, down the other side aisle, and back up the middle one. The audience flung coins at them, bits of copper and silver that would be swept up afterward by the attendants and presented to the groom in bags embroidered by some of the bride's closest friends. I tossed out a few copper bits of my own, but that wasn't my real gift. I had brought a sachet of pansy pat and rareweed and nariander—love, fidelity, and serenity—and while no one else was paying attention, I untied the strings holding the little bag shut. Then I tossed out the powdered herbs with the coins, so that my spell would be swept up with the money. More than that I could not give to anybody.

Once the newlyweds had finished their procession, the real mayhem began. Strong young ostlers and muscular guardsmen wrestled the pews to one side, stacking them high against the walls and swearing cheerfully as they did so. The kitchen maids went outside to fetch baskets of food and drink, and began to arrange their delicacies on a table near the altar. Somewhere I heard a musician tune a string. I decided this was my cue to exit.

"Lady Coriel!" a voice exclaimed behind me. I turned to find Shorro beaming at me. He was dressed all in black and silver, and he looked more freshly washed and clean-shaven than I had ever seen him. "Cloate'll never believe you came to his wedding! And his missus—lord, she don't even believe him when he calls you his friend. You'll have to come up and tell them hello."

There was a crowd packed tightly around the happy couple. I did not want to fight my way through or wait my turn. "I don't want to interrupt," I demurred.

Shorro took my arm in a completely unself-conscious hold. "Nonsense! He'll be happy as a hound dog to see you tonight. Make his wedding complete, it will."

So, I allowed him to pull me through the mob, which good-naturedly let me pass, waving aside my murmured apologies. Cloate indeed looked delighted to see me, his dour gray features lightening to a pleasant benevolence.

"Lady Coriel! You're here!" he exclaimed, and made me a deep, if unpracticed, bow. I heard my name echo in low voices behind me, and various others bent their heads to acknowledge me.

"Oh, please, none of that," I said. "But Cloate! Don't you look grand! And this is your lovely bride. I'm so pleased so meet you."

Though I had glimpsed the girl several times, I had never actually been introduced to her, and it seemed unlikely that I would get a coherent sentence from her on this particular occasion. "I—my lady—so good—" were the words she managed to choke out. I laughed, and drew her into a quick embrace, managing to scatter the remaining powdery seeds of pansy pat along the back of her dress.

"Best of luck to you both," I said. "I think you each did well."

I had thought I would be able to escape then, but, of course, I had reckoned without Shorro. He happily took my arm again.

"Dancing now," he said. "Don't even bother telling me you don't like to dance, because I can tell by the way you move that you do. Of course, there're no fancy dances here with the serving folk, but I believe you'll catch on fast enough. You're a quick study."

I couldn't help it, I started laughing. "I bet I know the country dances better than you do," I challenged him. "You forget where I spend the greater portion of my life."

His dark eyes lit up; if he'd been a puppy, he would have frisked. "Well, then! The first five dances with me!"

And, as the music had just started and dancers were already on the hastily cleared floor, we were able to show our mettle without any more time wasted. As I might have expected, Shorro was an energetic and flirtatious dancer. He held me close when the music called for hands to be linked, and he grinned at me suggestively when our pattern caused us to step apart. I swear, once he almost kissed me, but he remembered just in time who I was. But he seemed unabashed as he drew back, and the look in his eyes said he might, a little later in the evening, allow himself to forget.

I had planned to make good my escape as soon as the fifth dance with Shorro ended, but I found that I could not refuse when my hand was solicited next by Clem. So, I took a turn with him, and then a turn with Estis, and then I danced a few numbers with guards whose names I could not have called out if theirs were the last faces I should see before I died. I could not remember another time I had enjoyed myself so much. Maybe the release felt so good because of all the preceding days of cruelty and despair. Maybe, during some more ordinary week, I would have found the wedding celebration tedious. But this night I danced, I laughed, I flirted, and when Shorro claimed me for a sixth time, I let him kiss me as the music ended.

I drew back smiling, and he laughing. "No, and Cloate won't believe that either unless he saw it, which I know he was too busy to do," he said. "I've got an idea! There's a bench outside, where it'll be nice and cool. We can sit awhile and talk—"

I had no illusions about Shorro's idea of "talking," so this time I was the one to laugh. "I think I'd better stay inside, thank you very much. Or, better yet, go back to my room—"

"No, no, don't go!" Shorro begged. "One more dance! Two more!"

"But not with you," said a voice behind me. We both spun guiltily to face the speaker. It was Roderick, dressed in formal black and white, and looking both taller and more severe than usual. I could not keep the blush from rising to my cheeks, and even the bold Shorro looked a little chastised.

"Now, Roderick, there's no harm in Lady Coriel being here, no harm in my having a dance or two with her—"

"No harm at all," Roderick agreed in an amiable voice that still seemed threaded with reproof. "No one's likely to blame you for her conduct, in any case, since it's pretty well known she does what she wants."

At that, I stiffened. "All I did was attend the wedding of friends. Among the kind of company I keep nine months out of the year. And prefer," I added.

Roderick was looking down at me with the faintest smile lurking around his mouth. "So do I prefer it," he said, "and I have seen my share of the gentry over the past year."

"Excuse me a moment," Shorro said and disappeared into the crowd.

Left alone with Roderick, I tried a tentative smile. "It was a very nice wedding, wasn't it? Not as grand as the one we'll see in a week."

"But destined for greater happiness, I would think."

He kept his voice neutral, but I imagined I could detect a tone of bitterness. I studied him. "You'll be leaving, then, I suppose, as soon as the vows are spoken?"

He hesitated, and his face grew even more impassive. "That was my plan," he said. "Now I think I may stay awhile longer."

"Because?"

He shrugged. When he answered, for some reason I was sure he was lying. "Because I think the prince may have need of me. He lives in troubled times."

"He creates troubled times."

"Perhaps."

I took a step forward and touched him lightly on the arm. "And he draws my sister straight into his own whirlwind. If you could somehow see your way to guarding her while you are guarding him, I would take that as a great kindness. She is so completely vulnerable."

His gaze dropped to my hand then rose to meet my eyes again; there was no change of expression on his face. "I have always thought," he said, "that your sister knew exactly what she was doing by marrying the prince."

"That is how it appears," I said. "That she is marrying for position and glory. But I think it is because she can see no way out. She does not love Bryan, I know that."

"That does not mean she wants to be saved from him."

I shrugged, unable to explain. "Just protect her from the dangers that swirl around him. There are so many. Could you? Would you watch out for Elisandra as you watch out for the prince?"

His face was completely inscrutable, but somehow I was convinced he was angry at me. It led me to pull my hand away and bury it in the folds of my dress. "I will do what I can for your sister," he said at last. "As much as I am able."

I smiled now, oddly relieved. "Good! Then I will see you at the wedding—and, I suppose, everywhere Bryan goes for the next few days—"

It was meant as the prelude to a goodbye, as I had started edging toward the door, but he caught my arm. "Oh no, you don't," he said, and now his face was open and smiling. "You've danced with every other man here. I think you owe me at least one opportunity."

I'm sure I stared. "I didn't know you danced!"

He took my hands and tugged me toward the dance floor. The music had already started, but these were no formal figures such as you would find in the court ballroom; no, couples just twirled around madly in any chaos they chose. "I didn't know you did. Please, Lady Coriel, honor me with this dance."

He did not wait for a reply, just pulled me into the middle of the milling throng. He was not as spirited a dancer as Shorro, and nowhere near as elegant as, for instance, Kent, but he had a certain relaxed grace that made him an enjoyable partner. He did not flirt with me as Shorro had, but he kept his attention on me, noticed when I missed or faltered, and dexterously moved me out of the way when other couples came careening too close.

I thought, *If he watches Elisandra as closely as he is watching me, I shall have nothing to fear for her.*

The music came to a flourishing close. Roderick bowed, I curt-seyed, and we both came up smiling.

"Now, I really must go," I said.

"I'll walk you back to the main doorway."

"Oh, no! I prowl around alone at night all the time."

His eyebrows lifted. "Which is, I suppose, how you have become so friendly with all the guardsmen?"

I grinned. "Well, they do tend to be patrolling the area at that hour."

"I admire a woman who can make friends wherever she goes."

"Well, that's nice to hear. I didn't think you admired me at all."

His smile grew until he could no longer contain it, and his laughter escaped. "You're a scamp."

"Fine way to talk to a court lady," I said in a mock-haughty voice.

He glanced around expressively at our surroundings. "Fine court lady you are."

I picked up my green skirts and gave them a little shake. "It's what's in my heart that makes me fine," I said. "Thank you for the dance. And for your promise."

He walked me slowly to the door. "Are you sure you don't need an escort?"

"Sure."

He opened the door, glanced outside as if to check for immediate danger, then gave me a nod of farewell. "Then go quickly. And take care."

I nodded in response, and slipped out into the summer night. After the heat and noise of the hall, the air outside seemed wonderfully cool and quiet. My hard-heeled shoes made a loud tapping noise across the cobblestones, but I was the only source of sound, the only source of movement, in the whole courtyard. Even the moon seemed breathless, watching me with her round open mouth. She seemed astonished that, after the events of the past few days, she could actually see me smiling.

FAR TOO EARLY the next morning, the regent expressed a desire to see me.

Cressida carried the news in along with a breakfast tray, hours before I was ready to get up and consider the world. "You don't look like you've been in bed long," she commented as I glumly spooned up some fruit and cream.

"Four hours, maybe," I said. "What does Matthew want?"

"The lady Greta did not share that information with me," she said. "I think perhaps your blue dress. It makes you appear sober."

"If I look at all like how I feel this morning, anything would make me appear sober."

I bathed and dressed as quickly as I could, and, after a glance in the mirror, decided the smallest application of cosmetics would not come amiss. Therefore, it was close to an hour later before I made my appearance in Lord Matthew's somber, book-lined study. I was surprised to see Kent there as well as his father. The two of them were engaged in a low-voiced conversation when I entered the room, which they broke off when they saw me. Kent's eyes went instantly to my tired face, and the smallest smile crossed his own. He knew my night habits.

Lord Matthew, of course, was not smiling. "Coriel. Please sit. We have some things to discuss."

I flicked a glance between the two men, but settled my gaze on the regent. "Yes?" I said cautiously.

Matthew was studying some papers before him, which I took to be letters. "I believe I told you some time ago that Ordinal of Wirsten is planning to attend my nephew's wedding. He will arrive today and stay with us a week or so after the ceremony. He has not visited Castle Auburn in nearly five years, so this is a great mark of favor. I want you to be especially polite to him while he is here."

I sat up straighter in my chair. "I always strive to be polite to all your guests, Lord Matthew," I said in a level voice.

The regent looked at me with those completely humorless eyes. "Sometimes with better results than others," he said dryly. "You did not charm Hennessey of Mellidon as I had hoped. I had wished to cement an alliance between our provinces, but he has instead chosen to marry a girl not far from his brother's court. A mistake, I think, but I suppose there are Mellidon lords to placate."

"And is Ordinal of Wirsten someone to placate as well?" I asked sweetly.

"He is someone to court," Matthew said bluntly. "His cousin is viceroy but relies heavily on Ordinal for advice. Ordinal has seen two kings and a regent sit on the throne in Castle Auburn, and he knows the value of peace in the realm. He is a strong voice of reason—but he has been outspoken in his criticism of the prince. He is one of the best allies we could find if we could win him completely to our side."

I glanced at Kent but he was watching his father; he would not

meet my eyes. If Ordinal of Wirsten had lived long enough to see
Bryan's grandfather on the throne, he must be as old as my grandmother. "I just want to make sure I perfectly understand you," I
said in a reasonable voice. "You are hoping to make an alliance—a
wedding—between me and Lord Ordinal? Is he looking for a wife?"

Matthew looked surprised, as if he could not believe I was so
stupid I needed things put into plain words. "Yes, of course, a
marriage is what I am after," he said. "And I know Ordinal is
looking for a bride. He's been haunting Tregonia ever since his wife
died six months ago."

"What makes you think he would be interested in me?"

Now Matthew did smile, though it was not a particularly pleasant
expression. "Your face—your lineage—and your dowry," he said.
"It's rare that a young woman so winningly combines all three."

At that, Kent's eyes did flicker from his father's face to mine,
more in astonishment than complicity. From Matthew, that was a
compliment of fawning proportions. He had never said anything so
approving to me in my life.

"Then no doubt he will be most ready to fall in with your
schemes," I said, earning another quick look from Kent and a second
smile from his father.

"Of course, you must do your part and treat him with particular
attention," Matthew added. "But he knows I am interested in this
alliance. I do not think he will be difficult to snare."

"And if my personal allure is not enough, I could mix a potion
or two," I offered generously. "I know a few spells of attraction."

Matthew frowned. "No, I would not like to see you resort to
that sort of trickery," he said. "Your name and your money should
be intoxication enough. And your charm of manner, of course."

I rose to my feet, even though he had not dismissed me yet,
because I was not sure I could carry on even a few more sentences
of this conversation without screaming. "Well, I shall do what I can
to make his visit here memorable," I said.

Matthew nodded and said, "Good, good," but Kent at last turned
his eyes my way. He knew me well enough to distrust my meekness,
well enough to guess that my unforgettable behavior might not be

all that the regent hoped. But I would have to be very careful. If I were to be banned from the court for life, I wanted it to happen after Elisandra's wedding. Something told me I had to be present for that.

IN THE NEXT few days, hundreds of guests arrived at Castle Auburn. I had never seen the castle so full, or so busy, not even the previous year at the grand summer ball. But the marriage of the man who was to be king—this was not something even the nobility had a chance to witness often in one lifetime. No one wanted to be left out.

There were seemingly hundreds of events filling up every minute of those next seven days. We had breakfasts in the garden, musicales in the salon, nightly theater performances in the ballroom, which had been transformed into a stage. The ladies played genteel games on the south lawns; groups of men left every day on organized hunts. Every dinner was more sumptuous than the last, every new arrival more glittering. I could not imagine that the castle could hold one more soul.

Ordinal of Wirsten had arrived the very evening of the day of my conversation with Matthew. I was not surprised to find him my dinner partner that night, and less surprised to find Greta sitting across the table from me so she could watch my every move. Ordinal was exactly what I had expected him to be, an aging, powerful man of no charm or subtlety, so convinced of his own importance that it did not occur to him to wonder if others found him quite so magnificent. Oddly enough, I did not dislike him; I was relieved that he had no sensibilities that my behavior might offend. I was also relieved that he was unlikely to notice how completely disinterested I was in him, so he would not be complaining to Matthew of my attitude. I treated him civilly, did not pay much attention when he talked, and never gave him a second thought when he was not in my immediate vicinity.

Other guests, as far as I was concerned, were equally unwelcome. Megan of Tregonia, for instance, was very much in evidence from the moment she arrived at the castle. She had improved greatly in appearance since I had first noticed her four years earlier. She was still pale and, to my way of thinking, vapid, but she had developed a certain flickering presence that caught men's attention whenever she walked into a room.

Nearly every time I saw her, she was hanging on Kent's arm, or seated beside him at the dinner table, or turning a corner to conveniently step into his path. Judging by the expression on his face and his unfailing courtesy, he was always pleased to see her. I spent a great deal of effort convincing myself that his manner was only polite, and that he liked her no more than I did.

Though it was nothing to me whom Kent did and did not like.

Also at the castle for these heady days were several other nobles I had met in the past, and Marian and Angela were often paired with some of these lesser lords. Indeed, more than once I saw Angela smiling decorously at Lester of Faelyn, who was highly eligible, and flirting madly with his cousin Jude, who was not. Marian had already been unofficially betrothed to Holden of Veledore, but that announcement was not to be made until after the prince's wedding, so she had been instructed to spread her favors around. She did so, but not too willingly; she had formed a real attachment to the handsome young lord, and I wished her all the best. I had already made up a wedding kit for her, filled with herbs for happiness, serenity, and fertility. I did not think she could want for more.

Elisandra walked through these final seven days as a dreamer only lately wakened from her bed. She was much sought-after and constantly being pulled from one conversation to grace the participants in another. She could not speak more than five sentences to someone without being interrupted by someone else who absolutely had to have her attention. She smiled faintly and impartially at everyone, extended her hand to be kissed a hundred times a day, graciously accepted good wishes from obsequious strangers, and seemed to satisfy everyone's notion of a fairy-tale princess.

But I thought she looked paler and more ethereal with every passing day. I thought she had given herself up to the reaching hands and insincere embraces with the hope that so much contact, so much squeezing and pressure and stroking, would wear her away so that, by the time the day of her wedding dawned, there would be nothing left of her at all.

During this week, Bryan and Elisandra were seldom together in the same room—seldom at the same event, except for dinner. He rode all day in the hunt, and in the evenings gathered with his uncle and the other lords to discuss politics in one of the libraries, when she was listening to music in the salon. Even over dinner, though they sat side by side, they rarely exchanged a word. Of course, they were attended by a succession of important nobles to whom they had to give all their attention, but to me it seemed more deliberate than that. They had nothing to say to each other. I had long suspected that Elisandra despised Bryan, but I could not believe that he, that anyone, could feel for her anything except a famished fascination. And yet he sat beside her and ignored her; he could not have seemed less interested in marrying her if she had been a gilt and onyx statue set beside him to pretend to dine.

Which did not augur well for the success of their marriage. But then, nothing did.

ALONG WITH THE nobles, aliora came to the castle during that busy week in high summer.

I had asked Jaxon once how many aliora there were in captivity, expecting a rough estimate, and he had surprised me by giving me names. One hunter had captured ten aliora in his lifetime, who had been sold to the viceroy of Tregonia and his lords; another hunter had captured sixteen, and these had been parceled out to the lords in Chillain and Wirsten. Jaxon himself had snared thirty, all of whom had been bought by the residents of Castle Auburn or sold at Faelyn Market to nobles whose names Jaxon could still recite. A handful of others had successfully trapped one or two aliora and sold them for fabulous sums. Of the sixty-seven captured, five had escaped and eight had died in the service of their human masters. Nine, now that Andrew was dead.

Fifty-three aliora in captivity. One night, uninvited, I went up to the slave quarters at the top of the castle and crept through the room of sleeping creatures. I had sprinkled myself with siawort, which did not exactly confer invisibility but tended to distract the watcher's gaze and made him look the other way involuntarily. No one stirred as I passed through the room, though the humming sounds of their musical dreaming paused and altered as I crept past. I had to step carefully, for though the aliora were sleeping two and three to a bed, there were still a dozen on the floor.

All in all, I counted fifty-three bodies. Every single one of the captured aliora was in Castle Auburn for my sister's wedding.

I stood there for a moment in the middle of the musical, moonlit room and counted again. Fifty-three. I wished with all my heart that it had been fifty-four.

Stealing from the room, I made my way down to the lower reaches of the castle, out the broad front doors and into the warm, scented night. I exchanged absentminded greetings with the guards and strolled over to the fountain. It had been strung with colored lights, candles inside of multihued glass globes. It looked gaudy and festive under the still night sky. I perched on the edge and dabbled my fingers in the water. But it was late and I was not in the mood to swim.

"I thought you had given up your nocturnal rambling," Kent said. I looked up in some surprise to see him standing before me. I had not heard him approach across the cobblestones, and he did not usually move so quietly. Or perhaps I had been too deep in thought to have heard anyone. "I have wandered the grounds for three nights running and not come across you."

I pulled my skirts aside so he could sit next to me, and he did, settling his long frame easily on the cool stone. "And what has driven you out to roam the castle at night?" I asked.

"Questions that have no answer, puzzles that have no end," he said most unhelpfully.

"You have not convinced Elisandra to run away with you, I see," I said.

"No. I did try, though."

I glanced over at him, my brows high over my eyes. "You *did*? When was this? She said nothing to me."

"A few days ago. Offered her the sanctuary of my estates if she wanted it—and the protection of my name if she wanted *that*, though there were no conditions. She could marry me or not, and still live on my property. But she refused me."

I inspected him by the jaunty colors of the overhead lamps. He looked both indifferent and weary, as if he had cared too long about something he no longer had a hope of changing. "I think better of you," I said.

"That's why I did it."

"So, what did she say? What reason did she give?"

He smiled faintly. "That I had better uses for my life than to throw it away protecting her."

I thought that over. "A noble reason, I suppose," I said slowly. "But I would rather she wasted your life than ruined hers."

He gave me a sardonic bow from the waist. "I shall try not to be insulted by that."

"I'm sorry. It's just that—what will become of her? I dread this marriage. And I know she does."

"She will not admit that. She told me she knows what she's doing. She seemed very calm about it."

"Elisandra is always calm. That is no way to gauge."

"Perhaps she thinks it will not be so bad—not much different than it is now."

I stared at him. "She will be *married* to him. Sharing his *bed*. Forgive me for disagreeing, but I think that is much worse."

Kent glanced at me, looked away, glanced back. "Last night," he said slowly, "Bryan took to his bed a young lady traveling in the entourage of Megan of Tregonia. Not a noblewoman, mind you, but not a servant, either. She was sent on her way this morning."

I could not speak for the shock. I had no illusions about Bryan's virginity, not after the episode with Tiatza last summer. Still, I had hoped for some fidelity to a bride so beautiful as Elisandra.

Kent continued, "Elisandra knew about the episode. She knows about countless others. I think she thinks perhaps he will not make conjugal demands upon her."

"He must," I said through a strangled throat. "He must have a legitimate heir."

Kent nodded sharply twice. "Then perhaps once she has produced this heir, he will ask nothing more of her. I think that is what she hopes."

I passed a hand over my face. "But even so—he will have her watched closely. He will not want her to—to take lovers of her own. For any child born to the queen will be considered legitimate and a potential heir to the throne."

"I know," Kent said soberly.

I stared at him. "Then what kind of life is that for her? Ignored by her husband, surrounded by spies, unable to find a moment's affection for the rest of her life—"

"It is a life many of the noble ladies of Auburn endure," he said quietly.

I watched him for a long time in silence. The light from the red lamp overhead made the right side of his face look ruddy and jovial, but the reflections from the blue light gave his left cheek a solemn, brooding air. "This is my last summer at Castle Auburn," I said at last.

He nodded. "I know."

"How did you know?"

"You have been too unhappy here for too long. You do not like us."

"Some of you I like a great deal," I said in a voice scarcely louder than a whisper. "But living here is too painful. I do not think I could stand it another season."

"And then what becomes of Elisandra?" he asked. "If she does not have you to look forward to, what will she live for?"

"I'll work that out," I said.

"I think your uncle Jaxon can be counted on here," Kent said, his voice losing a little of its solemnity. "I'm sure Elisandra can persuade him to invite you both to Halsing Manor. He has much less interest in your political pretensions these days. He no longer cares if he pleases Bryan *or* my father."

"An excellent idea!" I approved, my own mood lightening a bit. "We shall stay there for months at a time, lolling about and reading badly written romances. We will grow fat eating all my uncle's food, and we will be so lazy that the aliora queen will beg Jaxon to send us home."

"It sounds idyllic."

"Perhaps we will allow you to come for a day or two, when we have grown bored with each other's company and require entertainment."

He smiled. "I was hoping you would invite me."

"But you must be amusing," I warned him, "or we will not let you stay for long."

He stood up and held out his hands to me. I allowed him to pull me to my feet. "People do not generally welcome me because I am amusing," he said regretfully. "It is because I am sober and well reasoned and do not make hasty judgments that people seek my company."

"Then perhaps we can have you settle our disputes over which color of embroidery thread looks best in a certain pattern, and ask you to determine who has been cheating at cards."

"Ah, there I am your man. There I am exactly what you are looking for."

He had not released my hands. I did not want to pull away, and I did not want to ask him to let me go. I stared up at him in the colorful dark and could read nothing in the patchwork of his face.

"And don't bring Megan with you when you come," I said suddenly.

He laughed out loud, clearly caught by surprise. "You need have no fear of that," he said cheerfully. "I will not marry her if you do not marry Ordinal of Wirsten."

"Then we have a bargain," I said dryly. "I think I will marry no one, for marriage does not seem like such a good arrangement to me."

He looked down at me, and I wondered what secrets my face revealed under the gaily colored lamps. "That would be too bad," he said. "Would you not marry even for love?"

"Love does not seem to bring anyone much happiness, as far as I have observed. So I think the lesson learned is never to love."

"The lesson is to love wisely," he replied.

"I'm not sure that is possible, either," I said.

"You're cynical tonight," he said.

"Sad."

"I wish I could cheer you."

I smiled faintly. "Study your juggling and your sleight of hand. Then you can cheer me when you visit us at Jaxon's."

"I meant, tonight."

I was silent a moment. He still had not dropped my hands, and it amazed me how desperately I did not want him to let me go even now. "I cannot be cheered tonight," I said finally. "I can only be distracted."

"Comforted?" he suggested and slowly, as if waiting for a protest that did not come, he drew me into his arms. I leaned against his chest and his arms wrapped around me. I felt safe and warm and hopeful as I had not felt in weeks. I turned my face into the cloth of his shirt and felt the tears rise. I knew that I would not be able to stop them, and knew that he would feel their wetness through the cotton to his skin, and knew he would know why I was crying and that he would not care. We stood embraced that way for minutes, hours, I could not guess how long. I cried and he held me and neither of us spoke a word.

The following morning, just four hours after dawn, my sister Elisandra married Prince Bryan of Auburn.

15

We were up at dawn, seemingly hundreds of us gathered in Elisandra's room to make her ready for the wedding. In addition to Elisandra and me, the room was filled with Greta, Angela, Lady Sasha, Cressida, two other aliora women, Daria, the castle seamstress, two of her assistants, and countless other servants coming and going at someone's command. We needed food, hot water, new hairpins, more thread, a completely different petticoat than the one that had been specially sewn for the gown because suddenly it had acquired a rip along the hem. We needed hair ribbons, pearl rings, net gloves, silk shoes—all of which had been procured in advance, of course, all of which had mysteriously been mislaid. I never saw such a whirlwind of energy and purpose, such moments of hysteria and hilarity, and all in one confined space. Through all the commotion, Elisandra stood calm, almost unmoving, arms extended as the women dressed her, head tilted as they combed her hair. She looked serene, at peace, unmoved and rested, and no one would have suspected that she had not slept for even an hour the night before.

I happened to know this, because I had come directly up to her room after leaving Kent at the fountain. I had meant just to check and make sure she was sleeping, and offer to keep her company if she was not, but in fact, she was not in her bed. She was nowhere in her rooms at all. I quickly searched my own apartments, just in case she had fallen asleep in my bed, awaiting my return, but she was not there, either.

Had she sought solace with her mother? With Cressida? I had never known her to go to the aliora for refuge, but then, she probably did not know how often I frequented that high, crowded chamber. Had she run away? Unlikely as it seemed, I hoped for the last possibility; but just in case she planned to return, I went back to her room and curled up in her bed.

I was dozing when, not long before dawn, I heard her enter. "Where have you been?" I demanded to the shadow in the dark.

"Corie?" she asked, her voice unsurprised. "Light a candle."

I complied, and she crossed the room to drop onto the bed beside me. "You've been gone all night," I complained. "Where have you been?"

She made an indecisive gesture with her hand. "Checking on things. The flowers in the chapel. The food in the kitchen. The arrangements in the royal suite. Everything I could think of."

"You should have been sleeping," I scolded.

"I couldn't sleep. How long have you been here?"

"A couple of hours."

"Did you need me for something? I'm sorry I was gone."

I sat up, pulling the covers around my waist. Did *I* need something—? "I came to talk to you," I said slowly. "To tell you—if you don't want to marry Bryan, there are options. I have skills that will allow me to start a practice in any town. We could bring your clothes and your jewels and sell them on the road. That would give us enough money to get started. And then we could rent a small house in some little village where nobody knows your name, nobody knows mine. We could live that way. No one would ever be able to find us."

"Corie." She leaned over and put a hand on my cheek, as if to reassure herself that I was real, as if marveling that such a miracle could have transpired when she was not paying attention. "What a thing to offer me. I am touched and grateful. But I will not allow you to give up your life for mine."

That was what she had told Kent; and I gave her the answer I had given him. "Better to do that than see yours ruined."

She dropped her hand. "I'll be fine. I know what I'm doing."

"He'll destroy you," I whispered.

"I don't think so," she said.

"He destroys everything."

"I'll be safe," she said.

"If you ever change your mind," I said. "At any time. Married to him or not. Come to me, and I'll make a home for you."

Now she leaned forward again, this time to kiss me on the cheek. "I'll remember that," she said.

I don't know if I would have repeated my arguments, useless though I knew them to be, but at that moment, there was a brisk knocking on the outer door followed immediately by Greta's entrance. Elisandra had closely timed her return to her room. She had known when her mother would arrive to begin the day's ablutions.

After that, of course, there was no time for private conversation. The room filled with women, and I was sent off on my share of errands. Angela, who was dispatched along with me to track down the errant petticoat, seemed as delirious as if the wedding were her own. "Isn't this exciting?" she exclaimed more than once. "Your sister is marrying the prince!"

Although Elisandra was the key player in the upcoming tableau, eventually the rest of us had to attend to our own toilettes. While Daria continued fussing over Elisandra, the aliora helped the rest of us dress. I wore a deep-hued gown of gorgeous cinnamon, which brought out the rich colors of my skin and my hair, while Angela was lustrous in shimmering gold. The hues provided a dramatic foil for Elisandra's dress of antique lace, layer upon layer of fragile web-like fabric the exact color of yellowed ivory. Greta had sniffed and said we were dressed for an autumn wedding, not a summer one, but I had felt the colors were appropriate for the event, which seemed to me to mark the withering end of a bitter season.

Greta and Lady Sasha were dressed in much livelier colors, ame-
thyst and sapphire, joyous jewel tones. I wondered how anyone could
find this an occasion to celebrate.

Once we were all dressed, we observed the ritual that, among
the highborn and the low, was common between the bride and her
attendants. One by one, we approached Elisandra and gave her a
simple gift, something of personal significance, though it need not
be expensive. Angela, for instance, gave the bride a handkerchief
embroidered on every square inch with intertwined *E*s and *B*s. Lady
Sasha gave her a prayer book to kiss when she spoke her vows. Greta
gave her a simple locket in the shape of a heart, on a chain so
long that the pendant slipped out of sight into the décolletage of
the dress.

"A heart so you know my heart goes with you," Greta said,
kissing Elisandra on the cheek and wiping her own eye with one
gloved finger. I had never seen Greta cry before. I tried not to
stare, though I found myself uncharitably wondering if the emotion
was real.

When it was my turn to give my sister a gift, I handed her a
small, flat sachet bag made of white silk and lace. "Slip it into your
bodice, next to your heart," I told her.

She did so, giving me a quizzical look. "And what magical herbs
have you mixed in this little bag?"

I smiled. "Too many to name."

"What are they meant to bring me?"

I came close enough to touch her, laying one finger upon her
lips for each gift I had given. "Courage. Strength. Protection." I
dropped my hand and leaned in to whisper in her ear. "Love." I
kissed her on the cheek and backed away.

Greta glanced around the room as if she had never seen it before,
as if she would never see it again. "Are we all done here?" she asked.
"Then it is time to go."

Greta, Angela, and Lady Sasha were already outside the door
when Cressida stopped Elisandra with a hand on her arm. "I wish
you would take a gift from me as well, Lady Elisandra," the
aliora said.

"Gladly," Elisandra said. "But your good wishes are enough."

The others were in the hallway. I could hear their high voices and nervous laughter, but I stayed to watch this exchange. Cressida handed Elisandra a small net bag tied with a bit of string—a sachet, much like mine, but less fancy.

"It is something the aliora keep beside them at all times, even in captivity. I have my own bag, that I carry in my pocket by day and place under my pillow at night."

Elisandra took the sachet and sniffed at it before tucking it into one of her dripping lace sleeves. "And what is the herb, and what will it bring me?" she asked gently.

"It is a common flower, found on the forest floor. You have another name for it, but we call it haeinwort. It is said that, when you are lost or confused, you need merely take a breath of it, and it will remind you who you are. It brings you back to yourself."

Elisandra smiled. "Then, as my life becomes so strange and so demanding, I will welcome such a gift. I am sure I will often want a simple way to come back to myself. Thank you, Cressida."

"You're welcome, my lady."

But I knew haeinwort, and I knew Cressida was not telling the truth. Oh, some herbalists did tell you that its secondary benefit was restorative, that it would help you focus your mind and, as Cressida said, "bring you back to yourself." But it was primarily sold as a more active and optimistic drug: It conferred hope. It was a hedge against despair. I could well believe that all the imprisoned aliora needed such a potion, but I was amazed that Cressida had found the resources to produce such a charm for Elisandra. For it was *not* a common flower, and Cressida did *not* live in the forest where she might harvest it for herself. My only guess was that she had given her own portion to Elisandra, deeming that the bride would need it more than she.

"A generous gift," I said to the aliora, meeting her gaze with a level look. She gave me a small, private smile; she knew I was witch enough to understand the symbolism.

"The lady has always been generous to me," she replied. "Good luck to you all."

*   *   *

THE CHAPEL WAS full to overflowing. Before we began our ceremonial procession down the center aisle, I peeked in through the back door to get a glimpse of the throng. The audience was arranged by rank, all the great nobles sitting in the front pews and the lesser gentry behind them. You could have done a genealogy chart of the eight provinces just by writing down who sat where to observe the wedding.

Bryan, Kent, and Holden of Veledore were waiting for us outside the chapel door, as were Roderick and Damien. Greta reared back in dismay when she saw the latter additions to the party.

"What are *they* doing here? This is a wedding, not a brawl."

"My personal guard goes with me everywhere," Bryan replied coolly. "What better time to make an assault on the prince than when he is at his most happy—and his most unguarded?"

"Fine, very well, then, at least he gives you some consequence. But this little man—your taster—"

Bryan regarded her out of very measuring eyes. "The ceremony is sealed with wine and sealed with water," he said. "I do not put anything in my body that has not been tested first."

I wondered, not for the first time, if Bryan had any idea how many slow-acting poisons were available to do him in long after Damien had survived the first few bites. Now did not seem like the time to bring it up.

"You arrogant boy," Greta hissed. "You will make a fool of yourself and my daughter before every noble of the eight provinces if you do not even trust yourself to take a drink of the wedding wine."

"I will not, however, make a fool of myself before you, if you make one more comment," Bryan said suavely. "My guard will be happy to escort you from the chapel if you feel you cannot observe my actions."

At that, Greta blanched and fell silent. This was the grandest day of her life, and even to prevent Bryan from disgrace, she would not say another syllable and run the risk of missing it.

"Mother, it's fine," Elisandra said, patting Greta kindly on the back. "Damien will taste for both of us. He protects me as well."

Greta turned huge eyes her daughter's way. You could just see the words shouting in her head: *But you do not need protection in such a setting!* But not for the world would she utter the words.

"So, my bride, are we ready?" Bryan said, addressing Elisandra for the first time, and in a jaunty voice that was somehow very disturbing. It was as if he had, within seconds, laid aside his icy mood and assumed a jocular one. It made him seem unstable—a little frightening.

Elisandra did not seem put off. She nodded serenely and laid her hand upon his crooked arm. "Ready, my prince," she said.

And, two by two, we entered the chapel.

First, Greta and Lady Sasha entered, signaling to the musicians and flower bearers before hastily taking their seats in the back of the chapel. They would be the first ones out, rushing to the kitchens to give instructions to the cooks. Once the music started, and the flower bearers had tossed rose petals down the center aisle, Bryan and Elisandra entered. Kent and I followed, and Angela and Holden came behind us. Damien and Roderick formed the last pair, an unconventional couple to trail behind this grand procession.

The ceremony itself seemed endless. I had been to my share of weddings—most of them, it is true, the rough-and-tumble, three-quick-vows affairs that you would most often witness in the village—but none which was as interminable as this one. The four attendants were required to speak up at various points during the ceremony, stating our belief in the rightness of the marriage and the fidelity of the two people most involved. I managed to say my pieces on cue without choking on the lies, despite the fact that my mind had not taken in a single word the priest said before he looked at me and asked, "And do you, Lady Coriel, affirm this?" Beside me, Kent's responses were solemnly spoken. Bryan and Elisandra answered every question with clear voices that must have carried to the back of the room.

Three times the union had to be sealed with wine and water. I was alert enough to pay attention to these interludes, which Bryan obviously had discussed beforehand with the priest, for they were handled very smoothly. Beside him on a small, lace-covered table, the priest had set a pitcher of water and a bottle of wine. As we watched, he recited each of the three vows, pouring the liquid from the containers to the silver goblets. He asked Bryan and Elisandra to swear their fidelity. They did. Then he sipped from each goblet.

"True in water, true in wine," he said. "So let the witnesses attest." He handed each goblet first to Damien, who took a shallow swallow from each. Angela and her partner next were proffered the drinks, then Kent and me. Elisandra drank from the cup after I did. The priest took his time making the circuit, so that perhaps seven minutes had passed between Damien's taste and the time Bryan brought the cup to his lips. That was a shorter lag than the one that occurred at every meal, but evidently long enough, for Bryan did not hesitate to take the cup and drink from it.

Elegantly done, I thought, and admired the priest for his diplomacy. Then I drifted into my haze again, unable—unwilling—to focus on the events unfolding before me. My back ached from standing so long. My feet hurt in the new, tight shoes. I wanted this hour to be done with, this day to be erased from the calendar. I wanted to be anywhere but here.

"And do you, Lady Coriel, affirm this?" the priest asked me.

"Yes, Holy Father, I do."

Once the ceremony finally proved to be finite, the bride and groom made the traditional parade up and down the aisles. I had not thought that, in a wedding of nobles, the audience would observe the ritual of throwing gifts at the newlyweds, but I was wrong. The air glittered with tossed diamonds and lesser jewels; I heard the sweet clink of gold as bags of coins fell to the floor and spilled onto the stone. Had I known, I would have brought another sachet with me, to untie and sprinkle at my sister's feet. I would have liked to seed her fortune with the treasures I had given to Cloate and his wife.

Finally Bryan and Elisandra exited the chapel, arm in arm, on their way to the great ballroom which, for a few hours, would be the scene of their reception. Greta and Lady Sasha had already hurried out, but I felt no need to rush. The next few hours would be deadly dull, as the prince and princess sat upon large thronelike chairs and every single guest came forward to offer congratulations. Nothing for the rest of us to do but mill about and sip from the wine that the servants would carry through the room.

This in fact was what we did for the next three hours. Angela and Marian and I found a place in the back of the room to watch the currents of the crowd and make admiring or spiteful comments about the gowns the other women were wearing. Megan of Tregonia, for instance, was dressed in a daring gold dress that showed off both her complexion and her figure, but the three of us chose to find it ill-suited for her on counts of color as well as cut. The fact that she attached herself to Kent early in the afternoon and looked like she might stay sutured to his arm for all eternity did not endear her or her clothing choices to me, either.

It was not to be hoped that we could entirely escape notice for the whole afternoon, which was intended, after all, as a social gathering. In fact, Angela left us for a good half hour to flirt with Lord Jude, while Marian and I endured the company of Ordinal of Wirsten for even longer. He had been stalking the room when we first arrived, clearly hunting for someone, and I had had to go to extreme shifts to keep my back to him for as long as possible. But, as I expected, he eventually tracked me down.

"A fine business, this," he said, after greeting both of us with brusque, insincere compliments. "A wedding's a good thing. Ties everything together."

"A good wedding's a good thing," I said.

"Every wedding's the same," he said. "You may bargain for more or less land when you arrange the marriage portions. You may marry a girl with connections to the squire or connections to the king. That's your own business. But once you're home in your house, no difference. A man's a man, a woman's a woman. Every marriage is the same."

I wanted to contest that hotly—*surely* a union for love brought more joy to it than one for position—but he was far more experienced than I was in this arena. For all I knew, he was right. Maybe there was neither magic nor mystery. Maybe there was only an exchange of properties and the sober, unexciting business of begetting heirs.

I forced myself to smile. "Well, you have been married three times yourself, Lord Ordinal," I said, for I had learned this bit of information during our first conversation. "You should be the expert."

He looked surprised. "Nothing to be expert about. Everyone's born the same way, knowing the same things. Not something to make a fuss about the way all those"—he seemed to search for a word opprobrious enough to convey his meaning—"those poets do."

I tried a flirtatious glance, just to see if he'd notice. "Sometimes women like all that fuss," I said. "Sometimes they like to think their lives are a little more—poetical."

He gave a sharp crack of laughter. "Yes, that's a woman for you. Nonsense to the core."

I couldn't stop myself. "And have you never been nonsensical? Just the tiniest bit? To make someone else happy?"

He finally seemed to understand my game, and he gave me a close stare. "Oh! Well. I can't write a poem, if that's what you mean. Can't get out one of those harps and play a song on it."

"Could you pick flowers from the garden?" I hazarded. "Bring a lady a gift of rubies just because they were her favorite gems?"

His gaze was unnerving. "I could do that. Do you prefer rubies?"

I gave a light laugh and turned my head away as if I was embarrassed. "Oh! Me! I wasn't talking about myself. I just wondered how you might be moved to treat *some* young lady—if you cared enough to win her heart."

"We have extensive gardens at Wirsten Castle," he said seriously. "More flowers there than you could pick in a year."

"You see?" I said, trying to keep the teasing note in my voice, though I was finding this conversation exceedingly tiresome. "You could be romantic if you wanted to."

Fortunately Angela drifted back to us a few minutes later, looking a little misty-eyed from her own, much more prosperous flirtation. She liked Ordinal; he reminded her of her father, and she knew much better than I did how to entertain him. So, I let the two of them talk while I spent a few minutes watching the activity in the room.

Nothing had changed since I had last paid attention. Bryan and Elisandra still sat on the two heavy, ornate chairs set up on a small dais at the far end of the room. The line of greeters was perhaps a hundred people long and moving very slowly. Every person in the eight provinces, or so it seemed, wanted to personally wish the prince and the new princess the very best. From this far away, I could only see Elisandra's coiled black hair; I could not make out the expression on her face. But I knew what it would be: tranquil, gracious, unwearied. She would thank everyone as if she meant it, and she would remember everything anyone said to her.

I could not see Bryan's face clearly, either, but even from this distance he looked flushed and overexcited. While I watched, he signaled Damien to bring him a glass of wine, which he drank in a few quick swallows. I wondered how many glasses he had already finished off. I wondered if Matthew, or Kent, or anyone else was paying attention.

Well, better perhaps if he drank himself sick this afternoon and at the banquet. Better if he slept and belched his way through his wedding night, through every night he shared his bed with Elisandra. No doubt she felt the same way.

As the long afternoon dragged to a hot close, I finally tugged Angela's arm, and she and Marian and I joined the reception line. We were nearly the last three to pay our respects to the newlyweds, first Marian, then Angela, then me.

I rose from my curtsey and went up on tiptoe to kiss Elisandra on the cheek. "Best of luck," I whispered. "You're a beautiful bride."

"Thank you," she said. Her smile seemed completely normal, but she did not lavish it upon me for long. She was already greeting the nobleman in line behind me.

I turned to the groom, extending my hand. "Congratulations, Prince Bryan. You have won the very best of your kingdom."

He caught my hand in an unexpectedly rough hold and pulled me unceremoniously toward him. I almost tumbled into his lap, and had to brace myself with a hand against his shoulder. "That's too tame a way to say hello to your brother-in-law!" he exclaimed. "Come, give me a kiss."

He tugged me into his arms and kissed me full on the mouth.

I did not struggle or scream, but I wanted to do both. He smelled like wine, he tasted like it. I could feel the heat of his skin through the plush pillows of his lips. I lay against him for a moment, so that my disgust did not immediately show, then I laughed and pushed myself away.

"No, no, brother Bryan, you do not want to ruin my chances with the other eligible men here," I said, freeing myself completely and stepping back. "What would Lord Ordinal think to see me flirting with the prince?"

"The prince flirts with all the pretty girls," Bryan said grandly. "That is why it is good to be prince!" He laughed loudly and took another swallow of his wine. I smiled, took a step backward, and then turned away as quickly as I could without appearing to run.

The first thing that caught my eye was the still, silent figure of the prince's personal guard, standing a few feet away from the throne and watching me, watching Bryan, watching Elisandra with an unwavering and unsmiling attention.

I turned away from him to see the prince's cousin also watching me, also wearing a stony, unreadable expression. I wondered who had displeased Kent—Bryan or me—and I walked by him without bothering to ask.

THE NEXT EVENT in the simply unending day was the banquet. This had been in preparation for more than two days, for there were literally thirty courses. Six kinds of meat, ten types of vegetables, fruits, cheeses, breads, pastries, cakes, pies. There was no way to sample even a small bite of everything that the servants brought around. The main dish—if one could be singled out from such an array—was a venison stew that was Bryan's favorite meal. He himself had hunted the deer that had been dressed and cooked to provide the basis for the stew, and Elisandra had stayed in the kitchen, at

Bryan's instruction, to make sure that the recipe was properly followed. I knew she had fretted for days over the preparation of this particular entrée, knowing how carefully Bryan would taste it as his first meal as a married man. I had worried with her—until I saw him at the reception, drinking so much wine that he would be unable to taste even the most flavorful combination of spices. Excellent or awful, Bryan would have no way of gauging the success of his favorite meal.

I was right about that. As always, Bryan was offered the first taste of the new course—which naturally ended up on Damien's plate, in Damien's mouth. Elisandra took a helping next, and the venison stew was presented up and down the high table before more dishes were brought around to the rest of us. I noticed, not to my surprise, that more men than women took large portions of this delicacy; it was a fairly hearty stew, with a gamy taste that some women could not abide. But I was a country girl and had grown up on such meals; I took a portion and ate it with relish.

There was more to come, of course—pigeon pie, baked chicken, pork in orange sauce, lamb and veal. Bryan (and Damien) took helpings of all of these as well, though Elisandra only tried the chicken. I was saving room for dessert, so I passed on all the other meats.

"An excellent pigeon pie," Ordinal commented to me, for, of course, he was seated beside me. "My cooks don't understand game birds—the meat's always overdone. This is just right."

"I believe there's a sauce specially made for the pie," Greta interposed helpfully, for, of course, she was seated across from us so she could supervise our romance. "I could ask our cooks for the recipe."

"Do that. Make sure Lady Coriel has time to study it," he said, and addressed himself again to the pie. Greta had to hide a smile of satisfaction. I had to hide an expression of disbelief.

"I'll certainly do that." Greta almost purred. "And just let me know if there's any other dish you particularly like."

"No, so far everything else has been ordinary enough," he said. "But I do like that pigeon."

Eventually we had all stuffed ourselves beyond the point of rational thought, and the servants had begun to clear away the dishes. More bottles of wine were brought out and set on every table; ewers of water were refilled. Matthew came to his feet and clapped his hands for silence.

"Friends—loved ones—noble gentry—I thank you all for coming here today to witness one of the greatest events of our times," he said in annoyingly pompous tones. "The wedding of a prince! The beginning of a new dynasty! The crowning of a new princess and the guarantee of new life and hope for our eight provinces!"

The crowd cheered. I thought perhaps Matthew himself had had a few too many glasses of wine. Once the applause died down, he proceeded in this vein for a few more fulsome sentences, then he raised his water goblet in a dramatic gesture.

"Long life and health to Princess Elisandra! Sealed by water!"

"Sealed by water!" the crowd roared back.

"Sealed by wine!"

"Sealed by wine!" the audience shouted. We all gulped down the appropriate liquids. Bryan, I noticed, raised his water glass politely when everyone else did, but did not bring it to his lips. The wine, however, he drained from the glass, which he then switched with the glass in Damien's hand, full except for the single sip taken by the taster.

Matthew was not quite done. "And to Prince Bryan, shortly to be our king! Long life and health to him! Sealed by water—sealed by wine!"

The regent proposed a few more toasts to lesser mortals, then Kent rose to his feet and made a few speeches of his own. After that, it was anybody's guess who would leap to his feet next, calling for the prosperity of Tregonia, the fertility of the Cotteswold farmland, the safekeeping of travelers who would be on the road tomorrow, the continuance of pleasant weather and the well-being of all our souls. After the first few toasts, I gave up on the "sealed in wine" part and only made my affirmations in water, because I knew one more swallow of alcohol would send me keeling over into Ordinal's lap. Many of the other ladies, Elisandra included, had reached similar conclusions and barely touched their wine for the rest of the evening. Most of the men, however, seemed to have no problem emptying their glasses for one toast and filling them for the next. Kent, I saw, was not one of them; he tasted his wine every time a new pledge was made, but the level in his glass barely dropped.

Just when I was beginning to think that the inexhaustible number of vows needing our endorsement would drain the castle of all liquid resources, there was a lull in activity. No one hopped to his feet to cheer on the proliferation of rabbits in Chillain or the perfection of the greenery in Faelyn.

Matthew rose somewhat unsteadily to his feet again. "The prince, the princess, and I ask you to join us now in the ballroom, where we will hear a symphony composed to commemorate this event. The orchestra is ready—let us all attend."

So, the whole mass of people transferred slowly from the dining room to the ballroom, where rows and rows of chairs had been set up facing a makeshift stage. The entire room had been festooned with streamers of white flowers, which scented the air with a sweet, wistful aroma; dozens of petals had floated down to land on the chairs and the stones of the floor, so many that we appeared to walk into the remnants of a summer blizzard. The musicians were tuning their instruments, a strangely discordant activity, and suddenly the last thing in the world I wanted to do was sit here through a long, pretentious concert. My head hurt, my stomach was complaining about too much food, and I didn't care much for formal music at the best of times. I sat in the very last row, thinking to make an early exit.

I glanced around the room as the other guests settled in, and realized that I was not the only one disinterested in this final segment of the celebration. At least a third of the people who had been present in the dining room were missing now, and I saw a few stragglers linger in the hallway and then turn away from the doors. Ordinal appeared to be one of those who had opted against further entertainment, for he was not beside me, and I did not spot him anywhere in the crowd. Angela had somehow eluded me as well.

Elisandra, of course, had no hope of escape—she and Bryan were seated in the very first row, facing the orchestra, forced to listen to every note of the composition written in their honor.

I did stay long enough to hear the first somber movement of the symphony, a slow, ponderous piece in a minor key. I supposed this symbolized the dreariness of their lives before they were joined in matrimony, but it did not make me eager to hear the rest of the music. It was having a soporific effect on the other guests as well, for I saw a few heads nod to one side, while a number of other bodies were slouched as comfortably as possible in the low chairs. Food, wine, and dull music; it would be a wonder if anyone was awake for the finale.

Eventually I rose to my feet and slipped noiselessly out the door. At last, at last, this long dreadful day was over—for me at least. I hurried through the quiet corridors, one hand pressed to my aching head, the other laid across my protesting stomach. I wanted nothing so much as to lie down and sleep away the rest of my life.

Once in my room, I lay down briefly, but my stomach was by this time in knots. "Please, no. Please, no. Please, no," I whispered over and over again, for more than anything in the world I hated to vomit. I curled up into a little ball on the bed, hoping the nausea would subside, but, of course, it did not. You couldn't eat and drink with such abandon for an entire day and not expect your body to revolt. I had three quick sessions over the chamber pot, and felt immensely better. After that, when I laid back down, I fell instantly into a blessed and dreamless sleep.

I WOKE ABOUT THREE hours later, at a time I judged to be about two in the morning. My head still echoed with the reminders of pain, and my stomach did not feel entirely normal, but all in all I did not feel so awful as I swung myself to a sitting position. I would have liked to go back to sleep, for I was tired to the bone; but there was much to be done, and this was the only night to do it.

I rose, cleaned myself up and combed my hair before changing into a simple, comfortable gown. By candlelight, I sorted through my satchel of herbs, then sifted a few into the pitcher of water that always stood on my bedside table. Eventually I poured the whole mixture into a large jug that I had stolen from the kitchen for this purpose. I sniffed at the opening—it could have been fruit juice inside—then stoppered the top. I quickly donned my shoes, and I was on my way.

I passed the silent castle corridors, where all signs of reveling had died down at least an hour ago. I heard nothing behind any of the closed doors; even the late-night arguers were too exhausted after this day to air their grievances. No one stirred in the servants' quarters, no one was up late browsing in the library. The first wakeful souls I saw were the two men on guard at the front door.

"Good evening to you!" I greeted them merrily. "And a long day of celebration it has been!"

"Good evening, Lady Coriel," one said.

The other, sounding just a little miffed, answered my second observation. "No celebrating for us. They said the prince was sending a keg of wine down to the guardhouse, but *we* don't get any. Oh, no, *we* can't drink on duty."

"That is a shame," I said sympathetically. "Can you have some berry juice? I brought some down with me, just in case they hadn't let you in on the festivities."

"Berry juice!" the first one repeated. These were men I was familiar with from the past two summers of late-night wandering. I had often brought them treats mixed by hand. "Like that stuff we had two weeks ago?"

"That was good," the second guard agreed.

I pulled out the stopper. "Hand me your canteens," I said gaily. "You can have as much as you like."

I poured out liberal portions and watched them drink, then poured them each a second helping.

"Save some for the gate guards," I laughed, when they would have taken more.

"But it's so good."

"If there's any left, I'll come back," I promised. Then I skipped down the steps, hurried past the fountain, and followed the flagged path all the way to the outer gate.

Shorro and Cloate were among the four men on guard there, and they all greeted me with enthusiasm. I had not seen the new husband since his wedding, so while I handed out my celebratory concoction, I asked how he was enjoying married life.

"*Don't* let him say a word, I beg you," Shorro interrupted before Cloate could answer. "All day long, constantly, we don't hear a word but how wonderful that woman is. Her cooking is so tasty, her temper is so kind, her loving is so sweet—I appreciate a good woman as much as the next man, but this woman, I swear, she has him bewitched. He's not a sane man anymore."

Cloate gave me that small, bashful smile that on him passed for exuberance. "I like married life just fine," he said.

"So, how was the prince's wedding?" Shorro wanted to know. "Grand? Exciting?"

"Interminable. Tedious," I corrected. "It took the entire day."

"And it'll take the entire night," was the guard's wicked response.

I smiled, though I did not want to. "Hush. You should not talk that way to the sister of the princess."

"You don't care how I talk," Shorro scoffed.

Cloate turned on him. "Well, still, you should treat her with some respect. Try to show you've got some manners, even if you don't."

That sparked a quick, halfhearted argument, which the rest of us ignored. The other two guards held out their canteens for more juice, and one of them asked me what activities were on the schedule for the morrow.

"I'm not sure," I said. "There's a hunt, I think, but not till late in the day. A lot of the guests will be leaving in the morning, so I understand. Pretty soon the castle will be empty again."

"Too bad," said the other, smothering a yawn. "I like it all stirred up like this."

"It has been fun," Shorro agreed, suddenly abandoning the fight with Cloate. "All those nice young ladies' maids from Tregonia—"

"Damn, Shorro, don't you ever think of another single thing?"

"What else is there to think of, I ask you?"

I laughed as the wrangling started again and held up my free hand for peace. "Goodnight, my friends, it was a pleasure to see you all again. I'll come visit again some other time."

They all called out their goodnights as I strolled away. Pausing by the fountain, I perched on its stone ledge and rinsed the jug thoroughly in the falling water. The multicolored lamps of previous evenings had not been lit tonight, but I could see well enough by the quarter moon that lay with a supine, lazy abandon on the velvet cradle of the night. The light breeze was warm and sultry, high-summer air, but I could detect the faint, crisp current of fall underlaying the heat. Autumn soon. I would not be sorry to see it come.

I lingered at the fountain no more than five minutes before rising and heading back to the castle, back up the grand stairway. The two guards stationed at the door were already asleep.

16

I ran down the main corridor, up the back stairs, up every stairwell to the top story of the castle. Here, as always, there was the muted hum and click produced by aliora sleeping. The sound was quieter than usual this night, due to exhaustion, I supposed. The aliora had been kept busy from sunup till midnight, dressing the grand ladies, decorating the vast halls, serving wine, serving the banquet. They would have tumbled into their crowded beds the very minute they had been released from duty.

I stood for a moment outside the curtained doorway, listening to the low music of communion. Then I lifted the gold key from its hook outside the door and stepped inside the room.

I moved among the sleeping bodies till I found the form I wanted. I had never tried to rouse a sleeping aliora; I did not know if they screamed or started as they were jerked to wakefulness. I placed my hand on her shoulder and shook her slightly. "Cressida," I said.

She came awake and to her feet in one single, soundless motion. One moment, she was prone and unconscious, the next she was standing beside me, gaunt, silent, and questioning. Her eyes looked huge in the moonlight that filtered in through the window. She did not say a word.

I showed her the key, gripped between my thumb and forefinger. "Give me your hand," I breathed.

She merely stared at me and did not move.

Impatiently I reached for the chain that ran between the shackles on her hands. She crossed her wrists against her stomach and shook her head. "The guards," she said, her voice as low as mine. "At the door and at the gate."

"Sleeping," I said.

She stared even harder.

"I can unlock the shackles," I said. "I can get you to the outer gates. After that, I cannot help you. Can you make it from there?"

"All of us?" she asked.

"Every single one."

"What time is it?"

"About three in the morning. The human servants will be up in another three hours, but I doubt any of your masters will call for you for another half a day."

"Three hours would be enough to get us safely on our way."

"Then let us waste no more time," I said, and reached again for her chain. This time she let me pull her hands up so I could see the lock and insert the key in the small opening.

The first shackle split into two hinged halves and fell from her arm.

She smothered a small cry as the metal fell to the length of the chain and bumped against her thigh. The noise was so small I couldn't imagine that anyone else could hear it, but suddenly there was a stirring all around us. Heads rose from their mattresses, thin voices called out a series of questions.

"Be quiet," Cressida said, and there was no more noise. One by one, the other aliora in the room sat up or came to their feet, and every single one of them watched us.

"Your other hand," I said calmly, and she held that out to me. Within seconds, it too was freed from its shackle. Cressida gave her wrist one sharp shake, and the chain fell with a tiny clamor to the stone floor. Everyone in the room gasped or cried out, then a sudden deathly silence descended once more.

"Gather what you need," I said to Cressida. "And explain to the others that they can trust me. We must move quickly."

Some of them had already guessed, or convinced themselves to hope, that a rescue was in effect, and a half dozen aliora had already lined up before me with their wrists extended. I moved from one to the next as fast as I could, two quick turns of the key and the sound of falling metal. Around me I could sense hurried, purposeful movement as Cressida and the newly freed aliora bundled up clothes, shoes, water jugs, and other necessary items.

"I did not have time to steal food for you," I told Cressida over my shoulder. "I don't know that it is wise to take time to stop at the kitchen."

"We can forage. We can make it to the forest."

The last chain was undone; I had a pile of broken fetters at my feet. I turned to face Cressida again. "You will be on foot. They will have horses."

She smiled, a fey, peculiar smile I had never seen on her face before. I realized she had never before had a reason to exult before me. "We can blend with the land. When we are cautious enough, and clever enough, we can hide in an open valley and a man will ride right by us."

"Andrew could not," I said.

She pointed to the small tower of open handcuffs at my feet. "Metal interferes with our ability to move, to change, to grow invisible. Andrew was hampered. We will not be. They will not find us."

Another aliora came forward and put his hand on Cressida's arm. He said something to her—her name, I think, her true one—and added, "We must go."

"We must," I said, and led the way to the door.

That was a strange, perilous, and exhilarating journey through the silent, shadowy hallways of Castle Auburn. Never had any corridor seemed so long; never had my footsteps sounded so loud. Behind me, the parade of aliora was absolutely silent. If I had not glanced back from time to time, I would have believed they had all stayed behind, cowering on the upper story of the castle, afraid to trust me, afraid to run. But they followed me, all fifty-three of them, down the stairways, through the halls, into the grand foyer, and out the great doorway.

Where the two guards still slept, slouching against the doorframe. They would not believe, when they woke, that they had slept at all. Their dreams would be of brief, desultory conversations with their fellow guards, frequent glances at the sky to gauge the level of the moon, sips from their canteens, idle games of dice. They would swear they had been awake all night—these two here, the four at the gate. Six corroborating testimonies. Would they be believed?

We descended noiselessly down the broad steps, fanning out to move in a group across the courtyard, past the fountain, and up to the main gate. Cloate, Shorro, and their friends stood and crouched by the great stone archway, seemingly caught in a moment's brief inactivity. The aliora slowed and glanced doubtfully at the still figures, but I shook my head and strode on.

Out through the gate; the first steps toward freedom.

I was the first one to stop, but the fifty-three aliora streamed past me. Their pace picked up as their feet crossed that visible boundary from castle grounds to open land. I doubted they would stick long to the main road. It was man-made; it would interfere with their magic. They would drift onto the grass and the soil, melt into the groves of trees that dotted the countryside from here to Faelyn River. I did not think it would take them three hours to disappear. I thought it might take three minutes.

Only one aliora stopped beside me as I stood at that gate and watched them go. Cressida stood before me, placing her hands on either side of my face. With the restraint of the shackles lifted, her touch was even more powerful than usual; I felt the shock of her aura resonate through me, past my cheekbones, through my skull, down my spine. Heat rose along every inch of my skin. I expected my flesh to begin glowing.

"Thank you, Corie," she said in her sweet, grave voice. "You have given a gift even greater than you know."

I managed a smile, though I felt like sobbing. "Aren't you going to ask me why?" I said.

She shook her head. "I know why. You could not save your sister, and you had to save something."

I put my own hands up to touch the contours of her face. It seemed softer than my own, more springy, as if the skin was not laid over a structure of bone but a framework of twigs or vines or petals. "Even if I could have saved her," I said, "I would have done this. But this was the only night to try, when every aliora in the kingdom was gathered in one room."

She spread her fingers wider, taking in more of my face, sending tendrils of a heartfelt longing curling into my brain. "Come with us," she said suddenly. "To Alora. There is no winter there, no heartache, no illness, no despair. You will be loved and welcome all the days of your life. The trees will brush their hands through your hair to greet you in the morning and the birds will sing lullabies to set you dreaming at night. You will be at home. You will be content as you have never been."

It was not the words, it was the desire conjured up by her words. Especially for someone like me—who had had too many homes, half homes, partial lives spent between two entirely different worlds— her invitation was almost irresistible. To belong, to be beloved, to go always in sunshine and in peace in a place of eternal beauty . . .

"I have to stay here," I heard myself say, though the words were strangled and unconvinced. "I am not ready to leave the mortal realm."

"You could come back here anytime you chose," she said, her soft voice compelling, insistent. "You would be free to leave us and return whenever you wanted. We would not hold you."

I took a step back from her and her hands fell to her sides. "Not as we held you, in chains and against your will, but you would hold me," I said, my voice stronger. "I cannot go with you. There is too much unfinished business here."

She watched me gravely a moment in silence. I could no longer see any of the other aliora; I hoped she would be able to catch up with them. "Anytime you change your mind," she said. "We will welcome you gladly. We will make our home your home—I will take you in as my own daughter. We would celebrate to have you among us. You would be our communal joy."

"Thank you," I said, backing away still more. "Someday, perhaps—thank you. Now you must go forward, and I must go back. You must run—the others have already disappeared."

She smiled. "I will find them. We will reach Alora together in a few days' time. Thank you again, Corie. I have no stronger words than those."

"You do not need them," I said, and stepped back through the gate. Back into the world of men, safe from the siren call of the aliora. One more moment she watched me through that stone portal, then she lifted her hand in a gesture of farewell.

"I will look for you," she said, and turned on her heel. Though I watched as closely as the darkness would permit, I could not follow her more than three steps down the road. That quickly she blended with the night, or was absorbed into it; that completely was she gone.

I stood a few minutes with my sleeping companions, Shorro, Cloate, and the other guards, and allowed myself to feel a moment's comfort in their undemanding presence. They—had they been awake—would have welcomed me as surely as the aliora would; they would have offered me their flasks and allowed me to deal a hand of cards. They would take me in, they would amuse me and—if it were in their power—they would protect me from distress and calamity. I need not feel so bereft just because the aliora were gone. Love and friendship could still be found in the world.

It was warm out, but I suddenly shivered, and my stomach twisted violently once more to remind me of its unhappiness. I hurried back toward the castle, past the fountain, past the sleeping guards at the door, up all those flights of silent stairs. Back in my room, I threw up once more, then lay in bed a long time, shaking. It was nearly dawn before my eyes finally stayed closed and I drifted off to sleep. Had I known it would have taken so long to fall asleep, I would have sipped from the guards' canteens as I slipped past them. This was a night I could have used some easy dreaming.

*   *   *

AN ANGRY SHRIEK woke me late the next morning. My room was filled with lazy golden light, enough of it to let me know the hour was far advanced. For a moment I could not think why I was so tired and why I should feel such dread for the revelations of the day. Another cry in the hallway was answered by a series of shouts. I sat up in bed. Suddenly I remembered.

I did not trouble to dress before running to the door and sticking my head out. The hallway was filled with people milling uselessly about; I identified Greta and Daria and a few of the noble guests.

"What is it? What's wrong?" I called out. Daria hurried to my side.

"Such terrible things!" she exclaimed. "Everyone is sick and the aliora are missing and the regent is accusing one of the noble lords of having been careless with the keys—"

"What? What? Who's sick? And the aliora? They're *missing*? How can that be?"

Daria nodded vigorously. "That's what everyone wants to know! But all the shackles are in a heap on the floor of their room. Dirkson of Tregonia says Lord Matthew did it on purpose, and the prince wants to ride out after them, but he's so sick he can't get out of bed—"

That caught my attention. "Bryan's sick? What's wrong with him?"

"Some kind of problem with his stomach. The princess said he was up all night with—with unpleasant episodes," she ended delicately. Apparently she did not want to offend my sensibilities by saying the prince had been retching out his guts.

"How strange. I had a little trouble last night as well," I said.

She nodded again. "Yes, so did many of the guests. The regent and Lord Kent also were sick, though it seems the prince suffered more than anyone. He is still unwell this morning and cannot even get up. Although the princess says he is determined to ride in the hunt for the aliora—"

The aliora! If Bryan was truly too sick to ride, it was unlikely Matthew would organize a hunt in his stead—not that the regent wouldn't want the aliora back just as badly as Bryan would, he just wouldn't run the risk of leaving the castle if Bryan were truly ill. This would have bought the fugitives half a day, a day—perhaps their freedom. Although one of the other lords might easily organize the hunt instead—unless they were all too sick to ride—?

"Who else has been infected? Has Giselda been called in? Has she identified the illness?"

"She has been with the prince since early this morning, but she says she cannot tell what the disease is. He has a fever as well, and his face is beginning to show spots of red color."

"Huh," I said, thinking it over. Well, fever, nausea, rash—that could be any number of illnesses, some dangerous, some not. It seemed likely that one of our charming guests had ridden in from the outer provinces carrying a malicious germ which had infected the whole palace. I smiled to think that I had attributed to nerves and overeating my own "unpleasant episodes" of the night before.

"Do you think she needs my help?" I asked Daria. "Tell her I'm willing to join her if she wants my opinion. I have to dress first, but I'll be ready in a few minutes."

"Certainly, Lady Coriel."

I jerked a head at the knot of noblewomen still wailing and gossiping in the hall. "And what's all the shrieking about? Who was making such a noise before?"

Daria tried very hard to hide a smile. "That was my lady's mother. She learned that Cressida would not be available to dress her this morning. She was not very happy."

"I thought from the sound of it somebody must have died."

"No, but she is quite distressed."

"I guess you'll have to help her, then."

Daria's face showed a faint alarm. "I must return immediately to the princess," she said quickly.

I laughed. "So would I, if I were you. But first give Giselda my message."

I withdrew into my room and began to dress hurriedly. No Cressida to bring me warm bathwater, so I made do with the pitchers of cold water in the room and decided I would just have to wash my hair later. I braided it back from my face, put on a plain, serviceable gown, and sallied out into the castle to see what I could discover.

The knot of agitated noblewomen had dispersed so I had to go farther to find activity, but once in the breakfast room, I was in luck. Angela was there with her parents, and she immediately came over to join me.

"*Tell* me what's going on," I demanded in a low voice as we found a table somewhat apart from the crowd. I had never seen so many in the breakfast room at this hour. Apparently the disasters of the night before had thrown people from their usual routines and caused them to band together in confused, useless groups.

"You know about Bryan? And the aliora?"

"Yes, but just the barest outlines. Bryan is sick? Is it serious?"

Angela spread her arms. "Giselda doesn't seem so sure. He's been vomiting all night, and now he has a high fever and this black rash—"

"Black rash," I interrupted. "You mean black spots? In the center of red spots, or appearing all by themselves?"

"Black spots within red circles," she replied promptly, for of course she knew. "On his hands and his face and, curiously enough, on his feet. And even though he is burning with fever, his hands and feet are so cold to the touch that nothing they can give him will warm his toes and fingers."

Every word she said made my own skin grow colder. I could feel the prickles of fear and disbelief skittering across my scalp and down my spine. "His breathing?" I said, my own breath coming slowly and with difficulty. "Is he wheezing? Coughing?"

Angela looked at me wonderingly. "Just this morning, he started having trouble breathing," she said. "But Giselda seemed more concerned about the rash."

I nodded. I felt like a stone statue that had been set in a winter garden—chilled, frozen, unable to turn my head or lift a limb. "Is Damien ill?" I managed to ask.

Angela shook her head. "No, for he was the first one Lord Matthew checked on this morning when he learned about Bryan. Damien said his stomach hurt during the night, but by this morning he was fine."

I shook my head slightly, for that made no sense. "Are you sure?"

"Yes—well, it's not the sort of thing the regent would be mistaken about! So, Giselda thinks it's some pox from one of the low countries, though she hasn't seen it take quite this form before. She's been run completely ragged, poor thing, because, of course, Bryan's not the only one who's afflicted. But no one else seems quite as sick—only Goff of Chillain has a high fever, and no one but Bryan has a rash."

I had to think. I had to do something. Giselda had not recognized the symptoms. It was a low country import, well enough, but it was not a disease; it was poison. If treated immediately it could be counteracted, but if the rash had already appeared, it was probably too late for Bryan.

"Where is Lord Matthew right now?" I asked through stiff lips.

"In his conference room shouting at his guests," Angela said with a laugh. "Dirkson of Tregonia is *so* furious that his aliora disappeared into the night! He only has the three, you know, and he paid some unbelievable price for the one he acquired just last year. He's convinced Lord Matthew was somehow careless and let the aliora escape. And, of course, Lord Matthew will not take that kind of accusation calmly—"

I allowed myself, for just this minute, to be distracted from the larger problem. "And what does the regent think happened? How does he think the aliora got free?"

"*He's* blaming Thessala of Wirsten."

"I didn't think they had any aliora at Wirsten Castle."

"No, that's it exactly. Thessala is some kind of reformer who believes it's sinful to domesticate any wild creatures—aliora, hawks. I think she even has a problem with hunting dogs because she says they were originally wolves of the forest. Anyway, Matthew thinks she had something to do with releasing the aliora. But Thessala is denying it, and all the viceroys are arguing—at least they were. That was an hour or more ago—"

"And how did they get off the castle grounds? Does anyone know? Did they just walk out the gates?"

"That doesn't seem possible, since all six of the guards say they were alert and attending all night. Someone's checking the gardens for footprints but so far no one's found anything."

"You don't seem too upset," I remarked. "I mean, about the aliora. You liked that little Phyllery, didn't you?"

Angela nodded, her blue eyes sober and her pleasant face creased into a frown. "Yes, but— Actually, I'm sort of glad that they're gone. Poor Phyllery was the sweetest thing and I loved her to death, but she—she was so miserable. She would come into the room and sometimes I would just want to cry. You know how aliora can generally sort of heal you—lift your spirits—just by touching your hand? She would do that—she would *try* to do that—and it would just make me sad. I can't explain it. I hope they make it to safety. I don't think I want another aliora in my life."

This from Angela, the shallowest woman I'd ever met. I gave her a quick hug, which surprised her. "That's how I feel," I whispered in her ear. "But I thought I was the only one."

"I think my mother feels the same way, though she hasn't said so."

"Will there be a hunt?"

She shrugged. "Dirkson and Holden wanted to organize one, but they were arguing with Matthew about what road to follow. And with Bryan so sick some of the other lords thought it would be disrespectful to go off sporting. Then someone else said, 'It's hardly sport, I paid half my fortune for that aliora—' "

"So, it might be awhile before a hunt actually gets under way."

She nodded. "Of course, the aliora are on foot—"

"I know. Well, we'll just have to hope for the best."

She said, "For everyone." She looked significantly toward the open door, where Lord Matthew had just stalked in. He looked angry but under control, and the cadre of noblemen who followed him looked equally as stirred up. Angela lowered her voice and whispered in my ear, "I think this will be a strange day."

I agreed, stood back against the wall to escape the regent's notice, and eventually slipped from the room as unobtrusively as possible. I knew where the royal suite was situated, in the middle level of the main portion of the castle, but I had never been there. This was where Bryan had had his bachelor's suite, and where Lord Matthew and his son lived. I had never been invited to visit. The right wing was my territory, the right wing and the upper reaches of the castle—and the stables and the servants' quarters and the weapons yard. . . .

When I found the newlyweds' new quarters, it was full of people.

Elisandra was in one corner of the outer parlor, talking seriously with Giselda, while nearby hovered Daria, Greta, Lady Sasha, Giselda's assistant, and two of the kitchen servants who appeared to have been pressed into nursing duty. In another corner stood Kent, Roderick, Holden of Veledore, and some of the male servants to whom Kent appeared to be giving instructions.

Greta was the first one to see me, and she hurried over. "What are you doing here? There are too many busybodies interfering as it is. We don't need any more people cluttering up the room."

I stood my ground, trying to get Elisandra's attention. "I thought I could help Giselda. I thought I could take a look at Bryan."

Greta inhaled one scandalized breath. "An unmarried woman examining a sick man! Have you lost your mind? And you, a common witch woman, not trained like Giselda—"

"I know some things Giselda does not."

Greta shook her finger in my face. She was so small and pale that even her rage seemed ridiculous. "Go on back downstairs! Offer to help the regent any way you can in this crisis."

"The regent is too busy even to listen to my offers for help."

"Then go visit with that nice Lord Ordinal. With the castle turned all upside down like this, he'll be needing someone to entertain him—"

I brushed right by her, as she continued talking, and approached the group surrounding Elisandra. She looked calm as ever but deathly pale. Her black hair made a smooth coronet around her white, white skin; even her lips seemed bloodless.

When Elisandra caught sight of me, she broke off her conversation with Giselda in midsentence. "Corie," she said, and came over to lay her head against my shoulder. From the self-possessed Elisandra, this was nearly a complete hysterical breakdown. "I am so glad to see you."

I hugged her tightly until she pulled away. "Poor Elisandra," I said, inspecting her face. "What a dreadful night for you."

She smiled faintly. "More dreadful for Bryan. I have never seen anyone be so sick in my life."

I glanced at Giselda. "How long have you been here?" I asked the apothecary.

"Since about five this morning."

I raised my eyebrows. The feast had come to an end around nine in the evening, and surely the music had not lasted much past midnight. If Bryan had first gotten sick around the time I had, he had been vomiting and burning up with fever a long time before the medic was called in.

Perhaps Elisandra read my look, for she said, "Over and over I begged him to allow me to send for Giselda. He kept refusing. Finally against his wishes, I sent the guard for Giselda, and she has done what she can, but he only seems to get worse—"

The room was too full of people; I could not voice my suspicions and risk the maelstrom that might be set into motion. Instead, I said to Giselda, "What have you given him?"

She rattled off an impressive list of medicinal herbs, but none of them would counteract the poison I suspected. I said, most casually, so that the tone of my voice would alarm no one, "And have you tried ginyese?"

"No," she said, sounding distracted and worried. "I've never used it for a fever. Do you think it might be of some use?"

"I've seen it work in about half the cases," I said. This was a lie. "It might not help, but it couldn't hurt."

"I don't have any," she said.

"I do. In my room," I said, most pleasantly. "Shall I go get it?"

"Why, yes—if you would be so kind—" she said gratefully.

Elisandra clutched my arm. "Corie, what is this ginyese? Why is it so important?"

I smiled and patted her hand. "Just an herb that has been known to be effective in cases like this."

"What kind of case is this? Is this a disease you recognize?"

No, for it was no natural disease. "I have seen symptoms like this a few times," I said. "Sometimes the ginyese has helped. Sometimes it has not. Let me fetch some, and we'll hope it does some good."

"Lord Goff has a fever, too," Giselda reminded me. "Do you have enough to dose both of them?"

I nodded. "I think so. I'll be right back."

I moved to go, but Elisandra's grip on my arm tightened so painfully it turned me back. "Corie," she said in a fierce undervoice. "What is it? Why do you talk so strangely?"

I smiled and kissed her very gently on the cheek. "Bryan has been poisoned," I whispered in her ear before drawing back so I could see her face again. "Remember the gifts I gave you," I said. "In the sachet. Have courage. Be strong. Now let me go see what I can do for the prince."

She released me, still staring. I hurried for the door, catching from the corner of my eye a swift movement from Kent's side of the room, as if someone started after me. I did not stay to see who. Outside the door, I picked up my skirts and ran.

With every hurried step, I was remembering an incident from a year ago, when I had returned to my room to find my satchel ransacked. At the time, I had assumed some lovesick young girl had stolen pansy pat or jerron weed to use on a reluctant swain. Had I been wrong? Had the intruder stolen halen root instead—and waited all this time to use it?

Once in my room, I did not bother to sort through my satchel, just grabbed it by the handle and went careening back out the door. The stone floors of the castle seemed slippery under my feet, and I skidded around more than one corner. Ridiculous, pointless, stupid to rush so; nothing in my satchel, nothing in Giselda's herbal store, would be sufficient to save Bryan.

I was half a corridor from the bridal suite when I turned a corner and slammed into Kent. He grabbed me by my arms to steady me, and it took me a moment to catch my breath.

"What are you doing? What do you know?" he demanded.

I had to suck in a few lungfuls of air before I could answer him.

"Bryan's been poisoned," I gasped at last. "All the symptoms point to it."

"Poisoned!" he exclaimed. "But—that's not possible."

I nodded. "I know. I can't figure it out, either. If it was something in his food, Damien would be sick, too. But Angela said he's fine."

"He is. A little stomach trouble in the night, but nothing like—" His voice trailed off and he shrugged expressively.

"A dozen other people got sick last night," I said. "They must all have eaten whatever Bryan ate that had the poison in it. But everyone else seems to be recovering."

"We all ate what Bryan ate. And anyway, why would he be so sick if everyone else is fine?"

"Something he ate more of than anyone else?" I hazarded. "Maybe something in his wine?"

"Damien tastes Bryan's wine as well."

"I know. He tastes everything."

Kent shook his head. "You have to be wrong, Corie. It's a germ, a disease, just like Giselda says. Otherwise, we'd all be as sick as Bryan. At least Damien would be."

"I'm not wrong. He had something the rest of us did not. Although I can't think—unless—was Bryan taking any medications? Anything that someone could have slipped poison into?"

"Not that I know of. We can ask Elisandra."

"Discreetly," I said. "We don't want to start a panic."

"I think we do!" he said indignantly. "If someone has come here to celebrate the prince's wedding and poisoned him instead—*that's* something that better be shouted out from the castle roof—"

"If I were you, I'd first make sure I knew who the poisoner was," I said softly.

He stared at me. Finally he dropped his hands. "What do you mean?" he asked at last, his voice much quieter than I expected.

I shrugged. "Who has the most to gain from Bryan's death?"

Now his head reared back and there was a flare of anger in his eyes. "Me, I suppose—next in line for the throne—"

I shook my head. "You'd be the last person I'd suspect."

"Then—a lot of the lords hated Bryan, but to murder him—that is—" He stopped and seemed, for the first time, to understand what I had said a minute ago. "Who has the most to gain from Bryan's *death*. But—is it fatal—I mean, this poison, if you've seen it—then you must know—what—"

I had never seen Kent so shaken. "It will kill him," I said quietly.

He pointed to the bag in my hands. "And—whatever it is—that drug you went running off to find—won't it help him?"

"No."

He did not seem to be able to take that in. He just kept staring at me, his face growing thinner and more bleak as I watched. "Bryan will *die?*" he asked in a child's voice. "How soon?"

"I don't know. Two days at the most. Possibly not that long."

"But—"

I nodded. "I know," I said.

"But he can't die," Kent said. "He's to be king."

"I know," I said again. "There's nothing you can do."

And, apparently, no answer he could make. I waited a moment longer, just to see if he'd come up with one, but he did not. I walked around him and finished the short trip to Elisandra's room.

The suite was still overfull of people, but Giselda had been watching for my reappearance. She hurried up to me and, standing in the middle of the room, we opened the satchel and sorted through its contents.

"Dissolve five or six grains in water twice a day, and make him drink all of it. For Goff, only one or two grains, I think, unless he seems to be getting no better."

She nodded once rapidly, then took the packet of herbs from my hand and rushed away. She disappeared behind the door that led, I presumed, into the bedroom of the dying prince. I snapped shut the clips on my satchel and looked around for Elisandra.

But before I could take one step from where I stood, the door was flung open and Lord Matthew strode in.

I did not even have time to wonder who had roused the look of fury on his face before he stormed across the room and grabbed me by the arm. "You traitorous, baseborn *filth*," he said in a murderous but deadly calm voice. "I want you out of here within the hour."

"Father!"

"Lord Matthew!"

"My Lord Regent!"

I distinguished a few of the individual cries of disbelief, heard a loud background mutter of stupefaction, and felt the other occupants of the room surge and regroup around us. But I really had attention for no one but Lord Matthew. His grip on my arm was bruising, but I actually felt fortunate. By the look on his face, he would have preferred to have his fingers wrapped around my throat.

"What have I done?" I asked in a low voice.

He shook me so hard my vision blurred. I heard shocked protests coming from Kent, Elisandra, others in the room. Someone stepped forward, but Matthew pushed him unceremoniously back with his free hand.

"You know what you have done," he growled fiercely. "You have freed the aliora." Fresh gasps at this news. "Freed them! Loosed them from their chains and led them from the castle—"

"What's your proof?" I asked coolly.

He thrust his hand into his breeches pocket and pulled out the gleaming gold key that had for so long hung outside the door to the aliora quarters. "*This* was found this morning in a pocket of *your* dress. The laundress brought it to me fifteen minutes ago, as soon as she discovered it. *She* knew what it was, well enough. *She* knew what it meant—"

The key. Yes, that had been clumsy. While I vividly remembered unlocking every single one of the metal shackles, I had no memory at all of what I had done with the key afterward. Obviously I had stuck it in my pocket and forgotten about it.

Kent had had the courage to approach his father a second time, though he did not come close enough to be shoved aside again. "You have no way of knowing if Corie put that key there, or if someone else slipped it in her pocket—precisely so you would ascribe this crime to her," Kent said.

Matthew spared a moment to glare at his son, and then turned his ferocious gaze back to me. "The guards saw her. Late last night."

"They did not see me with any aliora at my back," I said.

"You're a witch—a foul, sorcerous witch—you cast a spell over them to turn their eyes away."

"Father!"

"I don't know those kinds of spells," I said.

"Lord Matthew." Elisandra's voice, soft and appealing. She must have been standing behind me, because I could not see her. "Corie would not have done such a thing."

"She has not denied it!" he thundered.

"You have not asked her. You have only accused," Kent said.

Matthew shook me again, his menacing eyes blazing down at me. "Did you, Coriel Halsing, free the aliora last night using this gold key?"

"Yes," I said.

Another burst of amazement from the crowd, this one louder and more sustained. Someone went running from the room, presumably to spread the news elsewhere. A small part of my brain hoped Angela was the first to get the gossip. The rest of my mind was engaged in hoping Matthew did not strike me dead with the hand that was not clamped around my arm.

"You thieving bastard," he said in heavy, bitter accents. "You have cost me—my lords—half the noble families in the kingdom fabulous sums of money. You have *stolen* from us, we who took you in and raised you as our own—"

"I did not want to be one of your own," I said, my voice raised to be clear over the murmur of the crowd. "Not the way you treat your own sons and daughters."

At that he did slap me, backhanding me across the face with so much force that I staggered. Elisandra shrieked, and Kent leaped forward, trying to wrestle his father aside. Matthew shook him off, but he did not strike me again. He was breathing heavily and his whole body was bulging with hatred. I think if I had not been in a room of witnesses, he might have killed me on the spot.

"Get her out of here," he flung at someone behind him, and four guardsmen moved forward from the doorway. I had not even noticed they were there; I had been too intent on watching Matthew's face. "Take her to her room, let her pack. Have her down in the courtyard in thirty minutes. She is gone from here. She is banished, and she is not to return."

There was a long wail of grief, I assumed from Elisandra, and a flurry of arguing from Kent, but I did not stay even to trade glances with my allies in the room. I gave Matthew one swift, smart nod, then turned on my heel and marched out the door. The guards formed a phalanx around me.

And so went my last, ignominious trip through Castle Auburn.

We were in and out of my room in less than twenty minutes. There was very little I wanted to take back with me to Southey Village—one or two of my fancy dresses, a few shoes, and, of course, the small gifts Elisandra had showered upon me in the past few weeks. I already had my satchel in my hand. In a few short minutes, I was done, and we were parading down the stairs and out to the castle courtyard.

Where a huge crowd had already gathered. I was reminded of the time Tiatza—long since murdered by the dying prince—had left under similarly ignoble circumstances, and how so many of the guards and servants had turned out to watch her departure. I could not tell if I should be mortified or gratified that my reception was so much augmented from hers, for it seemed like every single soul in residence was present to watch my ejection. There were the visiting gentlefolk gathered for the wedding (I was tempted to wave at the astonished Ordinal, but I did not); they were jostled together next to the lords and ladies who lived at the castle and served the prince. In addition, there were the servants and the guards, some of the maids actually weeping and several of the guards looking exceedingly grim. I swear I saw Shorro blow me a kiss, though I was attempting to stare straight ahead and look at no one. One or two people called out my name—"Corie!" "Lady Coriel!" "Goodbye, Corie!"—which I did not remember occurring when Tiatza made her abrupt exit. But I did not look around to identify my well-wishers.

I headed straight for the plain black coach that had been drawn up outside the castle door. There was a driver and two guards, neither of them my particular friends, but I was glad to see them anyway. That meant Matthew was not sending me wholly unprotected across four provinces to my grandmother's. I would not have been completely surprised if he had set me out penniless and on foot.

But Matthew, I learned a scant moment later, had not ordered the coach: Kent had. For Kent was standing at the door, waiting to help me inside. I did not look at him, either, but tossed my small bags onto the floor and accepted his hand for assistance.

"Corie," he said in a low insistent voice, and pulled down on my arm so I could not step into the coach.

I looked up at him, my face completely expressionless. For the first time I was understanding how Elisandra had been able, for all these years, to appear so serene. There was nothing to fret about, nothing that could be altered by worrying or trying. Calm was easy to achieve when despair was so complete. "I can't think of anything you could possibly say to me," I said.

His hand tightened. I expected to have a series of bruises down my arm tomorrow morning from where everyone had clutched at me. "I will make my father reverse his decision," he said.

I almost laughed. "I doubt it."

"Elisandra cannot get by without you. She will need you more than ever during this tragedy."

"Elisandra," I said, "will not need me at all now."

"I need you," he said.

That did bring the surprise to my face, but I did not reply.

"When I am named king," he added. "I will need your advice. Your common sense."

"My peasant's perspective," I said, recovering a little.

"Your good heart."

"You will have your father. You will have countless other advisors. You will not need any words of mine."

"I will need you for more than words," he said.

Behind us, as if a herd of stampeding horses was thundering down the great stairwell, we heard a great rushing commotion of feet. *"Kentley!"* Lord Matthew's voice boomed behind us. "Put her in that carriage *now!*"

"Say goodbye," I said, "before he kills us both."

"Goodbye," Kent said, and bent down and kissed me on the mouth.

That was a shock like no other I had received in my life. My body stung with amazement, every inch of my skin exposed to the eyes of the watching crowd. My blood ran through its heated corridors and painted red banners on my face. The kiss was as brief as a chuckle and as long as a sleepless night. When he straightened again, he was smiling.

"When I am named king, we will have more to talk about," he said, handing me into the coach. He folded my fingers over a small, bulky package, nodded at me once in the coolest manner imaginable, and slammed the door while I was still staring at him. I heard his father's furious questioning mingle with the driver's cry and the single sharp crack of the whip. The coach lurched forward, and we were on our way.

Out past the formal gate. Down the first few miles of paved road. Through the lazy green countryside of Auburn. On my way back home.

For good.

I was not sure I would ever be able to stop crying.

It was a good ten miles before I had the strength to unclench my hand and see what Kent had given me in those final seconds. Whatever it was had been wrapped in a fine lawn handkerchief embroidered with the initial *K* and the twining arms of the House of Ouvrelet. I unrolled the object slowly until, finally free of the cloth, it dropped into my open palm.

A heavy gold ring set with a sapphire and bearing on either side of the gem the carved patterns of the House of Ouvrelet and the royal stamp of Auburn. It was a ring I had seen Kent wear every day of his life.

I felt the heat flood back along my cheekbones and skitter through every vein in my body. I tried to come up with reasons he would have honored me with such a gift. It was a gesture of friend-ship, a token of faith. A reparation for his father's harshness, a replacement for the wealth and gaiety I was leaving behind, forever, at the court. Nothing more significant than that. Nothing more personal.

I leaned my head back against the thin padding of the seat. I was tired, tearful, hungry, alone, and just a little afraid. My skin felt scratchy and dirty, since I had not had a chance to truly clean up that morning, and I knew my unwashed hair would make me crazy before the day was half over. I hoped Matthew or Kent had made provisions for us to stop for the night at a decent inn. I hoped that the trip would not seem as long and tedious as it usually did. I hoped that my grandmother would be pleased—or at least, will-ing—to see me again.

I hoped that, despite everything, my heart did not truly break.

17

Fall came late that year as though summer, idle intransigent girl that she was, could not summon the golden strength to rise from her bed along our hills and meadows and go sauntering off to some more southern site. When it did come, autumn was glorious, a fiery riot of colors spilling down over every hillside with a wanton display of fervor. The harvest was spectacular, and spirits in the village were high. Good profits tucked inside hidden purses, good seeds stored up for next spring, good ales brewed right in one's back room, good meals served up on every table. And good weather to bolster everyone's mood still more.

I had taken a room in the village with the seamstress and her daughter, and hired on as a barmaid at the largest tavern. The rent was not high and the work was not hard—and besides, I was able to make a little money on the side selling cures and potions. I had bought a fairly comprehensive supply of herbs from my grandmother, who was always delighted to sell anything to anyone; and I had discreetly told a few acquaintances in town that I could help them out if they ever had certain problems. I thought Milette might be a little miffed at losing the business I diverted, but my grandmother did not seem to mind. There were plenty of old-timers who would still insist on making the trek out to the cottage to see the *real* wise woman, the herbalist who had practiced her craft for decades. Those who came to me wanted only small favors, simple tonics, something they would trust to an amateur. This suited me just fine.

It had been clear to me that I could have made my home with my grandmother for as long as I chose, though it would have been an unpleasant home since Milette had grown sulky and self-assured during my most recent absence. My grandmother, I was happy to see, was not willing to choose her apprentice over me—but then again, she was not willing to choose me over Milette, and the house almost immediately began to seem too small. But my tiny room in the village, barely large enough to contain a bed and a small chest of drawers, seemed just right. I liked my landlady and I liked my job, and I thought I could settle in here for a good long while.

Or until I decided what I wanted to do with my life. Suddenly that was less clear than ever. But I would work for a year, think about it for a year, and then move forward on the strength of my savings and my intuition.

In the two months that I had been gone from court, news had filtered back to me slowly, sometimes in the form of ordinary gossip brought in by merchants and other travelers, sometimes in letters sent by my friends back at court. The news of Prince Bryan's death was brought by the candlemaker's son, who ran a carting business from the southern provinces to the northern and spent most of his life on the road. Official word came three days later as the regent sent criers throughout the eight provinces to bawl out the shocking tidings in every market square. Everyone in our village, or what seemed like everyone, gathered on the green to hear the proclamation.

"If Prince Bryan is dead," someone shouted back to the official messenger, "who will rule in his place?"

The messenger had obviously answered this question many times already. "Lord Matthew Ouvrelet continues as regent until Prince Kentley Ouvrelet can be crowned."

"Kentley Ouvrelet? What, Prince Bryan's cousin?"

"Yes, the regent's son."

"And what's he like?"

"He is fit to be king," the crier answered coldly.

"Aye, but what is he *like?*"

The messenger fielded that and a dozen questions like it with the stone-faced diplomacy you might expect. I, at least, was convinced Kent would make a far better king than Bryan ever would have. Not something I wanted to leap in front of the crowd and declaim, however. I found it strange—on that first day and in the weeks that followed—to hear Kent referred to as the prince. Even more odd was to think of him as the king. He had never seemed so majestic as all that. Thoughtful, intelligent, evenhanded, kind, but not majestic.

But then, Bryan had never seemed very regal, either. Romantic, not regal. I supposed one brought to the table whatever traits one had, and then did the best one could to grow into the role one was given.

More intimate news arrived in my hands via letters that came sporadically, depending on the time available to the authors and the availability of couriers coming my way. Elisandra wrote immediately and often, though her tone was guarded; I wondered more than once if Greta, or Matthew, was censoring her correspondence.

Her first missive told me of Bryan's death, which had occurred two days after my abrupt departure. *All I could be grateful for was that, as he got sicker, he seemed to suffer less,* she had written. *He had been in great distress when he first fell ill, but as the days passed, he seemed to grow calmer and less sensate. Giselda said she did not think he was in any pain at all when he died. That was a comfort to Lord Matthew as well as to me.*

I skimmed the descriptions of the mourning and the burial ceremony; all eight provinces had shared in the public displays of grief, draping black banners over city gates and flying black flags from the public buildings. Some of the more romantic young girls had dressed in mourning from which they refused to emerge for weeks on end, but most of the villagers had no real cause to grieve for the prince. They had never met him; they neither loved him nor hated him; the politics and personalities at court held very little real significance in their daily lives. The prince was dead and the new prince would soon step forward. The realm remained whole and united. That was all they cared to know.

What I really wanted to know was what would become of Elisandra next, and in a later paragraph, she addressed that very issue. *It seems strange to think I am a widow when I have scarcely been a bride,* she wrote. *Lord Matthew does not seem to know what to do with me, though I am sure he will come up with some sort of plan. Kent assures me that I have inherited Bryan's personal fortune, although, of course, I will not have access to the royal jewels and coffers. Matthew has hinted that I shall need to wed again. As for myself, I think, "I have had one disastrous marriage. Let me wait awhile before I embark upon another."*

I looked up from the page I was reading. Of course. *Halsing women have always provided the brides for the royal house.* Elisandra was a Halsing woman, and Kent was now the last living descendent of the Ouvrelet royal house. Even from hundreds of miles away, I could sense Matthew's brain engaged in its usual plotting. Decency required him to wait a short interval before handing Elisandra over to the new prince, but decency was not a consideration that had long tied Matthew's hands in the past. Soon enough, we would be hearing news of Elisandra's betrothal to the new prince.

It was what I had hoped for and tried to bring about for so long. I couldn't imagine why the thought depressed me so much now.

From Angela, I received much more gossipy letters describing the emotional flux at the court in the days following Bryan's death. Megan of Tregonia had had to be confined to her room, sedated, because of the strength of her despair. Three of the other young ladies, all of whom had seemed to be insanely attached to Bryan, had been sent home even before the funeral, because they had disrupted meals and councils with their hysterical sobbing.

The visiting noblemen, on the other hand, had not seemed quite so dismayed, *and the half-secret political meetings that took place* the very day of Bryan's death *were occurring in rooms all over the castle. I never saw poor Kent look so grim and harried, for, of course, everyone* instantly *wanted to call him friend. He is too polite to treat anyone with rudeness, so he allowed himself to be cornered every five minutes by some backwater lord who fancied a position at court. I must say he handled himself well enough, except for looking so tired. Even Elisandra, who has worries enough on her own, has grown concerned about him. Just yesterday she insisted that he come to the dinner table for a meal, since he had missed both breakfast and lunch.*

The question now appears to be when exactly Kent will be crowned. Since he is over twenty-one, there is no need to name him "prince," so when he ascends the throne, it will be as king. (King Kentley, is that not divine? It makes him sound so much more impressive *than our sweet, grave Kent.) Everyone says that Matthew has delayed in setting the date because he wants a smooth transition from regency to royal, but I myself wonder if Matthew is not quite so eager to hand over all his power at once—and to his son.*

No one was editing Angela's letters, that was obvious. I loved to receive them, and I wrote back faithfully so that she would not forget me. I had less to tell, of course, though I tried to make my stories amusing. I described the wild dance at the fall festival, and the traveling monkey show that had come to town. I also told her about some of the more outlandish requests I had received from the villagers who sought my professional advice (*Goodwife Janey, who's sixty if she's a day, came to ask for help conceiving a child. . . . Red Brotton, as he's called, wanted to know if I had any spells for increasing the size of his—well, he called it his "manfinger," so I suppose I should do the same. . . ."*).

To Elisandra I sent back shorter, more personal letters, asking about her health, reassuring her about mine, and expressing hope that I could see her again, somehow, soon. Into the folds of each of these letters, I sprinkled grains of nariander and stiffelbane, herbs that would lift her spirits and keep her serene. She seemed well enough, but with Elisandra, you never knew; and it was a simple thing to do and g..ve me great comfort.

My other correspondent this fall was a new one: Kent. He had never, in the twelve years I had visited at Auburn Castle, sent me so much as a solstice greeting when I was back at my grandmother's cottage. Indeed, the first time a letter arrived at the seamstress's house, I did not recognize the handwriting. I had to pry off the seal and turn to the signature before I could identify the author. I could not believe it when I saw Kent's name.

But the letter itself held nothing that should have sent my heart skidding so precipitously against my ribs. In fact, it was fairly short: *Corie—The carriage returned empty and the guards were all alive, so I presume you made it safely to your grandmother's cottage. There has been much chaos here, as I'm sure you can imagine. My father and I have been in endless conversation with the viceroys and their advisors as everyone looks on the prince's death as an opportunity to test and restructure old alliances. I am not used to having so many people ask my opinion, and I have been cautious about the replies that I have made, but I find that I usually have decided ideas about every topic that is brought up and I am convinced that my way is usually the most reasonable. The makings of a despot, don't you think? Nonetheless, I have mastered the art of listening with a serious, intent look upon my face. Even when I am not actually listening, I have managed to maintain the look. I expect this new trick will come in handy more and more often as the days progress.*

Other than that, we are all well here. Elisandra is quiet but does not seem unhappy. I have less time to spend with her than I would like. My father, who first seemed stricken at Bryan's death, now seems revitalized by the challenge of turning me into a king. On some days I am excited, on other days a little frightened, but most of the time I am just tired. I do miss you. Kent

Not "Kentley," I was glad to see. And he missed me. I sent him back a note even shorter than his own, but I did not say I missed him. I did not thank him for the ring. But I did dust the letter with a variety of crushed seeds, designed to endow him with wisdom and patience and strength. He would not notice the gesture, but it cheered me, and I sent the letter off with a light heart.

MY LIFE DID not consist solely of gossipy letters recounting court intrigue. My job at the tavern perfectly suited my personal schedule, for I went in during the early evening, worked till midnight or later, than came home to read herbal books and mix up experimental potions. I went to bed sometime after three and slept till noon the next day. And I loved the tavern work. I loved the simple routine of waiting on customers, flirting harmlessly with the men, sympathizing with the women, and bringing everybody food. When I noticed patrons who were ill or in trouble, I was not above seasoning their beer with restorative herbs, once I had managed to learn exactly what their problems were. Consequently most repeat customers were a healthy, happy lot who associated the tavern with thoughts of ease and renewal. This meant business picked up significantly with every passing week.

Darbwin, the barkeeper, noticed the trend. "Everybody likes you," he observed late one night as we closed up. "Days you're not here, they ask about you. Days you are here, they stay longer and order more."

"I guess you'll have to give me a raise, then," I said, grinning. I was counting the day's take, which was substantial. Darbwin was the richest man in town.

"That or marry you," he said. I looked up. He laughed. "No, in my experience, a good barmaid makes a lousy wife."

I laughed. He had not had as much experience as Ordinal, it was true, but he had been married twice. His first wife had died young, the second had run off, and he had shown no inclination to replace her. Both of them, if I remembered right, had started out as his employees. "From what I hear, you're a better boss than husband," I retorted. "So, thank you very kindly, but I think I'll just take your money."

I had handed him the stacks of counted bills, and he pushed one of them back across the table at me. More than I usually took home at the end of the week, but I did not point this out. Darbwin never miscounted dollars; this was a deliberate gesture.

"Though I do wonder," he said in a casual voice, "how long you'll be staying. Don't you usually go up to Auburn in the spring?"

I stood up and shook the crumbs out of my apron. "Used to. Not anymore."

He leaned back in the booth and watched me move around the tables, straightening chairs and blowing out candles. "So, you're planning to be here the rest of your life? Year in, year out?"

"I haven't made any plans," I said. "I suppose I'll go visit my sister now and then. You'll give me a little time off if I ask for it, won't you?"

He nodded vigorously. "Sorry to see you go, but happy to see you back. You've got a job here as long as you like it."

I smiled at him in what had become the near-dark of the tavern. "Glad to hear it," I said. "But I'll be here for a while yet. Not to worry."

"Through solstice, anyway, I hope," he said. "That's my busy time."

"Solstice I can guarantee." I took off my apron, laid it across the back of the booth, and smiled at Darbwin again. "See you tomorrow night," I said, and left.

It was a short walk home through the quiet streets, though the air was chillier than I expected. Winter before long; solstice before we knew it. I would have to write my uncle Jaxon and see if he was inviting Elisandra to Halsing Manor for the holidays. I could think of no reason he would not allow me to join them for a visit— once the actual celebration was over, of course. I could not abandon Darbwin during his busy season, after all.

But there was a letter waiting for me on the table outside my room, and it obviated any possibility of visits during the winter holidays. It was from Elisandra, and it was the longest one I had received from her yet. Also the most frank; she must have written it in secret and sent it out by a trusted hand.

Corie: The strangest news has just arrived today from the steward on Jaxon's estate. It seems Jaxon and Rowena have left—vanished. They were there one night and gone the next, all their clothes removed from the closets and all their personal effects missing. The servants say they heard nothing in the night, that Jaxon and Rowena retired to their room as usual, but in the morning, they were both gone. The steward says he made discreet inquiries at various inns and posting houses in the neighborhood, but no one remembers seeing them. Oh, and none of the horses are gone. Only Jaxon and his wife.

Is this not odd? What are we to make of it? I have only gotten one note from Jaxon since he left last summer, saying he was not sorry Bryan had died though he hoped it had not caused me any sadness. I burned it immediately, of course, for I did not want either my mother or Lord Matthew to find it. He said nothing about any plans to travel—or disappear!—and I feel quite disturbed and shaken. As if we might not ever see him again.

And I cannot help but wonder about Rowena's role in all this. She is the queen of Alora, after all, and the alora have gifts and powers that I do not believe we have ever understood. She made a strange bargain with Jaxon a year ago. Could she have come to regret it? Could she have done anything to harm him?

I have told Matthew that I would like to go to Halsing Manor to see for myself how the situation has been left, but he told me flatly that I was not to leave the castle. I was quite astonished, I assure you, and asked him with some hauteur what right he had to attempt to confine me anywhere. And then he told me—it was a day of shock piled upon shock—that I was the widow of the true prince and any children of my body would be considered the next heirs to the throne, and that until nine months had passed from Bryan's death, I must be carefully watched. Otherwise I might in secret bear a child that was either Bryan's, and thus rightful heir, or that I pretended was his, and attempted to put on the throne in Kent's place! Can you believe this? I was never more amazed. I told him that he could consult with Daria, who would inform him that I had had four monthly courses since my wedding night, but he said maids could be bribed and such signs could be misleading, and in any case, the law required a nine-month waiting period and he would observe it to the last day.

So this answers all sorts of questions that I have had, though I have not raised them—one being why he has not insisted Kent be crowned immediately, and another being why he has not shown more active interest in finding me a new suitor. I must confess, I still have no taste for another beau of Matthew's procuring, but I was surprised at his slowness in this area. But now I understand. I understand everything.

Oh, Corie, I miss you so much! I think so often about what you said to me, about living in some small cottage in a tiny village, raising herbs and earning enough to feed ourselves. How I would love that life and the chance to be near you always. Matthew has vowed that you shall never return to Castle Auburn, but I shall not let that keep us apart. I will come

to you, or you must meet me somewhere, as soon as my nine-month sentence
is lifted. Till then, think of me often, write me whenever you can, and
know you are always in my thoughts. Elisandra

This was a letter that needed to be read more than once, and I
did so, standing beside my bed and holding the paper to the candlelight. Jaxon and Rowena vanished! But there was no mystery there
at all. She had taken him back to Alora, that place of rest and
delight for which he had hungered ever since he spent that one
brief, fateful visit inside its borders. Or perhaps for even longer—
since his first glimpse of one of those frail, exotic creatures; since
the first time one of them touched a wondering finger to his cheek
and set in his heart that inescapable, inexplicable desire. I remembered what deep longing Cressida's touch had fired in me, that night
I released her from Castle Auburn. Even now, months later, I would
wake sometimes in the night weeping and wretched, homesick for
a place I had never seen. I knew where Rowena and Jaxon had
disappeared. We would not be seeing them again.

I skimmed the letter a third time, frowning as I came to the
second half. Yes, indeed, the possibility that Elisandra had become
pregnant on her wedding night would have loomed huge in Matthew's mind. Though even he must realize it was a slim chance,
considering how sick Bryan had been. And nine long months for
Elisandra to wait before she could make any moves, any changes in
her life! Nine months of limbo Kent would have to endure as well,
treated as the next king though still without any real power. Nine
months of waiting for me before I could see my sister again.

Well, four and a half months had already passed. We were half-
way there. I sat up another two hours, writing letters, before I sought
my bed that night.

THE SEASON ADVANCED; the sun grew small and ungenerous, parcel-
ing out a few watery hours of light every day. The nights turned
long, bleak, and frigid. Companionship and firelight were the only
weapons we had with which to combat desolation. The tavern was

crowded every night, and no patron ever seemed to want to go home, back out into that black and icy silence.

Even Darbwin, habitually cheerful, often seemed lost in melancholy thoughts from which he could not be easily shaken. I suggested we hire another barmaid, then began looking about for suitable candidates. My choice was a middle-aged widow with a curving smile and an ample body who knew how to handle herself around men. She was warmhearted, filled with laughter, and had turned away four offers of marriage that I knew about since her husband died five years ago. I was not surprised when she and Darbwin immediately struck up an easy, bantering friendship. In fact, when I had the chance, I used illicit seasonings to spice up their food— and their relationship.

I tried to spend a couple of evenings a month out at my grandmother's, where the turning of the season had little real effect. She and Milette were busy drying herbs and bottling up mixed potions. All the long nights meant to them were a few more hours to study by candlelight. Since I had moved into the village, Milette had grown a little friendlier to me, and we actually spent a few evenings consulting on some more arcane texts and discussing what the elixirs could possibly have been intended for. My grandmother watched the cessation of hostilities with a small smile, though she said nothing.

The three of us celebrated the solstice together, though I did not get to the cottage till midnight, since I waited tables at the tavern till eleven. Then I hurried down the frosty roads under a grinning quarter moon to arrive, shivering and grateful, into the bright heat of my grandmother's house. The three of us stayed up till dawn on that longest night of the year, tossing herbs into the fire and chanting the rituals that would ensure an early spring and a bountiful year. We slept till noon, then hiked into the village for the festival going on there—games, feasts, songfests, fortune-telling, and bazaars. The day was cold but exceptionally clear, and the wind had whipped color into everyone's face, so that the whole village appeared to be full of vital, jovial folk. Indeed, Solstice Day was generally my favorite of the year for that very reason—it put everyone into a good

mood, a mood of hope and expectation. From this day forward, till
the very green heart of summer, the light would stay longer and
the days would stretch themselves, one minute at a time, into the
night. That was something to celebrate indeed.

In the evening, I returned to my rented room, too exhausted to
stay up as late as usual. There I found two packages and a letter
awaiting me. The letter was a short solstice greeting from Angela
with no real news. One package came from Elisandra and contained
several yards of ocean blue silk. Too fine for my daily use, living as
I did, but I would use it to line my new cloak and it would make
me feel deeply loved.

The other package was from Kent and contained a gold locket
set with a sapphire that matched the one in the ring. His solstice
greeting was also short and very traditional, wishing me health and
a light heart. I looked at the locket a long time and did not know
what to do with it. Ultimately I put it in a small silver box which
also contained his ring, and hid the whole collection in the back of
my dresser drawer. I scattered a few grains of siawort around the
feet of the dresser—to distract thieves and make them turn their
eyes elsewhere—and then told myself to forget the whole thing.

WINTER PASSED WITH its usual, creaking slowness, an arthritic old lady
whose only delight was to inconvenience others. Just when we thought
she had been routed by the playful infant spring, she regathered her
strength and blanketed us all with a wet, messy coverlet of snow. It
took two days to dig out; the tavern did not even open that first day.
I went into the streets with the village children and played cannonballs
and targets. We were all soaked and freezing when we went back into
our respective houses, wet and chilled but happy. I fell into bed early
that night and slept with profound exhaustion.

The week that spring truly arrived, we had a wedding in the
village. Darbwin and the new barmaid spoke their vows in the tiny
chapel, then invited all the residents to come celebrate at the tavern.
I had had the responsibility of catering the dinner, which was to
feed at least three hundred and for which I had enlisted the help of

ten other women. The celebration went on for two full days and was followed by a week's vacation as Darbwin closed the tavern and took his bride on a honeymoon journey. I spent the week at my grandmother's cottage, sharing with Milette some of the recipes I had been taught for the wedding banquet. I still was not much of a cook, but the other women in the kitchen had been willing to share all their secrets. Milette, I learned from my grandmother, had been courted by a young man who lived three villages away, and she appeared to be considering what dishes she might set forth at her own wedding.

"A boy from so far away!" I exclaimed, staring at my grandmother. She hushed me impatiently and glanced out the doorway, for she had imparted this news while she and I were inside building up the fire. Milette was in the garden, pulling weeds.

"Well, thirty miles. It's a trip he can easily make in a day."

"But—if she marries him—have you thought what will happen? All this time, you have expected her to take your place!"

"Oh, *that's* settled," my grandmother said comfortably. "He wants to hire on at the stableyard and be an ostler."

"I didn't know they were hiring at the stableyard."

My grandmother grinned wickedly. "Well, if they're not, they soon will be," she said. "Milette has no ambition to move from this village. I've no fear of her leaving."

And indeed, two weeks later, I learned that a new man had been hired at the stables. Milette's future appeared to be settled.

Spring brought a bumper crop of new babies. I was kept busy more nights than I could count, rushing herbal mixtures to the midwives who were hovering over panting young women in painful labor. Darbwin bought the property next to his and began building an inn to attach to the tavern. The chapel spire got knocked over in a storm and had to be rebuilt in a community effort that caused equal amounts of dissent and satisfaction.

And nine months and one week after her wedding, my sister Elisandra rode into the village looking for me.

18

"Someone out front to see you," Darbwin told me.

"Who is it?"

"Didn't say. A young lady and a young man. On horseback."

My clients didn't usually come from so far away that they needed to ride in, for my reputation was decidedly local. I shrugged, dried my hands on my apron, and ducked out into the sunlight.

To see Elisandra standing beside her horse, watching the door hopefully.

"Corie!" she cried, and flung herself into my arms. I shrieked with delight and disbelief, and hugged her, and drew back to stare at her, then shrieked and hugged her again.

"Elisandra! What are you doing—oh, it's so good to—why didn't you *tell* me! How long can you stay?"

Her responses were just as disjointed, and we finally drew apart, laughing and clinging to each other.

"Tell me," I commanded. "What are you doing here? How did you convince Matthew to let you go? How did you *find* me? What's going on at court? How long can you stay?"

"Oh—it's so complicated—it's so exciting—!" she exclaimed, and I thought I had never seen her so animated. She was positively radiant, happiness spilling across her face and lighting its every angle. "Matthew had watched me all this time, and, of course, I wasn't pregnant. On the nine-month anniversary of my wedding, I told him I was coming to see you. He made a big fuss, and said how you were banned forever, and went on and on about how I had a duty to marry some man with a noble lineage. I just walked out of the room. Walked out. I've never done that to anyone in my life."

"I'm so proud of you," I said admiringly. "How did you find the courage?"

"I pretended I was you."

We both laughed. I said, "And your mother? What did she think of this little flare of rebellion?"

"I just told her I was leaving. Packed my luggage while she paced around the room and wept. I did kiss her goodbye, but that did not calm her. So, I don't know if she'll actually come visit me."

"Come visit—" I paused, momentarily struck dumb by shock, then rushed on. "You mean, you've *left*? For *good*? You've come to live with me? Oh, Elisandra, how wonderful!"

She was laughing again. "No, no, no, not with you. I'm going to Jaxon's estate. He's renounced his claim to it. Has declared himself legally dead."

"Has—" It seemed I could hardly comprehend what she was saying, let alone complete a sentence. "You've heard from Uncle Jaxon?"

She nodded. "I received a letter about a week ago. It seems he's sent copies to his steward and the local squire, as well as Matthew. In it, he renounces his citizenship, his claim on Halsing Manor, his right to inherit property from any other source, and, essentially, declares his status as a—I think he called it a 'nonliving person.' It was very strange."

"He's gone to Alora," I said.

"Yes, that's what I think, too. You should have heard Matthew ranting, but nobody else seemed surprised. Kent suggested that he might someday regret his decision and want to live among men again, but I think—"

"Never," I said. "He'll never leave Alora. The stories I have heard of the place—the stories he has told himself—he's with the aliora forever now."

"Which means that I've really and truly inherited Halsing Manor." She gave me another quick hug. "You and I have inherited," she amended, "because anywhere that is my home is your home, too."

I was thinking hard, trying to remember. "But wait. There was something odd about the entailment—I remember. You can only inherit property from Jaxon once you're married."

She nodded again, a great smile spreading across her face. "I know. I've come here to be married. I want you to be my bridesmaid, for the second time in less than a year."

"Married—!" I breathed. "But to—"

And then I thought to look to her companion, who all this while had stayed seated motionlessly upon his horse. He was not dressed in castle livery, so I had assumed he could not be one of the royal guards, sent to protect her on this most hasty of journeys. But he was, and a guard I recognized: Roderick, the prince's personal defender.

I felt my mouth drop open in astonishment.

"I know you realize what a wonderful man he is, for he has told me of your great friendship with each other," Elisandra's voice was saying, faint and faraway in my ear. I could not stop staring at Roderick, who gazed back at me with absolutely no expression on his face. "Whoever else scoffs at me, I know *you* will understand."

I made an effort to shut my mouth, and I looked back at Elisandra. "But how did this come about?" I asked stupidly. "I never even saw you together. You never mentioned his name."

She was blushing prettily; she looked as sweet and lovestruck as any village girl. "We went riding that one time—you and I—and you fell off your horse. You remember that day?"

"Oh, yes."

"And Roderick had come riding with us, and he saved your life."

I glanced once more, sideways, at the silent guard. I was ready to swear now that the slightest smile played across his lips, but still he sat quietly upon his horse and did not speak. "Well," I said, "he did carry me back to the castle. As for saving my life—"

"And that fall he traveled with Bryan and me to Tregonia. He was so alert and careful on the road that I always felt safe with him beside us. And he saved Bryan's life that one time—and he was so brave and thoughtful when Andrew was captured. Oh, there are so many times he has done such wonderful things!"

It was becoming clearer to me as she spoke. Roderick had a country charm to him, that I would absolutely admit, and it was true that the more I had come to know him, the more I had liked him. No doubt it had been the same with Elisandra. I just had not been able to picture the first few meetings, the chance encounters, the unexpected conversations that had sparked interest, then affection, then passion, between these two most unlikely lovers. But once the affair had begun—oh, I could see it well enough.

"And then, I suppose, once he was made Bryan's personal guard, you saw him every day—" I mused.

"Every day. In every setting. And day after day, week after week, he exhibited such strength, such nobility of character, that I could not help but fall in love with him."

I sent another sideways glance in Roderick's direction. He was definitely grinning now, though he tried to wipe the expression off his face when he caught my gaze. I tilted my head and watched him a moment. "So, I suppose Daria was acting as a courier on your behalf when she brought him notes and remembrances," I said. "I suspected the maid."

Elisandra laughed. "No—you didn't! You thought Daria was flirting with Roderick?"

"It seemed a more logical explanation than the truth."

She came a step closer and put her hand on my arm. "But Corie—you understand, don't you? Nothing in the world will change my mind, nothing will change my heart, but I— If I do not have your support and your approval—it means so much to me that you accept him, accept us, stand up with us on our wedding day—"

I laughed out loud and held my hand out to my new brother-in-law-to-be. "I prefer him one hundred times over Prince Bryan!" I said gaily. "There is no one I would rather give you to than him."

Elisandra actually squealed in my ear and clutched tight at my arm. This was the signal Roderick had been waiting for. He swung down from his horse and came over to me in three quick strides.

"I'm happy to see you, Lady Corie," he murmured, and lifted me off the ground in one brief, bone-snapping hug. "Yours was the only opinion that mattered."

"That's a first in my life," I said breathlessly when he set me on my feet. "Now! Come inside for a drink. We have a wedding to plan."

DARBWIN WAS MOST interested to meet my sister—as was everyone else within earshot. They all knew my history and my lineage, of course. So, once I pronounced her name, everyone in the tavern knew that the prince's widow was sitting nearby, having run off with a commoner. It was just the sort of news to make every yeoman in the eight provinces feel pride in his own virility, so Roderick and Elisandra were instantly the most popular couple on the premises. There was no hope of planning a wedding or even holding a conversation in private, but Elisandra, that most regal of women, did not seem to mind. She nodded as the serving girls debated wedding attire and the farmers conferred about the best venue and the innkeeper's wife suggested a reception feast which featured squirrel stew as its primary component. Elisandra's cheeks richened with color, her eyes sparkled with mischievous laughter, and her rare, delicate laugh filtered through the smoky air of the tavern more times than I could count.

"You'll be needing a few days off, then, to plan this affair," Darbwin said late in the evening, when we were both back in the kitchen at the same time. I have to confess, I was feeling a bit disoriented by this time—too many surprises, too many changed reference points.

"Yes—I suppose—except I don't think they're in any mood to wait. A day or so, maybe, and then I think they want to be wed."

"Copley will wed them any day they say—that's no problem," Darbwin said, dismissing the first of my many concerns. Copley, the village priest, was a great friend of Darbwin's, despite the fact that the tavern owner was a complete heathen. "They'll need a place to stay for their wedding night, of course, and Jake's inn is full up with the traveling season begun again."

"I know," I said worriedly. "They could have my room, I suppose, though it's small for two. I could sleep out at my grandmother's."

"You could bed down here in the kitchen if it came to that, but it won't," Darbwin said. "I've got two rooms completely framed in on the new inn. Windows aren't in, but we can cover the holes with good heavy quilts, and build up the fire real nice. Bring in a bed from my house, just for the night—they'll be all snug and cosy. Not a soul around to bother them, either, which is just what they'll be wanting on their wedding night."

I thought for a moment of Elisandra's first wedding, an affair attended by so much pageantry that Darbwin would not believe it if I recounted half of the details now. I thought of the bridal couple's royal suite, the furnishings of the room hand-carved by master carpenters, the curtains made of velvet, the marble floor covered in exotic fur. I thought of the noble lords who had toasted her health, the noble ladies who had wept over her good fortune, the soldiers who had guarded her rest.

I thought of the secret poison racing through her husband's blood, malicious enough to mark him for death almost as soon as he had swallowed it.

Then I thought of Darbwin's unfinished village inn, quilts on the windows for curtains, an old mattress for a matrimonial bed.

"It will be perfect," I told him. "Thank you so much for offering."

IT WAS, IN fact, a simply charming wedding, held outdoors in the market green because the weather was so fine. Every soul in the village turned out for the event—because this was a rare match indeed!—and stayed afterward to participate in the ring-toss games and drinking contests and other customary entertainment. Even Milette and my grandmother had walked into town to see the proceedings for themselves.

Elisandra wore one of my old dresses, hastily fancied up with ruffles of antique lace by my landlady, the seamstress. Roderick wore a dark jacket supplied by Darbwin and a fine cotton shirt that he produced himself. The priest, Copley, a bit intimidated by his unexpected commission, spoke his prayers and masses in an almost inaudible tone; but both the bride and groom gave their responses in firm, cheerful voices. When the ceremony concluded, Roderick snatched Elisandra up in his arms, swung her around in three wide circles, and then kissed her heartily. The audience cheered.

After the congratulations and the feasting and the games and the toasts, they retired to Darbwin's unfinished inn and made themselves truly husband and wife. I had wondered, watching them the past two days, if they had not in fact already taken that final physical step sometime on the road from Auburn—or even before—but I did not ask Elisandra. There were still questions that that happy, carefree woman would not answer.

I had had very little time to talk with her alone in the two days preceding the wedding, though she had stayed with me in my tiny room and we had whispered in bed at night until we fell asleep. Trouble was, we were both so tired that we had fallen asleep almost instantly both nights. We had managed to stay awake long enough that first night for me to ask a few of the questions that had vexed me for the past nine months.

"What about Kent?" I asked. "How is he faring?"

"Oh, he's been absolutely lionized! Especially as it became more and more obvious that I was not going to bear Bryan's child. You should have seen the lords fawning over him—even Matthew, who does not offer anyone more than ordinary courtesy—"

"I meant," I interrupted. "This marriage. Does Kent know about it? How will he take the news?"

She was silent a moment. "He might know. It is hard to tell," she said. "He knew I was coming to see you—he knew who my escort was—and I told him I planned to marry. In some ways, I think it was a relief to him to see me go."

"A relief! But he—but you have always been such close friends! And now—with Bryan gone—I just assumed that you and he would marry. And surely Kent assumed so, too."

"Matthew did, I know. But Kent—I don't think Kent ever wanted to marry me." Even in the dark, I heard the smile in her voice. "Even when he proposed to me last summer. To save me from Bryan. No, I do not think Kent will be sorry that I am gone."

I doubted it. Nothing would convince me that the serious, kindly new prince had not always loved my sister. But that was a tangle between them, and not one I had any hope of unraveling now. Against my will, I yawned mightily.

"And Bryan's death?" I said, with all the urgency I could summon at this hour. "Matthew never asked—never wondered—"

"As far as Matthew knows, as far as anyone knows, Bryan died of a fever. Giselda never even hinted otherwise."

"And Lord Goff? Did he recover?"

"Yes, but slowly."

I fought to keep my eyes open. "And no one muttered the word 'poison'?"

"No one but you."

"But it was poison," I said sleepily, and felt myself drifting away.

I heard her whisper, "I know."

But she did not say how she knew.

I had even less chance to speak with Roderick, who was always off with the village men on those mysterious male pursuits—hunting, dicing, drinking, or discussing one of the three. I finally caught up with him late in the evening of his wedding day, as he was laughingly refusing a challenge to down an outsized stein of beer in one swallow.

"Beer makes a man lusty," his new friend boasted.

Roderick chuckled. "Beer makes a man—" He saw me and obviously changed the word he was going to use. "Sleepy," he said. "This is a night I wish to stay wide awake."

I stepped forward and took the mug from the man's hand. "Let me," I said, and gulped the whole thing down successfully if somewhat messily. There were cheers and catcalls all around me as I laid the mug back on the table and was unable to repress a couple of coughs. Roderick grinned and pounded me on the back.

"And to think I was ruing the fact that Elisandra had no brothers," he said admiringly. "But who needs them when she's got you?"

I coughed once more and then looked up at him with as much dignity as I could muster. "Good. Then you understood me," I said.

He nodded. "You're tough enough to protect her if I do her wrong."

"Though I have to say I think you're less likely to harm her than her previous husband."

"Far less likely," he said dryly. He glanced down at me, hesitated, then spoke. "What nobody seems to realize is that Elisandra is tough enough to take care of herself."

"I do realize it," I said, "but it took me a while."

He smiled lazily, that old familiar smile that made him so attractive. "But she seems happy now, does she not? Everyone will tell you she chose foolishly, but it's a wise girl who knows what will make her content."

I glanced over at Elisandra, accepting a posy of dried flowers from a five-year-old village girl. She was flushed and smiling; her dark hair, which she always wore pulled back in a severe style, was loose and tumbling about her shoulders. In my refurbished gown, which was just a touch too small for her, she looked a little awkward, a little tentative, completely unsophisticated.

"Oh, yes," I agreed softly. "She has never looked better."

Two days later, the whole village turned out once more to see the newlyweds on their way. Everyone shouted and waved and tossed handfuls of rose petals at them. Indeed, I began to think even the court had not mustered so much excitement for Elisandra's first wedding. I had hugged Elisandra so often that I was afraid I would break her bones if I took her in my arms one more time, and still I did not want to let her go.

"Come to Halsing Manor," she repeated. "As soon as you can. We'll be settled in no time. Come soon and stay as long as you like."

"I will—soon. I will—goodbye, goodbye, goodbye—"

I watched them ride out of sight, then retired to the back of the tavern and burst into tears. Darbwin's wife found me there an hour later when she came in to begin cooking the evening meal. She offered no comments or condolences, just handed me an apron and said she thought a few of the back tables needed to be wiped down. I was grateful for her unspoken kindness and the chance at a distraction. For the rest of the day, I worked as hard as I ever had.

I was less depressed the next day and actually cheerful by week's end. After all, what was there to mourn? Elisandra was happy and I could see her whenever I wished. She was not married to the man I had expected to see her wed, but perhaps she had chosen for herself more wisely than I would have chosen for her. She was, as Roderick had pointed out, very well able to care for herself.

Villagers were still talking about the event, as I assumed they would until the world itself came to an end. Even Darbwin, harder than most to overawe, would now and then make some reference to the wedding and its participants.

"Nice young man, that Roderick," he said more than once. And now and then: "Very open, for such a noble lady. Very friendly. We'd all have a higher opinion of the gentry if the rest of them behaved so well." And once, toward the end of that week: "So, it'll be your turn next, will it?"

I had not been listening closely. It was late, and I was counting receipts, and I was tired. "My turn for what?" I asked absently.

"To wed."

That did catch my attention. I looked up at him in surprise. "Who exactly do you think I would be marrying?"

Darbwin shrugged. He was sitting across the table from me, checking inventory logs. "I suppose you're the one who'd know the answer to that. But that nice young man, he said you had a beau yourself."

"*Roderick* said that? What beau?"

"Well, he wasn't rude enough to name names," Darbwin said with an assumption of hurt dignity. As if he hadn't pried for every bit of information he could get. "He just said I'd best be looking for a new barmaid because he thought you'd be marrying soon."

I could not for the life of me guess who Roderick thought I would be pairing up with. Shorro, perhaps, with whom he had seen me dance at Cloate's wedding? Ordinal of Wirsten? Surely he realized I had put myself beyond the pale of the gentry by releasing all the aliora into the wild. Or maybe it was that romantic streak that a wedding seemed to wake in all people, and he merely desired to see me as happy as he undoubtedly was himself.

I went back to my receipts and tallied up numbers again. "I don't think you'll have to worry about it," I said shortly. "I see myself staying here for a long time."

The next few weeks passed in a swift blur of work, sunshine, and easy contentment. The only exciting word that spread throughout the provinces was news of King Kentley's approaching coronation. I could imagine the feasts and jousts and balls that would be held to commemorate this grand event. I was just a little sorry that I would not be there to witness it. (Banned for life from the castle. No chance of sneaking back for this.) I debated sending Kent a small gift of congratulations, then decided against it, then changed my mind. I bought a small silver incense ball from a peddlar and filled it with a compilation of herbs. Luck, courage, wisdom, patience, mercy. Bryan had had none of these. I sewed a purple velvet bag to hold it, and covered the bag with gold thread and silver lace. Then I boxed the whole thing up and sent it to him anonymously. Perhaps I needed an herbal dose of courage for myself.

Descriptions of the coronation filtered back to us in the usual way, through the stories of merchants, soldiers, and other travelers. I, of course, waited impatiently for Angela's letter, which would give me the truest and most interesting account of the proceedings. It came five days after the new king was crowned.

Kent looked quite *splendid, much more regal than I'd ever thought he could look, though he frowned through the whole ceremony as if he were imagining the direst circumstances. Now, if I'd just been crowned queen, I would have been laughing and dancing and blowing kisses, I would be so happy. But Kent does not show much lightheartedness these days. Matthew stood beside him and looked so smug that I wanted to hit him, but, of course, I did not. Oh, and the funniest thing! Greta was not treated at all as a member of the royal family, but relegated to a seat in the back of the chapel, just like any visiting noblewoman. But I think that was Matthew's doing, not Kent's, for Kent made a point of speaking with her ten whole minutes at the reception afterward. That was more time than he gave to anyone, even Megan. . . .*

Who nobody *could help noticing, because she was dressed in the brightest yellow gown trimmed with violets. Everyone stared at her anytime she crossed the room. Marian said the color looked hideous on her. But I think she wore it as a foil for Kent, who dressed in royal purple and gold—and indeed, when they stood side by side or when they danced (which they did three times that night) they made quite a striking combination. . . .*

Oh, I could not read such letters, could not learn such news. I folded the pages tightly together and promised myself I would finish the letter in the morning. But I did not. I left it in the drawer and told myself I had forgotten it.

TWO WEEKS AFTER the coronation we had a spring fete in the village—an affair I had always missed, since I had always, by this time, been on my way to Castle Auburn. It was a grand market as much as a celebration of the season. Dozens of villagers rented stalls for selling cakes and pies and needlework, and peddlars came from miles around to vend their wares. Milette and my grandmother set up a booth on the village square and sold potions, and my landlady made a small fortune off the lacework she'd made during the long dark winter nights.

At the tavern, we were absolutely swamped with business, and Darbwin hired two more girls to work on a temporary basis. They were pretty but stupid, and spent more time flirting than waiting on customers. Both Darbwin's wife and I wanted to wring their long, thin necks.

"And that one girl—the blond one—oh, I could slap her senseless," Darbwin's wife muttered to me as we passed each other in the kitchen.

"Too late," I said.

She laughed tiredly. "Well, she's supposed to be waiting on the back tables *and* the booths. But there's a new customer at the last booth, and I know she hasn't said a word to him. So, could you—"

I picked up my damp rag so I could wipe down the table. "Right away," I said, and headed back out into the warm, noisy, cheerful bar. I dodged past outflung arms and answered greetings and made my way as quickly as I could to the final booth in the back of the tavern, where a lone man sat studying his menu.

"Sorry to take so long, sir, we've been busy," I said, cleaning the crumbs from the table. "What will you have? The cider's the best in the eight provinces and the stew is better than your own mother makes, though we're running low. However, the chicken pie is excellent."

"Stew, if you've got it," he said, in Kent's voice. "But I've no objection to pie."

I dropped my rag and stared at him. Kent grinned back at me. He was dressed in plain dark clothes—though finer than you'd see on the backs of most yeoman this far into the country—and he appeared perfectly at ease. His face seemed thinner—etched with finer lines and much older than one year should have made it—but he did not, at this moment, look particularly burdened by care. In fact, he was smiling at me quite broadly.

"And a glass of cider," he added. "I'd like to try the best in all the kingdom."

My knees would not hold me and so, even though one should not sit uninvited in the presence of the king, I dropped into the seat across from him. "What are *you* doing here?" I demanded.

"Looking for you."

"But you—but why—but how did you *find* me?" was my next fabulously intelligent question.

He seemed amused. "I've been writing you letters for almost a year, or hadn't you noticed? I knew your address. And I had your map."

Which made no sense. "My map?" I repeated.

He reached into a pocket of his dark coat and pulled out a much-folded and antique drawing of the road from Castle Auburn to Southey Village in Cotteswold. I felt my face burn with mortification.

"I was fourteen when I drew that," I said.

He carefully refolded it and slipped it back into his pocket. "I know. I've kept it all this time, thinking someday it might prove useful. And you see, it has."

I shook my head. "But you have—but still—I mean, *why* did you come look for me?" Then suddenly I knew, and I felt even more dreadful than I had a moment ago. "Elisandra," I said. "You've found out about Elisandra."

Now he looked interested. "Is there fresh news? Last I heard, she and Roderick were safely installed in Halsing Manor, and everything seemed to be going quite well."

I stared at him. "She and—you *knew* about Roderick? How did you learn? Did she tell you? Kent, I'm so sorry. I'm so sorry. I know it is you she should have wed—"

His expression was imperturbable. "I think I knew about your sister and Roderick the day after Bryan died," he said. "When my father suggested that, now that the prince was dead, there was no need for the prince's personal guard to follow the widow from room to room and from palace to courtyard. Roderick answered, cool as you please, that Bryan had made him swear to protect Princess Elisandra should anything ever happen to him. Which you know," Kent added, "it would never have occurred to Bryan to say. So, I knew about them then—or rather, I knew how Roderick felt about your sister. Not until Elisandra let him trail her for the next few weeks did I realize how she felt about him."

"But you—weren't you upset? Because I know you—you were always so close to Elisandra. And last summer you asked her to marry you—"

"Which I did at your behest, as you very well know," he answered calmly. "I was never in love with your sister. I never wanted to marry her in the first place. Even less did I want to marry her after her first husband died. Of poison. Administered at her hands."

I stared at him for a very long time, while the sounds of the tavern faded to empty gray noise around me and the edges of my vision blurred. I felt as if I had been turned to brick, and at the same time I felt as if every nerve in my immobile body had begun jumping violently inside its sheath of skin. He was the only thing I could focus on, and I kept my eyes riveted to his face. He gazed back at me with no expression whatsoever upon his own.

"There, now. I see Corie's found an old friend," Darbwin's wife said at this juncture, coming up unexpectedly with a tray in her hands. She placed a pitcher of cider and two mugs on the table, and laid out plates and silverware for both of us. I gave her one quick, stricken look, but she merely smiled at me. "Would you like the stew? Or the chicken pie?"

"The stew for me, thank you very much," Kent said politely. I merely nodded. She smiled again and left.

I finally found my voice. "Why do you think Elisandra poisoned Bryan?"

"Because of what you said. Because she was the one who would profit most from his death." He laughed soundlessly. "As to that, there are any number of us who might say the whole realm profited from his death. Bryan was a terribly flawed man. He would have made a very bad king. And a very bad husband."

I did not answer, and Kent picked up the pitcher of cider. "Would you like a glass? I hear it's the best in the kingdom." Without waiting for my reply, he poured for both of us and then took a long swallow. "This *is* good," he said, glancing at the glass as if it were decorated with the secrets of its ingredients, and then taking another deep drink.

"Does she know you suspect her?" I asked finally.

He shook his head. "We never talked about it. She may not think I believed the accusation. She may not think I even know what you suspected." He took another drink. "What I cannot figure out," he said, "is how the poison was administered. Admittedly she sat beside him at the dinner table and perhaps she could have slipped the drug onto his plate while he did not notice. But Bryan was so afraid of poison, I cannot see him being so careless. And Damien tasted everything Bryan ate—everything he drank—how can Bryan be dead and Damien not?"

I had asked myself these same questions so often, particularly on that interminable drive home from Castle Auburn, that it was a relief to finally be able to answer them out loud. "As for where the poison was placed," I said, "I believe it was in the venison stew. Elisandra had a hand in making it, because Bryan wished her to prove her domesticity. Ample opportunity there to season his food with enough toxins to kill him three times over."

"Yes, but nobody else died! Goff was sick, of course—many of us were—but she could have been looking at a massacre! Was she just counting on the fact that Bryan would eat more of that particular dish than anyone else would? That's too chancy even to be credible."

"She was counting on him refusing to drink the water," I said in almost inaudible tones.

"She was—" Kent stopped abruptly and frowned at me. "Bryan hasn't drunk the castle water for four or five years."

I nodded. "So, that is where she mixed the antidote. It has no color or flavor. She could have poured gallons of ginyese into the water barrels and none of us would have known."

"Yes. I see. Of course. Many people ate the poison, but only one did not also take the antidote. Very clever." He shook his head. "Very chancy still. Very—" He shook his head again. "It takes a woman with an absolutely iron will to accomplish a task as desperate as that."

"I could not do it," I said.

"I am glad to hear it," he said. "Nor could I." We both sipped at our cider a moment, mulling things over. "But still," he said. "How did she obtain the poison? How did she learn about the antidotes? That was the reason I stayed silent, you know."

"What was?" I asked, totally bewildered.

He pointed at me across the table. "Who at that castle knew more about herbs and elixirs than you? If the word 'poison' was to be bandied about, you would have been the first one to be suspected.

I was glad my father banished you so quickly. I wanted you safely away."

I smiled faintly at that. "I'm afraid she learned of the poison from me, though I never guessed that she would use the knowledge in such a way," I said. "One night I was describing for her all the contents of my satchel, and halen root was one of the herbs we discussed. It's a poison, though it has many other uses. I'm sure I mentioned that it could be bought in any apothecary's shop in Faelyn Market."

He was frowning. "She spent some time in Faelyn Market—"

"I know. A few weeks before her wedding. She told me in a letter how she shopped for days on end. I just did not realize what she was picking up at the bazaars."

"Does she know that you suspect her?" he asked.

"I haven't said so," I replied. "I doubt if I ever will."

He nodded. "So, you see," he said in a conversational tone of voice, "why I was not eager to marry your sister. I did not want to be poisoned on my wedding night. Or, indeed, at any time."

I forced myself to smile. "And yet the king must marry."

"And traditionally he has taken his bride from the house of Halsing."

I just looked at him.

"You," he added, "are the only marriageable daughter of the house of Halsing that I can think of."

I continued to stare.

"So, I have come here today to ask you to be my wife."

I watched him another long moment in silence. He did not seem particularly uncomfortable under my searching gaze. He did not fidget or look away; he did not even seem nervous. He gazed back at me, his own expression serious and considering, and waited for my answer.

"That's not a good enough reason," I said finally.

A slight smile softened his face. "What, tradition? No, I suppose you're right. For you it is not."

"It is not good enough for you, either," I said. "I'm baseborn. That's hardly a traditional match for the king."

"Yes, and there will be a certain consternation when I ride back to the castle to announce our betrothal," he said, as if I had actually accepted him. "My father will—"

"Your father!" I exclaimed, because, for a minute, I had forgotten Lord Matthew. "He has banned me from the court for life!"

Kent was grinning. "Yes, that's why I waited till after my coronation to propose to you. Now that I am king, I can reinstate anyone I choose. I can order my father to welcome you, and he will have to do so."

I smiled somewhat bitterly. "Your father would never welcome me at the court. And I have no desire to return there. Do you think I miss it? Do you think I long for its pomp and pageantry—its intrigues? I don't. Never. Not a single day. I am happy here."

He was studying me much as I had studied him earlier. "That is not the right reason to refuse me any more than tradition is the right reason for me to propose," he said slowly. "I was the prince's heir—I have lived my whole life under the shadow of politics. I have seen every friendship, every marriage, every alliance of any kind forged because of expediency. I had assumed that my own life would be bounded by such considerations. I could make my father happy by marrying Megan of Tregonia tomorrow—or Liza of Veledore, whom he also favors.

"But I am king," he said, even more slowly. "And the well-being of my kingdom depends on my sound judgment and clear head. And those things depend on my state of happiness. And I have known for a long time that my state of happiness depends on you."

He leaned forward across the table, suddenly urgent and intense. "I was a man long before I was king, and I fell in love with you," he said. "If I was a farmer in Cotteswold, I would want you beside me to help me run the business and raise the children and get the livestock ready to ship to Faelyn Market. I would want you beside me because I love you and my life would be so much harder without you in it. Now that I am king, I want you beside me to help me outmaneuver my viceroys and sit in on judgments and debate declarations of war. I admit, the job is harder. But it is essentially the same job. To live with a man and share his life with him and love him and have him love you back. You do not decide first if you want to live in a village or a court. You decide if that is the man you want to live with, and then you say yes or no."

"Yes," I said, and then looked around to see who had spoken.

Kent sat back, grinning broadly. "Excellent! I will meet your grandmother this afternoon, and we can start back for Auburn tomorrow."

"Wait," I said.

"We can wait a few days," he said agreeably. "I'm sure you have affairs to tie up here and people to say goodbye to—"

"No—I meant—wait. I have not thought about this long enough—"

He tilted his head to one side. "You mean, you are not sure you wish to marry me."

"I mean, I have not thought of it before now! It did not occur to me as a possibility! You have been plotting for a year, but I was here in the village, getting accustomed to a quiet life—"

"Do you love me?" he asked.

I fell silent.

"For the rest of it is glitter and noise," he said. "At the heart of it all is love. You make that choice, and you go forward from there."

I thought of the complex, wicked, brilliant life at court, and wondered if it could really be that simple. I had been happy here for the past year—content, surrounded by friends, touched by few worries. But half of my heart had still been elsewhere. I had lived for the letters from Elisandra, from Angela, telling me stories of the world I had left behind. If Matthew had lifted his ban, I would gladly have returned as the visitor I had once been. Or would I? I had defied Matthew's machinations before. I did not want to fall victim to them again.

I had no particular desire to be queen. It had not ever occurred to me that it was a role that would come my way. Whatever Kent said, it was not a part that could be separated from the one he offered me—I could not simply be his wife. He was not merely a peasant farmer, counting his bushels of grain and heads of cattle. His life was far more complicated.

But if he were that farmer? Would I marry him, then? Oh, yes, in a heartbeat. To see that kind, serious face every day of my life; to rely on his sweet temper, good heart, and deep sense of responsibility; to have him watch me, attentive and hopeful as he was now, and know I had the power to make his face light with happiness. That was a life I would accept any minute, any day. I could find someone else to love, and he could find someone else to be queen, but those would be second choices. Those would never be as good as the world could hold.

"I do love you," I said at last.

"And will you marry me?"

"I will."

YOU CANNOT IMAGINE the uproar that followed in the next few hours. Elisandra's wedding had nothing on it for sheer excitement and incredulity. For the *king* had come to our village to sweep away one of the tavern maids and make her queen. There was simply nothing that could compare to that story. The feasting and congratulations went on all night. I swear every single soul who lived within the village came by at some point to touch my hand and bow to the king. Darbwin could not have been happier if it were solstice all over again. Even the fact that I had worked my last shift did not seem to perturb him, though he insisted on paying me my last set of wages late that evening, while his wife was next door fixing up the best room and the farmers were still buying the king another round.

"Never know when a little extra cash will come in handy," Darbwin said, laying an additional stack of bills beside the first. "Even the queen needs to buy something now and then that she might not tell her husband about."

I leaned forward and kissed him on the mouth. "Don't tell your wife," I said.

He kissed me back. "Don't tell the king."

The next morning, we rode out to visit my grandmother. We were followed by the twelve guardsmen who had accompanied Kent on his mission and who had been waiting outside the tavern while he made his proposal. I was delighted to find, among his escort, several of my old friends, including Cloate and Shorro. Cloate was reserved with me, now that I had attained such high status, but Shorro could not have been more pleased had he been the one elevated to the royal house. He rode beside me for the whole three miles and regaled me with stories of events that had transpired in the past year. I laughed till my sides hurt. Kent gave me a sidelong look, and at one opportune juncture leaned over to whisper, "I think I know how the aliora escaped past the guards that night." I gave him an innocent look and continued bantering with Shorro.

When the royal entourage pulled up in front of my grandmother's house, she and her apprentice were out front, fertilizing the garden. They stared, dumbstruck, as the fourteen of us came to a halt. Kent lifted me from the saddle. "King Kentley of Auburn and his bride-to-be!" Shorro bawled out, and the two women dropped hasty curtseys. Kent gave each of them his hand and offered a grave hello. Milette, at least, looked awed into silence. I waited somewhat nervously for my grandmother's response, however, for she could not always be counted on to behave as one would like.

But she merely accepted Kent's hand and came to her feet and gave him one of her curt nods. "And if you're really taking her to wife, you got the best bargain from her mother's house *and* her father's," was what she said.

"I think so," Kent replied. Then he followed her into the cottage.

We stayed for an hour, politely drinking tea and talking, though the conversation was strained from the fact that so many of the people in the room had nothing in common with each other. It was a relief to finally stand up and prepare to leave. I was actually a little surprised when my grandmother came over to hug me goodbye.

"I knew you'd never stay to be a witch's apprentice," she said in my ear. "He seems good enough, but it's hard to tell with men. You know you've always got a home here if you need it."

Which was as generous a thing as she'd ever said to me. I hugged her tightly in return and said, "I'll visit. Often."

She stepped back. "I know you will," she said briskly. "Now, do you need any provisions for the road?"

Five minutes later we were on our way.

Back to Castle Auburn, but it would not be the same place it had been when I left a year ago. Bryan was dead—Elisandra was gone—the aliora had disappeared—and I was to be married to the king. Not the same place at all.

Unconsciously I dropped my hand to the saddlebag behind me, where I had packed my satchel with all my herbs. I would need an elixir or two to get me through the next few months, I thought, mentally running through the store of dried plants I had brought with me.

"What are you thinking about?" Kent asked. "You look so purposeful."

I smiled at him. "The brews I'll need to mix up to give me the qualities I need at court."

"What qualities?"

"Courage. Strength. Will."

"Love," he said, smiling.

I reached out my hand to him and he took it—no simple maneuver for lovers on horseback. "That I have without a potion," I said.

He kissed my hand. "So much happiness with so little witchcraft," he marveled. "Who would have thought it possible?"

I laughed, squeezed his fingers, and would have dropped his hand except that he would not release mine. We rode that way, handfast, for the rest of the trip. It was the shortest and most direct journey I had ever taken in my life.

Epilogue

My own royal wedding was even more lavish than my sister's, though many of the same people attended and many of the same scenarios played themselves out. I sprinkled myself with nariander for serenity and moved among my guests—my subjects—with a majestic calm. So far, so good.

Gifts arrived from all over the kingdom, exotic and beautiful things—clothes, jewels, tapestries, sculpture, illustrated books, decorative boxes, rare pet animals—too many to count. I opened every box myself, had Daria keep a record of who sent what, and spent the next six months of my life writing gracious letters of acknowledgment.

One box came with my name written on the front but no return address and no card from the sender to be found.

Inside was a box within another box within another, each container progressively smaller and more ornate until the tiny final one appeared to be made of hollowed ivory encrusted with a mosaic of gems. The lid was tied in place with a length of silken cord, and the whole thing weighed practically nothing at all.

I opened it cautiously, and instantly the room was filled with the sweetest of scents. A small mesh bag was nestled inside the box and tied with a red ribbon, and from this bag rose the most delicious and tantalizing medley of spices. I sniffed several times, trying to identify them all. Some were ornamental, for fragrance only, but a few came freighted with a sorcerous significance. For that was surely pansy pat, for true love, and rareweed for fidelity, mingled with the nariander and stiffelbane I used so frequently myself. I took another sniff.

There was something else mingled with the more lighthearted herbs, something gorgeous and foreign and seductive. I closed my eyes and inhaled deeply. Images of the forest evergreens rose around me in their silent, emerald clamor. I smelled the earth and the trees and the winding, beguiling wild vines, heavy with their summer blossoms. I had a sudden urge to kick off my satin shoes, lift up my heavy embroidered skirts, and run gaily from the castle toward the river, toward the woods.

This was the perfume of Alora, packaged by a master hand, sent to reward me or charm me or mystify me. Who knew? I thought it might be Rowena's way of saying, more elegantly, what my grandmother had said: *If you find you are unhappy with the choice you have made, you will always have a home here.* I inhaled again, greedy for that magical scent, that hallucinogenic wash of primeval exuberance. Then I set the lid firmly in place.

"And who shall we be thanking for this lovely gift, my lady?" Daria asked respectfully.

I tied my handkerchief around the little box and carried it to my dresser drawer. It would be safe enough in the very bottom, at the very back, where I would not accidentally come across it more than twice a year.

"Nobody," I said. "No reply is expected. Come, let us see what we have received from Hennessey of Mellidon and his bride."

The embroidered silk tablecloth was much more to my taste, and much less problematical. I sat down that very afternoon to thank the couple for their exquisite gift, and signed my name with the flourish that I had begun to affect: *Coriel, Queen of Auburn.* It made me smile to write such a ridiculous thing.

But the scent of Alora still lingered in the room, caught in the whorls of my fingertips, perhaps, or sparkling invisibly through the air. I scrubbed my hands three times with the strongest lavender soap, but still the forest smells drifted around me.

"We will finish this tomorrow," I told Daria, and left the room looking for Kent. I found him fifteen minutes later, reading over his own mail and making a list of people to whom he owed replies. He greeted me with an absent smile, but let me perch on the edge of his chair and run my fingers through his hair while he continued to frown over his correspondence. His rough curls scrubbed away the last clinging scent of Alora; the perfume evaporated into the room. I wrapped my arms around his neck and rested my cheek on the top of his head. I was content.